PROTECTOR

A WITCHES OF CLEOPATRA HILL NOVEL

CHRISTINE POPE

Dark Valentine Press

PROTECTOR

ISBN: 978-0692393246
Copyright © 2015 by Christine Pope
Published by Dark Valentine Press

Cover design and book layout by Indie Author Services.

To learn more about this author, go to
www.christinepope.com.

PROTECTOR

CHAPTER ONE

THE HEADACHES HAD STARTED THE WEEK AFTER HER fifteenth birthday. Caitlin McAllister remembered the day very clearly because she'd dozed off while watching TV, and then had a horrible nightmare about some tourist taking a turn too quickly off Main Street and ending up at the wrong end of Boyd Willis's driveway, the car a wreck, and the garage door and the tourist not in much better shape. It wasn't really that strange, after all, since it wasn't the first time a tourist had taken a header into Boyd's garage. Except…

…it hadn't been a dream.

At first Caitlin had shrugged off the incident, telling herself that she'd probably overheard her mother talking about it on the phone with one of the other clan witches, and only thought she'd dreamed the whole thing, but that wasn't what had really happened.

She'd fallen asleep during a repeat of *Charmed,* which was on at four, and the accident occurred at four-fifteen. And the gossip about the accident hadn't started making the rounds until at least a half hour after that. Caitlin had sat on the living room couch, staring blankly at the television, while her mother was on the phone with Rachel McAllister, the two of them were agreeing that *something* had to be done about the situation with Boyd's property.

That "something" turned out to be Margot Emory casting the strongest spell of illusion she could on Boyd's driveway, making it look as if a stone wall stretched across the opening. There weren't any more incidents with wayward tourists after that.

But Caitlin knew something else was wrong, because her head was pounding after she woke up from that not-dream, and the headache didn't go away until sometime the next day. And then, about a week later, she wasn't even dreaming, but gazing moodily out the window during her geometry class, and she saw one of the oily rags Micah Landon had lying around his studio burst into flame, burning down half the room before the volunteer fire department swung into action and put it out. Everyone believed the fire was Micah's fault, since he often walked around with his head in the clouds instead of attending to practical matters, such as making sure those turpentine-soaked rags had been stored properly. That might have been true, but the really scary thing about the incident was that Caitlin had witnessed the whole scene in her head approximately fifteen minutes or so before it happened.

That vision...or whatever it was...resulted in another headache.

She knew she should tell someone, but the mere notion of revealing that she'd begun to see things that came true scared her far more than the visions themselves. The McAllister clan had been without a seer for some time, and they needed one desperately, what with the threat of the Wilcox clan always hanging out there on the horizon, like the smoke of a far-off grass fire. It was Caitlin's responsibility to let her parents and the elders know that the McAllisters finally had the seer they so desperately needed.

Except...a clan seer couldn't call her—or his, although seers tended to be female—life her own. People always wanting to know what the future held, the elders always bringing her in for consultations...Caitlin knew she wanted none of it. Her power had revealed itself very late; most witches in her clan began to show signs of their latent abilities sometime around ten or eleven, but here she was, fifteen and being confronted by something she most decidedly did not want.

And so, even though she knew it was wrong, she hid what was going on, dosing the headaches with aspirin or ibuprofen or whatever happened to be in the house at the time, and by around a year or so later, they mostly disappeared. Not altogether; if something big was happening and she had a vision about it, her head would pound for a day or so afterward. When Great-Aunt Ruby died, Caitlin had stayed home sick from school for a day, the pain was so bad, and when Damon Wilcox kidnapped Angela McAllister, the new prima…well, that was the worst, Caitlin's head aching so much she almost threw up. Or maybe the real cause of the nausea was simply guilt at her own cowardice. Maybe if she'd spoken up, she could have rallied the clan in time to stop the kidnapping. True, she hadn't known exactly what was going to happen, only that it was something very bad. Again there had been that sensation of something oppressive looming over the tiny hillside town of Jerome, like a thunderstorm with such extreme low pressure that it felt as if it was sucking all the air out of your lungs, crushing down on your sternum. A feeling that something terrible was approaching, although she couldn't tell what it might be. That was probably Damon's own power at work, concealing his actions. He'd been so very powerful. Surely no one could have expected her own puny abilities to pierce the dark veil of magic he'd wrapped around himself.

Well, of course no one had expected her to do anything, since no one knew she was capable of seeing the future.

In the end, that had all worked out better than anyone could have imagined, so Caitlin tried to reassure herself that if she'd interfered, she could have kept Angela McAllister from being with Connor Wilcox, and that would have spelled trouble for both the clans. Even she was forced to admit that was a rather self-serving argument, but "all's well that ends well" seemed a good enough excuse to Caitlin for keeping her mouth shut. Besides, now that the clans had been more or less mingling for the past two years, the McAllisters could always call on Marie Begonie, the Wilcox seer, for all their soothsaying needs.

The visions never went away, but they did seem to become somewhat less urgent...although that could simply have been because life had been remarkably placid up here on Cleopatra Hill for some time. Not to say that there weren't squabbles in the clan, or marriages falling apart or bad business decisions or the sorts of things that seemed to affect everyone at some time or another, witch-born or no. However, there was nothing catastrophic, nothing to tax her abilities or bring on one of those sudden, piercing headaches.

Until now, some six years after the first vision had visited her, letting her know that her life would never be the same again.

The bad feeling was back, that sensation of something dark looming on the horizon, but even when Caitlin tried to will it into revealing itself, into giving her more detail, she saw nothing. Maybe the visions were something that couldn't really be forced. She didn't know, because she still hadn't told anyone her secret, was still living the lie that she hadn't inherited any special abilities, despite her mother being such a strong weather-worker that she'd been called to take over as elder for Margot Emory when the other witch wanted to step down so she could marry Lucas Wilcox.

And there was no reason for feeling as if the mountainside was about to crumble, or a plague of locusts was going to descend on Jerome. Everything had been sailing along just fine. It was a beautiful spring morning, and Caitlin was packing to go to Tucson for a few days with her friends Roslyn and Danica. Their own mini spring break, so to speak. All right, so Roslyn wasn't even in college, since she'd gotten her AA a year ago and decided that was enough, that she'd rather hang out in Jerome and wait tables at Grapes in between singing gigs at a variety of local bars and clubs and wine-tasting rooms. Her mother was less than thrilled with her, but since Roslyn actually was earning a living, there wasn't much else her mom could do.

Danica was a Wilcox, and she and Caitlin had become friendly when Roslyn's brother Adam began dating Danica's sister Mason. In fact, they'd become so close that last summer Danica and Caitlin had decided they were done with dorm life and had gotten an apartment off-campus.

Anyway, even if Roslyn might not deserve a spring break, strictly speaking, Caitlin knew that she and Danica had definitely earned one. It had been strange to transfer to Northern Pines, to be someplace where she wasn't surrounded on all sides by people who'd known her all her life...but it was also liberating. No one knew anything about the secret she was hiding. And since most of Flagstaff was made up of civilians—non-witches—most of them probably wouldn't give a rat's ass about the way she'd hidden her powers from her clan members. School was challenging, the coursework much more difficult than the classes she'd taken at the local community college, but she enjoyed it. She enjoyed feeling normal, even though she knew she wasn't. Not really.

"Almost ready?" Danica called out, and Caitlin hopped on her suitcase to smash it closed tightly enough that the locks would engage. It weighed a ton, but she only had to get it down the apartment's stairs and into Danica's Land Rover. Danica's parents had bought it for her used, but Caitlin still felt a twinge of jealousy every time she looked at her roommate's SUV. She drove a hand-me-down Honda her mother had given her, and knew she should be glad she even had that much. No McAllister witch was poor, but neither were they conspicuously wealthy like the Wilcoxes.

Caitlin rolled out her suitcase, and carried the small weekender bag with her leftover odds and ends in her free hand. Traveling light was a skill she hadn't quite mastered. "Ready!"

Danica was waiting in the living room, a leather jacket slung over the lightweight cotton top she wore underneath—a concession to the thirty-degree temperature difference between Tucson and Flagstaff. At her feet were her own suitcases, a lot newer and less shabby-looking than Caitlin's own. "Roslyn just texted me. She's all packed and ready, too, so we need to get moving."

"No problem," Caitlin said. It was not quite an hour drive to Jerome, and sort of out of their way, but they hadn't wanted to take two cars down to the condo they were renting in Tucson. Or rather, the condo that Danica's parents were renting for them.

"Oh, you girls just worry about your food and gas, and we'll take care of the condo," Danica's mother had said, and although Caitlin had thought she should protest such over-generosity, she couldn't really think of a good reason why, so she'd let it go. In a way, she supposed she should be glad Danica's parents had relaxed enough about the whole McAllister/ Wilcox thing that they hadn't batted an eyelash about their daughter going off for a debauched four days in Tucson with a couple of McAllister girls. Funny how having your daughter married to someone from a different clan—Mason and Adam had gotten married last fall—could mellow a person.

They put their suitcases in the back of the Land Rover and headed down I-17, driving in companionable silence while Danica's favorite retro metal played on the satellite radio. Caitlin tuned it out as best she could; if the worst that could be said about Danica was her terrible taste in music, then Caitlin figured she really didn't have that much to complain about.

Not according to Roslyn, though. After they pulled up in front of the big Victorian house on Paradise Lane where she still lived with her parents, she tossed her luggage in the cargo compartment, got into the Land Rover, and wrinkled her nose. "Seriously? Am I going to have to listen to this noise all the way down to Tucson?"

"Yeah," Danica replied. "Because I'm sure as hell not listening to that Taylor Swift crap you like for three straight hours."

Roslyn shot a beseeching look in Caitlin's direction, and she shrugged as she fastened her seatbelt.

"Sorry, Ros. I think I'd rather listen to Black Sabbath than Taylor Swift, too."

"You know, there's good retro and bad retro," Roslyn said darkly. But her expression was resigned. Danica's car, Danica's rules.

Caitlin smothered a smile as they headed down the hill and back toward the freeway. Even the impulse to smile faded soon enough, though, as that sensation began to creep over her once more, the way thunderheads would pile up above the Mogollon Rim to the east of the Verde Valley, presaging a wild summer storm.

Maybe she should have begged off and stayed up in Flagstaff, or come home to Jerome to spend a few days with her family, the way her mother had wanted her to. At the time, though, the trip to Tucson had seemed like a good idea. The plans had been made long before she began to get these vague feelings of unease. And, once those plans were made, she didn't want to be the one to back out, since she was sort of the glue that held the other two together. Roslyn and Danica got along, but they were friends because they'd each been friends with Caitlin first.

"The little sister brigade," Adam had called them once, and it was true. All three of them were the youngest child in their families. It was something else they had in common, something that helped them to bond. Roslyn probably had it worst, since she was the youngest of three, but even so, they all knew what it felt like to not be taken all that seriously half the time.

"Especially since Mason is such an overachiever," Danica had complained once. "She can call fire out of the air and could make a river reverse its course if she wanted to, but of course that's not enough—she has to get married and be working on her master's degree at the same time. So I figure I'll have to hang on and get a Ph.D. in physics or something before my parents take me seriously."

At the time, Caitlin had just grinned at her friend's exasperated expression, but she understood. Her own brother had always possessed an innate sense as to which flavors worked well together, a subtle magic, but one that had gotten him a chef position at one of the hottest new restaurants down in Cottonwood. He'd always known exactly what he wanted to do, whereas she....

Well, she'd been lying to everyone, including herself, for the past six years.

By the time they reached the outskirts of Phoenix, Danica relented and switched the station to one that played the sort of Top 40 pop Roslyn preferred. Caitlin wasn't overly thrilled with the switch, since she preferred more alternative stuff, but she decided not to protest. They only had an hour to go, and if it really started to drive her crazy, she could dig the earbuds out of her purse and listen to Pandora on her phone.

The readout on the dash said it was eighty-one degrees outside. She shook her head, always surprised by the difference in the weather between Flagstaff and Phoenix, or even Jerome and Phoenix. This time of year, Jerome was still lucky to reach the mid-sixties, and sometimes you got hard frosts even into May. But Phoenix? It never seemed to cool down. Not really.

Their destination was even farther south, but because of its elevation, it tended to be a couple of degrees cooler than Phoenix. *Big deal,* Caitlin thought. *Like you can really tell the difference between seventy-nine and eighty-one degrees.*

In contrast to the bright, sunny day outside, she felt cold all over. It could have merely been that Danica was blasting the air conditioning…or it could have been something else entirely. She reached over and shut the vent that was blowing on her. It helped, sort of.

Then they were at the condo, retrieving their keys from the resort office, unloading the Land Rover and getting everything situated. It was a full one-bedroom, not a studio, so there were two queen beds and a fold-out couch. They flipped for who would get the couch, and Roslyn lost.

"You swear you didn't put a whammy on that quarter?" she asked, giving Danica the side-eye.

"Witch's honor," Danica replied, putting her fingers in an upside-down "V" near her nose.

"I think it's supposed to go the other way," Caitlin said, although she wasn't completely sure. Her mother didn't think reruns of *Bewitched* were a very good viewing choice, considering how the show's portrayal of witches was completely unrealistic. But Caitlin hadn't really watched it because of the way it portrayed witches, but because she was fascinated by the styles and the technology (or lack thereof), and the sense of it taking place so *very* long ago.

"Is it? I haven't seen that show since I was a little kid. Talk about giving me a skewed sense of what it means to be a witch. I kept trying to wiggle my nose and have a unicorn show up in the backyard or something, but it never worked."

They all laughed at that, then decided it was late enough that they could justify going out for margaritas. After doing some quick research on Yelp, they found a Mexican restaurant within walking distance that sounded decent and headed over.

"Ah, this is heaven," Roslyn sighed as she took a long pull on her strawberry margarita, once they'd all settled themselves in a booth. "And it feels so good to be able to wander around in flip-flops. My toes have been yearning for freedom."

"Well, they look pretty free now," Caitlin said, after taking a quick look under the table and noting her friend's bright turquoise polish, complete with sparkly flowers on her big toes. Although her own classic margarita on the rocks tasted great, Caitlin still was feeling prickly and on edge. Never mind that a brightly decorated Mexican restaurant in Tucson was probably one of the last places she'd expect to meet any kind of trouble.

"Mmm…look over there," Danica murmured, giving the slightest jerk of her chin toward a table with three young men around their own age, maybe a few years older. "Tasty, huh?"

Caitlin shifted in her seat so she could get a better look without actually appearing as if she were staring in their direction. At the same time, she felt a tingle along the back of her neck, her witch sense telling her that the guys in question must be warlocks. "Do you think they're de la Pazes?"

Taking another long sip of her margarita, Roslyn seemed to think it over. "Must be," she said, then reached for a tortilla chip. "Tucson is still part of their territory, right?"

"Well, I think we're about to find out," Danica said in an undertone. "Because they're getting up and coming over here."

At once Roslyn abandoned her margarita and hastily rearranged her long honey-blonde hair so it draped gracefully over her shoulder. Caitlin forced herself not to react. Yes, from what she could tell in the dim bar, the guys were cute, but she wasn't going to act like a complete moron just because they were headed in her direction.

As they approached, though, the wrongness she'd been feeling all day seemed to coil in the pit of her stomach, making even the few sips of margarita she'd had so far burn like acid. Not sure what she should do, she reached for her water and drank some of that, telling herself that she needed to calm down.

The trio of strange young men stopped a foot from their table. One of them stood slightly in front of the other two. He was extremely good-looking, with thick black hair and well-muscled arms. A tattoo of a snake wound itself around his throat.

"Hi," he said. "We couldn't help noticing—"

"Neither could we," Danica said in that casual yet take-charge way of hers. "We're not trespassing on your territory or anything, though. Our families checked with Maya de la Paz, and she said it was fine—"

"Whoa," the stranger cut in. "We're not here to check your credentials or anything. It's just that we hadn't seen you before. You from up north?"

"Yes," Roslyn replied eagerly, toying with a lock of her hair. "Caitlin and I are from Jerome, and Danica's from Flagstaff."

Might as well have given them our phone numbers and addresses, Caitlin thought sourly, but there wasn't much she could do about it at this point. Roslyn never had possessed exactly the best judgment when it came to good-looking men.

"Two McAllisters and a Wilcox," the strange young man said. "We don't see too many of you down here in Tucson." He smiled, and although he had very straight, shining white teeth, something about that smile made a shiver go down Caitlin's back. She wished she could think of some excuse to get herself and her two friends out of there. "I'm Matías, and this is Jorge and Tomas." The other young men smiled as well, but Caitlin didn't feel very reassured.

"Hey," Roslyn whispered to her, "scooch over so they can sit down with us." Tilting her head to one side, she let her dimple show as she said more loudly, "Why don't you join us?"

Caitlin had no intention of "scooching," but that didn't really matter, because Matías said, "Actually, we were wondering if you'd be interested in coming back to our place. We won't water down the margaritas like they do here, and we were going to barbecue some carne asada."

Alarm bells started going off in Caitlin's head, and she opened her mouth to protest, to say that maybe it would be better if they just stayed here. But Danica and Roslyn were too quick for her, both of them saying that sounded like a lot of fun. What the hell? She could believe Roslyn going for such a scheme, but Danica? Usually she had way more common sense than that.

But Danica was smiling up at Matías, too, her dark eyes shining as if she'd just seen the promised land. This was not good.

And somehow they were gulping down their margaritas so they wouldn't be wasted, then dropping a couple of twenties on the table so they could get out of there without waiting for the server to come back. Before she could really figure out what was happening, they'd emerged from the restaurant into the warm sunshine and were walking down the sidewalk, Matías in the middle, with Danica on one side and Roslyn on the other, and Caitlin sort of uncomfortably sandwiched between Jorge and Tomas.

Every nerve ending was screaming at her to get away, which on the surface sounded completely ridiculous. Wasn't this what spring break was supposed to be about—getting out and having fun, meeting guys, maybe hooking up if everyone involved was amenable and knew there wouldn't be any strings attached?

Never mind that the mere thought of kissing any of these guys, let alone going to bed with one of them, was enough to make her want to throw up.

They passed the condo complex where the girls were staying and kept walking. Well, that wasn't so very strange; there were a lot of complexes like that in the area, and the odds of the guys staying in the same one where they were renting were pretty low.

"So," Caitlin managed, even though she found it hard to get the words out past the tight knot of worry in her throat, "are you staying in a condo, too?"

The guy on her right—she couldn't remember if he was Tomas or Jorge—shook his head, looking amused. "Oh, no. We live here in Tucson. Our house is just down the next block."

House. For some reason, that sounded ominous. It seemed far more innocuous to be going back to a rented condo rather than a house they lived in. "Oh," she said faintly. "So you guys are all roommates?"

"Yeah," he said, his gaze moving from her face to the half-revealed curve of her breasts in the lightweight top she wore. "Tomas and I, we're brothers, and Matías is our cousin."

Caitlin forced down a breath. Maybe he really hadn't been looking at her chest. Maybe she was just imagining things because she felt so crappy. "That's cool," she said, hoping she sounded casual and not as if she was about to gag. The sensation was pressing so heavily on her now that it felt as if she could barely pull in enough air to speak. "Roslyn and I, we're cousins, too. Her dad is my mother's older brother."

"Yeah, we witches, we're all related somehow," Jorge said, and for some reason Tomas seemed to find that amusing, because he began to chuckle.

If only she had enough breath to ask him what was so funny. At the moment, she felt as if she were about to pass out at any second. And of course Roslyn and Danica weren't paying any attention to her, were still staring up at Matías with that gaga expression on their faces, which didn't make sense at all, because although he was good-looking, he wasn't *that* good-looking. Not really.

They turned a corner into a residential tract with modest one-story homes, most of them built in the Southwest style with flat roofs, and all of them with gravelly front yards planted with cactus and other drought-tolerant species. It all appeared relatively normal, if somewhat exotic to her eyes. She was used to the Victorian architecture in Jerome, or the wood-framed houses common in Flagstaff. But nothing here seemed particularly strange, especially for Tucson.

It felt like it, though, worry running up and down her skin as if every ant within a square mile had started to march over her flesh. She knew she should be saying something, should be reaching out to her friends and grabbing them by the arms so she could pull them away from Matías, but for some reason she couldn't give voice to her worry, couldn't do anything except follow the group up the front walk to a stucco house painted a pale rosy tan color.

Inside it was very clean and neat, decorated in a simple, neutral style that had hints of the Southwest without being kitschy. The place certainly didn't look like a house that had three twenty-something guys living in it. Caitlin had been to Roslyn's brother Adam's apartment once or twice before he got together with Mason and moved to Flagstaff, and it sure as hell hadn't been anywhere near as tidy as this.

"Margaritas," Matías announced.

Everyone headed into the kitchen, which also showed no sign of anyone actually using it. Well, except for a bowl of limes on the counter, and a bag of tortilla chips. Jorge got some salsa out of the refrigerator while Matías got to work with the blender, and Tomas wandered off into the next room. A few seconds later, some jaw-rattling hip-hop started to play, and Caitlin winced. She hated that crap.

And she knew Roslyn hated it, too, and Danica only sort of tolerated it, and yet both of them were grinning like Tomas had just put on their favorite song. What the hell was going on?

She stood off to one side as Roslyn chattered away about the house and how it must be so awesome to live in a part of the state where it was warm all the time, and the guys kept exchanging knowing grins that made the blood in Caitlin's veins feel just about as frosty as the concoction inside the blender. But every time she took a breath and attempted to speak, the words got caught in her throat, choking her to the point where she began to cough.

"Hey, let me fix that," Matías said, sounding a little too solicitous. He handed her a margarita, and she set her purse down on the floor so she could take it from him.

"Yeah, Cate, you okay?" Danica asked. The question seemed almost automatic, though; Caitlin couldn't detect any real concern in her voice.

"Fine," she managed to croak. The margarita glass sat in her hand, cold, inviting. She'd just watched him mix the drink, so there couldn't be anything wrong with it. And she needed to drink something to get that lump out of her throat.

She lifted the margarita to her lips and swallowed, watching as Roslyn and Danica did the same. As soon as the frosty tang of it hit her stomach, though, Caitlin knew she shouldn't have drunk it, that something was horribly wrong. Suddenly, it wasn't cold at all, but burning, a strange, insidious heat that began to lick its way all through her, making her feel....

"That's better," Matías said. He nodded at Jorge and Tomas, and they moved toward Roslyn and Danica, Jorge with his arm around Danica's waist, Tomas with Roslyn, both of them pulling the girls toward them and kissing them hard, hands roaming upward to fondle their breasts. And neither of them reacted, did anything except moan and push closer to the guys manhandling them, when Caitlin knew that even Roslyn would have kneed anyone else in the nuts for pulling something like that on such a short acquaintance.

And then Matías was coming closer to her, dark eyes glittering. "You sense something, don't you?" he murmured. "It doesn't matter. Soon, nothing much will matter at all."

His mouth was on hers, lips hard and hot, and although she knew it was wrong, knew she should be pushing him away, the signals her mind was sending to her body didn't seem to be getting there. She let him kiss her, let him lead her out of the kitchen to a room attached to the back of the house, an empty space that probably had been intended as a sun porch. There was nothing in the room now, though, except an intricate tracery in colored chalks on the cement floor, a pattern that not only looked wrong, but felt wrong, the patterns off somehow, the arrangement of colored candles around its circumference wrong as well, although she couldn't say why.

Tomas and Jorge brought Roslyn and Danica in with them, both girls looking dreamy and flushed. Danica's shirt was half unbuttoned, and Caitlin knew that was wrong as well, that Danica would never be standing there in front of a bunch of guys she didn't even know with her bra showing and her breasts about to spill out.

Matías smiled. "The blonde one first."

Tomas nodded and pulled Roslyn forward, positioning her at the edge of the circle. Silvery metal flashed in the bright light pouring into the room, and Caitlin realized then that he'd pulled a knife from somewhere, was pressing it against her friend's exposed forearm.

"No!" she screamed, somehow forcing the syllable past the constriction in her throat, past the strange fuzziness that seemed to have settled on her brain. Roslyn blinked at her, as if puzzled why Caitlin would have a problem with Tomas slicing her open with a knife.

"Calm down, *chica,*" Matías murmured, his breath hot against Caitlin's neck. "He's not going to kill her. We just need something from her."

"You can't...." She made herself gasp in a breath, hoping the extra oxygen would make her brain begin to work properly. "It's wrong. We don't—we don't do that kind of magic."

"Maybe you don't. But we do." He nodded, and Tomas drew the blade across Roslyn's arm, a quick, sharp cut, barely more than inch long. Deep crimson blood dripped from the wound onto the circle chalked on the ground.

Faint tendrils of pale gray smoke began to drift upward. At the same time, Caitlin could feel the wrongness of the thing they'd drawn twisting through her, cold, hungry…strong. It was more than chalk on the ground.

It was alive.

"Roslyn!" she screamed. "Run!"

But Roslyn only looked at her with foggy blue eyes, and Danica wasn't watching at all, had her eyes shut as Jorge kissed her neck and stroked her bare arm. She didn't seem to have heard Caitlin's cry, or, worse, was ignoring it.

"I don't think they mind, *chica,*" Matías said, chuckling into her ear. "And you won't, either, when your time comes."

Help. She had to get help. From where or from whom, she didn't know, because she was in the heart of de la Paz territory, and here were three guys from that clan engaging in the sort of magic that had been forbidden for centuries. But she knew Roslyn and Danica were lost to her for the moment, and so the only thing she could think of to do was to run.

The next part didn't require thought, only instinct…and the strength to overcome the fog of confusion which had come with that margarita she'd sipped. But she'd only had a little. Besides, damn it— she was a McAllister.

She twisted in Matías' arms, bringing her knee up into his groin as hard as she could. He grunted, then cursed. Sharp pain flared in her side, and she saw he'd been holding a knife that whole time, had just plunged it into her. Because the angle was off, it barely penetrated more than an inch, but oh, Goddess, it hurt.

Crying out, she brought her elbow up into his chin, connecting squarely. He cursed again, but, more importantly, he let go of her.

That was all she needed. Mentally asking Roslyn and Danica for forgiveness, Caitlin bolted from the room, then ran through the house and out the front door. Without bothering to stop and close it behind her, she pounded down the walkway and back to the sidewalk, retracing her steps, knowing she had to get back out to the thoroughfare where the restaurant was located.

Not that she was sure she could make it that far. The restaurant was blocks from where they'd turned into this residential district, but between here and there, she'd noted there were other businesses, places where people had to be working. Normal people. Ordinary people. They'd see she'd been hurt and call an ambulance. Surely she'd be safe in the hospital, wouldn't she?

Behind her, she heard running feet, but no shouting. No, that would probably draw too much attention. All she could do was run, glad that she hadn't worn her flip-flops and instead had on a pair of ballet-style flats.

Don't look back, she told herself. The pain in her side was searing, but it seemed to clear her head, get rid of that horrible fuzziness. Or maybe it was just that she'd put enough distance between herself and Matías that whatever spell he'd cast—and it had to be a spell—wasn't working as well anymore.

And there was the street, and cars whizzing back and forth. She let out a sobbing little breath, thinking she'd never been so glad to see anything in her life. Something wet was dripping on her jeans, and she glanced down and realized the blood from her wound had flowed from her side and had stained all the way to her thigh.

But she couldn't think about that, think about how much it hurt. Now she had turned on to the sidewalk that paralleled the street, and it seemed harder and harder to keep running. She slowed to a walk, risked a look behind her. Matías stood on the corner, fists balled at his side, but he made no motion to come any closer. She guessed that he couldn't, not with this many witnesses around. So his powers had some limits.

Just up ahead was a large building, a store of some kind. Her vision was becoming blurry, so she couldn't see what its sign said. But there were cars in the parking lot, and people coming and going. And she couldn't walk much farther. Surely someone here would help her.

She pressed her hand against her side, attempting to conceal as much as she could of the blood that stained her clothing. Limping now, she staggered past the parked cars and went into the cool, air-conditioned interior of the building. Around her, she could hear gasps as the shoppers in the store appeared to take in her condition, but she couldn't focus on any of them. Not really. Just up ahead was a tall young man in a white dress shirt, the sleeves rolled up to his elbows. He looked handsome and friendly, with kind dark eyes.

Summoning the last of her strength, Caitlin went to him, grasped his arm. Her hand left bloody prints on his white shirt. His eyes widened, even as he reached out to catch her.

"Please," she whispered. "Please help me."

The world went dark.

CHAPTER TWO

ALEX TRUJILLO SHOVED THE CLIPBOARD UNDER HIS ARM and went back to the stockroom. Just as he'd expected, the bags of rice Luis said he couldn't find were stacked right where Alex had known they would be, on the rack on the west wall. He tried not to sigh. It probably would have been easier if Luis was actually that stupid. He wasn't, though...just lazy. And because he was Alex's cousin, Alex couldn't exactly fire him.

Just another day at Mercado Trujillo.

For most of his life, Alex had known this was where he'd probably end up, but that didn't mean he had to be happy about it. His one chance at escape had been that kiss with Angela McAllister. If he'd turned out be her consort, he would have been up in Jerome... doing what, he wasn't sure...but at least it wouldn't be managing the store that had been in his father's family for three generations now.

But he hadn't been Angela's soul mate. No, that role had gone to Connor Wilcox, of all people. Lucky bastard. It wasn't as if Alex had thought he was in love with Angela or anything. He barely knew her. What he'd seen, he'd liked, and at the time he'd thought they could have been good together, if fate or the Goddess or whomever had seen fit to smile on their pairing. She'd been destined for other things, however, and so Alex had let it go. Mostly.

It wouldn't have been so bad if his brother Diego could have shouldered part of the burden here. He was the oldest son, after all, and so he really should have been the one to take over the store, or at least the larger part of managing it. But last year he'd finally gotten around to getting married, to a woman whose family owned a vineyard down in Bisbee, and he'd gone to work there instead, using the excuse that Letty was an only child and that he was needed to help shoulder some of the burden.

Burden, Alex thought. *Yeah, it must be really rough to spend your whole day tasting wine.*

Intellectually, he knew there was more to managing a vineyard than that. And Diego's new wife was a civilian, which meant Diego had to be on guard all the time. Maria knew about the de la Paz clan, that her husband's family wasn't exactly typical, but her own family didn't have a clue about the de la Pazes. And they needed to be kept in the dark, for obvious reasons.

"Besides," Luz Trujillo had pointed out to her son, probably trying to be helpful but in fact just making things worse, "why did you get those degrees in marketing and communications, if not to be more valuable to the store? I'm sure you'll have all sort of ideas!"

He'd had ideas once. Unfortunately, none of them really applied to running a neighborhood *mercado*, even if said *mercado* had a thriving side business that most of its regular customers didn't know anything about. Through a side door that most civilians thought led to another stockroom or possibly an office, you went into a second store, smaller, but stocked with the sorts of items the witches and warlocks in the area might need: crystals and other stones of power, herbs and floral essences, candles and saints' icons and all manner of arcane items. Luz Trujillo, whose gifts included a facility with minor illusions, had cast a spell on that doorway so the civilians never quite noticed the parade of people going in and out during the hours the *mercado* was open for business.

"Luis," Alex said to his cousin, who was lurking in the dry goods aisle, attempting to look busy but really eyeing a pretty girl who was inspecting the spice display, "the rice is on the shelf to your right as you go in the stockroom." He'd tried to sound mild, but he couldn't help letting an edge creep into his voice as he added, "The same place it's always been."

The girl giggled, and Luis gave Alex the evil eye. At least he didn't argue, though, but headed back where he was told, albeit with excruciating slowness.

And that's the problem with hiring family, Alex thought. Things would have been so much easier if he could have just gotten some regular help around the place.

Frowning, he emerged from the dry goods aisle and began walking toward the front of the store. His frown deepened, though, as he heard gasps and murmurs from up near the entrance. In the next moment, he saw the source of the disturbance: a young woman with long red hair was staggering toward him, eyes blank, glazed. For a second or two, he wondered if she might be drunk, or possibly high, and then he saw the stain of bright blood against her pale blue gauzy top, the way that blood had run all the way down her side and onto her jeans. And in that same instant he felt the slight tingle that told him he was in the presence of a witch, even as she reached out with a bloody hand to grasp him, her hoarse voice pleading for help right before she slumped into his arms.

He couldn't stop to think. The better place to take her would be the hidden side of the store, the one where the witches shopped, but he wasn't sure his mother's spell could hold up, not with so many curious eyes on him. So he lifted the strange young woman, saying to the clerk, "Manuela, call 911!"

Since Manuela was another witch, she would know he didn't really want her to call emergency services, but instead their local healer, who lived approximately ten minutes away. She nodded, picked up the phone, and made a show of dialing 911...but instead was putting the call through to the healer. Luckily, this wasn't the first time the clan had had to indulge in this sort of subterfuge, so the healer would know to come right away, no matter what Manuela might be saying on the phone.

Without pausing, Alex went on into the stockroom and through it, to the small break room at the back of the building. He laid the wounded witch on the couch there, then hurried to get some towels from the supply closet. After wetting a washcloth, he went back to the sofa before gingerly tugging her shirt upward a few inches so he could wipe away the blood and see where she was hurt.

And there it was—a small but deep gash in her left side, piercing the smooth, pale skin.

A knife wound. Shit.

He'd never seen her before, but, judging by the warm red hair that flowed over the shabby pillow where her head currently rested, he guessed she must be a McAllister. Most of them tended to be much fairer than the members of the Wilcox clan.

"Who are you?" he wondered, belatedly realizing he'd spoken the words out loud.

Her eyelids fluttered, and she stared up at him, face white and taut with pain. Then she seemed to focus on his features, and a spasm of panic went over her. She pushed at his hand and tried to sit up, wriggling away from the washcloth he had pressed against her side.

"Hey," Alex said, wondering what in the world had set her off. Yes, she'd been attacked, but even in her wounded state, she had to sense that he was a fellow witch and that he meant her no harm. "Stay still. You've already lost enough blood."

"You—you're one of *them*," she whispered, her voice cracking with fear.

"One of who?" he asked. "I'm—my name is Alex Trujillo. I'm Maya de la Paz's grandson."

That declaration seemed to calm her a little, although he noticed that she remained wedged up against the other end of the couch, as far away from him as she could manage. "Maya?" she echoed.

"That's right, Maya," he said, attempting to keep his voice as calm, as soothing, as he could manage. "She's helped your clan before. You're a McAllister, right? What's your name?"

"C-Caitlin."

Her voice shook, and her entire frame was wracked with shivers. Going into shock, probably. There was a blanket folded up at the top of the storage cabinet here in the break room. He should get that and cover her up. The healer would be here soon, but—

"Do you want a blanket, Caitlin?"

She nodded, and seemed relieved when he moved away from her to the cabinet. When he came back, he was careful to avoid touching her as he spread the blanket over her. With shaking fingers, she pulled it up to her chin.

He knew he should really be holding that washcloth up to the wound in her side to slow the bleeding, but he also knew that whatever had happened to her, it was traumatic enough that she seemed to be having difficulty recognizing a friendly gesture. Instead, he moved a foot or so away, then told her, "The healer is on her way. She'll have you fixed up in no time."

The smallest of nods. Her eyes, a clear, mesmerizing blue-green, seemed to be fixed on the window in the wall opposite, and as he watched, he saw tears fall from them and slide down her pale cheeks. "I left them," she whispered, her voice ragged.

"Left who?" Alex asked. Something was going on here, that was for sure, but he couldn't begin to make any sense of it. Maybe once Valentina got here and had this Caitlin McAllister put back together, they could figure out just what the hell had happened.

Almost as if his thoughts had summoned her, Alex heard a soft knock at the door to the break room. He went to answer it, letting the healer in. She was a tall, slender woman a few years younger than his mother, serenely beautiful.

"Over there," he murmured, inclining his head toward the sofa. "Her name is Caitlin."

That serenity appeared a little shaken when the healer approached Caitlin and realized the wounded young woman in question was a witch, too. Still, Valentina gathered herself and said softly, "Caitlin, I am Valentina. I will need to lay my hand on your wound. Will you allow me to do that?"

Silently, Caitlin nodded. Tears still leaked from her eyes, but she didn't pull away, didn't move or flinch as Valentina touched her. And that took some doing, because Alex knew from experience that although Valentina's healing magic was powerful and effective, it wasn't pain-free...more like you had to experience all the healing a wound or injury required as she brought her powers to bear. It could be intense.

Caitlin's small white teeth clamped down on her lower lip as Valentina continued to press her hands against the wound in her side. Gradually, though, the young witch became less tense, until at last she expelled a breath and nodded.

"Thank you," she said, her voice still hoarse. She placed her hand against her side, against the flesh that had knitted itself together, and gave a small wince. The spot would probably be tender for a few more days. "That's...amazing."

"You clan doesn't have a healer, I recall," Valentina said, straightening so she could move a few paces away from her patient, her work done.

"No, we all have to get patched up at the Verde Valley Medical Center," Caitlin replied. Her gaze moved from the healer and came to rest on Alex. "I'm sorry I reacted like that. You're Alex—the Alex who tried to be our *prima*'s consort. I should have recognized your name."

"It's all right," he said, vaguely wishing she'd heard of him some other way. Not that there was anything shameful in not being a consort, if it wasn't your fate. But still.... He shook himself. That wasn't important right now. "You've had a shock. Can you tell us what happened?"

Her entire body seemed to tense, and she winced again. That involuntary reaction had probably hurt a good deal. "I-I'm not completely sure. I mean, I know *what* happened, but I still can't explain it."

Alex flicked a glance at Valentina, and she gave the tiniest lift of her shoulders. She'd healed Caitlin's wound, but that didn't mean she had any more idea of who had inflicted it—and why—than he himself did. He offered Caitlin what he hoped was an encouraging smile, saying, "Well, just tell us as best you can, and we'll go from there."

She hesitated for a few seconds. "Can I—could I have some water first, please?"

"Of course," Valentina replied. She went to the break room's refrigerator, where they kept some bottled water for the store's employees. After pulling out one of the bottles, she took it to Caitlin, who accepted it with a grateful nod.

She drank deeply, almost a quarter of the bottle. "That's better. It's getting the rest of that...whatever it was...out of my throat."

Alex could feel his eyebrows lift at that remark. What exactly *had* happened to her?

Now looking a little more composed, Caitlin shifted slightly on the couch so she was sitting more upright. That must have hurt as well, but she gave no sign of being in any pain, save for a quick tightening of her fingers around the water bottle she held. "There were three of them," she said at last. "I was here with my friends. Roslyn McAllister and Danica Wilcox." She pronounced the names carefully, as if wanting to drive home that her companions had been fellow witches. "We went out for drinks. Spring break, you know?"

Alex nodded. Of course, he'd never been able to cut too loose during his own vacations, mostly because his getaways in the greater Phoenix area had been made under the watchful eye of his grandmother, and so news of any debauchery he'd indulged in would have reached her ears soon enough. Not that Alex had much taste for debauchery. That had been more Diego's thing.

The McAllister witch continued, "There were these guys at the bar. They came up to us. Sort of flirting, you know?"

That didn't seem terribly strange. Even pale and drawn as she was now, he could see that Caitlin was extremely pretty. And that head of gorgeous red hair was sure to attract attention pretty much anywhere she went. He opened his mouth to reply in the affirmative, but she kept talking.

"Only...I knew there was something wrong about them. I *knew*, and yet I let Danica and Roslyn go with them anyway."

"'Knew'?" Valentina repeated. "How is it that you knew?"

Caitlin's face seemed to crumple as fresh tears sprang to her eyes. Her fingers clutched the blanket, knuckles showing white against her already fair skin. "I could tell they were warlocks, you know, the way we can always tell when we're around witch-kind. But it wasn't just that. They felt off. Bad. Wrong.

Whichever word you want to choose." Her gaze fastened on Alex, and there seemed to be something both pleading and ashamed in those blue-green eyes of hers, too bright now because of the tears that still shimmered in them. "And I'm sorry about the way I reacted to you. It's just that they were about your age, and also—" She broke off, staring down at her fingers where they were knotted in the blanket.

He had a pretty good idea of what she'd been about to say. "Mexican?" he suggested.

A nod. "Well, I was going to say Hispanic, but yeah. Yes. I didn't know if you were one of them, too."

"Can you describe them?" Valentina asked, her tone troubled.

"There were three of them." Caitlin drew in a hitching little breath, as if even attempting to recall the faces of the young men who had assaulted her was physically painful. "The leader, his name was Matías, and the other two were Jorge and Tomas. They said they were brothers, but I don't know if that was true or not."

"But you're certain they were warlocks," Alex cut in. None of this made sense. He didn't know anyone in Tucson, or in his extended family in Phoenix, named Matías. Jorge and Tomas were more common names, but again, among his cousins, he didn't have any brothers who shared those names.

He might have said one or two of his wilder cousins were capable of messing with some *gringa* witches who'd come down to Tucson to party, just to show them whose territory they were in...but certainly not to the extent of physically assaulting them.

"Yes, they were definitely warlocks," Caitlin replied, her voice barely above a whisper. She drank some more of her water. It seemed to revive her, because she sounded stronger as she continued, "They took us to their house, which is in that residential area just past the traffic light, the one where there's the closed-down gas station on the corner. You know, that way?"

She made a vague gesture toward the wall with the window in it, which was in completely the opposite direction from the neighborhood he thought she was talking about. But that was all right; Alex knew which one she meant. And he also knew that none of the de la Paz witches or their extended families lived there. So who the hell were these strange young men she was talking about?

Caitlin continued, "Matías was the tallest. He was probably about your height." Then she hesitated and seemed to study Alex a bit more closely. "Well, maybe a little shorter. He was good-looking, I guess. Black hair and brown eyes. He had a snake tattooed around his neck."

"There's no one in our clan with a tattoo like that," Valentina said, her tone troubled. She shot a significant glance in Alex's direction, one that he knew most likely meant she wanted to call his mother now, before this went any further. He supposed it made sense, since his mother was Maya's daughter and the *prima*-in-waiting, and Maya was in Scottsdale, more than an hour away.

Without taking his focus from Caitlin, he nodded slightly at Valentina. Murmuring that she needed to make a call, she headed out the back door, no doubt so she could get her cell phone out of her purse and make that necessary call.

After she'd gone, Alex said, "What about the others?"

"Jorge and Tomas? I guess you could say they were good-looking, too. Not as tall as Matías. They had tats, too—a bunch of symbols I'd never seen before. And Tomas had what looked like a ring of roses and barbed wire around one of his biceps." For some reason, the recollection seemed to upset her; Alex saw her hand begin to shake again as she lifted the bottle of water to her lips.

All good details—and he was sort of surprised she'd been able to remember that much, considering how shaken up she was, how much blood she'd lost. Even so, he could tell there was something else she didn't want to talk about. Yes, she'd recognized that the young men who'd approached her and her friends were also witch-folk, but that didn't explain how she'd sensed they were bad...and it sure didn't explain the knife wound in her side.

Maybe with Valentina gone, Caitlin would feel more like opening up, now that it was only the two of them in the room. He guessed she had to be a few years younger than he was, maybe as much as five, but they were still a lot closer in age than Valentina, who was old enough to be Caitlin's mother.

"And so...you said they felt wrong. How did you know that?"

A blank expression seemed to settle on her pretty features. Her gaze shifted to the wall, to the calendar from one of their produce supply companies and the overly bright still life of pears it was showing for the month of March. "I just knew. I sensed it."

He got the feeling she didn't want to say anything more than that, and he wasn't going to push it. After all, he didn't know her. He'd leave the poking and prodding to his mother, who was all too skilled at extracting information from her children and pretty much anyone else she set her focus on.

"So you went to their house...."

"Yes. The guys said they were going to make margaritas. Danica and Roslyn really wanted to go, and I could tell I wouldn't be able to talk them out of it. Also, they were acting strange."

"Strange how?"

With a nervous gesture, she reached up to push some of the heavy hair that hung over her shoulder back a little, so it wouldn't be lying against her neck. Alex had a sudden flash of what it might feel like to have those silky dark copper strands running through his fingers, brushing against his face, and then frowned. Where the hell had that come from? Sure, she was pretty—beautiful, really, or would be, once she wasn't so shaken and pale—but they had far more important things to focus on right now.

"Strange like…almost like they were drugged or…."

"Or under a spell?"

A nod. "Yes. Like Matías had cast a spell on them. And I could feel it, too, or at least feel *something*, but for some reason it didn't seem to have the same effect on me. That is, I went along, and some part of me was trying to fight it, but I couldn't open my mouth to really say anything, to tell them to stop, that we shouldn't go to the guys' house. Every time I tried, I felt as if I was choking."

That did sound like a spell, a dark one of compliance, of control. Alex didn't know of anyone who possessed those kinds of powers. It was the sort of spell Damon Wilcox might have cast back in the day, but he was long gone. And anyway, if anyone in the de la Paz clan had attempted to meddle in those sorts of things, his grandmother would have sniffed them out immediately.

Well, she would have, once upon a time. Now....

His expression must have darkened, because Caitlin asked, voice sharp with worry, "What is it?"

"Nothing," he said immediately. His clan had been careful to keep hidden as much as they could about the truth of his *abuela*'s condition, and he didn't think it was his place to discuss it now. "I mean, there's no one in my clan who can do that sort of thing. Did they say they were de la Pazes?"

"Well, no," she admitted. "I just kind of assumed...."

He wanted to be annoyed with her for making that assumption , but he knew he probably would have done the same thing, had he been in a similar situation. Witches and warlocks always stuck to their clans' territories. Sure, you'd get some visiting from time to time, but always with permission. Since he wasn't privy to all of his grandmother's affairs, he didn't know for sure that Caitlin and her two companions had contacted her directly, but you could be damn sure someone in her clan had reached out to her, just to make sure it was all right for the girls come visiting in de la Paz territory. For all he knew, Maya had passed the information along to his mother, since she was sort of in charge down here in Tucson.

Which meant she was not going to be happy when she found out that a trio of unknown warlocks had been using some kind of forbidden magic right under all their noses.

"Anyway, that doesn't matter," Caitlin went on, pushing at the blanket that covered her, then sliding her legs off the couch. Her mouth tightened in pain, but she went on, "We need to go find them. Goddess only knows what those bastards are doing to Danica and Roslyn right now!"

"Hey," Alex said, and took a step toward her. "We can't just go charging in there if we don't know what we're dealing with."

She shot him an impatient look and got to her feet. For a second she seemed to teeter a bit, as if she wasn't quite as steady as she'd hoped, but then she straightened. When he saw her standing like that, he realized she was taller than he'd thought, unbending and slender. Of course, the impression of strength was marred somewhat by the unsightly bloodstains that marked her blouse and jeans.

"I left them," she said, and her tone had shifted from impatience to a sort of desolate pleading. "I shouldn't have done that."

He moved even closer, putting a hand on her arm. She tensed, and he let go. Even so, he maintained eye contact with her, hoping he could find a way to convince her that she'd done the right thing.

"If you'd stayed and tried to fight them, you'd prob-ably be dead now, Caitlin."

Her mouth compressed to a tight line, but she didn't argue. Encouraged, he went on,

"Running away was the smartest thing you could have done. You came here, got help. We're not going to abandon your friends. We're just waiting for reinforcements."

"And they're here," his mother said crisply, com-ing in through the back door, Valentina a few paces behind. Alex had been so focused on the young witch before him that he hadn't even heard the door open.

Neither apparently had Caitlin, since she star-tled, but then seemed to regain some of her compo-sure. "Who are you?"

"I am Luz Trujillo, Alex's mother—and Maya de la Paz's daughter. You might say I'm the deputy *prima* for Tucson." Her gaze moved from Caitlin to Alex and back again. "Now, tell me more about these warlocks you met."

CHAPTER THREE

THERE WAS SUCH A NOTE OF COMMAND IN LUZ Trujillo's voice that Caitlin didn't quite have the courage to continue with her protests, but instead gave a quickly truncated account of what she'd already told Alex and the healer, Valentina. Like Valentina, Alex's mother was darkly beautiful, her shining black hair pulled back into an elegant ponytail that hung halfway down her back. She was wearing a simple bright pink dress that complemented her olive complexion, and low-heeled sandals.

Really, it looked like she'd come here from brunch with friends or maybe early drinks at the country club, and it felt somewhat incongruous to be talking to her about spells of coercion and spiked margaritas. But as Caitlin went on, and did her best to describe the circle she'd seen chalked on the floor in that empty sunroom, Luz Trujillo's elegant arched brows kept pulling together into a deeper and deeper frown.

Once Caitlin was done with her account, explaining how Matías had stabbed her after she'd kneed him in the groin, all was silent in the room for several seconds. Three pairs of dark eyes were fastened on her, all of them troubled, and she didn't know quite what to do with her hands. She ended up crossing them in front of her; at least that covered up some of the bloodstains on the peasant-style blouse she wore. In a way, Alex's concerned regard was the worst, just because she still felt awful for thinking that he could have been connected in any way with Matías and his cronies. Alex practically radiated good, and she could see how worried he was about her, even though they'd just met.

At last Luz said, "Can you take us back to this house? Do you remember where it was?"

The image of it was burned permanently on Caitlin's brain. She nodded, then asked in diffident tones, "So...only the four of us will be going?" It seemed rude to come right out and say she didn't think they would be enough to combat those three warlocks, but she had to voice her concern somehow.

An amused smile spread over Luz Trujillo's full mouth. "Actually, it will only be the three of us. Valentina is...not one for confrontations. But I think you'll find you will be well protected."

Confused, Caitlin looked over at Alex for clarification. His expression had turned grim, and he gave a small nod at his mother before saying, "You'll see, when the time comes."

Well, that was reassuring. But she didn't want to waste any more time talking; she just wanted to get out there and pray that Roslyn and Danica were still all right. Or at least as all right as they could be, given who they were with.

Luz appeared to sense her impatience. "Lead us there, Caitlin. Valentina will wait here for us."

Each step seemed to jolt the tender spot in her side, the place where Matías had slid his knife in, but Caitlin ignored the pain, instead taking Alex and his mother from the room in the back of the store, across a stretch of asphalt that appeared to be both the loading area for the business and the employee parking lot, and over to the street. At first she wondered why they hadn't driven, but then she noted how Luz walked with her hands spread before her, as if she were sensing the psychic currents in the area.

When they got to the corner where the main street intersected with the smaller road that led into the residential area, Luz paused. "Now, Alex. I can feel…something…but I am not sure what it is."

He nodded, then told Caitlin, "Come in a little closer."

Mystified, she did as he'd instructed, while his mother did the same thing on his other side, standing a foot or so away from him. He pulled in a breath, dark eyes somber, and then—

— and then the air seemed to somehow shimmer around them, forming a kind of dome approximately seven or so feet high and around ten feet in diameter. Caitlin could see through it, although the world appeared slightly distorted, as if she were viewing it from inside a soap bubble.

"What is that?" she breathed.

"His talent," Luz said, sounding as proud as if she'd conjured that strange transparent dome herself. "Nothing can get through it."

"Nothing?"

"Well, air, obviously," Alex replied, and his tone, in direct contrast to his mother's, was almost embarrassed. "But nothing else. Rain. Sticks. Stones. Spells," he added significantly.

"Wow," Caitlin said, impressed despite the situation. She'd never heard of a talent like that before. No wonder Luz hadn't been concerned about going back to the evil warlocks' house with only her son and Caitlin at her side.

"So lead on, please, Caitlin," Luz said in that commanding way of hers.

It wasn't far. Down this short feeder lane, then left onto a street lined with one-story houses.

Nothing appeared to have changed since she'd run past here—maybe a car was now in one driveway, and had left another. Just the typical coming and going you'd see on any weekday.

And there was the house, looking perfectly ordinary, with its neat walk and carefully arranged succulents in the yard, and one graceful palm as an accent. Even so, looking at it made the blood in Caitlin's veins go cold all over again, as if she'd just had another sip of Matías' tainted margaritas.

"It's all right," Alex murmured. "There's really nothing they can do to get through the shield."

"How long can you hold it?"

"At least an hour."

That reassured her a bit. Luz nodded, and Caitlin began moving up the walk, Alex right next to her, his mother shifting so she was a few paces ahead of them. When they got to the front door, it stood slightly ajar. What the…?

Luz paused there, seeming to breathe in the air and taste it, as if somehow by doing so she could divine who was in the house and what they were doing. At the same time, Caitlin attempted to force that unruly sixth sense of her own to tell her what the warlocks were up to, but she felt nothing. Well, not precisely nothing. Even though she knew Alex's dome was protecting the three of them, her hands still shook, and cold fear seemed to be eating away at her stomach. But she'd run away once; she wouldn't do that again.

At last, Luz reached out and pushed the door open all the way. That was strange, seeing her hand go through the dome to touch the door handle and then come back inside the bubble of Alex's spell. She sent an inquiring glance in his direction.

"It's sort of like one-way glass, I guess," he told her in a murmur. "We can reach through it and not harm ourselves, and even cast spells through it, but it doesn't work the other way."

"Handy."

But then Luz was moving forward, and so Alex had to move with her, Caitlin sticking close to his side. It should have felt strange to be so near someone she'd only just met, but instead his presence felt safe, comforting. He smelled good, too.

Of all the things to be thinking about right now, she scolded herself, even as she crossed the threshold into the house, halfway expecting some sort of magical attack to begin assaulting the dome that surrounded the three of them.

Nothing happened, though, and she looked around in some mystification. The house was dead silent, except for the background hum of the central air conditioning system.

"Where?" Luz whispered.

"Down the hall is the kitchen, and then off that is the sun porch with the—with the circle." Caitlin didn't know how else to describe it. The thing had been some sort of summoning device, some sort of gateway, that much she knew, even if she had no experience with that kind of dark and terrible magic. But "circle" worked well enough to describe what she had seen.

Luz nodded and moved through the living room and past the dining room, then into the kitchen. No sign of the three warlocks, or of Danica and Roslyn. Even the counters were clear, the blender's mixing container washed out and set back on its base.

This whole thing was wrong, but for some reason that cleaned-up blender felt the most wrong of all. How could the warlocks have so quickly gotten rid of any trace of their being here? It couldn't have been more than twenty minutes or so since she bolted from the house.

Worse, she could feel Luz and Alex giving her puzzled glances, as if they were wondering whether she'd screwed up and brought them to the wrong house or something. But she knew that wasn't the case—this *was* the right place. See, there was the bowl of limes on the counter, sitting exactly where she remembered seeing it.

Without thinking, she stalked past Luz, almost through the dome's protective membrane. Behind her, Alex moved quickly, making sure she stayed even with the bubble. He didn't say anything, didn't reprimand her for being so careless, but even now, tense and worried as she was, she knew that had been a stupid move.

Not that it really mattered, because when they got to the sun porch, it was empty as well. No circle. No ring of colored candles. And definitely no warlocks or captive witches.

"It was right here," Caitlin protested. "I saw it. I swear."

"We're not saying you didn't," Alex said quietly, his tone reassuring. "*Mamita,* you feeling anything?"

Luz held herself very still, breathing in and out. Then her nose wrinkled, as if she had just smelled something foul.

"Drop the spell for now, Alex," she told him. "There is no one here, and it is getting in my way."

At once the dome shivered out of existence. Luz stepped forward so she was standing nearly in the center of the room, almost exactly where the circle had once been, although no trace of it was left. Caitlin didn't bother to wonder how Luz had managed to do that—she was Maya de la Paz's daughter, after all, and most likely the next *prima.* Her talents must be very strong.

"Yes," she said at last. "It was some kind of summoning spell. Black, and made blacker still by being mixed with blood. What they were summoning, I can't say for sure. Perhaps the spell was interrupted by your running away, Caitlin. That frightened them, I think, or at least compelled them to leave this place so they would not be caught. I'm not sure if they knew the *mercado* was owned by witches, but I think perhaps they did. And they knew if you sensed that, then you would soon be bringing help."

"But I *didn't* know," Caitlin said, wondering why Luz Trujillo would think she'd gone to the store on purpose. "I just went to the first place that looked safe."

"Ah, that is what you think happened," Luz replied. "But there was another restaurant and a dentist's office between that street corner and our store, and yet you headed straight for the *mercado*. Your witch senses instinctively sent you there because it was the one place you were certain to find help."

Was that what had happened? It was hard to know for sure. She'd been in so much pain and frightened out of her mind, so Caitlin knew she hadn't been thinking clearly. And yet she had gone into that one particular store, and straight to the young man she knew would help her.

Alex. He was watching her carefully now, expression sober. Goddess, but he was good-looking. Angela must have been awfully disappointed when it turned out Alex wasn't her consort. Well, she'd done all right in the end, but at the time....

And that's a ridiculous thing to be thinking about now. So what if Alex is good-looking...and kind...and powerful? Roslyn and Danica are still missing.

Caitlin pulled in a breath and tore her gaze away from Alex so she could focus on Luz. "So...what now? Can you sense where they've gone?"

The older woman didn't reply at first, only stood there in the center of the room, her hands still spread in that gesture Caitlin was coming to recognize as her "divining" one. Then she shook her head. "Not really. Maybe the faintest trace of some kind of energy pulling toward the south. But nothing beyond that."

"But what do we do now?" Caitlin asked. She knew she sounded frantic, but she didn't much care. Her friends were still missing, taken the Goddess only knew where by a trio of warlocks who clearly had no compunction about using them to power their own hideous rituals.

"We don't panic," Luz said. Her expression softened, and she came back over to where Caitlin stood next to Alex, then laid a hand on her arm. "We are certainly not going to let the matter go. Valentina promised to contact Maya while we came over here, so she knows of the situation. I think now we should go and speak with her."

"Go up to Scottsdale?" Wait, what was the point of that? She couldn't leave Tucson, not if her friends might still be hidden somewhere within the city limits.

Sensing her turmoil, Luz pressed her fingers against Caitlin's arm for just a second, as if to reassure her, and said, "My dear, Maya will most certainly want to speak with you. We will send out the word here in Tucson, so that all of our clan members in the city will be on the lookout for your friends and the warlocks who have kidnapped them. You will not be abandoning your friends, only leaving for a few hours. You can come back here afterward."

"I don't know if it's a good idea to have her staying in a condo by herself after what happened," Adam began, his tone dubious, and Luz broke in, saying,

"Of course not. It would probably be best if she stayed with you."

Caitlin felt her eyes widen. Had Alex's mother seriously just suggested that she stay with her son?

He didn't look all that enthused by the prospect. Not making eye contact with either of them, he said, "Are you sure that's such a good idea?"

"You are the best suited to protect her," his mother said, her tone so matter-of-fact that it didn't leave much room for argument. She glanced over at

Caitlin. "Unless you would prefer that we send you home to Jerome so your family can watch over you?"

No, that didn't sound good at all. Never mind that she didn't actually live in Jerome anymore, but in the apartment she shared with Danica in Flagstaff. That sounded even less secure than going back to her old room in her parents' big Victorian house on Paradise Lane. Yes, she supposed the Wilcoxes would make sure she was looked after…if her parents would even agree to her going back up to Flagstaff after what had happened…but that was the coward's way out. Hide up in northern Arizona while those bastards still had Danica and Roslyn with them? No way.

"No," Caitlin said, her tone firm. All right, it would be beyond awkward to go and stay with Alex Trujillo, but at least she'd still be here in Tucson. "I don't want to go to Jerome."

"Well, then," Luz said. "I think we should be on our way to Scottsdale."

After leaving the house the warlocks had so briefly occupied, Alex and his mother took Caitlin back to the store. Just for a few minutes, enough so he could tell Manuela that family business had come up and that she'd have to keep an eye on things for him, and so he could trade the shirt he wore, the one with Caitlin's bloody handprints on the sleeve, for the fresh one he kept hanging in the office, just in case he spilled something on himself during the workday.

Manuela nodded and said it was no problem, but he could tell from the inquisitive gleam in her eyes that she really wanted to know what was going on, and would probably be on the phone the second they left, trying to ferret out what she could from the family grapevine.

Good luck with that, he thought, *because no one else knows anything about all this. Except Valentina, and she knows how to keep secrets.*

His mother had already asked him to drive, so they all got into his shiny black Pathfinder, Caitlin in the passenger seat, and his mother in the back directly behind her. As they pulled out of the parking lot, his mother said, "Caitlin, I can cast a small illusion to hide the stains on your clothing. Or would you rather we stopped at the mall on our way out of town, so you can buy something new?"

In the seat next to him, Caitlin brushed at the bloodstains on her jeans. "Couldn't you just take me back to the condo? All my luggage is there."

Luz hesitated, then said, "I suppose that would work as well. But we will need to be on our guard, just in case the warlocks who took your friends have gone there for some reason."

From the way Caitlin paled, Alex guessed she hadn't considered that particular angle. But she lifted her chin and replied, "I hope they have. Then we can catch them and put an end to all this."

"Perhaps," Luz allowed.

Alex doubted it would be that simple. Still, he cast the spell of protection around the three of them once again as they got out of his SUV and followed Caitlin to her rented condo. It was a nice one, not some cramped studio, but a regular one-bedroom with a full kitchen and a shaded patio. Scattered around the main living space were various bits of luggage; it looked as if the three girls had just dumped their suitcases and gone out looking for a good time, figuring they could always unpack later.

For some reason, looking at that abandoned luggage upset him, since it seemed to bring home the reality of the situation, that two of the girls who'd brought those suitcases here to Tucson might not ever need them again.

You don't know that, he told himself. *What those warlocks were doing was terrible, but from what Caitlin said, it didn't sound as if they intended to kill those girls.*

Yet, anyway.

Looking pale and grim, as if a similar thought had crossed her mind, Caitlin gathered up two of the suitcases and disappeared into the bedroom. She shut the door quietly behind her.

Alex glanced over at his mother. "Are you going to tell her about *abuelita?*"

Jaw tight, she shook her head. "She will see for herself soon enough. Perhaps we shouldn't have kept so quiet about this, but...."

"Grandmother said she didn't want the news to get out. The situation isn't the same as it was two years ago, but you know she still doesn't want to appear weak."

"I know." His mother, usually so serene, so calm and in control, now just looked tired. Shadows seemed to have appeared from nowhere to touch the smooth skin under her eyes. "And we've all respected her decision. But no secret can remain hidden forever."

That much was true. And how much more of the burden would his mother have to carry now, with this latest crisis? He didn't know. She was strong—everyone in his clan was strong—but he knew she'd always believed she wouldn't have to take the mantle of *prima* from her mother for many years yet to come.

"At least relations between the clans are very good now," he ventured, but she appeared far from reassured.

"They have been. But once the McAllisters and the Wilcoxes learn of what has happened to their daughters while visiting our territory?" Her shoulders lifted, and he realized then how she had lost weight over the past few months, how those shoulders now seemed much thinner and narrower.

"That was not our fault," Alex argued. "No one could have foreseen anything like this happening."

"You can say that, and in our case, it is partially true. We have no seers among us right now. Even so, there was a time when *mamita* could have sensed a strange witch or warlock entering our territory and given the alert. The *prima* of the McAllisters and the *primus* of the Wilcoxes both know she had this ability once upon a time, and so they will want to know how such a thing could have occurred now."

It still sounded strange to think of Angela and Connor in such a way, but he knew his mother referred to them by their formal titles as a sign of respect. Alex couldn't claim to know Angela well. However, he'd interacted with her enough to believe she'd listen to what the de la Pazes had to say for themselves and wouldn't immediately think the worst. Connor he didn't know at all, but the reports seemed to indicate he was fairly level-headed as well, and more or less the polar opposite of his brother, who'd always been quick to take offense and never met a scheme he didn't like.

The door to the bedroom opened then, and Caitlin emerged, looking far more in control than the disheveled girl who had left them five minutes earlier. She'd changed into a fresh pair of jeans and another one of those peasant-style tops, this one a fresh yellow with turquoise embroidery, and she'd brushed her hair and put on a little makeup, some lip gloss and maybe mascara. Gold hoops gleamed in her ears.

She was stunning.

Alex realized he was staring and said, his tone probably too casual, "You ready?"

If she'd noticed the way he was looking at her, she didn't give any indication of it. "Yes, thank you. I feel—well, not all the way better, but better."

"Good," Luz said in approval. "Then we should be on our way."

Caitlin made a strange abortive step toward the coffee table, then stopped and shook her head. "Sorry," she said. "It's just—I was about to grab my purse, and then I realized I left it back at the war-locks' house when I ran. So now those bastards have my phone and my wallet, my debit card...." She trailed off, looking so worried that Alex had to fight the impulse to go and give her a hug, to tell her it was all right.

Instead, he stayed where he was and asked his mother, "Shouldn't Caitlin call that in? They could be using her credit cards."

"No, I don't think so," Luz said, so emphatically that a little of the worry seemed to leave Caitlin's face. "If they use any of her credit cards, then they will give away their position. And what they have in their favor right now is that we don't know where they are."

"I should still call, though...."

"Later." Luz appeared to hesitate, then went on, "My dear, I would be more worried about any personal items you had in your purse. With the dark magic these warlocks are using, it's possible they could use something as innocent as a strand of hair from a brush, or a family photo, to attempt to do you harm."

The color seemed to drain from Caitlin's cheeks, making the bit of blush she must have applied while freshening her makeup stand out against her white skin. But her voice was firm enough as she said, "I did have a hairbrush in there. I'd just changed out my wallet, though, and hadn't transferred over a lot of the personal stuff. So they won't find too much, unless they want to abuse my Walgreens reward card or something."

Hearing this, Alex wanted to smile. Yes, she was scared, and worried, but he could tell she wasn't going to lie down and give up. Those McAllister witches were tougher than they looked.

"That's good to hear," Luz said. "But let's gather up your things and bring them with us. That way, when we are done at Maya's house, you can go directly to Alex's place. Do we need to wait for you to pack anything?"

"No," Caitlin said. "I put everything back as I used it. Just give me a sec to go get my bags—I left them sitting on the bed." She headed back into the other room.

Alex gave his mother a sharp look, and she smiled. "Worried, my son?"

"Worried" probably wasn't the exact word. Disturbed...on edge...unsure of himself. Was he ready to have a beauty like Caitlin McAllister camped out in his house for the indefinite future?

"I'm fine," he said shortly.

Right after that, she came back in, a hard-sided suitcase in one hand and a smaller weekender-style bag in the other. She lifted her chin, and her shining hair fell over her shoulders as she announced, "I'm ready."

Once again Alex wondered what it would feel like, those rivers of molten copper slipping through his fingers, and a not entirely unpleasant shiver went over him. This wasn't good. He shouldn't be attracted to her. He couldn't, not with his mother inviting her to come stay with him so she would be safe.

All right, maybe she'd be safe from those unknown warlocks if she was staying at his house.

The question was, would she be safe from him?

CHAPTER FOUR

EVERYTHING WAS HAPPENING SO FAST, MOVING SO QUICKLY. Now they were back in Alex's SUV, heading north toward Scottsdale and a meeting with Maya de la Paz. Somehow that felt wrong, as if she should be calling her parents to tell them what had happened, or at least Roslyn's parents—belatedly, Caitlin realized she didn't even have a number where she could reach Danica's mother and father, now that her cell phone with all its stored contact information was gone—but when she'd tried to suggest doing so, Luz Trujillo had only shaken her head and told her that it was Maya's duty to inform the *prima* of the McAllisters and the Wilcox *primus* that something terrible had happened to two of their witches while visiting in de la Paz territory.

That had made a little sense, but Caitlin still thought it was wrong that her Aunt Lysette and Uncle

Marcus didn't know anything of what had happened to their daughter, and neither did Olivia and Joseph Wilcox. But there wasn't much she could do about it now. If she'd wanted to call anyone, she should have done it while she was back at the condo and had access to a landline.

And maybe those warlocks had looked up Lysette's and Marcus' number where it was stored in her contacts, and had already called. Maybe they'd made a ransom demand or something. No, that didn't feel right. Those warlocks hadn't been after money. They'd wanted Roslyn and Danica…and Caitlin herself, only she'd somehow been lucky enough or crazy enough or whatever to get away. Something about the blood…she didn't know what it was for sure. A whisper of a whisper, the sort of subject that was always carefully avoided whenever impressionable ears were around. Blood magic was the darkest kind, one that had been forbidden for generations. What were those three warlocks trying to do?

She stared out at the unfamiliar landscape passing by outside the SUV's windows. How dry and dusty it was here, how inhospitable-looking. No, that wasn't exactly fair. At this time of year, there were wildflowers blooming along the edges of the highway, in shades of bright coral and pale, pale lavender and purest white. Even the desert had its blooms,

although sometimes you had to look harder to find
them.

On the way out of town, Alex had stopped at a
drive-through and gotten iced teas for everyone. Luz
had asked if Caitlin wanted anything to eat, and she'd
shaken her head. It had been a long time since the
burger she'd eaten on her way into Phoenix, when
Danica had pulled over at an In-N-Out on the outskirts of the suburban sprawl, but at the moment,
the thought of trying to force some food down her
throat only made her feel vaguely nauseated. At
some point Caitlin knew she'd have to eat, but not
now. Right now, she just had to get through this
interview with Maya de la Paz.

That notion was almost as frightening as the
thought of confronting those three warlocks again.
Caitlin had never met Maya, or even seen her, but
she'd heard stories about what a tough woman the
de la Paz *prima* was, how no witch or warlock with
a healthy sense of self-preservation would ever think
about going up against her. She was sure to ask questions, hard questions, and Caitlin had no idea how
she would ever begin to answer them.

She sipped some of her iced tea and then closed
her eyes, once again willing the strange ability that
slept within her to wake up and tell her where her
friends were. But she saw nothing, only the glare
of the bright afternoon sun coming in through the

car's windows, a glare that somehow managed to penetrate her closed eyelids, burning down out of a hard, bright blue sky with not even a single cloud in it. You couldn't hide under a sky like that. It exposed everything.

Trying not to sigh, she opened her eyes just in time to see Alex pull off the freeway and head slightly northeast, along wide boulevards planted with cactus and palm trees in the center dividers. It looked very unlike Jerome. Well, to be fair, so did Flagstaff, but Flag had a certain wild woolliness in common with Jerome, whereas Scottsdale might as well have been on another planet, with its expensive homes and upscale-looking shopping centers, and equally upscale and expensive cars on either side.

Maya's house was intimidating as well, a handsome Santa Fe–style compound with an actual courtyard with a fountain in it. Everything about the place made Caitlin feel small and shabby, like a poor relation coming to visit some rich great-aunt in the city or something. Which was silly, because it certainly didn't matter how rich Maya de la Paz was or wasn't, or how homespun the McAllister witches might seem in contrast to all this splendor. The important thing was whether Maya could help her or not.

Luz didn't seem inclined to stand on ceremony, but only led Caitlin and Alex through the courtyard with its bright-blooming flowers and on past a massive front door of aged timbers banded in black iron. As they entered the foyer, fully two stories tall, Luz called out, "*Mamita!* We're here."

"In the living room," a soft voice replied, so whispery and dry that Caitlin could barely hear it.

The three of them entered the living room, where a tiny woman sat on one of the leather couches there. A knitted afghan covered her legs, and a glass of water was sitting on a lap tray on top of that, as if she didn't have the strength to even reach as far as the coffee table to get her refreshment.

It took everything Caitlin had in her not to stare. This—*this* was the fabled Maya de la Paz?

For the woman before her looked as dry and shriveled as if she'd been left out in the Sonoran Desert for fifteen years, her hair white, her olive skin cut through with deep furrows, as if rain had pressed it into the sorts of gullies Caitlin had seen in the washes and canyons near her home. Her hands, where they rested on the tray, were covered in raised veins and age spots, and seemed to tremble.

Somehow Caitlin found her voice, managed to say, "Hello, Mrs. de la Paz."

"Maya," the woman said in that soft, whispery voice, which sounded like a rustle of brittle leaves. "You seem surprised."

"No, I—"

A lift of her hand. "You should be. This is not how I should be…or how I would choose to be. My clan has not spoken of it to anyone."

For the first time, Caitlin tore her gaze away from Maya's withered form, saw the naked worry in Luz Trujillo's face, the sadness in Alex's dark eyes. Whatever had happened to their *prima*, it seemed to be something more than merely old age or illness or infirmity. No wonder the de la Paz family had done its best to conceal the condition of their matriarch.

"But this is not why you are here," Maya went on. "I wish to speak with you of what happened to your friends. Come, sit here on the sofa."

Not daring to protest, Caitlin moved away from Luz and Alex, and took a seat on the couch, sitting down carefully so as not to jostle the fragile old woman. Seen up close like this, she appeared even more brittle, as if she might snap in two if Caitlin made too sudden a move.

For all that they were framed in wrinkles and bags, and so deeply shadowed they looked almost sunken, Maya's black eyes were very bright. They glinted now as she looked at her daughter and grandson. "You two—there is some fresh lemonade in the kitchen. Go and get yourselves some. I wish to speak to Caitlin alone."

That was the last thing Caitlin wanted, but she knew she didn't dare protest. Neither, it seemed, did

Luz or Alex, because they nodded and headed out of the room, Alex giving Caitlin a single backward glance as he did so. Something in that gaze felt very warm and friendly, and somehow, meeting his eyes, she didn't feel quite as nervous about being left alone with Maya as she might otherwise have.

The *prima* didn't miss that look, either, it seemed; her mouth, surrounded by deep lines, seemed to purse in apparent amusement, and possibly approval. "My Alex, he is a very good boy."

Not sure how exactly she should respond to that remark, Caitlin ventured, "He's been very nice."

"Nice?" Maya chuckled, but the laugh turned into a cough, and she had to drink some of the water from the glass on her tray before she could continue. "Well, I suppose we can leave it at that for now. Valentina has related the basics to me, but I want to hear from you what happened."

Again? Caitlin thought, but she took a breath and then dutifully recounted everything that had occurred after she and Danica and Roslyn walked into that Mexican restaurant. Well, almost everything. If she could get away with not revealing anything of her own strange visions and feelings, she would. None of that was Maya's business.

When she was done, Caitlin shifted on the couch, her mouth dry. She wished she could have some of the lemonade Alex and his mother were currently off drinking in the kitchen. Why Maya hadn't offered her some, or at least a glass of water, Caitlin wasn't sure. Maybe she'd intended the apparent oversight as a subtle show of power. If that were the case, Caitlin knew she wouldn't allow herself to show any signs of discomfort. At least she was reasonably hydrated, considering the iced tea she'd finished off right before Alex parked his SUV in front of Maya's house.

"Ah," Maya said, after a protracted pause. That could have meant anything...or nothing. The old woman lifted the glass of water from her lap tray and drank slowly before setting the glass back down. "Tell me, Caitlin McAllister...do you truly intend to keep hiding your gifts from everyone?"

Her mouth was dry, and Caitlin wondered if she'd been too hasty in thinking she'd be above asking for a glass of water of her own to quench her thirst. Maya's black eyes were fixed on her, far too penetrating, too keen.

"What gifts?" Caitlin managed.

A pair of sparse salt-and-pepper eyebrows drew together, and Maya responded, "You can lie to your family, and you can lie to yourself, but I will not allow you to lie to me."

Crap. Since she didn't have a glass she could fiddle with, or a purse strap or anything else along those lines, Caitlin had to settle for knotting her fingers together and slipping them over one knee. "I don't know what you're talking about."

"Oh, I think you do."

The sharpness of Maya's dark gaze disconcerted Caitlin. It could have been the contrast between their all-too-knowing gleam and her overall decrepit appearance. Once again Caitlin found herself wondering what had happened to Maya to cause such a degeneration. Surely no one in the McAllister or the Wilcox clans seemed to have an inkling of the sea change the de la Paz *prima* had undergone. Unfortunately, Caitlin knew she could sit here and speculate all she wanted, but in the end it wouldn't matter—Maya wanted answers, and apparently seemed content to sit here and wait for as long as it took to get them.

"I—" Caitlin floundered, wishing she had a plausible lie to cover up the very obvious holes in the story she'd told Maya. None of it made sense if you didn't factor in the seer abilities she'd tried so desperately to hide. And the *prima*, weak as she might be, was certainly no fool.

"You what?"

Desperation clear in her voice, despite her best attempts to hide it, Caitlin said, "I don't know what gifts you're talking about."

"Of course you do," Maya replied calmly. Again she drank from her glass of water, although this time the palsy in her hand was far too evident as she set the glass back down on its tray. "No ordinary witch could have sensed the evil in those young men—certainly your friends did not. And no ordinary witch would have had the ability to see past the spell this Matías cast and strike out at him so she could get away." The elderly witch's gaze sharpened, and Caitlin wondered if those gleaming black eyes might actually bore holes right through her, so piercing they seemed. "You do not have to tell your family, if that is your wish. But you need to tell me."

No way out. Oh, she could keep on lying...and Maya would only continue to stare at her, every tightening of her lips and lift of her eyebrows handing those lies right back to her. Caitlin broke the eye contact and looked out the large triptych of windows on the opposite wall, which showed a view of the courtyard. The sun was beginning to drop toward the west, glinting and glittering in the falling water of the fountain outside.

"They started about six years ago," Caitlin said at last, not looking at Maya, but keeping her gaze focused on the way the water splashed and danced in the fountain, the way it caught glints of gold and copper and bronze from the westering sun. "I'd see things, and they'd come true. Or sometimes they'd be coming true at the same time I saw them. It's not always consistent. But I do see things. I guess that makes me the McAllister's next seer. But I don't want to be that. I don't want people always asking me for advice and wanting to know what their futures will be. Why would anyone want to know that? The future is scary."

She broke off then, hands still knotted where they rested on her knee. She didn't want to look at Maya, see the disapproval on her face. No witch was supposed to deny the gifts that were her birthright, that ran as deeply in her blood as the genetic markers which dictated her hair color or the shape of her nose. No, those with witch blood were supposed to embrace those gifts, no matter what they might be. But Caitlin didn't want to know the future, especially Maya's, which was all but written in the weary lines of her face.

Silence then, broken only by the faint ticking of the clock on the mantel. If Alex and his mother were talking where they waited in the kitchen, they must have been speaking in low tones, or were far enough away that their voices couldn't carry all the way to the living room.

At last Maya said, her own voice soft, "When they came to me and told me I would be the next *prima*, I didn't want to believe it. My own mother, she was a strong witch—a *curandera*, a healer—but nowhere near strong enough to be *prima*. No, the title came to me from my cousin Luisa, and, like your own *prima* Angela, I was young when I had to take up that role, for although Luisa was my cousin, she was some thirty years my senior. I didn't want it. I wanted to live my own life, choose my own man, and not have to take the consort fate decreed should be mine."

These revelations made Caitlin sit up a little straighter. She had never even stopped to think that perhaps Maya, the redoubtable head of the de la Paz clan, had not wanted to take on that role, because everything Caitlin had heard made it seem as if Maya had been born to it. In that same moment, she also wondered who that consort was, as Caitlin had seen no evidence of a husband here in the house, and neither had she ever heard anyone mention him by name. "But you didn't say no."

"Of course not. Just as Angela did not say no when that mantle fell to her. She knew what she had to do and did not shrink from it."

Although Maya's tone was mild, Caitlin couldn't help thinking there was just a hint of disapproval in it. "So I'm a coward."

"Would a coward have fought back against a warlock such as Matías?" Maya shook her head, then went on, "'Coward' is too simple a word to use here, I think. I can understand why you would not want to tell anyone of the gifts that had come to you, for in some ways I think it is even more difficult to be the seer of a clan than to be its *prima,* or one of its elders. The visions can intrude when you do not wish them to, and everyone, even the *prima* herself, will be coming to you for advice."

"So what should I do?" Caitlin asked, and hated herself for the quaver of worry she heard in her voice.

Maya smiled sadly, then reached out to touch Caitlin's hand. Only briefly, and even that gentle brush felt more like the whisper of a frail, bird-like wing than actual fingers. "You will have to ask yourself whether the lives of your friends are worth revealing your gift to your clan. Because I will tell you, Caitlin McAllister, that this is only the beginning. You cannot hide what you are, or even a part of it. You must embrace it fully. It is your sight that can save them…if you'll let it. For if you do not, nothing else on earth can save them."

This was the thing she'd feared all along, that the visions and feelings and vague sensations of foreboding were the only things that might somehow lead her to wherever Danica and Roslyn had been taken. And even then it might be too late, if Matías and his cronies determined that the powers they were summoning needed a greater sacrifice than just a few drops of innocent blood.

"I don't—I don't know how to use it," Caitlin whispered at last. "I've spent so many years trying to hide it that now…I guess I'm afraid to even try tapping into it."

"That's not surprising," Maya said, and instead of sounding disapproving, her tone was gentle, if a little sad. "But your gift wants to manifest itself, which is why you've had visions, even if you've tried to suppress them. All you must do is take down the barriers you've built up."

All. Caitlin thought of the past six years, of how she'd tried to close her mind down whenever those unwanted images began to pop into it. That didn't always work, of course; instead, her gift had edged its way into her dreams, or the unguarded moments when she was thinking of something else entirely. But it had never abandoned her, and had even tried to protect her, back there at the bar when Matías and Jorge and Tomas approached her and her friends. If only she had trusted in it more.

Seeming to sense her inner turmoil, Maya said, "Let it move through you now. Don't try to direct it. Think of your gift as a river—it knows where it must flow. Trying to redirect it will only cause harm. And remember—*always* remember—that your gift is part of you. It is not some alien thing attempting to act on you from outside."

That was a little more reassuring. Even so, Caitlin didn't quite know what she should be doing with herself. Should she close her eyes? Choose one object in the room and focus on it? Always before, the visions had come without her bidding them, without even knowing exactly where they had come from.

But then it didn't matter, because the room around her suddenly seemed to blank out. No, that wasn't quite right. It was more as if another image overlaid the one she had just been seeing, obscuring the leather couch and the faded Persian rug on the floor, the dancing waters of the fountain outside in the courtyard. Instead, she saw a small room, around the same size as the living room in the apartment she shared with Danica in Flagstaff, similarly furnished in the kind of shabby hand-me-downs that Danica had referred to as "early Salvation Army."

And there was Danica herself, sitting on a truly hideous plaid sofa, with Roslyn next to her. Both girls had their eyes open, and yet Caitlin had the uneasy feeling that neither of them was truly *there*, as if their individual selves had either fled or were so deeply buried that they might as well not be there at all. Roslyn's arms showed several cuts, but Danica's were still unmarked. Maybe wherever the strange warlocks had fled wasn't suited for a summoning, or maybe they simply hadn't had enough time to redraw the circle and begin all over again.

"Fucking *puta*," Caitlin heard Matías say, and even though she knew this was a vision, that the warlock was probably miles and miles away, she gasped.

At once the image of that shabby living room, and of her two friends, faded away.

"You saw them." It was a statement, not a question.

"Yes. I think—I think it must have been an apartment somewhere, although I couldn't tell where. Both Roslyn and Danica seemed okay, but still…." The words seemed to evaporate into the air, since Caitlin couldn't quite bring herself to say the word "enchanted." No, they weren't enchanted. That was far too pretty a term for what was being done to them. Hexed, or bespelled, or good old brainwashed? Any of those words seemed far more appropriate to the situation.

"They are not themselves," the de la Paz *prima* said.

That was an understatement. "No. Whatever this hold is that Matías seems to have on them…it's strong."

Maya's thin, dry lips seemed to stretch even tighter as her mouth compressed. "He is using a kind of magic that has been forbidden for generations. And I know he is none of mine."

"So…where did he come from?" Caitlin asked, perplexed. The witch clans had their territories, and everyone more or less stayed in theirs, except in certain cases, and that was that. For a warlock of unknown origin to suddenly appear in de la Paz territory and begin wielding the sort of black magic that had been outlawed years and years ago was more than terrifying. It meant that the rules the witch clans had been following all these years had suddenly been abandoned.

"As I have not seen him, or experienced the magic he uses firsthand, I can only guess." Maya sighed, and Caitlin fancied she could hear that breath rattling in the older woman's narrow chest. "But I fear very much that he is one of the California warlocks whom Angela and Connor fell afoul of several years ago, or at the very least is associated with them in some way. Símon Santiago does not keep as close an eye on the witches and warlocks in his clan as he should. True, it is difficult, with a territory as large as his, but...."

This was the first Caitlin had heard of any trouble with warlocks in California. True, her *prima* and *primus* had been pretty well occupied for the past few years, what with first breaking the Wilcox curse and then having twins to raise, but you'd think they would have said something. Or maybe they did, and the elders—Caitlin's mother among them—did know, and had decided for whatever reason not to pass that intelligence along to the next generation. It was possible they'd thought no trouble would come to them, with the Wilcox and McAllister clans now more or less joined, and California and its problems so very far away.

But trouble had come, even if it had taken a few northern Arizona witches to go to Tucson before disaster struck.

"Then shouldn't you approach this Simón Santiago and let him know what's going on?" Caitlin asked. Strange that the Santiago clan had a warlock in charge, when almost every clan save the Wilcoxes had a *prima* at its head. "Maybe, even if he couldn't help directly, he would be able to give us some information on how to track down Matías. I mean, yes, I just saw him in a vision, but a crappy-looking apartment with a very ugly plaid couch isn't a lot to go on."

Despite everything, Maya smiled slightly. Her expression turned grim quickly enough after that, though, as she replied, "I fear it is not quite so easy. You see, Simón is not actually the true head of the clan—his wife Graciela is the actual *prima*. But she suffered a fall some years ago, and while they have a healer, she is not a very strong one, and was unable to make the Santiago *prima* whole. Graciela has been in a wheelchair for twenty years now, and Simón more or less runs the clan. I was never able to learn precisely what his particular gift is, but whatever it might be, clearly it is not well-suited to him being in charge of the Santiagos' territory."

"This just gets better and better, doesn't it?"

A rusty chuckle. "Yes, I fear that we will not have much luck going to them for help. Perhaps we will still have to try, if that is what the kidnapped girls' parents and your *prima* and *primus* want." Maya went still then, her dark eyes focused on the bright colors of the flowers in the courtyard, the fountain dancing in the last light of the afternoon, completely oblivious to the turmoil within the house. "And I will admit to you, Caitlin, that is not a phone call I will enjoy making. But it is my responsibility."

"Just as it's mine to keep looking for Roslyn and Danica," Caitlin said, and was gratified to see the de la Paz *prima* give her an approving look.

"Yes, I fear that task will fall to you. The Wilcoxes have a seer—"

"Marie Begonie," Caitlin supplied.

"Yes, Marie. And no doubt she will wish to help, as one of her clan's own has been taken as well."

It would be a relief to have Marie involved, even if Caitlin had to admit to herself that she'd never warmed to the Wilcox seer. Apparently she was miles friendlier than she used to be, now that she'd been reunited with the love of her teenage years, but even so, the woman could be awfully prickly at times. Somehow, though, Caitlin got the feeling that Marie wasn't going to be all that much help here. For whatever reason, the universe seemed to have decreed that this task would fall on her own woefully unprepared shoulders.

Her expression must have shifted, because Maya said, "But you don't think Marie will be of much assistance."

"I—I'm not sure. But...." Caitlin lifted her shoulders. "I'm getting a feeling."

"And you should trust it." With a trembling hand, Maya took her glass of water and drained the rest of its contents. "But now, I am afraid I will have to make some phone calls. If you could go to the kitchen and send Luz to me? It's down the hall, toward the back of the house."

"Sure," Caitlin said, rising from the couch. Maya's request had made it clear enough that their audience was over. And although Caitlin experienced a slight stab of relief at being released from this interview, she was not looking forward to the inevitable fallout of those phone calls the de la Paz *prima* was about to make.

Still, she'd worry about that later. For now, it was enough to make her escape.

CHAPTER FIVE

"They've been in there a long time," Alex said, glancing over at the digital clock on the microwave.

"I imagine they have a good deal to talk about," his mother replied, her tone somehow managing to be simultaneously mild and reproving. "It does no good to sit here and fidget."

He knew that, but he'd never been much good at sitting around and waiting. But since there wasn't much else to do, he drank some more of his lemonade and wished it was something a little stronger. A shot or two of Reposado might go down pretty well right now. But his *abuela* didn't keep spirits in her house, and even if she did, Alex knew better than to go in search of something he hadn't been offered.

If this wait felt torturous to him, he could only imagine what Caitlin must be going through. Getting grilled by Maya de la Paz was not something most people would particularly enjoy. Having to do it after being attacked by a trio of strange warlocks? No, thanks.

Even so, he hoped his grandmother was having better luck at extracting information from Caitlin than either he or his mother had. The girl was hiding something; he could tell that much, even if he couldn't quite figure out what it might be. That seemed like a foolish move on her part. How could he and the rest of the de la Paz clan help her get her friends back if she wasn't willing to tell the entire truth of what had happened?

Movement at the entrance to the kitchen caught the corner of his eye, and he shifted in his seat in the breakfast nook to see Caitlin standing there. For someone who'd just spent a good half hour having her story picked apart by his grandmother, the McAllister witch looked remarkably calm. She even smiled at Luz as she said, "Maya would like to talk to you now."

"Thank you, Caitlin," Luz said, sliding out of her seat and taking her glass of lemonade with her. "Alex, would you get Caitlin something to drink? She must be parched after all that talking."

As Caitlin murmured her thanks, Alex got up from his own chair and said, "Is lemonade all right, or would you rather have some water? I don't think my grandmother has much of anything else."

"Lemonade is fine," Caitlin replied, watching as Luz shot her an encouraging smile before going down the hallway that led to the living room.

Alex poured a glass and inclined his head toward the chair his mother had just vacated. "Want to sit down?"

"Definitely." She took a seat, then managed a half-smile as Alex handed her the glass of lemonade. After sipping some, she nodded. "That's better. Although right now I could use a margarita." She paused. "No, scratch that. After what Matías did, I don't think I'm going to want a margarita for a long time."

Frowning, Alex sat down. Even though she'd taken him and his mother to the house where the warlocks had brought the girls, shown them where the circle had been drawn, Caitlin hadn't been very specific about exactly what had gone down in there. "What *did* he do?"

She bit her lip and looked away, out through the stained-glass-bordered windows in the nook, the ones that had fascinated Alex when he was younger. One finger drew a line through the condensation on the outside of the glass as she appeared to contemplate the desert-y loveliness of the back garden, with its gravel walks and careful plantings of native flowers and shrubs and cactus. At last she said, "I told you he brought us back to that house for margaritas, right? Well, they were drugged or something. I had just a sip of one, and it made the spell he had cast so much worse. It was so hard to fight it." Shuddering slightly, she picked up her glass of lemonade and drank deeply, as if by doing so she could erase the taste of the tainted drink Matías had given her earlier that afternoon.

"But you did fight it," Alex reminded her gently, wishing he'd left it alone. He didn't like to see her so upset, eyes tragic, her jaw set. In that moment, he realized he'd barely seen her smile so far, and certainly never laugh.

He wanted to hear her laugh.

"I did," she said. "I still don't know how, exactly, but…." Looking up from her drink, she faced Alex squarely. In the warm late-afternoon light, her eyes seemed to glow almost green. "I wasn't telling you the truth earlier."

Puzzled, he asked, "You weren't?"

"Not really. I mean, I was trying to dance around the issue. The reason I knew something was off about Matías and his gang, and maybe part of the reason I was able to get away, is that I'm a seer. I *felt* how awful he was. In fact, I knew something terrible was going to happen even before we left Jerome. I just didn't know what it was, and I didn't want to tell anyone, because then they'd know."

"So…no one in your family knows you're a seer?"

She shook her head, and he tried not to stare at the waves of coppery hair that seemed to dance with the movement. "I couldn't tell them. I know it was wrong. But…I didn't want to be a seer. I still don't. But I will, because otherwise I don't know how we'll ever find Danica and Roslyn."

Right then he wished with all his soul that he knew Caitlin better. If that were the case, maybe it would be all right to get up from his chair and go to her, take her in his arms and give her the hug he thought she so desperately needed. This whole thing had to be so rough on her, from losing her friends to realizing that the one thing she had wanted to keep secret was the only thing that might save them.

But he was too chickenshit to do that. Or maybe cautious was a better word. Diego probably would have gone to Caitlin and given her a hug, but he and Diego were very different people. Alex had to settle for a completely inadequate, "I'm sorry."

Even that seemed to floor her. She blinked, then said, "You don't think I'm a jerk?"

"A jerk? Why would I think that?"

"Because I should've told someone I'm a seer! I've been hiding it, pretending that I can only do the small, regular things—you know, lighting a candle without a match, unlocking a door without a key, whatever—when all this time I could have been helping my clan."

It was clear she'd been beating herself up over this for some time, so Alex didn't see any reason why he should. "Well, I suppose that's between you and your clan elders," he said mildly. "And you're going to use your gift to find your friends, so...." He let the words trail off, mostly because he wasn't sure what else she expected him to say.

If Caitlin intended to argue further, that resolve appeared to have faded. She wrapped her hands around the glass of lemonade but didn't drink. "I'm going to try, anyway," she murmured, then added in clearer tones, "I'm not sure how much good I'll be. Not really. I've spent way too much time trying to repress my gift, and now I don't even know how to use it properly."

"It'll come to you," he said, trying to sound encouraging. "Our gifts, talents, whatever you want to call them—they want to be used. A little practice, and you'll be amazed at what you can do."

At first she didn't reply, only stared at her fingers where they still encircled the tall, moisture-beaded glass. She had pretty hands, with strong but delicate fingers, although the pale pink polish she was wearing had already started to chip off. No rings, which relieved Alex a little. She did seem a bit too young to be married or even engaged, but witches and war-locks tended to marry early, so it wasn't outside the bounds of possibility for her to already be commit-ted to someone.

Like that should even matter. No matter how pretty she was, they'd only just met. He didn't know anything about her.

Well, except one thing. He thought he liked her, liked her odd combination of toughness and vulner-ability. As if she had a lot more to her than even she realized.

"What about you?" she asked, and he tilted his head.

"What about me?"

"When did your gift show up?" A shy smile. "It's a pretty cool talent. I've never heard of it before."

Neither had anyone in his clan. He rocked back in his chair and grinned. "I was eleven. I was play-ing soccer with some friends from school and some other kids from the clan. Nothing formal—just kick-ing the ball around on a Saturday afternoon. Well, Humberto Almeida—he was this big kid, older than most of us, almost fourteen—he launched that ball right at me. Hard. I could tell it was going to hit me right in the face, probably break my nose. You know how you can see something about to happen, and you know there isn't anything you can do to stop it?"

Caitlin nodded, a small smile playing around her mouth. It was a pretty mouth, with that defined Cupid's bow at the top and the full lower lip, all overlaid with a faint gleam of soft peach lip gloss. And Alex realized he'd better stop staring at it.

Somehow he managed to tear his eyes away and drink down the rest of the lemonade in his glass. "Well, it was like that. This ball coming right at my face. And then at the last minute, this shield or whatever you want to call it shimmered out of thin air and surrounded me, and the ball bounced right off. At first everyone was too shocked to say anything, but then the kids started calling out, 'Do it again! Do it again!' and running for the spare balls we had sitting off to one side so they could start throwing them at me."

"Ouch," Caitlin said.

He grinned. "Yeah, something like that. Because the shield or whatever it was didn't come back. I took off for home, running like I had the zombie horde or something after me, and told my mom what had happened. I asked her why the shield hadn't come back, and she thought about it for a minute and said it was probably because I didn't think I was really going to get hurt, not like I would have if the ball Humberto had kicked had really gotten me in the face."

"So how did you start practicing with it? Have someone throw knives at you?"

Her tone was wry, but really, she wasn't that far off from the truth. "Not knives. Not at first, any-way," he added, and her blue-green eyes widened. "But having Diego come at me and threaten to pile-drive me was pretty effective. He was in wrestling in high school."

"Double ouch."

"I might have had a few bruises that needed explaining away. Gradually, though, I got control of my gift instead of having it control me. And now I can summon it when I need it, instead of having it pop up out of nowhere while watching the 3D ver-sion of the latest *Avengers* movie or whatever."

Again she smiled slightly at that image, but her expression turned thoughtful as she said, "I like that. Having control of my gift instead of letting it con-trol me. I guess that's what I was letting it do when I was so afraid all the time of what the next vision would be, and when it might show up."

Privately, Alex wondered how pleasant the next round of visions would be for her, considering she was going to use them to track down the warlocks who'd kidnapped her friends. He decided it was bet-ter to let that go for now. "It makes a huge difference. And maybe you'll find out that being the McAllister seer isn't so bad after all."

The dubious glance she gave him spoke vol-umes about what she thought of that prospect, but she didn't contradict him. She didn't really have the chance, because his mother entered the kitchen, her expression troubled. In one hand, she held a cordless phone.

"Caitlin," she said. "Your mother would like to talk to you."

Some of the pretty color drained from Caitlin's cheeks, but she raised her chin and nodded. "I had a feeling she would." She extended her hand, and Luz gave her the phone while at the same time shooting Alex a worried glance.

He wasn't sure what to do—get up from the table and give Caitlin her privacy? Stay where he was and pretend he couldn't hear every word she was saying?—but she solved that problem by standing up from her chair and moving out of the breakfast nook and past his mother, going to pause in the corridor.

"Hi, Mom."

A long silence, during which Luz shook her head slightly, which led Alex to believe that Caitlin's mother, who seemed to be one of the McAllister elders, wasn't being quite as zen about the revelation of her daughter's powers as Caitlin had hoped she would be.

"That's not going to happen," Caitlin said, her voice firm and carrying clearly enough down the hallway. "I know you're worried. *I'm* worried. But

I can't help Roslyn and Danica by hiding in Jerome and letting everyone else do the heavy lifting."

Another long pause.

"Fine, if Connor and Angela want to bring Marie in on this, there isn't much I can do about it. That's their call. But I'm pretty sure she won't be able to help."

Alex lifted his eyebrows at his mother, and she shrugged slightly. Even though Caitlin had told him she was going to stay down in Tucson until this thing was settled, some part of him hadn't believed she'd really stand up to her family and do it.

Which meant it looked like she actually was going to be crashing at his house for a while. That could get...interesting.

"...you know Angela won't tell me to go back to Jerome. That's not how she does things. Maybe that makes all you elders crazy, that she's not laying down the law right and left. But unless she comes down here and point-blank tells me to go home, I'm not changing my mind. It'll be—well, maybe 'fine' isn't the right word, but they're all looking after me here. You have nothing to worry about."

Brave words. Alex hoped they were true. Oh, he and his mother and everyone else in the clan would do whatever it took to solve this problem, not out of any loyalty to Caitlin or the McAllister family as a whole, but because it reflected badly on the de la

Pazes to have something this awful happen on their home turf.

"I'm hanging up now, Mom. You do whatever you have to on your end, but I'm staying. My phone's gone, but I suppose Luz Trujillo gave you a number—right. She'll be able to get ahold of me." A *click,* and Caitlin came back into the kitchen, looking annoyed. Her expression smoothed itself slightly as she handed the phone back to Luz.

"Well, she's not happy with me, but I don't think she's going to send anyone down here to hogtie me and drag me back to Jerome."

"That is good," his mother said, her voice grave, although a certain glint in her dark eyes seemed to indicate she was somewhat amused by Caitlin's declaration of independence. "Then we should be going. Maya takes her dinner early, and my cousin Raisa will be here soon to cook her meal."

Was it really that late? A glance at the clock on the microwave told him it was a quarter to six. The whole day had practically slipped away, a day in which almost anything could have been happening to Danica and Roslyn. But there wasn't much they could do about that, except hope that Caitlin's visions would be of some help now that she wasn't actively trying to block them.

They all left the kitchen, stopping in to the living room to say their goodbyes to his grandmother. She still sat on the couch with her glass of water, but her eyes were closed, as if she had dozed off after Luz had returned to the kitchen. As soon as they entered the room, however, she blinked, and focused a sharp enough gaze on all of them.

"So you're back to Tucson now?" she inquired.

"Yes, *mamita*," Luz replied. "I believe the Wilcox seer will be coming to speak with you tomorrow."

Maya nodded, hands twitching at the knitted afghan in her lap. Her expression was weary, but at the same time almost amused. No doubt she never thought she'd see the day when a Wilcox witch would be approaching her openly, particularly for advice. "Well, that should be…interesting."

Luz flashed her mother a smile, then bent down to give her a goodbye hug and a quick kiss on the cheek. Once she had stepped away, Alex bent down to do the same, while Caitlin lingered in the background, looking uncomfortable. Well, she wasn't the only one who felt uncomfortable; he had to force himself not to wince at how frail his grandmother seemed as he embraced her, how cool and papery her cheek was against his lips. He'd had almost six months now to get used to her condition, but he was beginning to think he'd never fully accept it.

After Caitlin said a quiet goodbye to Maya, they all went back out to his SUV and got in. It would be almost seven-thirty by the time they got back to

Tucson, and that was if they didn't hit any traffic. Should he take Caitlin out for dinner somewhere, or fix something at home? For all he knew, his mother would want them both to come back to her house. Alex wasn't sure he liked the idea of that; he'd rather have Caitlin to himself for a while, if for no other reason than she looked tired now, and having to be "on" around his mother and father and sister for dinner might be more wearing than she would like.

They were all quiet during the drive, as Phoenix finally dropped behind them, even while the sun began slipping down to the horizon. He was grateful for that, since he got the distinct impression Caitlin was fairly talked out and didn't need his mother grilling her all the way back to Tucson. For himself— well, he wanted to talk to her some more, but not with his mother around.

To his relief, Luz only asked, "Is there anything else you need, Caitlin?" once they were off the freeway and headed back to the store.

The McAllister witch shook her head. "No, thank you, Mrs. Trujillo."

"Luz," his mother corrected her gently, and beside him, Caitlin managed a weary smile.

"Thanks, Luz, but I have everything I need in my luggage. Right now I think I just want to sleep for a hundred years."

And dream? Alex wondered, but he didn't ask. Caitlin hadn't gone into a lot of detail, so he wasn't sure what kind of visions she had, whether her "sight" visited her when she was asleep, or whether she had waking dreams as well. Witches could experience both kinds, depending on how their powers manifested, or so he'd been told; the last de la Paz seer had died when he was still a toddler.

"I can imagine," Luz said, her tone gentle. "Well, the spare room at Alex's place is very comfortable. I'm sure you'll be fine there."

Caitlin nodded, a lukewarm response, but Alex found he didn't mind too much. If she'd acted too enthusiastic about staying over at his place, that might have sent up warning flags to his mother. On the other hand, maybe having Caitlin McAllister shacked up at his house was exactly what Luz wanted, since God knows his mother had been pestering him about settling down ever since Diego finally got himself hitched. Whatever her motives, Alex decided he was too tired right then to figure them out.

They pulled into the parking lot at the *mercado,* two spaces down from where his mother had parked her silver Lexus. By then it was full dark, except for the faintest dark orange smudge on the horizon. "I'll go in and check to make sure everything is okay," Luz said.

"Why wouldn't it be?" Alex asked. "I left Manuela in charge."

"Yes, and she has a good head on her shoulders. But it never hurts to check in." Luz put her hand on the door handle but didn't pull on it. Instead, she looked toward Caitlin where she was sitting quietly in the passenger seat, then said, "We will talk more in the morning. But for now, try to get as much rest as you can." She didn't bother to add, *You'll need it,* but her meaning was clear enough.

"I will, Luz. And—thank you."

"You are most welcome, Caitlin." Then Luz finally did get out of the SUV, closing the door behind her before she strode purposefully through the back entrance to the store, through the break room.

Alex didn't quite let out a sigh, but he knew he'd be lying if he didn't admit to a certain sensation of relief. Not that he didn't get along with his mother, but he could tell Caitlin wasn't as inclined to talk openly when Luz was around. "So," he said, as he turned the key in the ignition, "you hungry?"

Caitlin nodded but didn't say anything.

"We could go out, or we could go straight back to my house and fix something there. I have some carne asada in the fridge—we can have a little bar-becue. Does that sound okay?" Was that too casual? He was desperately trying to sound normal, even though nothing about this situation was even close to normal.

Another nod. Then she said, her voice small, "I'd rather not go out. I don't have my I.D. or anything...." She let the words trail off, but he got her meaning. If anyone probably needed a drink right about now, it was Caitlin McAllister, and she sure wouldn't get it at a restaurant, not without being able to prove she was over twenty-one.

"No problem," he said with a grin, backing the Pathfinder out of its space so he could head out onto Sixth Avenue. Since she was still looking tired and worried, and he wanted to see her smile, he added, "I promise I won't card you."

And she did smile at that remark. Just a little, not much more than a lift at one corner of her mouth, but it was a start.

He hoped someday he'd be able to make her smile for real.

CHAPTER SIX

THEY DROVE FOR A WHILE, FAR LONGER THAN CAITLIN had anticipated. For some reason, she'd thought Alex's house would be closer to the store, but that didn't seem to be the case. Maybe he'd wanted some separation between his home and his work. Since it was dark, she couldn't get more than an impression of businesses of all types sliding by past the car windows—restaurants, medical buildings, a mall, the inevitable Starbucks, grocery stores and drugstores and auto parts stores. At last they were turning, moving into a more residential area where the road sloped upward almost impercep-tibly. Did he live up in the hills somewhere? She had to admit that her knowledge of Tucson and its environs was basically nil; since she hadn't been the one driving when she came to town, nothing had left much of an impression on her.

Finally, they turned into a housing tract, one composed of large, new-looking homes, or at least as best she could tell in the subdued street lighting. After winding through a few more streets, Alex pulled into a driveway, then touched the remote clipped to the sun visor of his SUV. A garage door began to open, revealing probably the most spare and uncluttered garage Caitlin had ever seen. Almost everyone she knew in Jerome used their garage for storage, not to actually put their cars in.

But that didn't seem to be Alex's mode of operation. He parked the Pathfinder in the right-hand bay, close to a door she presumed led into the house. "Here we are," he said, quite unnecessarily, but she figured he spoke more to fill up the silence than because he'd expected to startle her with that revelation.

"It'll be good to get out of the car," she replied. "I think I've spent most of today driving around." Which, she realized, was only the truth. First the drive from Flagstaff to Jerome, then Jerome to Tucson… and then to Scottsdale and finally back down here. Hard to believe she'd done all that in the space of a day…and harder yet to believe everything that had gone on during those few short hours. Her mind had a hard time acknowledging that she really had just set out from Flag earlier that morning.

"Well, stretch your legs all you want," Alex said, then headed back to the cargo area so he could retrieve her luggage.

Caitlin felt as if she should protest, should tell him she could take care of that herself. But she realized Alex was only trying to help. Anyway, she was tired. Exhausted, really. If he wanted to carry a couple of suitcases, she should let him.

So she remained silent as he got out her two bags, then waited as he went past her and led her into the house. As she followed him, she had to prevent herself from gawking at the place like some rube from the country who'd never been to the big city before. The place did look practically brand-new, and so did all the furniture. Travertine floors, and bronze and alabaster glass light fixtures, and—well, it was about as different from the big Victorian house she'd grown up in as a person could imagine. And she wouldn't even bother to compare it to the shabby apartment she shared with Danica. The garage here was nicer than that.

Feeling somewhat cowed, she tagged along while Alex led her into a largish bedroom furnished with an oak daybed and matching dresser and nightstand. He set her bags down on the floor, which was covered in a fine-weave Berber carpet. "Here you go. I hope it's okay."

Hope it's okay? She cleared her throat and replied, "It's nice. I mean, really nice." As soon as the words left her mouth, she wanted to kick herself. "Really nice"? Seriously?

Either Alex didn't seem to have noticed the inanity of the remark, or was telling himself she'd had a rough day and so couldn't really be expected to be all that eloquent. He went on, "The bathroom's across the hall. There's soap and clean towels, but if you need anything else—"

"I'm fine," she said quickly. "I have all my shampoo and stuff."

"Then how about some dinner?"

A few hours ago, she would have said she never wanted to eat again. Now, though, her stomach was telling her that it needed something to keep going. She wouldn't be much use to Danica and Roslyn if she was so faint from hunger that she couldn't concentrate.

"Sounds great," Caitlin replied, and Alex smiled.

"Then let's get that going."

She trailed after him as he headed down the hall and then back into the huge space that seemed to be a combination living room/dining room/kitchen. Down a short hallway off to one side, she spied what seemed to be the family room, as one wall was dominated by a large flat-screen TV.

How much had this place cost? She was the first to admit she didn't know anything about real estate, beyond what she could afford for half-rent on a dumpy two-bedroom apartment, but she guessed it had to be a lot. Did managing a grocery store really pay that well?

Not that she would ever ask such a rude question. No, she waited off to one side, near the enormous granite-topped breakfast bar, and watched as Alex pulled a paper-wrapped package of meat from the refrigerator. "We'll go outside to grill this," he told her, then seemed to give the lightweight cotton top she was wearing a second look. "It gets cold pretty fast once the sun goes down. Do you have something to put over that?"

Despite how hungry and tired she was, and the way the ever-present worry for Danica and Roslyn kept pushing at the back of her mind, Caitlin couldn't help smiling. "I've been living in Flagstaff. Anything above sixty is going to feel downright balmy."

Alex didn't argue, but only grinned in return. "If you say so."

They went outside, to an enormous covered patio with ceiling fans and spot lighting built right into the roof. It was furnished out here, too, with an outdoor sofa and chairs and cocktail table, and a little ways from that, a round table with four chairs. A pool glimmered blue-green in the dusk, and the whole place looked like something out of a magazine.

Ignoring all that inviting furniture, Alex headed straight for a big stainless-steel barbecue and popped open the lid. "The carne asada cooks pretty fast, so we won't have to wait too long."

That sounded good. In fact, it sounded so good that her stomach growled. Chagrined, she clapped her hands over her belly—as if that would shut it up—even as Alex chuckled.

"Not a moment too soon, I guess." His expression sobered, though, as he asked, "Do you want to sit outside, or should we eat indoors?"

"Eat out here," she said. To her, the air wasn't chilly at all, but gently cool, soothing on her skin. And if it did get too cold, well, she could always run back inside and grab the denim jacket she currently had folded up inside her suitcase. "You have a gorgeous view."

And it was gorgeous—the faintest glimmer of dying sunlight still etched the very edge of the horizon, while above big, bright stars were beginning to glitter in the velvety dark blue sky. The faint outlines of jagged mountains were a deep black against navy, giving structure to the night.

"Okay." He paused, then asked, "Can you keep an eye on the meat while I run inside for a few things? Just flip 'em after a few minutes."

That sounded easy enough. Anyway, she'd baby-sat plenty of burgers at McAllister Fourth of July gatherings in past years. "Got it," she said, picking up the tongs Alex had left sitting on the slate counter to the right of the built-in barbecue.

He gave her a thumbs-up and went back inside. Was it strange that she felt this easy around him? Her surroundings were like nothing she'd ever experienced before, or even imagined, but despite that, she wasn't uncomfortable. It felt good to stand here and smell the unfamiliar spices rising from the sizzling meat, to have the mild air flow over her bare arms. She could almost forget what had happened to her earlier that day.

Almost.

Even though she knew she was safe here, her entire body tensed as she recalled the way Matías' black eyes had mocked her, the way he had held her. She had gotten away, true, but what was he doing now to Danica, to Roslyn?

No way of knowing, if the visions chose not to come. And she'd already discovered that they would only appear on their own timetable, and not hers.

Scowling, she flipped the meat over. It did look close to being done, probably because it was cut so thin. She'd had carne asada before, in quesadillas and burritos and whatnot, but never like this, plain.

Or almost plain. She saw Alex coming out through the sliding glass door, his hands full with a tray that held not just plates and napkins and flatware, but also bowls of what looked like cut-up cooked peppers, rice, some kind of cheese...and a bottle of wine and a couple of glasses. Thank the Goddess.

"You were busy," she said as he started setting everything out on the patio table.

"This?" His shoulders lifted. "Most of it's just stuff from Trader Joe's that I nuked."

"Well, it still looks good."

He came over to her then and cast a practiced eye over the skirt steak sizzling away on the grill. "Speaking of which, that looks about done. Let me dish it up."

She handed over the tongs, and he picked up the carne, then deposited it on a plate. Standing this way, he was very close to her, and she shivered. In a good way...but still.

Seeming to notice, he inquired, "Getting cold?"

"No," she said hastily. "Just hunger pangs, I guess."

"Well, let's fix that."

They went and sat down, and he dished some rice and beans on her plate, along with a tortilla.

"I usually roll it in a tortilla and put some peppers on top. It's good that way."

Caitlin thought that sounded better than good, so she assembled her food the way Alex had described while he busied himself with uncorking the wine and pouring some into her glass.

"I hope you're okay with the wine. Back in the car, it sounded as if you were worried about getting something to drink."

Wincing, she said, "I hope you don't think I'm a lush."

"Hardly." He flashed her a smile, then added, "I don't know too many people who wouldn't need a drink after what you've been through today."

Maybe that was true. Right now she felt like a coward for sitting here on this fabulous patio and sitting down to eat with an equally fabulous guy. She should be doing something, shouldn't she? There had to be something she could do to help her friends.

Problem was, there *wasn't* much she really could do. Not until that third eye of hers...or whatever it was...woke up and started giving her some of the information she so desperately needed.

"Possibly," she allowed.

Alex seemed to sense her internal turmoil, because he leaned forward slightly and said, "I know this must be hard for you, but really, I think the best thing to do is relax as much as you can. Worrying won't change anything."

That was probably true. And it seemed the quickest path to relaxation was drinking some of that wine, so she lifted her glass. "Okay...I'll try."

"That's a start." He raised his glass and clinked it against hers, as if sealing some sort of agreement.

She took a sip. Wine was sort of a part of Verde Valley culture, but her parents had been strict about her not drinking before she turned twenty-one. It hadn't stopped her from trying alcohol, of course, since not everyone in town was as uptight on the subject of underage drinking, but she'd never been one of the party girls, the ones who managed to get wasted at almost every high school get-together. Anyway, no one drank wine at those parties. Beer and tequila shots and sometimes whiskey, all of which she'd thought were pretty nasty. Margaritas were a different story, but no one bothered with mixed drinks when it was so much easier to get drunk on the straight stuff.

This wine, though...it was smooth and dark and rich, and sent a comforting warmth down her throat. Some of the tense, knotted-up sensation seemed to leave her neck and shoulders, and she pulled in a breath.

"Better?" Alex asked.

"Starting to be," she replied, then sipped again before setting the glass down so she could get to work on that carne asada. Drinking too much on an empty stomach could be dangerous for a number of reasons. She sent a sidelong glance in Alex's direction, but he seemed intent on his food as well, eating a forkful of black beans before returning to his own rolled-up tortilla filled with meat and roasted peppers.

They ate without speaking for a few minutes. He seemed to sense that she didn't want to talk. Or at least, he was willing to sit back and let her initiate the next round of conversation, for which she was grateful. There were so many things she did want to talk about, but wasn't sure how to begin the dialogue.

A few more sips of wine gave her the courage to ask, "Alex—what's going on with your grandmother? I mean, I've heard Angela talk about her, and—" Caitlin wasn't sure how to say, *and she sure never mentioned how sick your* prima *was,* so she let the sentence break off half-finished.

But he seemed to know exactly how she had intended to finish the thought. Brows drawing together, he drank some more of his own wine, then replied, "We've been trying to keep it quiet. Most of the time there isn't all that much interaction between our clans, so it wasn't that difficult. And for the past few years my mother has been handling some of the 'go-between' kind of stuff for our *prima* anyway, so if Angela called to get permission for you and your friends to come down to Tucson and spoke to Luz instead of Maya, no one would think it was that strange."

He paused, and Caitlin held herself still, waiting for him to go on. From the way his fingers clenched the stem of his wine glass, and the way he wouldn't quite look at her, she could tell this was difficult for him. This wasn't just his *prima* he was talking about, but his own grandmother.

"I suppose it started about four months ago… right after *La Día de los Muertos*." The dark eyes slanted toward her. "You know what that is?"

"The Day of the Dead," Caitlin said promptly, recalling the candles lit for loved ones now gone, the sugar skulls she and Roslyn had bought from a vendor at the Tlaquepaque Village event a few years ago. "They have a festival in Sedona for that. I've gone a few times, when it didn't conflict with our Samhain observances."

"Right. So some years my family would go up to Scottsdale to take part in the rituals there, and sometimes we would stay down here, depending on what everyone's schedules were like. Last November we stayed in Tucson, mainly because there are more and more people who aren't willing to make the drive, and my mother, as the *prima*-in-waiting, handles things here." He toyed with the handle of his fork, but Caitlin could tell he didn't seem terribly interested in eating right then. "The next day we got a phone call from my Aunt Francesca, who said my *abuelita* had had some kind of seizure and that the healer was with her but couldn't seem to figure out what was wrong."

"That must have been frightening."

"It was. We all went up to Scottsdale, but by then the seizure had passed, and Maya seemed a little better." He shook his head. "'Seemed' being the operative word. She had another seizure soon afterward, began growing weaker, and yet still the healer couldn't find anything wrong. Valentina, who's our healer down here in Tucson, couldn't seem to figure it out, either. But she's younger than Alba, who's been the healer in the Phoenix area since long before I was born, and so she insisted that the *prima* go to a hospital for tests."

In Jerome, the McAllisters had been without a healer for long enough that using civilian medical facilities was something no one thought twice about, but Caitlin supposed she could see why it might be an entirely different prospect for a clan that had never been forced to rely on modern medicine. Voice quiet, she asked, "Did they find anything?"

Another head shake. This time he abandoned the fork and picked up his wine glass instead, took a fairly healthy swallow. "Nothing. They tested for cancer, for epilepsy, for Parkinson's and diabetes and a bunch of other things I can't remember, and nothing. Not one of those tests turned up anything. At last she said it was enough, that she wasn't going to be poked and prodded anymore. That was about a month ago. And since then…." He set his glass down and stared off into the distance, although it was dark enough by now that Caitlin wasn't sure what he could be looking at. "Well, you saw her. That's where it stands. She's not getting better. Every day, she gets a little bit worse."

And how horrible that must be for him. For his clan as well, but Maya was more than just his *prima*— she was his grandmother. Losing Great-Aunt Ruby had been terrible for the McAllister clan, but more because everyone knew their safety then depended on Angela, who'd been roughly the same age Caitlin was now when she had to take over as *prima,* than because it was a tragedy to lose someone at eighty-eight, someone who'd lived a full life. No, Angela's youth had been the real issue; most of the time, a new *prima* was much older, had a family and a life of her own before she was asked to assume the role of leader of her clan. At least in the de la Paz family, Luz seemed ready to take over for her mother, even though she shouldn't have had to worry about doing so for another ten or fifteen years.

"I'm so sorry," Caitlin said, since anything else would have probably sounded like false platitudes. From what Alex had told her, it sounded as if Maya was dying. Not quickly, but in a way that made every day another one where they had to worry about how much more debilitated she would be, how much more she'd have to suffer. And if neither the healers nor the doctors could figure it out, there didn't seem to be much hope for a cure, either.

"It is what it is," Alex responded, then scowled. "Actually, I hate that saying. And I hate what's happening to my grandmother. If it had been something sudden, like a stroke or a heart attack, it would have been terrible, but at least it would have been over." His mouth pulled into a tight line. "But I guess that sounds terrible, too. It's not that I want her dead, but—"

"But you hate seeing her suffering," Caitlin broke in, hoping he would hear the pity and compassion she felt. Growing up, she'd been very close to her paternal grandmother, who seemed to understand why her granddaughter spent so much time reading and dreaming about the world beyond Jerome, who never gave her pitying looks when it became clear that Caitlin had no defined magical ability—one she would admit to, anyway. Grandma Ellen was still very much alive and well, still making her beloved pottery and selling it in the local shops, and Caitlin didn't want to contemplate what it would feel like when she finally lost her. More than once she'd been tempted to confide in her grandmother, tell her about her unwanted gift, but Caitlin had always worried that Grandma Ellen would find that a secret too big to keep, and so she'd held her tongue.

Alex shifted in his seat, turning his full attention back toward her, and she had to force herself not to look away. Something in those dark eyes seemed warmer now, approving. Despite the somber tone of their conversation, a thrill went through her. Had anyone else ever looked at her like that? She wasn't sure. Admiring stares, sure, especially after she'd gotten through her awkward phase in junior high and her freshman year of high school, when she started to grow into her height and had begun to fill out a little. But now, in this moment, it seemed as if Alex was looking at *her*, not her hair or her eyes or her chest, or any one of the things she was used to having guys look at.

"Yes," he said after a long pause. "That's exactly it. And my *abuela*—she's a strong person. She doesn't complain. She doesn't want people to see that she's in pain. And…she worries."

"Worries?"

"It's one thing if a *prima* just…dies." He swallowed, then appeared to gather himself so he could push on. "A clan can deal with that. It's bad, but…it's what happens, you know? There's always someone waiting in the wings, ready to take over."

Caitlin wondered how he felt about knowing his mother was next in line, that once she took over as leader of the de la Paz family, she wouldn't exactly belong to him anymore. Yes, she'd always be his mother, but she'd also have to be there for the clan as a whole. And sometimes that could be difficult. Looking at him now, though, at the worry in those fine dark eyes, the tense set of his jaw, she knew she couldn't ask him that question. Not yet, anyway.

"But this?" he went on. He reached for his wine glass and took another one of those healthy swallows. Another couple like that, and he would end up draining the glass entirely. She couldn't blame him, now that she knew what he'd been going through with his grandmother. "When a clan's *prima* is weak, the clan is weak. We've seen that same problem in California."

"That's where Maya thinks Matías and his gang have come from," Caitlin said quietly. She hadn't had the opportunity to relay that information to Alex prior to this, and she watched as his eyes widened briefly before he nodded in understanding.

"That makes sense. Símon Santiago isn't the best caretaker of that clan, and things have gotten out of hand. My grandmother's strength was always enough of a deterrent to keep them away in the past, but now?"

"Now they're moving in." Despite the mild, gentle evening air on her skin, the feeling that this lovely patio and the shimmering pool beyond it seemed to exist in a world far from the evil of the magic she'd sensed earlier in the day, something deep within her went cold. How many of those rogue warlocks were there? Did they have any witches working with them? Caitlin hadn't seen any, but that didn't mean much. They could have been off someplace else... maybe at the shabby apartment with the ugly couch she'd glimpsed so briefly in that vision before it was torn away.

"It sure looks that way." Alex picked up his neglected tortilla and took a bite, and she forced herself to do the same thing, even though her appetite seemed to have deserted her for the moment. "Which is why it's so important that we find out where they are. It could be a lot more than just saving your friends—it could mean rooting out a cell of these bastards before it has a chance to take hold."

Great. As if she wasn't already feeling enough pressure. She set down her half-eaten tortilla. "I'm doing the best I can, Alex. I know right now that isn't much, but—"

At once he shook his head. "Shit, Caitlin, that's not what I meant. I'm not trying to pressure you. I know you can't force this kind of stuff. It's just—" He seemed to grit his teeth, then reached over and picked up the wine bottle, poured a good measure into his glass and another into hers, even though she hadn't drunk nearly as much as he had. "I just hate the idea that these guys are over here in my clan's territory, laughing at us because our *prima* isn't strong enough to sense their presence and send them straight back to whatever hole they crawled out of."

"I hate it, too," she said. Almost without thinking, she laid her right hand on his left, where it was resting on the glass top of the patio table. He jerked a little at her touch, then relaxed as she squeezed his fingers gently before returning her hand to her lap. "And we *will* do something about it. The situation isn't going to stay this way."

"I know," he replied, and again those dark eyes latched onto hers, holding her gaze. She saw trust there, a belief in her abilities that she sincerely hoped wasn't misplaced.

It couldn't be. Way too much was riding on those inconsistent dreams and visions of hers. All she could do was hope that the years she'd spent pushing them away, denying them, hadn't weakened them beyond repair.

CHAPTER SEVEN

AFTER THAT, THEY DIDN'T TALK MUCH, BUT ATE THEIR rapidly cooling food and drank the rest of the bottle of wine. By the end of the meal, Caitlin was feeling—not exactly light-hearted, but probably more relaxed than she should be, given the circumstances. In fact, the false sensation of well-being that came over her was so pronounced that she almost asked Alex to open a second a bottle of wine.

No, that would be a very bad idea. For one thing, she sure didn't need a hangover getting in the way of her next attempt to summon a vision, and for the other, it was hard enough forcing herself not to react when Alex looked at her, to pretend that the way her blood seemed to run a little hotter in her veins every time she caught a stray glance from him was perfectly normal and nothing she needed to worry about. She couldn't let herself be attracted to him. That was going to be difficult, considering the way just being around him made her heart feel as if it was in a perpetual state of flutter, but she'd do her best. How could she focus if she allowed herself to be so distracted?

So they finished their dinner, and she helped him clear away the uneaten food and the dirty dishes, and after that it wasn't quite late enough to go to bed, since it was barely a quarter to nine. Sitting down and attempting to watch TV as if everything was normal and her friends hadn't been kidnapped by a trio of dark warlocks was completely out of the question.

"Maybe I should try again," she suggested, as Alex closed up the dishwasher and turned to face her.

"Try for a vision?"

She nodded.

"I thought you couldn't force the visions."

"I can't...I mean, I haven't been able to in the past. But Maya—your grandmother said I just had to open myself to it, to let it flow through me."

"Like the Force?" Alex asked, an incongruous grin pulling at his mouth.

Caitlin tried hard not to look at that mouth. His lips were just full enough that she thought they would feel very good when pressed up against hers. Okay, and that was exactly the sort of thinking she was trying to avoid, so she pulled in a breath and said severely, "Maybe like the Force, you geek. I don't know. But I think I should try." Before he could cut in with another Star Wars reference, she added, "And don't hand me that line about 'do, or do not,' or I'll have to resort to physical violence."

"Whoa," he said, holding up his hands. The grin he shot her, however, told her he wasn't too worried about her ability to beat his ass.

Which, she had to admit, was severely lacking. She'd never roughhoused that much with her brother, so the finer points of getting in a good punch were not exactly in her wheelhouse, so to speak. Deciding it was better to let the subject drop, she announced, "I'm going to sit down now," and went over to the couch in the living room. It was soft bone-colored leather, and seemed to envelop her as she sank down onto it.

Alex followed, still wearing an amused expression. She was actually glad to see it, as that half-smile seemed to tell her he'd put his worries about his grandmother aside for now at least. A matching love seat was positioned a few feet away from the couch, and he lowered himself onto it, pushing an accent pillow made out of what looked like a miniature Navajo rug over to one side.

"So…how does this work?" he asked.

Good question. Maya had said Caitlin had to open herself to her gift, but the exact mechanism for doing so seemed to elude her. "Well, for one thing, it would probably help if you weren't sitting there and staring at me as if you expected me to turn into a toad or something."

"God forbid. I kind of prefer you the way you are."

Embarrassed blood rose to her cheeks. This seemed like a really good time to close her eyes and try opening herself up to her gifts. At least that way she wouldn't have to figure out the best approach when it came to dealing with Alex's intent gaze.

So she did just that—shut her eyes, took a deep breath, followed by another, and tried to will herself to a stillness she certainly didn't feel. In fact, it seemed as if the harder she tried to make her mind go quiet, the more her thoughts churned one after the other... fear for Roslyn and Danica, the hell she was probably going to catch when all this settled down and her parents had the leisure to read her the riot act about hiding her gifts, worry that the warlocks might decide to snag a few more unsuspecting witches and she'd have to track them down as well. And, above it all, and the last thing she should be thinking about, the young man who sat a few feet away from her, the way she thought she could hear him breathing, could practically hear the beating of his heart in his chest... and how much she wished she could go to him and lay her cheek on that chest, feel it strong and sturdy and reassuring against her skin.

Her eyelids snapped open, and she saw Alex still sitting there, his gaze seemingly fixed on something outside the window. She guessed, however, that he had been watching her right up until the moment she opened her eyes.

"Anything?" he asked.

"No," she replied, not bothering to keep the irritation out of her voice. "I know I'm supposed to relax, to let myself be a conduit for the visions, but the harder I try not to think about anything, the more I think about *everything*. Now I wish I'd taken that yoga class Danica tried to get me into. Maybe that would've helped with my focus."

Alex made a sound that might have been a chuckle, but which morphed into a throat-clearing as she narrowed her eyes at him. "Well, you've had a rough day. It's early, but maybe you should try to sleep. Try again tomorrow when you're better rested."

That sounded like good, practical advice. She knew she should take it. She just wished she didn't feel like such a failure for doing so. "Okay," she said reluctantly. "You're probably right."

When she got up from the couch, she could feel the heaviness in her limbs, the ache of weariness all through her. The wine had erased it for a little bit, but now it was returning, worse than ever. Why had she thought she could accomplish anything useful tonight? Her body was clearly telling her that it needed to rest.

Alex stood as well, but she noticed that he kept a careful distance from her. If she stumbled, would he put out a hand to steady her?

Probably, and no way was she going to attempt such a transparent ploy. Acting the helpless female was just not her thing. Chin raised, she walked out of the living room and down the hall to the guest room where Alex had dropped off her luggage earlier.

He stopped on the other side of the door, then asked, "Is there anything else you need? Toothpaste, whatever?"

"No, I'm good. I packed all that stuff."

"Okay. Well…good night, then."

A quick smile, probably meant to reassure her, and then he was moving away from her, going to his bedroom. He let himself in, and she got a quick glimpse of a room decorated in soothing shades of brown and blue before he closed the door. That was probably for her benefit, as she'd have to go across the hall to use the bathroom, and it seemed like he wanted to give her as much privacy as he could.

Which she appreciated. She closed the door to her own room, picked up the smaller bag, the one that held all her toiletries, and got out the cosmetic case that contained her toothbrush and toothpaste and the glycerin bar she used to wash her face. After setting those aside, she went into the other suitcase, pulled out the tank top and yoga pants she'd brought to sleep in, and got into them quickly. The jeans she'd been wearing could be folded and set on top of the chair in the corner, while she hung up her top. In a pinch she could wear it again, since she'd only had it on for half the day.

Then she darted across the hall to the bathroom and closed and locked the door, then performed her usual going-to-bed rituals. In the past she'd found following the routine to be vaguely reassuring, but now she could only keep thinking of Danica and Roslyn, of where they were, of what those warlocks were doing to them. Would they be allowed to sleep, to eventually wash their faces and brush their teeth? Or did Matías and his two buddies plan to only use them for a day or two, and so didn't care whether the girls would have a chance to take care of themselves?

Those thoughts tumbled around in her head, and when she looked into the mirror after she'd washed her face, Caitlin saw how bleak and frightened her eyes were, how drained of color her skin. Well, who cared? She wasn't here to win any beauty contests.

Even so, she put on some moisturizer and lip balm, then returned the products to the cosmetic bag when she was done. Afterward, she found a sponge under the sink and wiped down the granite counter. Everything here was so clean, so new and shiny and perfect, that she didn't want to leave even a water spot behind.

And then it was time to go back into the guest room, to quietly shut the door behind her and pull back the daybed's quilted coverlet, then fold it neatly at the foot of the bed. Something in her was loath to go to the light switch and flick it downward, although she knew she was perfectly safe here. No one except her parents and Luz knew she'd decided to stay at Alex's house, so even if the three warlocks who'd taken her friends were actively hunting for her, there was no way they'd be able to track her current whereabouts.

Well, unless they had a seer of their own.

Caitlin shut down that line of thought right away, then turned off the light before she could lose her nerve. To her relief, the room wasn't completely dark even then, as it had a flat sort of nightlight plugged into one of the outlets on the opposite wall. It helped her make her way back over to the bed and then slip under the cool sheets.

The mattress had to be that memory foam type, from the way it seemed to cradle every inch of her aching body. Right then she realized how much she did hurt. Valentina had healed the wound in her side, but a deep, throbbing pain still lingered, now that Caitlin had a chance to focus on it. A good night's sleep should do a lot to take care of that, though.

Closing her eyes, she breathed in deeply, letting the stillness of the house surround her. She was safe. Alex was just down the hallway, and this place was so new that nothing bad could have ever happened here to leave a lingering psychic stain. She could relax and give her body the time it needed to heal itself, and then tomorrow she would be rested and ready to allow her gift to guide her wherever she needed to go.

Sleep came quietly, stealing over her like a dark fog. She let it surround her, gentle and soft, her consciousness slipping farther and farther away from this room, away from the pale greenish glow of the nightlight and the luxurious mattress cushioning her body.

Deeper, deeper....

Until she wasn't in that bed at all, but someplace else, in a room she didn't recognize. In bed, yes, that much was the same, although it was bigger than the daybed on which she'd gone to sleep, and not nearly as comfortable. Something acrid and sickly sweet tickled her nose, and as she shifted, she realized the scent came from a joint burning in an ashtray on the nightstand next to the bed.

"You want some, *chica?*" a half-familiar voice asked.

To her horror, Caitlin realized it was Matías' voice, and that she was lying in bed next to him.

Half her body was covered by the sheet, but even so she knew she was naked. Dark hair slipped over her shoulder, and she realized that wasn't herself in bed with the warlock, but Danica.

"Mmm," Danica said, and Matías reached over and picked up the joint, then slipped it between her lips. He, too, seemed to be naked, and Caitlin could now see that the snake tattoo which encircled his neck continued over one shoulder and then looped around a pectoral muscle, the rattle centered squarely in his muscular chest. It seemed to move with a life of its own as he shifted so he was closer to Danica—Danica, who'd never done drugs in her life, but who was now taking a long pull on the joint as if she'd been smoking weed for years.

Danica, wake up! Snap out of it! Caitlin screamed at her, but she realized the words were only resounding in her own mind. Danica could hear nothing... nothing except Matías' insinuating voice.

Then he was taking the joint from her and inhaling deeply of it, right before he set it back in the ashtray. He exhaled, the cloud of smoke surrounding them both, right before he lowered his head to her breast, tongue slipping over her bare flesh, while at the same time his hand moved between her legs. Danica moaned, her eyes closing, and if there were any mercy, that would have been the end of it, and Caitlin wouldn't have to see any more.

But no, it was like viewing some strange multi-viewpoint porn film where she was forced to watch what Matías was doing to Danica, to listen to her friend spasm in pleasure as the warlock stroked her to orgasm, while at the same time seeing these things and feeling them as if they were happening to her as well. And after Danica climaxed, he told her, "My turn," and she sat up, reached out to touch him, then lowered her head to take him into her mouth.

A scream tore itself from Caitlin's throat. "No! No, Danica! No!"

And she wailed in agony, because she knew her friend couldn't hear her, and there was nothing she could do to stop what had to be happening to Danica right now.

Nothing.

It had been difficult, but Alex eventually fought his way to sleep, made himself stop thinking about the girl lying in bed just down the hallway from him. He'd closed his bedroom door to give her privacy, true, but it was also to avoid catching a glimpse of her in whatever she might have worn to sleep in. That would've kept him awake for hours.

At first it penetrated his sleep-fogged brain like the distant wail of an air-raid siren, a shrill noise that definitely had no place in his house. Then he blinked, his eyes opening as he realized it wasn't a siren at all, but Caitlin, screaming as if she was being axe-murdered.

He didn't stop to think, or worry that he'd been sleeping in his underwear and nothing else. No, he pushed back the covers and was bolting from his room within seconds, tearing down the hallway as he brought the protective dome around him, just in case there were any armed intruders in Caitlin's room.

But when he flung open the door and switched on the light, he saw nothing except the McAllister witch herself, huddled into a corner of the daybed frame, arms clutched around her as she rocked back and forth and let out a series of despairing cries that sounded like a litter of kittens being run over by a truck.

"Caitlin!" he said sharply, hoping the sound of his voice calling her name would be enough to snap her out of whatever state she was in.

No response, only that terrible rocking motion as her eyes seemed to stare at something only she could see.

He had no experience with someone being in a trance, or whatever was currently possessing her. However, he also knew that he couldn't let her remain in this state. She was obviously terrified.

Since they were clearly alone, he dropped the shield and went to her, grasping her by the arms. "Caitlin! Caitlin, please—you're here. You're safe."

Those last words seemed to penetrate when merely saying her name hadn't. The wild look began to leave her eyes, and then she blinked and looked around the room before returning her gaze to him. She drew in a shuddering breath and burst into tears.

Oh, hell. Dealing with crying women had never been his strong suit. But because she was so obviously in pain, he let go of her arms and pulled her close to him, holding her so she'd know she wasn't alone, that there was someone here to protect her. At the same time, he was doing everything in his power not to focus on the way her breasts were pushed up against him, separated from the bare skin of his chest by only a thin tank top. That loose-fitting peasant blouse she'd been wearing earlier had concealed some of the shape of her body, but now he could tell how rounded and full those breasts actually were.

Despite his best efforts to tell his body this was absolutely the wrong time, he could feel himself begin to stiffen. Great. It was a lot easier to hide that sort of thing in a pair of jeans than a pair of boxer-briefs.

Don't...just don't, he told himself, and his erection subsided a little. He could only imagine Caitlin's reaction if she noticed that he'd managed to give himself a boner when he was trying to comfort her.

"What was it?" he asked. "A vision?"

She nodded and pulled away from him slightly. Her eyes and nose were red, but he found he didn't care too much. She still looked so damn beautiful.

"I'm guessing it wasn't a good one."

That remark earned him a rusty chuckle. After wiping at her eyes with the back of her hand, she said, "I saw Danica."

"Was she—" He didn't complete the sentence, but he figured Caitlin would know what he was driving at. Surely nothing besides seeing her friend's death would have made her act like that.

"No," she whispered. A shudder passed through her, and she looked away from him, at the wooden blinds that concealed the window. "She was with *him.*"

"Matías?"

Another nod. She drew in a breath, then expelled it. Her body was still shaking, and he forced himself to keep his attention fixed on her face. "They were… they were in bed. You know."

Yes, he did know, although it had been a while. But he could understand why Caitlin would be so upset, seeing her friend having sex with the man who had kidnapped her. "Was she being forced?" That would explain the screams, especially if Caitlin had experienced the scene with the sort of immediacy that sometimes came with visions.

"No." The word was hardly more than a whisper. She cleared her throat, then went on, "I mean, I think he was still controlling her. She certainly wasn't trying to fight back. She looked like she was enjoying it. She—" The syllable seemed to choke her, and Alex saw her visibly swallow. "He had her share a joint with him. Danica doesn't do drugs. Ever. She hardly even drinks that much. That one margarita she had at the restaurant would've been it for her."

It definitely did sound as if Danica was still under Matías' influence, although Alex wasn't sure whether the warlock had cast an actual spell, or whether this was his gift—the ability to make those around him bend to his will. If so, that was an even more frightening prospect. No one in the de la Paz clan had that sort of talent, and although there were dark rumors of such things existing once upon a time, they hadn't been around for generations. Until now, it seemed.

"I'm sorry, Caitlin," Alex said. He hesitated, wondering how much he should press her. Still, at least she'd had a vision. That meant her own particular talent was attempting to assert itself. "Did you see anything else?"

She shot him a black look. "What, you don't think that was enough?"

"No," he said calmly. "What I meant was, did you see anything else of their surroundings, anything that might help us track down where they are?"

"Oh." She seemed to deflate then, and shook her head. "I'm pretty sure it was the same apartment, but it was mostly dark. There was...some kind of candlelight." A frown as she appeared to rack her patchy memory of the scene. "I think there were some of those saints' candles on a dresser across the room. A queen-size bed, and a nightstand. Curtains at the window, I think, not blinds. The room wasn't very big."

"Well, that's something," he said. "Did it feel more like an apartment or house, or a motel room or something?"

Her eyes shut, lashes dark russet against her pale cheeks. "I don't think it was a motel. It felt more like an apartment, although I can't say why." Then she blinked. "The door was open. There was light coming down the hallway, so unless it was a suite somewhere, it must've been an apartment or a house. And you'd think a hotel suite would have better furniture."

Alex fought back a smile at that comment. It was delivered in a wry tone that made him think she was beginning to recover from the nightmarish vision she'd just seen. "You're probably right. That narrows it down a bit."

"A bit," she repeated. "So how many rundown apartments and houses are there in Tucson?"

"A good number." *A lot,* he thought. *More than we could search in the time Danica and Roslyn probably have left*. But he didn't bother to say that out loud. He had a good idea Caitlin knew exactly how hopeless the situation was.

She didn't respond, only toyed with the sheet covering her lap. Then she seemed to focus on him—*really* focus on him. Her eyes widened, and she said, "Um…did you forget your pajamas or something?"

Thank God he didn't have the kind of skin that flushed easily. Holding her gaze…mostly so she couldn't look down…he replied, "I don't even own pajamas. You were screaming bloody murder, so I ran to help you."

"Oh." Her voice sounded very small. "Sorry about that."

"Don't be. That's why you're here—so I can help keep you safe."

"I'm still sorry I woke you up."

"It's all right." She did seem calmer now, so he pushed himself away from her and off the bed, glad that his body had decided to behave itself once their conversation got started. That would have been even more awkward than standing in front of her wearing only his underwear. "But if you're okay now, I'll go back to bed."

"Don't!" she exclaimed, then looked away from him, as if she'd surprised herself with that outburst. "I mean…I'm not sure I want to be by myself."

He couldn't really blame her for that. That vision had sounded pretty awful. And the worst part was that she didn't have much control over when those images invaded her mind. He wouldn't want to be alone, either, if their situations had been reversed.

"Then come stay in my room," he offered, and her eyes widened again.

"Sleep with you?"

"Yes," he said patiently, then added, "The operative word being 'sleep.' I have a king-size bed. You'll hardly notice I'm there. But at least you won't be by yourself if you have another one of those visions."

A long, long pause. She stared up at him, clearly conflicted. He supposed he should be glad that she was looking at his face, though, and not the rest of him. Or at least he didn't think she was.

Then, finally, "Okay." She pushed aside the covers and got up, giving him a better look at the way the tank top she wore clung to her breasts, the yoga pants that showed off the lines of her long legs and rounded ass.

Damn. He could feel himself start to stir again, and turned away from her, praying she hadn't noticed. "This way."

She followed him without comment back to his room. Since it was clear enough from the way the bedclothes were rumpled which side he slept on, she climbed under the covers on the right side of the bed, while he went to his usual spot and got in.

It did feel strange to have her there. He'd bought this house after he broke up with his last girlfriend, and so he hadn't had anyone in bed with him here. True, Caitlin was staying way, way over to the one side, leaving quite a space between them. Even so....

He said calmly, "Good night, Caitlin."

"Good night, Alex." She sounded far more composed now, although there was a tension in her voice that indicated she wasn't quite as relaxed as she would have liked him to think. Well, he couldn't blame her for that. They'd just met this afternoon, and now she was here in his bed....

Sleeping, he told himself. *Only sleeping.* At the moment, he was just glad he'd bought a king-size bed when he moved to this house. That put some nice, safe real estate between him and the body he'd been trying hard not to ogle a few minutes earlier.

He reached over and turned off the light. Darkness immediately surrounded them, save for the faint reflected glow of the nightlight in the *en suite* bathroom. Caitlin was lying so still that he could almost convince himself she wasn't there at all.

But he knew better.

CHAPTER EIGHT

CAITLIN OPENED HER EYES AND BLINKED UP AT THE ceiling fan above her head. It was off, the air against her face cool enough that a fan wasn't needed. For a second, she couldn't figure out where she was. The condo she'd rented with Danica and Roslyn?

Then she felt the bed shift slightly, and she looked over to her right, saw Alex Trujillo's dark head on the pillow next to her. Well, okay, not *right* next to her; the bed was large, and he was on his side, facing away from her. She could see the smooth golden-brown skin of his shoulders and back, underlaid with an impressive amount of muscle.

It all came back to her—the warlocks, the kidnapping. How she'd ended up here, in Alex's house. In his bed.

Nothing happened, she told herself. It was true. Nothing *had* happened. That didn't make the current situation any less awkward.

"Good morning," she said, since she could tell he was awake.

He turned toward her, propping himself up on his elbow. The fine lines of his jaw were now covered with dark stubble, and his hair was sticking out every which way, and he looked freaking gorgeous. "Did you sleep well?" he asked.

"Fine," she managed.

"No more visions?"

She shook her head, hoping she looked as adorably rumpled as he did, and guessing she probably didn't. Oh, well. "Nothing."

"That has to be a relief." His expression was sympathetic. "At least you were able to get some rest."

Yes, she had, although it had taken her what felt like forever to fall asleep, knowing that Alex was in bed with her, that all she had to do was reach out and...what? Pull him to her? That was insane. But once she'd heard his breaths deepen as he slept, she'd allowed herself to relax, to drift off, until eventually slumber had claimed her as well. It hadn't been easy, however.

"You want some coffee?" he asked, sitting up.

It was hard not to stare at his exposed chest, even though she'd gotten an eyeful of it the night before.

Then again, it was a lot brighter this morning, even though all the blinds in the bedroom were still shut. "I don't really drink coffee," she confessed. "Do you have any tea?"

He shook his head, but brightened a little as something appeared to occur to him. "I have a jug of iced tea from Trader Joe's in the fridge. Will that work?"

It would have to. She'd rather start off the day with a hot drink, but better some kind of caffeine than none at all. "Sure."

After pushing back the covers, he got up and promptly disappeared through a door in the sitting area off the bathroom. Apparently, that led to some sort of walk-in closet, because he came back out a minute later in a pair of faded jeans and a University of Arizona T-shirt. Much better. At least now his face would be the only thing distracting her.

"Is that where you went?" she asked, sliding out of bed as well. The clothes she'd slept in covered everything, more or less, but they also didn't hide much. And crossing her arms over her chest would be way too obvious. Tone casual, she added, "U of A?"

"Yeah," he replied, and, thank the Goddess, his eyes were on her face and didn't seem inclined to move any lower.

"Did you like it?"

He shrugged. "It was okay. I graduated, which is the important thing, I guess."

His attitude puzzled her. She'd been overjoyed at the prospect of finishing up college at Northern Pines, since it meant she could get a real degree from a real four-year university, something that had been denied the McAllister clan until the recent truce with the Wilcoxes. And here Alex had grown up in the town that had the best school in the state, and was acting as if it was no big deal.

"What did you major in?"

"Double major. Marketing and communications." Something in his expression told her he really didn't want to talk about it. He picked up the iPhone that had been sitting on his nightstand, then asked, "You ready for that tea?"

"Sure," she said, taking the hint. For whatever reason, the subject of college seemed a touchy one for him. Maybe she'd get to know him well enough that she could ask what that was all about.

Or maybe not. She was only here to help find Danica and Roslyn, right?

Frowning, she followed Alex to the kitchen. The travertine tiles were cold under her feet, and she wished she'd thought to pop into the guest room and slide on her flip-flops. Well, Alex was wandering around barefoot, so she'd do the same.

After setting his cell phone down on the counter, he got a glass out of the cupboard, then went to the fridge and retrieved a large plastic jug full of tea. Once he'd poured some for her and returned the jug to the refrigerator, he busied himself with getting a pot of coffee going.

Caitlin sipped her tea and tried not to watch him, although that was difficult. Something about the way he moved, the way he looked...everything... seemed to draw her eyes, no matter what she did. "So...what's the plan for today?"

"It depends, I guess." He turned away from the coffeemaker and leaned against the counter, arms crossed. "I'm supposed to work, but I'll get someone to cover for me."

She hadn't even thought about that. It was Thursday, a normal work day. Or at least a normal work day for most of the world. She knew a lot of the Wilcox clan had regular jobs, acted as if there wasn't anything particularly special about them, and it seemed to be that way down here in de la Paz territory as well. In Jerome, people worked, but even the shop owners tended to be fairly haphazard about their business hours. And since so many of the McAllister witches and warlocks were artists and artisans, they set their own schedules, such as they were.

The coffee began to perk. Caitlin inhaled the aroma, wishing coffee tasted even half as good as it smelled. But the jug tea was actually pretty good, and she could feel herself becoming more awake, more on top of things, as the caffeine started to flow through her bloodstream. There was a downside to being more alert, though; as her brain woke up, memory started to flow as well, the nightmarish images of Danica in Matías' arms, of her letting him touch her. Violate her.

"Hey," Alex said, the brittle note completely gone from his voice. He'd stepped closer to her, and she hadn't even noticed. "Are you okay?"

"Yeah," she replied, forcing a smile. "It's just… memory can be a bitch sometimes, you know?"

He reached out and ran a thumb over the back of her hand. Briefly, and purely out of a desire to reassure her, she knew, but warmth flooded through her at that touch. She remembered how he'd held her last night, how it had felt being pressed up against his bare skin, how she hadn't wanted to pull away but had done so because she knew it was dangerous to let him continue to hold her.

Yes, memory definitely could be a bitch.

"I know it's rough. But we'll get through this. Okay?"

She nodded, then made herself sip some more tea. Alex seemed to get the message, because he backed away and busied himself with retrieving a coffee mug from the cupboard and fetching a small container of cream from the refrigerator.

Just as he was pouring some coffee into his mug, his phone pinged. An email, it sounded like. He finished with the coffee, stirred in some cream, and then went to pick up his phone. As he read the message, he seemed to simultaneously relax and tense up.

"What is it?"

"The good news—I'm off the hook for work until this is all settled. My father's going to keep an eye on things."

"Oh? Doesn't he have another job?"

Alex shook his head, his mouth pulling into a slight frown. "No, he's sort of retired. That was his fiftieth birthday present to himself. He used to run the store, but now it's my turn."

He didn't sound too pleased about it, and Caitlin wondered if that was where some of the apparent bitterness about his education had come from. Someone with a double major in marketing and communications had probably planned to do something a little more exciting than manage his family's neighborhood store.

"And the bad news?" she asked.

His gaze returned to the email. "It sounds like Marie Begonie—that's the Wilcox seer?"

Caitlin nodded.

"Anyway, she's coming down to Tucson. My mother gave her directions, so I guess she's heading straight here to the house. It sounds like she'll get here a little after one."

Great. Well, it was probably to be expected. No way would Angela allow all this responsibility to rest on the shoulders of an untried seer, even though Caitlin knew deep down that Marie wouldn't be able to help. For whatever reason, rescuing Danica and Roslyn was Caitlin's responsibility.

She didn't tell Alex that; it wasn't as if he'd be able to stop Marie, not when she was coming down here at the express request of the McAllister *prima*. Well, at Connor's request, probably. Caitlin hadn't spent a huge amount of time in their shared company, but she could tell that relations between Angela and Marie were a bit strained, no doubt because Marie couldn't help seeing the daughter she should have had every time she looked at the McAllister *prima*, if only fate hadn't intervened. But Marie would never go against the wishes of her *primus*.

"Have you met Marie?" Caitlin asked.

Alex looked somewhat surprised at the apparent *non sequitur*. "Um, no. I haven't been up to McAllister territory since, well…." His eyes wouldn't quite meet hers as he let the sentence die away.

"Since you went up to find out if you were Angela's consort." The thought of Angela kissing

Alex in that age-old ritual sent an odd stab of jealousy through Caitlin, which was stupid. It was all just part of the tradition. They hadn't even known each other. And Angela was ridiculously happy with Connor—anyone with half-decent vision could see that. But Alex? Obviously, he wasn't married, and as far as Caitlin could tell, it didn't seem as if he was involved with anyone, either. She sort of doubted he'd have let her sleep in his bed, his role of protector notwithstanding, if he was in a serious relationship with someone else.

"Yeah, since then." His tone too deliberately casual, he continued, "Anyway, I met Connor once, and that's about it for the Wilcoxes. I know some of them have started coming to Phoenix to shop and whatever, and a few more are attending ASU, but none of them have made it all the way to Tucson."

"Until now," Caitlin said. She glanced at the clock on the microwave. They'd slept in; it was almost nine. Her stomach rumbled, and although she didn't want to impinge too much, she knew she needed to eat something so they could get on with their day. She really didn't want to risk Marie showing up while she and Alex were still running around in their equivalent of lounge wear. "Are you one of those breakfast-skipping types? Because I'll try to scrounge something if you are."

"Are you kidding? It's the most important meal of the day." His dark eyes glinted at her, and it seemed as if some of his good humor had been restored. "I've got some frozen breakfast burritos, and there are bananas if you need fruit."

Normally, she'd have yogurt and fruit, but a burrito sounded nice and sturdy. Caitlin had a feeling she'd need as much ballast as she could eat in order to face Marie Wilcox-Begonie.

Caitlin was nervous, that much Alex could tell. Obviously, she wasn't too thrilled about having Marie show up here, and he supposed he couldn't blame her. After all, she'd been hiding her gift from everyone, and so Marie had been managing seer duties for both clans for the past two years. From the tense, strained look in Caitlin's eyes, Alex thought she was expecting some kind of dressing-down. He could only hope that Marie wouldn't do that sort of thing in front of an audience, because he knew he wasn't about to leave Caitlin alone with the Wilcox seer.

They'd eaten breakfast, and taken their respective showers and finished getting ready. Since breakfast had been so late, they only grabbed some fruit for lunch. Well, Caitlin had; he asked if she wanted a sandwich and she shook her head, so he put together a quickie ham on wheat bread sandwich for himself while she munched on grapes and stared off through the sliding glass doors, expression troubled. Whether she was worrying about what might be happening to her friends at that moment, or stressing about what Marie was going to say to her, Alex didn't know for sure, and he didn't dare ask.

At five minutes after one, the doorbell rang. He slid off the stool he'd been sitting on at the breakfast bar and headed toward the front door, Caitlin a pace or two behind him. She'd spent some time on her appearance, that much was obvious—her hair hung in shining waves past her shoulders, and she was wearing darker, nicer jeans and a dark green knit top that hugged her curves without being too revealing. Even so, he'd had to work not to stare at her when she emerged from the guest bathroom earlier that morning. She was just so frigging gorgeous.

When Alex opened the door, he saw two people waiting outside: a severe-looking woman with straight black hair and elegant cheekbones, and a man about the same age, also dark-haired, a ponytail hanging halfway down his back. That must be Andre Begonie, Angela's father. Unlike his wife, Andre wore a pleasant expression, and smiled at Alex.

"I hope you don't mind both of us coming," Andre said. "I'm Andre, and this is my wife Marie, the Wilcox seer."

"Hi, Andre, Marie. I'm Alex. Come on in."

He stepped aside, pushing the door open a little wider at the same time. The Wilcox witches entered, Andre flashing a reassuring smile at Caitlin as she stammered a hello, while Marie only nodded and continued on into the living room.

Nonplussed, Alex brought up the rear. "Uh—can I get you anything? Iced tea? Water?"

"Some water would be very good. Thank you, Alex," Marie said in a cool, brisk tone. She sat down on the couch, and Andre settled himself next to her. Looking awkward, as if she didn't quite know what to do with her hands, Caitlin took her own place on the love seat.

Since he really didn't want to leave her alone with Marie and Andre any longer than he had to, Alex hurried with grabbing a couple of glasses, dispensing some ice into them from the freezer door, then filling them with water. When he returned to the living room, he was relieved to see that Andre was asking Caitlin if she was doing okay here in Tucson, and whether she needed anything.

"I'm fine," she said, wearing a hesitant smile. A quick glance up at Alex as he brought in the glasses of ice water and handed them to Marie and Andre, and she went on, "Alex has been taking very good care of me."

Something flickered in Marie's eyes at that comment, but she only said, "That's good to hear." After murmuring a thank-you to Alex for the water, she continued, "Any more visions?"

Caitlin bit her lip. Alex knew he wouldn't want to be her, to have to relate what she'd seen the night before to this cold-looking woman. Never mind that Andre was giving Caitlin an encouraging nod, as if trying to let her know that it would all be okay, that she didn't have to worry about what Marie would say in response to whatever report she might have to give.

"Last night," Caitlin said, her voice quiet, tense. "I only saw Danica. She was with Matías."

"You saw him?" Marie asked, her tone sharpening. "It was definitely him?"

A small shudder passed over Caitlin's slender frame. "Unfortunately, yes." Her hands knotted together in her lap, and Alex wished he could sink down next to her on the love seat and put his arm around her, give her a comforting hug. Since he doubted that would go over very well with Caitlin or her current audience, he remained where he was, leaning up against the arm of the love seat, watching but not actually participating in the current convo.

"What did you see, Caitlin?"

There would be no arguing with that calm, cool voice. Marie Begonie was obviously used to having her questions answered, and it seemed just as obvious that Caitlin knew she couldn't avoid providing some kind of answer. She seemed to brace herself, shoulders going rigid, and then, in a tight, dispassionate tone that didn't sound at all like her, she related what she had seen in the vision the night before. No embellishment, no pausing to make an attempt at interpreting those images.

Just the facts, ma'am, as his grandfather sometimes would joke.

Andre looked horrified, as one might expect, but Marie showed very little reaction at all, save the smallest tightening of her mouth. Then she said, "But you saw nothing else? Nothing that would indicate where they were?"

Caitlin shrugged. Frustration was clear in her voice as she replied, "No. I've been wracking my brains. There just wasn't enough detail. And nothing personal lying around that I could see—no photographs, no pieces of unopened mail. Nothing at all, except those saints' candles. Oh, and I think I saw Danica's earrings lying on the nightstand next to the ashtray. But while that helps to show it was really Danica I was seeing there, it doesn't give any more information as to where she might be."

"Any sign of Roslyn?" Andre inquired.

"No. Matías and Danica were alone. There was light coming down the hallway outside the bedroom, so somebody else might have been in the house…

apartment…whatever it was…but I didn't hear anyone or see anything."

For a long moment, neither Marie nor Andre said anything. They did share a single significant look, but as Alex didn't know them very well, he couldn't hazard a guess as to what they were thinking. Then Marie said, "Caitlin, do you have anything that belonged to Roslyn or Danica? Sometimes holding a personal item helps me focus in on someone."

Caitlin began to shake her head, then seemed to stop herself. "You know, I think I do. I borrowed a bracelet from Danica. It should be in with the rest of my stuff."

"Please get it for me."

Yes, Marie had said "please," but there was no missing the note of command in her voice. Caitlin got up from the love seat and hurried down the hallway toward the guest room. After she was gone, Marie fixed Alex with the sort of piercing gaze that made him think she must have noticed a stain on his shirt, or maybe a piece of ham sandwich stuck between his teeth.

"And what is your clan doing about all this?" she asked.

"Doing?"

"This…crime…happened on your territory. Surely your *prima* must be taking some action of her own."

Irritated by the note of cool accusation in her voice, he responded, "Besides having you come down here?"

"That was not something offered by Maya, or your own mother, who seems to be acting as her deputy these days." Something flashed in Marie's dark eyes. Anger? "This was something Connor and Angela requested, which is why I am here. But I want to know what your own people are doing. In the end, the responsibility for what happens to those two girls will fall on the de la Paz clan."

Was that a threat? It sure sounded like a threat. Although at first he'd been glad that his mother hadn't chosen to attend this meeting, had appeared to think Alex could handle things on his own, now he wasn't so certain. Inter-clan diplomacy wasn't exactly his forte. He'd seen something of how Maya ran things, just because she was his grandmother and so he'd been around her far more than your average member of the clan. Still, it wasn't enough exposure to give him the sort of experience he needed for this kind of situation.

"We're looking into it," he said, which was basically a non-answer, but better than telling Marie to go to hell. "And of course having Caitlin here is a big help, since we don't have a seer of our own."

The Wilcox witch's lips thinned at that remark. Maybe he should have kept his mouth shut; that

Caitlin had turned out to be a seer at all was probably a sore subject with Marie Begonie.

But then Caitlin returned, holding a bracelet of woven leather and turquoise beads. If she noticed the tension in the room, she didn't give any indication. Or possibly she'd decided the best thing to do was ignore it.

"Here's the bracelet," she said, handing it to Marie.

She took it, turning it over in her hand, letting a finger slide over the surface of a smoothly polished bead. "When did she loan this to you?"

"Right before we left. I said it would be cute with one of the tops I was packing, and she told me to go ahead and take it, since she wasn't planning on wearing it."

"Good. Then she's handled it recently."

Caitlin nodded and resumed her place on the love seat. As she settled herself, she looked up at Alex, her glance clearly questioning, but he knew he couldn't say anything in front of Andre and Marie. Alex knew he'd never been the best at concealing his emotions, so God only knew what was on his face right then. Irritation...worry? About all he could do was hope that Marie would think his expression stemmed from being troubled over the current situation and not anything she might have said.

They were all silent as Marie turned the bracelet over and over in her hand. Then she shook her head. "I'm not getting anything. Is there someplace where I can go to sit quietly?"

The house had three bedrooms, but Caitlin's stuff was in the guest room, and the other bedroom held his home office. Well, what he called his office. It was really more of a man cave, what with the big TV mounted on one wall and a console that held his various gaming equipment. Yes, it had a desk, which was where his laptop usually hung out, but it still didn't feel like the sort of place Marie was asking about.

"On the patio?" he suggested. "It's usually pretty quiet out there, and if you think it's too warm, I can turn on the ceiling fans."

"I'm sure it will be fine," she said, rising from the couch. Andre made a movement, as if to get up as well, but she made a quelling gesture with one hand and he subsided, not looking all that comfortable.

Alex decided to ignore that exchange and instead pointed toward the French doors that opened from the living room onto the patio. "Right through there. They're unlocked."

She nodded and went outside, letting in a waft of warm air. The day was clear, the sun bright. He had to hope she could either figure out the ceiling fans or would take off the sweater she wore over her T-shirt and denim skirt. That sweater had probably been necessary up in Flagstaff, but it sure wasn't needed here.

Out of the corner of his eye, Alex saw her pull out one of the chairs at the patio table and sit down, taking the exact spot where Caitlin had sat the night before. But since Marie obviously didn't want an audience, he made himself turn back toward Andre.

The older man seemed to recognize Alex's unease. "She can come on a little strong," he said. "I apologize for that. She's just worried. We all are."

Caitlin swallowed. "I am so sorry about not saying anything about my visions before this. I never thought—"

Andre held up a hand. "It's—well, I'm not sure if I can say it's all right, exactly, but what's done is done. The best we can do now is hope that your talents, combined with Marie's, will be enough to guide us to those girls before…before anything else can happen to them."

His expression was grim, and Alex couldn't blame him. For all any of them knew, what Caitlin had seen the night before was only the smallest taste of what Danica and Roslyn might be enduring even as the rest of them sat here, far away from any danger. Alex reminded himself that Andre was Angela's father, and very likely was putting himself in the places of Roslyn's and Danica's fathers, both of whom must be worried sick about their daughters, but who could only sit and wait while the elders of their clans attempted to effect some kind of rescue.

"I hope so, too," Caitlin said. "I've been trying and trying, hoping to get something else to come through, but...I just can't force the visions."

"It's all right," Andre told her, although some hesitation in his voice told Alex the other man wasn't quite as all right with it as he wanted Caitlin to think. Maybe he thought, after being married to Marie for the past few years, that the whole seer thing came that naturally to everyone who'd been born with the gift.

They all fell silent then. Alex wished he could think of something to say that would break the tension in the room, but every option that crossed his mind sounded worse than the last. *Glad to see you're putting that communications degree to good use,* he thought, even though he knew none of the classes he'd taken at U of A had exactly covered this type of situation.

The sound of the French door opening made everyone look up. A spark of hope flared in Caitlin's eyes as Marie entered the room, but the grim expression on the older woman's face told them all that she'd had no luck, even when granted the peace and quiet she'd requested.

"Nothing," she said, crossing the living room and setting Danica's bracelet down on the coffee table. "Normally, I should have been able to pick up something, even if I couldn't get a great deal of detail. But it's as if she's hidden behind some kind of dark curtain, some sort of barrier that my Sight can't penetrate." Marie's brows drew together, and she shook her head, lips compressing into a tight line that was already familiar to Alex. "If that had been Roslyn's bracelet, I might have understood it more. I don't know the girl—I might have seen her in passing at a family gathering here or there, but that would be the extent of our contact. But Danica? I've known her since she was born. I should have been able to detect some trace of her." Her gaze sharpened, that laser-beam focus falling on Caitlin, who flinched. "How is that you're able to have visions of her, when you've only been friends for a few months?"

"More than a year," Caitlin said. Her tone was quiet but firm, and her chin lifted as she looked up at the other woman. "We've been friends for over a year now. I wouldn't have moved in with someone I'd only known for a few months."

That show of defiance, mild as it was, made Alex think that Caitlin wasn't quite as ready to get walked over by Marie Begonie as he'd worried she might be. And Marie seemed to notice, too; she didn't quite scowl down at Caitlin, but her expression turned even more grim.

"Be that as it may, it still doesn't explain how you're able to see her when someone who's known Danica her entire life cannot."

"Maybe we won't ever be able to explain it," Andre said thoughtfully, and Marie's gaze shifted to him, then softened. Prickly she might be, but that prickliness didn't appear to extend to her husband. "We're talking about magic here, talents that run in our blood. This isn't science, where things can be measured exactly, and where certain inputs will always return the same results. Perhaps we're meant to trust in Caitlin's talents and see what they can do for Danica and Roslyn."

That sounded sensible to Alex, but, judging by the stricken look on her face, it seemed Caitlin didn't entirely agree. No doubt she'd been hoping that Marie would swoop in and pinpoint exactly where the two kidnapped girls had been taken, and that would be the end of it.

Unfortunately, these things were rarely that easy.

"You may be right," Marie said, and she let out a very small sigh, the first sign of anything less than absolute certainty Alex had seen in her. "At any rate, I can tell that I need to let it go for now. I'll try again— later tonight, most likely."

She nodded toward Andre, and he stood up.

Alex said, "Are you sure there isn't anything else you could try?" Not that he really wanted to prolong their visit, but at the same time, he hated the look of helpless worry on Caitlin's face, the realization that she really might have to do this on her own.

Well, not entirely on her own. He'd make sure he stuck with her until this thing came to its conclusion…whatever that might turn out to be.

"No," Marie said flatly. "Not now. There is no point in beating my head against a wall. As I said, I will try again when I've given myself a chance to rest."

Caitlin got up then as well, asking, "Are you staying in town?"

"For the night, yes. Although I doubt there's any reason for us to stay." She'd set her purse down next to the coffee table, and now she bent to retrieve it. "If I have any news, I will let you know. Alex, your mother gave me your cell number. I assume it's all right for me to call you if anything changes?"

"Sure," he said, although he could think of roughly a hundred other people he'd rather have his phone number than Marie Begonie.

Something around her mouth seemed to twitch, as if she'd guessed what he was thinking. But then her gaze moved past him to Caitlin, and Marie added, "If you should have any more visions, let me know immediately. My own cell number was in the email Alex's mother sent him this morning."

Caitlin nodded. "Of course. Even if it's the middle of the night?"

"Yes, even then."

Andre didn't look entirely thrilled at that prospect, but seemed to know better than to protest. "Thank you for letting us come by," he said.

"No problem," Alex said, the automatic response. After that, he led them to the front door, Caitlin a pace or two behind them. She gave one last reassurance that she would call if anything changed or she saw anything else, and then they were gone. He closed the door and let out a relieved sigh. "Well, we survived."

Caitlin gave a half-hearted nod but didn't appear entirely convinced.

"Come on," he said. There wasn't much he could do to help her at the moment, but he wanted to try, wanted to do something to help remove the anxious expression from her face. "While we're waiting for those visions to come, let me show you around a bit."

CHAPTER NINE

EVEN A HOUSE AS NICE AS ALEX'S COULD SEEM confining after a while. Caitlin was forced to admit that it felt good to get out, to let the sun warm her skin and the breeze blow through her hair. He drove them away from his neighborhood up in the hills, back down toward the center of Tucson proper.

"Anything in particular you want to see?" he asked, once they were driving south on the freeway.

By then it was around two-thirty, late for lunch, far too early for dinner. She thought she could eat something, but at the same time, she was feeling on edge after that meeting with Marie, her stomach sort of jumpy and nervous. Better to hold out on any real eating for a few more hours.

"The university?" Caitlin responded. That sort of came out of nowhere, but she thought it would be interesting to see where Alex had gone to college, and whether it was so very different from Northern Pines.

"Thinking of transferring?" he asked with a grin.

Maybe, if it meant being closer to you. Then she wanted to smack herself. A day around this guy, and she was already thinking about possible ways she could spend more time with him? It was ridiculous. Focus. She really needed to focus.

"No," she replied, taking care to keep her tone light. "It's just—Northern Pines is the only other university I've ever seen, and even that's super-recent. Up until a few years ago, it might as well have been on the moon."

He must have caught something in her inflection, because he glanced over at her for a second before returning his attention to the freeway. There was traffic, but it moved well enough. "I guess I always took it for granted that I could go to college—whether here or up at ASU. But you McAllisters didn't have any real universities in your territory, did you?"

"No, only a community college. That's where I was going, actually. But then everything changed." There was an understatement. A feud that had lasted for generations, wiped away as if it had never existed. Well, almost. Caitlin knew that among her own generation, most people, whether Wilcox or McAllister, didn't have too hard a time adjusting to the change in the status quo. With the older set, that sort of acceptance was a little more spotty. Her mother and father hadn't been terribly thrilled when she announced she was transferring to Northern Pines so she could get a real degree, but after some family drama, they'd eventually settled down.

"Let me guess—mass influx of McAllisters?" Alex asked, that same grin flashing at her, making her just weak enough in the knees that she was glad she was sitting down.

"I don't know about 'mass,' but there were a few…maybe enough to make someone at the registrar's office wonder why so many of their incoming students had the same last name." It was funny, because she'd never thought about it that way before. Then again, not all of her fellow clan members who'd transferred to Northern Pines even had the last name of McAllister, although of course they were all related in one way or another.

"Well, it makes sense. It would be a big deal to me, too, if I'd spent my life in a small territory like yours, and then had the chance to get out." He seemed to stop himself, adding, "Sorry—I didn't mean it that way. Jerome is great, from what I saw of it."

"I'm not offended," she replied, and offered him a smile of her own. "That is, our territory is a lot more than just Jerome, but compared to what the de la Paz clan controls, or even the Wilcoxes...yeah, it's sort of underwhelming."

"All the more reason for you to get out and stretch your legs." He pulled off the freeway then, crossing back under it before heading...east? Northeast? It was hard for Caitlin to say for sure, since she really hadn't gotten her bearings yet, and the position of the sun wasn't telling her much, either.

They were headed up a main street, she could see that much, and the area around the freeway didn't look too promising. It did improve, however, as they drove along, until suddenly on either side of the boulevard were official-looking buildings in a variety of different architectural styles.

"This is it," Alex said.

Caitlin blinked. "You mean...you have this big road just going through the middle of your campus?" Not that Northern Pines didn't have its own access roads, but the campus still felt somewhat segregated from the city around it. Here, the school seemed to have been plunked down right in the middle of town.

"Basically, yes. So what did you want to see?"

"I don't know...where did you hang out?"

He didn't exactly frown, but he also didn't look quite as cheerful as he had a minute or two earlier when he'd been teasing her about the McAllisters invading Northern Pines. "I worked part-time at the store the whole time I was in college, so I didn't do a lot of hanging out. But there was a coffee place I'd go to between classes. I think the Caffe Lucé espresso kept me alive during finals a few times."

"Oh," she said, her tone flat. She wasn't sure what she'd been expecting him to say, but telling her that a coffeehouse had been one of his favorite haunts hadn't even occurred to her.

"Right, you're not a coffee drinker. They have tea, though, and good pastries, if you can grab one before they sell out." A quick glance over at her before he turned right down another street whose name she didn't quite catch. "Does that sound okay?"

It sounded way more than okay. Right then she knew she'd never make it to dinner without having something a little more than the few handfuls of grapes she'd eaten while Alex had his sandwich. "You had me at pastries."

His smile returned, and after they'd gone another block or two, they came up to a row of shops dominated by a Trader Joe's. The street parking was dicey, but he found a spot just as someone was pulling out, and so was able to park his SUV there. "Right this way."

Because it was a dead time in the afternoon, they didn't have too much trouble finding a place to sit after placing their orders for coffee and tea. "Should I feel guilty for snagging the last coconut raspberry scone?" Caitlin asked.

"Only if you want to." Alex picked up his coffee and took a measured sip.

"Then I won't." She drank some of her iced tea, then broke off a piece of scone. "You want some?"

"I'm good. I had an actual lunch, remember?"

Caitlin nodded before popping the bit of scone in her mouth. It was very good, rich but not too sweet. Rachel McAllister would have approved. "I know I should have eaten something, but...."

"But you were mildly freaked about having to deal with Marie."

"Something like that." She washed the scone down with another swallow of tea. "Actually, for her, she was kind of mellow. I kept expecting her to rip me a new one for hiding my seer abilities from the clan." Alex's gaze slid away from her at that remark—just for a second, but enough that she thought he didn't entirely agree with her. "What...did she say something while I was off getting Danica's bracelet?"

"Not about that exactly." He picked up a stir stick and ran it through his coffee, even though he was drinking it black and didn't really need to stir anything. "She just...well, it wasn't as if she said it in so many words, but she made it pretty clear that the wrath of both the McAllisters and the Wilcoxes would fall on the de la Paz clan if we don't get Danica and Roslyn back safely."

Caitlin wanted to protest that he must have mis-understood her, that Marie had meant something else entirely, whatever she'd said to him. But although she couldn't claim to know Marie well, Caitlin did know that the other seer wasn't exactly the world's most tactful person. However you wanted to paint it, the kidnappings had taken place on de la Paz soil. That meant their clan was partially responsible, since if Maya had been fully functioning as a *prima*, she should have known interlopers from another clan were in her territory, and taken steps to have them sent back to wherever they'd come from.

However, Caitlin also knew that Alex knew all that as well, so there was no reason to point it out to him. Instead, she broke off another piece of scone, then said, "We all know that Angela and Connor will never retaliate. No matter" —her voice felt oddly dry, and she set down the bit of scone and instead took another pull at her iced tea— "no matter what might happen."

"Maybe they wouldn't. But what about your other clan members?"

He would have to ask that. Caitlin stalled by eating the piece of scone she'd broken off. "They wouldn't go against their *prima*'s wishes. And neither would the Wilcox clan."

"Are you sure about that?"

His dark eyes searched her face. She could see the doubt in his expression, the worry that Angela and Connor might be the *prima* and *primus* of their respective clans, but they were also, in the eyes of a lot of those same witches and warlocks, only a couple of kids in their twenties, not ready for the kind of responsibility this crisis had created.

"Well, I can't speak for everyone," Caitlin said, knowing she was hedging but at the same time realizing that she couldn't possibly give him a definitive answer. "But even though they haven't been the heads of their clans for all that long, no one can say they haven't been doing a good job. I'd like to think everyone would give them the benefit of the doubt."

For a few painful seconds, Alex didn't say anything. Then his shoulders lifted, although she got the feeling the shrug was intended more to show her that he didn't feel like arguing the subject, rather than because he agreed with her.

"The best thing we can do is find them," she went on. "Which is why it's so frustrating to sit here and know that I should be doing something besides having scones and tea. It's just not right."

"What else could you do?" he asked reasonably. "You've tried summoning the visions, and that didn't work. In the meantime, you still have to eat and drink and carry on like a normal person. I doubt you'll do them any more good by continually stressing until your focus is totally shot."

She couldn't really argue with that. At the same time, she couldn't help feeling angry with herself for being here and finding any kind of enjoyment in the pastry she was eating, or even simply being able to look across the table and see Alex's earnest gaze on her, the warmth of his voice. Something about the way he spoke always sounded unruffled, always in control, although she knew that wasn't entirely the case. There were things that worried and upset him, just as they would anyone.

"You're right," she said, trying not to sigh. At the same time, she couldn't help feeling impatient with that supposed third eye of hers, or whatever it was. If time was of the essence, why wasn't she being bombarded with a string of images that would lead her straight to wherever Danica and Roslyn were being held?

Alex's phone went off then—another email, judging by the alert sound.

"I'd better check that," he said. "That's usually how my mother gets in touch with me. She hates texting, and I hate getting interrupted by phone calls, so the emails are our compromise."

"Maybe she has some new information for us," Caitlin suggested.

"Yeah…or maybe she's emailing to give me a ration of shit about how that interview with Marie went."

"Ouch."

He smiled then. "Yeah, that about sums it up." But he reached into his pocket and dug out his iPhone, then unlocked it so he could access his emails.

Caitlin watched as he scanned the message from his mother, the movements of his eyes almost hidden under the dark sweep of his eyelashes. Was he even aware of how good-looking he really was? He definitely didn't dress all that flashy; when she'd first met him, he'd had on dark khaki pants and a white button-down for work, and today he was wearing nicely faded jeans and an untucked polo shirt along with some well-broken-in cross-trainers.

"Well, that's interesting," he said at last, setting the phone down on the tabletop so he could pick up his neglected coffee and take a sip.

"What is?"

"We have someone in the clan—my cousin Miguel, who lives up in Mesa—who's a private investigator. His talent is always being able to tell when someone is lying. Convenient for his line of work."

"I can imagine."

"Anyway, my mother had him look into that house where Matías and the others took you, to see if there was any kind of a connection between them and the house."

"And was there?"

Alex shook his head. "Not exactly. Turns out the place is owned by a couple of snowbirds from Chicago. They'd just gone back up north the week before, had the house listed with a rental company that specializes in short-term vacation rentals of houses and condos. But there's no record of anyone renting it yet, which means the warlocks were just using it, knowing it was vacant."

It would have been so much easier if Matías and his goons had rented the place legitimately. But that would have meant leaving some kind of paper trail, something Caitlin knew they would have worked hard to avoid. "So…do you think they were keeping an eye on available rentals in the area, knowing they could use one if the opportunity presented itself?"

"That sounds about right." Alex ran a hand through his thick, dark hair, pushing back the one bit that always seemed to droop over his forehead. "I mean, pretty much any witch or warlock can get into a locked house, so it would be easy. And since it's spring break for ASU—U of A is off next week— no one would probably think twice about seeing a group of college-age guys going in and out of a house that was up for rent."

There wasn't much Caitlin could find to argue with in that logic. But still…. "I suppose that makes sense. What I don't understand is how they were able to target us. I mean, the only people who knew Roslyn and Danica and I were even coming here to Tucson were your mother and Maya. I kind of doubt they'd be spreading that information around."

"No," Alex said at once. "I mean, your travel plans were your business, and if you'd come across any de la Paz witches or warlocks while you were here doing your thing in Tucson, they would have known you were here with permission and wouldn't have thought much about it." His brows drew together, as if he was mentally attempting to put the pieces together, and he continued, "But if any of those warlocks has the kind of talent my *abuela* has…*had*…they might have been able to sense you from much farther away than a regular witch or warlock could. I don't know why they would have been hanging around here in the first place, as you'd think they'd have better hunting up in the Phoenix area, but if one of them did have that gift, they would have felt you three as soon as you came into town. And then…."

Caitlin could tell he didn't want to finish the idea, so she did it for him. "And then they came after us because we were three witches a long way from home, without the support of our clan anywhere near us. Easy pickings."

Somberly, Alex nodded. "Yeah, I'm afraid that's pretty much exactly how it must have happened. And it never would have happened, if my grandmother still commanded the powers she once did. I'm sorry."

On an impulse, Caitlin reached out and laid her hands on his. He didn't try to move away, but rather wrapped his fingers around hers so they were intertwined. His skin was warm, his grasp strong. A tingling heat went through her, telling her that maybe this hadn't been such a good idea after all. No way would she pull her hands from his now, though.

She cleared her throat and said, "Alex, that's not her fault. No one is going to put that on her. She's ill."

"I know, but—"

"But nothing," Caitlin said firmly. She gave his fingers a squeeze and let go, then picked up her iced tea, as if that was the real reason she'd lifted her hands from his. Of course it wasn't; she was just too ruffled by the way his touch made her feel. He didn't need to know that, though. "The only people at fault here are Matías and Tomas and Jorge, and maybe Simón Santiago, if it turns out they really are from his clan, and he knew what they were capable of but didn't stop them from coming over here. That's it."

"I'm glad you see it that way." Alex didn't look particularly cheered up as he said this, however, and went back to stirring his undoctored coffee, which had to rapidly be going cold. "But will other people?"

"I know Connor and Angela will, and that's the most important thing, isn't it?"

"Maybe."

If she'd been in his position, maybe Caitlin would have felt similarly disinclined to cling to false hope. Unfortunately, there was no way of knowing how anyone was going to react to all this, just because nothing similar had ever occurred. At least, not that Caitlin knew of. Yes, Damon Wilcox had kidnapped Angela, stolen her right out of her bedroom, but that had turned out okay in the end, because of Connor. Somehow Caitlin doubted such a happy ending awaited her friends at the hands of Matías and his cronies.

It wouldn't come to that, though. Danica was... well, clearly Matías was using her as his personal sex toy, but the vision hadn't shown any cuts on her arms, or anywhere else. She seemed to be okay physically, although Caitlin prayed with all her might that her friend wouldn't remember anything of what she'd done with the renegade warlock once this was all over. At any rate, she didn't seem to be in any immediate physical danger.

Roslyn...Caitlin didn't want to think about that, because they *had* cut her. Did her absence from last night's vision indicate that she was already dead?

No. That couldn't be true. Caitlin wouldn't let it be true. The only reason she hadn't seen her cousin in the vision was that she'd been off in another room somewhere, probably with Jorge and Tomas. Then again, that wasn't a very encouraging thought, either.

She pushed away the remnants of her scone, appetite gone, and Alex asked, "All finished?"

"I think so."

He dug in his wallet and dropped a couple of ones on the table for the tip. "Then let's go. Maybe some more fresh air will clear both our heads."

Alex decided to take Caitlin out of Tucson proper and over the hill to the Old Tucson Studios park, partly because it was a nice drive, and partly because they needed something to fill up the time while waiting for her next vision to show itself. She gazed, wide-eyed, out the car windows, staring at the saguaro cacti that marched up and down the hillsides, standing there like silent sentinels.

"They're kind of creepy, don't you think?" she asked at last.

"The saguaros?"

"Yes…like they'd shift their positions the second you turned their back on them or something."

Well, that was a nice friendly image. He really hadn't thought about the cacti one way or another, even though he'd grown up with them all around him. His father grumbled about the saguaro, just because they were protected plants, and you couldn't cut them down or dig them up, even if one did happen to be in the way of your current landscaping project.

"That's quite an imagination you have," Alex remarked, slowing down as they began to wind their way up and over the crest of the hill, down into the valley where the studios were located.

She didn't smile, though, but only shrugged and said, "I suppose so."

Now, what was that about?

But the small frown that had been tugging at her pretty arched brows faded as she gazed out at the vista ahead of them. "Wow, it's...." She broke off, stared out the windshield, then said, "It's so beautiful. I guess I hadn't expected it to be like this."

"Because the southern part of the state is supposed to be hot and dry and dusty?"

"Yeah, something like that."

Well, at least she was honest. "You're coming at a good time of year. It was a nice rainy winter, so things are pretty green. But I'm glad you like it."

"What's it called?"

"The Santa Cruz Valley. We're not going too far into it, though, just to the studios."

"I still can't believe there's a movie studio out here."

Alex said, "Why, because we're not in Hollywood?"

"Something like that." Then she did smile, just a little. "But we have a recording studio in Jerome, so I suppose it all evens out."

"Seriously?"

"Yeah. It's on the lower level of the old high school. The other floors are rented out for artist studios now."

That sounded very cool. When he'd gone to meet Angela, to see if he was "the one," he'd driven straight in to Jerome and met her, shared that one ritual kiss, then basically turned around and headed for home. At the time he'd been fighting his disappointment and really didn't want to stop and look at any more of the town.

Now, though...now he didn't feel quite so disappointed.

"I'd like to see that," he told Caitlin, and her expression brightened even more.

"And I'd love to give you a personal tour."

"I'll take you up on that."

It would be good to get past all this, to spend some time with her without the fate of her two friends hanging over her head. What he was doing now was only a small stopgap, something to lighten her mind, if only for an hour or two. Last night's vision had come while she was sleeping, but who was to say one might not intrude when she was awake? He supposed he'd just have to hope it wouldn't hit her when she was out in public. Maybe coming here wasn't such a good idea....

Nothing he could do about it now. Alex pulled into the parking lot at the studio, which was moderately more full than it usually would be during a weekday. Tourists from the Phoenix area, most likely, visiting because their kids were out of school. He hoped the place wouldn't be completely overrun.

There was an open parking space not too far from the entrance. He stopped the Pathfinder there, and then he and Caitlin both got out. A warm breeze ruffled his hair, but that's all it was—warm, not hot. A perfect day for coming out here.

He turned toward her, and she came around the front of the SUV, her own hair blowing around her face in a cloud of brilliant copper. God, he wanted to run his hands through that hair, feel its silky strands slip through his fingers. Who knew he'd have such a redhead fetish? Before now, he wouldn't have really admitted to a preference when it came to hair color in women.

Or maybe it was just that it was Caitlin's hair, rather than its particular color.

"This way," he said, hoping his voice didn't sound as strained to her as it did to him. He really did need to keep it together.

She smiled and followed him into the park, eyes bright, interested. Clearly, she didn't think it was hokey or silly that he'd brought her here. And she maintained that wide-eyed appreciation the whole time, during the stunt shows and the staged gunfights and the tour that talked about all the movies and TV shows filmed in the facility and its environs.

Since Alex had been here several times before, he found himself focusing on Caitlin and her reactions to what was going on around them, rather than the shows and displays themselves. It was good to watch her forget, if even for a little while, the real reason why she'd come to Tucson. She needed this, he could tell. And he needed it, too. How long had it been since he'd gone out and done something for fun, just because?

Way too long.

And how long had it been since he'd felt like this when he looked at a girl?

Even longer. No, that wasn't exactly true. He wasn't sure he'd ever felt like this. Not really.

Just what he was supposed to do about it, he had no idea.

CHAPTER TEN

THE AFTERNOON WAS GONE, AND ALEX WAS DRIVING THEM back into Tucson proper after suggesting that they go downtown for dinner. That sounded good. Walking over the old movie sets and watching the shows and yes, even panning for gold like a silly tourist, had worked up quite an appetite.

"What're you in the mood for?" he asked.

By then she was so hungry that even the greasiest fast food would've sounded good. "You choose. It's your city. Whatever's your favorite. Except sushi."

"What, you're not into raw fish?"

She made a face, remembering the one time Danica had talked her into trying some sashimi. "Not really."

He grinned. "That's okay—neither am I."

Well, thank the Goddess for that. True, most Japanese restaurants had teriyaki and tempura, and she was okay with eating either of those. That didn't seem to be an issue now, though. She did have to wonder where they were going to end up, however, as they zigzagged off the freeway and headed into the heart of the city. They wound through the streets of downtown, some of which ran one way, and ended up opposite a structure that appeared to be an official building of some sort, maybe a courthouse. That clearly wasn't their destination, as Alex instead led her to a brick-fronted building with no obvious signs. It didn't look like a restaurant from the outside, but once he ushered her in through the front door, it was clear that's exactly what the business was.

And obviously it wasn't the first time he'd been here, since the girl performing hostess duties greeted him with a "hey, Alex!" and led them right to a table off in one corner, much to the disgust of the people who'd been waiting there ahead of them. True, they were a party of four, and Caitlin guessed the hostess could use that excuse as to why they hadn't been seated first, but....

"It's good to know people, isn't it?" she said to Alex as the hostess made her way back to her spot by the entrance.

He managed to look embarrassed. Sort of. "Yeah, I might have eaten here once or twice."

Caitlin decided to leave that aside for now. Her stomach had really woken up when it got a whiff of the savory smells that filled the restaurant, and pretty much everything on the menu sounded good—it was Mexican food, but an artsier kind than she was used to. "Do you recommend anything?"

"Their mole is really good, and pretty much any of the tacos, depending on what you like. And we definitely need to have some of their sangria."

That did sound good. A few glasses of sangria, the two of them tucked into this intimate corner… anything could happen.

And nothing should *happen,* she told herself. *You're eating because you're hungry. This is not a date.*

Then she remembered that she had no I.D., no money. Alex had paid for everything at Old Tucson Studios, and she hadn't protested because she didn't want to make a scene, but she couldn't let him keep on doing that indefinitely.

"And what about me having no driver's license to prove I'm of age?" she asked in an undertone. "They're totally going to card me."

"No, they won't," he replied, apparently not worried by the situation at all. "It'll be fine."

She raised an eyebrow at him, but didn't have a chance to protest further, since a waiter showed up right then and asked for their drink orders. "A mason jar of the sangria de rosé," Alex said without batting an eye, and the waiter just nodded and said, "Sure," before heading off toward the bar.

"What, do you have Matías' mind-control abilities or something?" she inquired. "I always get carded. *Always*."

"Like I said, they know me here. And they know I wouldn't be out on a date with someone under twenty-one."

A date. He called it a date. But had he really meant it, or just used the word as shorthand for whatever they were actually doing? "So have you brought a lot of 'dates' here?"

His gaze slid away from hers. "A couple."

Of course he had. Someone like Alex, good-looking, with a good job and an awesome house? He was probably knee-deep in girls wanting to go out with him. But had they been civilians, or the kind of distant cousins it was okay to have a relationship with? Probably a mixture of both, if her own experience was any indication. Having to hide the truth about who you were from a civilian could be a real pain, but having an ex who was also part of the extended family could be even trickier....

She was distracted from that line of thought by the arrival of the chips and salsa. Thank the Goddess. At least she'd have something to munch on along with the sangria.

Which appeared almost immediately after the chips, forcing her to make a quick scan of the menu and decide on the carne asada tacos, while Alex got the mole. He poured some sangria into her glass and then into his. She waited a second after she lifted her drink, wondering if he was going to clink glasses with her or something. But apparently he thought that wouldn't be in the best taste, considering their current situation, so she continued bringing the glass to her lips as if her hesitation had been for some completely different reason.

"So what now?" she asked.

He was munching on a chip, and waited to swallow before he replied, "I don't know—there are a few places nearby where we can listen to live music after dinner, if you want."

"That's not what I meant."

"No, I guess not." His fingers wrapped around his sangria glass, but he didn't drink. Instead, his dark eyes watched her steadily as he said, "What are we supposed to do? Obviously, my mother's working on it in the background, since she has Miguel snooping around and doing what he can, but I don't know how much that's really going to help. Even if someone saw Matías and the other two guys when they took you to that rental house, what good is that going to do?"

"I don't know," Caitlin responded. She'd never been much for reading mysteries or watching detective shows, preferred science fiction and fantasy instead. Head in the clouds, her brother used to tease her. It certainly hadn't prepared her for this sort of situation. Still, she wracked her brain, trying to think of something they might have missed. "Maybe… maybe if someone did notice the warlocks, then saw them drive away with Roslyn and Danica?"

Alex's expression brightened somewhat at that suggestion. "Okay. Did you see a car when you went to the house?"

Time for more brain-wracking, as little as she wanted to revisit those harrowing memories. She'd been sort of out of it at the time, thanks to Matías' grip on her mind. But she'd noticed what the house looked like, more or less, and as far as she could recall, she didn't remember seeing a car in the driveway or parked out front. She supposed they could have hidden it in the garage; even if they didn't have a remote, they could've opened the door from the inside once they had access to the rest of the house.

"I don't think so," she replied slowly, shuffling through her memories as she spoke. "It might have been in the garage. Or maybe they parked it a few streets over so they wouldn't be obvious."

"If they did that, there would've been more chance of someone noticing them taking Danica and Roslyn to it." He shifted slightly, and Caitlin realized he was getting his phone out of his pocket. "Do you mind if I email my mother, send our ideas along? For all I know, Miguel's already thought of it, but…."

"No, please, go ahead," Caitlin broke in. If nothing else, at least it would show that they'd done something today besides spin their wheels. Not that going out to the studios with Alex hadn't been fun, but it hadn't exactly gotten them any closer to finding Roslyn and Danica, either. On the way back into town, she'd closed her eyes for a bit, tried once again to empty her mind of everything and let the visions pour through her. It hadn't worked. Nothing came to her at all, and she could only hope that Alex had thought she was merely resting her eyes instead of proving what a crappy seer she was turning out to be.

While she sipped at her sangria, Alex tapped out an email, fingers moving with surprising dexterity on the tiny screen of his phone. Maybe it had really good auto-complete software. She wouldn't know, because she tended to get by with bargain-basement Android phones, not the gleaming silvery iPhone Alex currently held.

"All done," he said, then slid the phone back into his jeans pocket. "Here's hoping that's an angle they haven't thought of yet."

She nodded, but the memory of her failed attempt at forcing another vision still nagged at her. "Alex, what are we doing?"

"Having dinner?" he joked. But when she didn't smile, he told her, "We're doing what we can. It's like I told you earlier today—beating yourself up the whole time isn't going to help your friends. And awful as it is, thinking about what might be happening to them, they're still alive. Matías needs to keep them alive for that magic he's performing."

Just the mere memory of the strange circle and its unnatural symbols, the way Roslyn's blood had dripped onto it and made that horrible mist rise into the air, curdled Caitlin's stomach. Ignoring the sangria, she picked up her water glass and took a large swallow. It helped a little.

"What do you know about that, anyway?" she asked, pitching her voice low and shooting a wary glance at the couple sitting at the table next to them. Luckily, it looked as if they were on their first date or something, as they seemed to be doing the standard "what shows do you watch? Oh, you liked that movie, too?" sort of thing people tended to do when they were getting to know one another. At any rate, they didn't seem to be paying any attention to her or Alex, or to their conversation.

He obviously didn't miss that quick, sideways darting of her gaze. Lowering his own voice, he said, "Not very much. I mean, we all have slightly different flavors to our magic—the de la Paz clan came here from Mexico, so we use some rituals that are different from yours, just as you came from Scotland and follow a more Wiccan tradition. But dark magic, blood magic—it was outlawed everywhere centuries ago. We might be descended from the guys who used to throw human sacrifices off pyramids, but I promise we haven't done anything like that lately."

Caitlin couldn't prevent herself from smiling at that remark. "No, I guess that would be kind of conspicuous, wouldn't it? The problem is, that makes us fly even more blind, really, since we don't know for sure what they were doing, or why they needed blood for their spell."

His gaze didn't quite meet hers. "Well, we may not know, but I can guess."

She crossed her arms. "What aren't you telling me?"

"Not that I know firsthand or anything, but there are witches and warlocks in our clan who do know something of that kind of magic—not because they practice it themselves, but because it's important to know what your enemies might be up to." He drank some more of his sangria, and this time his eyes did flicker back toward hers, troubled and dark. "The doings of the Santiago clan haven't always been entirely on the up and up. Not as bad as this, at least not that I know of, but I've heard rumors. We've tried to be vigilant. The McAllisters are far enough away that the Santiagos' doings weren't much of a concern. Same with the Wilcoxes. Anyway, the Wilcox clan had a bad reputation for long enough that even the Santiagos wouldn't have wanted to tangle with them."

That made some sense, although she wondered at the way Connor and Angela had gone into Santiago territory several years ago, with no one apparently warning them about what they might be walking into. It was possible that no one had worried too much, because the combined power of a *primus* and a *prima* was certainly nothing to mess with.

"So what do you think Matías is up to?" Caitlin finally picked up her sangria and took a swallow as well, mostly because contemplating a new threat in the shape of the entire Santiago clan had left a definite bad taste in her mouth.

"Like I said, I don't know for sure, because I didn't see what you saw. But generally when a witch or warlock is doing blood magic, it means they're calling up something to assist them in casting a black spell. That would've been the mist you saw beginning to rise from the floor."

"You mean…it was *alive?*" she asked, her voice barely more than an aghast whisper. Yes, Luz had mentioned that the warlocks were summoning something, but at the time she'd been so shaky and out of it that she hadn't really processed the statement and its implications. Although it was warm enough in the restaurant, a river of ice suddenly seemed to run down her spine.

"Sort of, if not exactly the kind of thing most of us think of when we say 'alive.' But it was some kind of spirit...entity...energy...whatever you want to call it." He picked up a chip from the basket and broke it in two, but didn't eat either piece, instead staring down at them as if he wasn't sure what he intended to do with them.

"What were they doing with it?"

"I don't know. I'm sure my mother went back to that house with someone who knows more about that kind of magic, but if they discovered anything else, she hasn't told me." He hesitated then, as if he'd been about to say more but had decided to stop there, for whatever reason.

Caitlin thought she could guess the reason why. If Luz and whoever was helping her had dug up something really terrible, she might not want to frighten her son...or the unpracticed seer he was supposed to be protecting.

Another shiver moved down her spine, but then she had to sit up and act halfway normal, as the waiter showed up with their meals. She thanked him and stared down at the food on the plate before her, hoping she could reclaim some of her appetite. Right then her stomach was churning with an uncomfortable combination of worry and fear.

"It's all right," Alex said, apparently noticing her unease. "We're safe here. And even if something were to happen, you know I would protect you."

Well, that was true. Or at least she hoped it was. She'd seen the odd shimmering sphere that Alex could cast to surround himself and anyone near enough to him, but she'd yet to see anyone or anything challenge it. Luz had said nothing could get through it. Did that include strange mist-like entities called here from the Goddess only knew which dimension?

"Right," Caitlin said, and forced herself to smile at him, even though she knew it must have looked watery and weak. "I guess I'm just not used to this kind of thing. I mean, Damon Wilcox did some terrible stuff, but he's gone, you know? I suppose it was naïve of me to think there wouldn't be someone or something equally awful out there."

Alex nodded, but she noticed how he'd barely looked at his food, either, although his left hand was resting on his fork, as if he'd intended to pick it up and then got distracted. "Well...you McAllisters do tend to be kind of isolated. In a way, that's good. You're focused on your own clan, and there's nothing wrong with that. But there are a lot of other clans out there, some good, some...not as much, for whatever reason. At least with Damon, you knew exactly why he did the things he did, even if they were terrible. But this?" His shoulders went up, and at last he retrieved his fork and stuck it into the mound of chicken on his plate, even though he didn't make a move to lift it. "I can't figure out what their game is. Kidnapping a couple of witches from clans that are bound to retaliate isn't exactly the smartest thing to be doing."

"But we aren't retaliating, are we?" Caitlin asked, and Alex gave her a considering look.

"Not yet. But don't tell me that Angela and Connor won't do something about it, or at least try to, once we've located Matías and his buddies. I know I would."

Any protests she might have made died away as Caitlin considered Alex's point. Neither Angela nor Connor was the type to go flying off half-cocked, but they also both had a strong sense of right and wrong, and the unwritten rule of the witch world was that if someone messed with your clan, you found some way to bring them to justice. No matter what.

Since she wasn't sure how to respond, Caitlin finally picked up one of her tacos and took a bite, knowing if she didn't start eating, the food would soon get cold. In an abstract way, she realized it was very good, and so she took another bite. Strangely enough, eating something seemed to help settle the nervous churning of her stomach. After she washed the food down with a swallow of her sangria, she said, "Maybe they will retaliate. I can't speak for them. But I know that whatever they do, it will be measured. They won't do something stupid, just in the name of revenge."

Alex didn't respond at first, but followed her lead by eating a few bites of his own meal. Then he asked, "You think a lot of them, don't you?"

"Connor and Angela? Well, why wouldn't I? She's my *prima,* and he's her consort."

"True, but not everyone always agrees with their *prima,* do they? Even if they publicly go along with what she says."

Caitlin thought that over for a few seconds. "Maybe, but so far Angela hasn't done anything that would make me question her judgment. She and Connor are both kind of live-and-let-live types. I'm not saying she hasn't stepped in from time to time when someone's gotten out of hand, but she's definitely not some kind of dictator. Which is as it should be. I don't have any reason to think she'll do something crazy now, either."

The expression on Alex's face was hard to decipher. He didn't say anything at first, but from the way his eyes narrowed slightly, Caitlin wondered if he was trying to process her view of her *prima* with the girl he'd only met a few times, someone he hadn't seen for several years. And those were important years. Angela was now a mother, had a few years of being *prima* under her belt. She'd changed. But then, who wouldn't, after everything she'd experienced?

Finally, Alex said, "Well, that's good to hear. Because the last thing we need is a clan war on our hands."

Caitlin couldn't argue with that. "Even though Matías might turn out to be one of Simón Santiago's, I kind of doubt he'd do much to stick up for him, once the truth comes out about what Matías has been doing. You'd think Simón would wash his hands of him, if only to do some damage control."

"I hope you're right." The worried expression on Alex's features smoothed itself into something else entirely. There was even a hint of a smile playing around the corners of his mouth. "So, since we can't fix all the world's problems at dinner, why don't we let that all go for now?"

That sounded like a great idea. She raised her glass in agreement. "I'll drink to that."

It was a relief to shift gears, to watch some of the tension leave Caitlin's face as he purposely moved the conversation to something a little lighter, like how he'd found this restaurant, his favorite places to go in and around the city—anything except her kidnapped friends and the dark powers their kidnappers seemed to be employing. She asked about his family, and he told her how Diego was now living down near Bisbee, his wife already expecting their first child. "Nothing like not wasting any time, considering they just got married in June," Alex had remarked, and Caitlin grinned, a dancing light he hadn't seen before coming to her eyes.

She told him about her brother the chef, how his talent was coming up with amazing recipes and food combinations right out of thin air—or so it appeared to the foodies who had started flocking to Cottonwood to try his various creations. "Everyone was so amazed by Michael that they sort of missed how I hadn't developed any powers," she said. "Which was fine by me."

"Well, any powers you were willing to tell them about," he countered, and a bit of the twinkle in her eyes faded.

"Okay, you got me there. But yeah, I was just fine with letting my brother bask in the limelight. It made things a lot easier for me."

Alex reflected there might be something to that. His own brother charmed everyone within a twenty-mile radius, it seemed like, to the point that even when he married Maria and disappeared to Bisbee to make wine, neither of his parents were that upset with him. Then again, why should they be? There was always good old dependable Alex to pick up the slack at the store.

"Something wrong?" Caitlin asked.

This was a topic he really didn't feel like going into, so he just shrugged. "Not really."

"Oh, come on. For a split-second, you looked like you'd been sucking on a lemon or something."

Despite himself, Alex chuckled. "That bad?"

"Yeah. And since I've told you some of my secrets, it's only fair that you tell me at least one of yours."

Damn. She had been pretty honest with him so far, once she'd unburdened herself of the secret she'd been hiding from everyone for years. "It's not that big a deal. I just—running a store wasn't exactly how I thought I'd end up, you know?"

A look of confusion passed over her face. "But... it's your family business, right? Why wouldn't you end up there? I mean, I thought that's sort of how it works down here."

Not the sort of question most girls of their generation would have asked. But witch families followed their own rules, had their own traditions. Especially here in de la Paz territory, where things tended to be more rigid than in freewheeling Jerome. He hesitated, then said, "My great-grandfather started the store, and then my grandfather inherited it, and he passed it on to my father. He wasn't the oldest child, but he was the only son." He flashed a grin at Caitlin, who flushed prettily and picked up her sangria, trying to pretend she hadn't been affected by his smile. Not that he'd meant it that way, but her reaction was interesting. Maybe she wasn't quite as "all business" as he'd thought. "Four daughters, and then finally my dad. My grandfather was ready to tear his hair out."

"He could've left the store to his oldest daughter," Caitlin pointed out.

"Tradition. A woman wasn't supposed to run the *mercado*."

"That's silly."

Maybe to her, it was. The McAllisters seemed to have a more female-dominated culture than the de la Paz family. Yes, a *prima* ran things here...but that was sort of where the buck stopped, so to speak. "It's how it was. Diego was supposed to take over for my father, but he never wanted to. I have a feeling part of the reason he married Letty was that he could go help her with her family's vineyards and be safely away from Tucson and the store."

Caitlin's brows went up. "Isn't that a little, I don't know...cynical?"

You don't know my brother, Alex thought, but he didn't bother to voice the notion aloud. "Maybe. I don't know. Anyway, that left me. My little sister doesn't have any interest in running the store. Besides, it wouldn't suit her talent."

"What's that?"

"She can...well, 'talk to the animals' sounds sort of Horse Whisperer-ish, but that's basically what she can do. Knows how they're feeling, knows the best way to work with them. She's finishing up her degree in biology now, and then she's going to vet school."

An expression of not-quite envy passed over Caitlin's face. "That's a really cool talent."

"I know. But obviously it's not of much use when it comes to running a store. And my parents said to themselves, 'Hey, Alex just got his degree in marketing. He'll be perfect at running the *mercado!*'"

"So why the degree in marketing, if you didn't want to manage the store?"

He'd never confessed his goals to anyone before. Not completely, anyway. A marketing degree was a good one to have, and the communications degree on top of that was just the cherry on the sundae. But Caitlin was gazing at him so earnestly, one dark russet eyebrow arched at an adorable angle, that he found himself saying, "I wanted to work in local television—you know, one of the stations up in Phoenix?"

"Wow," she breathed. "Like a reporter or something?"

"No," he replied, knowing that was the expected reaction. "I would've gotten a journalism degree for that instead of the marketing one. I wanted to do more behind-the-scenes stuff, maybe producing, once I'd put in my time as an intern. Since I'm bilingual, I could've tried for some of the Spanish-language stations, too, if the right opportunity presented itself."

She sat back in her chair, looking impressed. "No wonder you're grumpy about having to manage the store."

"'Grumpy'?" he repeated. "Is it that obvious?"

"Right now it is. But before this, I probably wouldn't have guessed it was such a sore subject." Her gaze slipped away from his, and she toyed with the napkin in her lap. "I'm sorry."

"Sorry?"

"Sorry that you didn't get to do what you wanted to do. But I guess that happens to a lot of us."

She spoke simply, but he caught the trace of bitterness in her voice. "And what is it that you wanted to do? I mean, you're going to Northern Pines, right?"

"Right. I am." Still not looking at him, she added, "It's nothing. I'm babbling. Long day and too much sangria."

Alex wasn't so sure about that, since she'd only had a glass and a half, but he wasn't about to argue with her. "Well, if you're done, I can get the check, and we can go home."

"Sounds great."

Was it his imagination, or had he heard a hint of trepidation in her tone? Maybe she was worried about what they'd do when they got there, whether he'd press her to sleep in his room again, just to be safe. As much as he'd enjoy that, he'd let her make her own decision. She should know he'd never urge her to do something she didn't want to do.

After flagging the waiter down and asking for the check, he and Caitlin sat in a semi-uncomfortable silence until the rest of the ritual could be completed and he could drop the necessary number of twenties down on the table. Good thing he'd been carrying a decent amount of cash; waiting to have his credit card run would have been even worse.

They drove back to his place, still not talking. She looked out the window, seemingly staring at the clear skies above, at all the bright stars winking overhead. They couldn't be that new to her, though; Jerome had to have even less light pollution than Tucson, even for all his hometown's reputation as a dark sky city, a place that purposely cut back on its nighttime lighting so as not to interfere with the spectacular desert starscape.

He pulled into the garage and shut off the Pathfinder's engine. Even as he pulled the key from the ignition, Caitlin opened the passenger-side door and got out. She did have to wait for him to come around and unlock the door that led from the garage to the house, but once he'd done that, she pushed inside, as if afraid to be alone with him in the dark.

Two of the lamps in the living room were on timers, so they came on whether he was home or not. Their soft glow provided enough illumination to show Caitlin pausing next to the breakfast bar in the kitchen, her expression diffident.

"Thanks for dinner. It was really good."

"You're welcome," he said, the automatic response. He moved toward her, to the little bowl he had sitting on the end of the bar, where he generally dumped his keys at the end of the day. She stepped away—less than a foot, but enough to show she was uncomfortable with allowing him to get too close.

Damn. Talk about mixed signals. With the way she'd looked at him earlier that evening, he'd thought...oh, never mind what he thought. She was here to help find her friends and for no other reason.

"Do you watch *The Walking Dead?*" he asked, forcing his tone to be relaxed, casual. They had to do something to fill up the rest of the evening, since it wasn't even eight-thirty yet. Watching TV seemed the most innocuous thing to do.

For a second, Caitlin looked puzzled, and then what he could have sworn was a look of relief crossed her face. "Yeah, I do."

"Did you see this week's episode?"

A shake of the head. "No, I was down in Jerome having Sunday dinner with my family. Danica was supposed to download it for me, but...." She let the words trail off. They both knew Danica probably wasn't going to be downloading anything for a while.

Alex let it go. He knew nothing he could say would change anything or make it better. "Well, I've got it on my DVR. What do you say we go and put our feet up, and watch some people who have even worse problems than we do?"

For a second, she didn't respond, only seemed to be staring down at the toes of the somewhat scuffed ballet flats she wore. Then she looked up and smiled—a real smile, the kind that seemed to light something in those beautiful blue-green eyes of hers.

"I think that sounds like a great idea."

CHAPTER ELEVEN

It was sort of surreal to be sitting in here next to Alex, their feet propped up on the glass and metal coffee table, attention fixed on the flat-screen hanging from the wall opposite them. The thing was huge, too, way bigger than the 42-inch television her parents had bought a year ago. Again Caitlin wondered where the heck Alex got the money for all this stuff, but that was a question that could wait for another day.

For now, she was having a hard enough time keeping her attention fixed on the TV, on the admittedly gruesome scenes playing out there. But she'd never gotten grossed out by things she saw in the movies or on television, no matter how gory they might be.

It was the real-life stuff she had problems with.

Alex had gotten them both water, and he was drinking from his glass now, attention fixed forward so she could catch the fine outlines of his profile from the corner of her eye. The Adam's apple in his throat moved as he swallowed, and she made herself look forward again, to not think about the lean muscles of his neck and what it would feel like to place her lips against the warm brown skin there.

All right, this was getting out of hand. Her friends were still being held against their will by Matías and his gang, wherever they might be hiding, and right now she was watching some extra on *The Walking Dead* get his entrails ripped out of his stomach in a spectacular spray of Karo-syrup blood, and the only thing she could think about was kissing Alex's neck?

All she could do was pray he hadn't noticed her tension, hadn't seen the way her gaze kept wandering from the television set. He'd seated himself a respectable distance from her, at least a foot, and yet she fancied she could feel the warmth radiating out from his body even so. She knew she was acutely aware of every time he shifted, every creak of the couch and every movement of the sturdy biceps under the polo shirt he wore.

To distract herself, she bent forward and picked up her own glass of water, then planted her feet firmly on the rug-covered floor while she took a few swallows. There, that was a little better. If she drank enough, maybe she'd dilute some of the sangria currently swirling around in her stomach. To be fair, it really hadn't been that strong…just strong enough to have messed with some of her extremely hard-won composure.

"More?" Alex asked, and she started.

He grabbed the remote and paused the DVR. "Do you want more water?"

"Um…sure."

Setting the remote aside, he got up from the couch and moved from the family room to the kitchen, giving her a great opportunity to watch how his faded jeans clung to his ass and thighs. He was built just the way she liked—muscular but not muscle-bound, tall and broad-shouldered. After she'd hit her current five foot eight, she'd realized there were a lot of guys she wouldn't consider dating, just because they were too short. Call her shallow, but she wanted someone she could look up to.

Alex came back with her freshened-up glass of water in his hand, then gave it to her. She noticed he was careful not to let his fingers brush against hers, and felt a stab of disappointment. Well, what had she expected? She'd been acting like an idiot today, blowing hot and cold, being completely inconsistent in the way she was treating him. He'd probably decided it was much safer to keep his distance. And if she could just get her head screwed on straight, she'd put all these unwanted feelings and thoughts aside, and would regain some kind of focus. Maybe then the visions would return. For all she knew, she'd been unsuccessful so far because she was expending way too much mental energy on Alex Trujillo and not enough on letting her powers work through her.

"Better?" he asked, dropping down onto the couch next to her.

"Sure…thanks." She swallowed some water, and then some more. Whether it would be enough to clear her head, she had no idea.

He must have noticed something was wrong, because instead of picking up the remote and unpausing the DVR, he shifted so he was more or less facing her. "What's the matter?"

"Nothing."

His eyebrows quirked slightly, but he didn't say anything, only sat there, watching her. And that was the absolute worst, because not even a foot separated them now. No matter what she did, she couldn't seem to drag her eyes away from his, from their warm brown depths.

"It doesn't look like nothing to me," he said.

What was she supposed to say? An easy lie, one about being worried about Roslyn and Danica? It wouldn't even be a lie, not really—of course she was worried. But their predicament wasn't what occupied her thoughts right now, and Alex seemed to sense that.

"It's just—you're distracting," she finally blurted out, then wished she had rammed her fist into her mouth to shut herself up before she could say something so baldly honest.

Those eyebrows lifted even further. "Distracting? I think I kind of like the sound of that."

Oh, hell. She set down her glass of water, mainly because doing so gave her an excuse to break eye contact in a way that appeared more or less natural. When she straightened up, however, he was still watching her, didn't appear to have moved. "It's just that I feel like I should be focusing on Roslyn and Danica, and I'm trying, but every time I look up, you're there, and it's like you've managed to get in my head or something, and I don't know—"

She'd meant to say, *I don't know what I'm supposed to do about it,* but she didn't get that far, because Alex had reached out to her, had laced his fingers through hers and then pulled her toward him, his lips pressing against hers before she had a chance to even process what was happening. And, oh, Goddess, his mouth felt so good, strong and full, and he tasted even better. She opened her own mouth to him, let him deepen the kiss, found herself pressing against him, her breasts crushed against the strong muscles of his chest.

He let go of her hands, instead wrapped his arms around her, holding her close, his mouth still exploring hers, and it was all heat and need and a wild racing sensation through her entire body, so strong, so unexpected, that she found it hard to breathe. It had never felt like this before when someone was kissing her—not that she had a huge amount of experience. Even so, she was fairly certain she could have kissed a hundred guys, and none of those kisses would have come anywhere close to what she was experiencing now.

Gasping, she finally recovered herself enough to pull away, to lift her mouth from his, although doing so felt harder than anything else she'd ever done. But she knew she had to stop kissing him, or she'd never be able to get her spinning thoughts in order.

Alex didn't try to stop her; something in his expression seemed to show that he understood she needed her space right now. She set her hands down flat on the sofa cushion, felt the soft leather against her skin, the floor beneath her feet. Okay. That was a little better. At least now the world didn't feel as if it was spinning out of control all around her.

"What the hell are we doing?" she whispered at last.

He took her hand and held it in his. Maybe she should have tried to pull away, but she really didn't want to. His fingers were so strong, so warm. They felt real, something she could cling to in a world that had become strange and frightening.

"I don't know," he said at last, his voice also quiet, yet filled with its own urgency. "I've been trying to fight it, but when I looked over at you right then—I don't know…it just seemed like I couldn't control it anymore. Did you—did you not want me to?"

She'd wanted him to kiss her, more than anything. And that was the real problem. If she'd met him under different circumstances, then she wouldn't have minded one bit. Yes, there could be some difficulties in getting romantically involved with someone from another clan, but the McAllisters and the de la Paz family had always been more or less friendly. However, she hadn't stayed down here to Tucson so she could hook up with Alex Trujillo. She was here because, flawed and useless as she felt right now, she was her friends' best chance of rescue.

"No," she said, and his brows pulled together. Oh, crap. That wasn't what she'd meant. "That is, it's not that I didn't want you to kiss me. It's just that… we shouldn't be doing this at all. Not right now. Not with everything that's going on."

His face cleared a bit. "I get it. I feel the same way. But this pull…this attraction…whatever it is… it feels stronger. So I don't know what to say about that."

Caitlin didn't, either. After all, it wasn't as if she was a *prima* seeking her consort. That sort of connection was understandable…necessary, even.

But she wasn't the *prima* of her clan, and Alex sure as hell wasn't the *primus* of his, so she couldn't say their attraction was anything quite so cosmic, or at least foreordained. But it also went way beyond anything she'd experienced with anyone else. She'd had a couple of boyfriends, nothing serious, mainly because hiding her talents from her family was difficult enough without having to conceal those same gifts from the person she was romantically involved with. It could be that was part of this strange attraction to Alex—yes, he was good-looking and fun to be with, and kind and...all right, a whole bunch of positive adjectives—but he also knew the truth about her and didn't care, didn't even mind that she'd spent a good chunk of her life trying to avoid that truth.

"I don't know, either," she admitted. "And now, this" —she waved a hand in the direction of the kitchen, indicating the house in general— "is even more awkward. What are we supposed to do now?"

Without replying, he reached for the remote and turned off the TV altogether. After he'd set the remote back down on the coffee table, he took her hands in his again, his fingers twining around hers. Not tightly, though; he seemed to be telling her by the way he held her fingers that she could pull away anytime she wanted to, if she felt uncomfortable.

Strangely, though, she didn't. It felt right to have his hands wrapped around hers, strong and comforting.

"We don't have to do anything," Alex said reasonably. "I'm not going to lie and say I don't want you to sleep in my room tonight—just because I think it's safer, and not because I'm going to try anything." He paused then, almost as if he hoped she might say that she *did* want him to try something. She wasn't that crazy, though—not yet, anyway—and so he continued, "But I don't see a problem with you staying here in the guest room or wherever you want to be. It really is best that we stick together, you know?"

Yes, she did know. And as much as she wanted to stay with him in his room...in his bed...that was too much right now. She trusted him not to do anything, because he'd said he wouldn't.

She just didn't know if she trusted herself.

"Okay," she said at last. "But in the guest room. I don't...I don't want to go any further than we already have. I hope that's all right." Oh, Goddess, now she sounded like the world's biggest prude. She wasn't, or at least she didn't think she was, but kissing Alex was about all she wanted to commit to now. Soon she'd have to explain the truth behind her reticence, but for now it was probably best to let it go.

His fingers tightened around hers. "Of course it's all right. I hope you don't think that I'm trying to push you someplace you don't want to go."

"Oh, no," she replied at once. "But I'll be fine in the guest room. If I have another vision, well...."

"Then I'll come running, because you'll probably be screaming bloody murder again."

Despite everything, Caitlin grinned. *And it won't be so bad,* she thought. *Even if I do have another vision and start screaming my head off, I'll get a chance to see Alex walking around in his underwear again when he comes in to check on me....*

At least he'd convinced her to stay. That was something, although he could tell from the skittish, worried look in her eyes that it might not take too much more to scare her into running off to Jerome, even though she wouldn't be able to help her friends from there.

And he couldn't even blame her for returning to the guest room. He wanted her...his body was telling him exactly how much he wanted her...but he was willing to be patient. The way she'd felt in his arms, the way she'd tasted, the way the shape of her lips seemed to match his exactly...all those things told him she was the woman he'd been waiting for his entire life. But because he'd been waiting this long, he was fine with giving her some space, some room to think things over. Besides, she was right—their main goal right now should be finding Roslyn and Danica. He knew his feelings for Caitlin wouldn't change merely by putting off any further progression in their relationship for a few days. Or weeks, although he hoped for the missing girls' sakes it wouldn't take anywhere close to that long.

The king bed had always felt big to him, but tonight it felt even bigger, the expanse to his left where Caitlin had been lying the night before now empty, cold. He certainly didn't want her to suffer another horrifying vision, although some part of him thought that if she did, it might bring her back to him.

He began to stiffen at the thought, and he pushed away the vision of Caitlin lying next to him, her bright hair spread on the pillow, the curve of her breasts half-revealed by the covers. Of course, that thought only made his own situation that much worse, and he rolled over on his side, cursing his body. How long had it been, anyway? He and Lana had broken up what, almost ten months ago? Right after Diego's wedding.

And that had been the reason, because Lana had been his date at the wedding, and afterward she started pushing Alex to take the next step, to start planning for a real future together. She was a civilian, though, and hadn't known the truth about him. For some reason, he'd never found the courage to go into all of that with Lana...or maybe it wasn't that he'd lacked courage at all, but that he knew she wasn't the one, and so wouldn't risk revealing any of his clan's secrets to her.

Anyway, that was neither here nor there. It was just that, any way you cut it, it had been a *really* long time since he'd last been laid.

The house was quiet around him. No air-raid-siren screams from Caitlin, although she'd only gone to bed a half hour earlier. Plenty of time for the next vision of Matías' iniquities to invade her sleeping mind.

That thought made Alex think of what she actually had seen, of Danica apparently being coerced into having sex with Matías. No, that wasn't really correct, because she wasn't struggling, appeared to be a willing participant.

Only because of the way Matías is able to mind-fuck her, Alex thought, and he frowned, turning over onto his back, since trying to fall asleep on his side clearly wasn't going to work. And what was Matías' deal with that, anyway, except getting his rocks off in addition to however he was using Danica to fuel his dark magic?

But Caitlin had said she hadn't seen any cuts on the Wilcox witch's arms....

Alex wasn't sure what to make of that. Were they draining Roslyn first, and, once she was of no further use to them, would they move on to Danica? Possibly. He didn't have a clue how that kind of magic worked, not when you got down to the real nuts and bolts of it, and he didn't want to know. Any power that could be gained by participating in dark magic seemed to be canceled out by the damage it did to the magic-worker's soul. It just wasn't worth it.

Except...Matías apparently thought it was.

So what was his endgame? Surely he must know that provoking the de la Paz clan on its own territory—and involving the Wilcoxes and the McAllisters, too—wasn't going to end well. The problem was, too many pieces of the puzzle were still missing. Alex knew that he and Caitlin would never be able to figure it out if they didn't dig up some more of those pieces.

Exactly how, he didn't have a clue.

Bright morning sun peeking around the edges of the blinds told Caitlin that she'd managed to sleep the whole night through. More to the point, she hadn't had any visions. Not even any dreams she could remember.

What she did remember was the taste of Alex's lips, the feel of his arms around her. A thrill ran through her body, warming her, making her positively tingle with need for him.

Don't, she told herself. *You are not going there now. No way.*

She made herself get out of bed, then rummaged through her suitcase for some clean underwear and a fresh pair of jeans. A hot shower might help to clear her head. At the very least, it would get the day started, and she and Alex could decide what they wanted to do next. Something that didn't involve jumping into bed together.

Good luck with that.

After peeking down the hallway to make sure the coast was clear, she hurried into the bathroom and turned on the shower. The water came on hot almost immediately, so unlike the bathroom she'd had to share with Danica back at their cramped little apartment. The landlords swore up and down that every unit had its own water heater, but Caitlin had her doubts.

Anyway, it did feel good to shampoo her hair and get clean, not that she'd done much to exert herself the day before. When she emerged from the bathroom, she could smell the scent of coffee drifting down the hallway, and guessed that Alex was already up and dressed as well.

Sure enough, he was in the kitchen, pouring himself some coffee. "Iced tea?" he asked her.

"I'll get it," she said quickly. This was her second morning here, and she had no idea how long this stay might last. He certainly didn't need to keep waiting on her hand and foot.

He didn't argue, but cradled the mug of coffee in his hands while Caitlin fetched a glass, got some ice out of the freezer door, and then poured some tea from the jug into the glass. After she was done, she glanced out the kitchen window. It seemed to be another bright day, although the sky was speckled here and there with high, thin clouds.

"So," she said, not quite able to meet his eyes. Goddess, she hoped this awkwardness would go away soon. How could she and Alex get anything accomplished if they kept trying to dodge what had happened between them the night before? And that had only been a kiss. What would have happened if they'd ended up in bed together?

She decided she really didn't want to think about that now.

"So," Alex said, and then he shot her an inquiring glance. "I assume there were no visions last night?"

"Nothing," she replied, not bothering to keep her disgust at herself out of her voice. "Not even a bad dream. So I don't have anything new to offer."

He didn't appear all that disappointed. "Well, the day is young. Let's have some breakfast and worry about dreams and visions after our stomachs are full."

Since there didn't seem to be anything else to do, she went along with him on that plan, nuking another breakfast burrito, grabbing the last banana after Alex insisted she have it. They were sitting at the breakfast bar and finishing the last of their food when the doorbell rang.

"Are you expecting someone?" Caitlin asked, glancing at the clock on the microwave. Nine forty-five. A little early for visitors, but not horribly so.

"Not that I'm aware of," Alex replied. He hopped off his stool and headed for the front door, and Caitlin did the same, praying the visitor wasn't Marie Begonie, returned to give the wayward McAllister witch the chewing-out she should have gotten the day before.

But no, when Alex opened the door, Caitlin could see at once that the person outside wasn't Marie. She'd never seen this man before—he looked to be in his late thirties or maybe early forties, Hispanic, not quite as tall as Alex, and definitely not as in shape. His rounded stomach was obvious even under the baggy bowling-style shirt he wore.

"Miguel?" Alex said.

Miguel. The private investigator from Mesa that Alex had mentioned the day before. What the heck was he doing here?

"Morning, Alex." The man's dark eyes shifted from Alex to where Caitlin stood behind him. "Caitlin."

She started at his casual use of her name, and Miguel seemed to smile at her discomfiture.

"Luz sent me. Can I come in?"

"Sure," Alex said, then stepped aside. Caitlin did the same, moving over so Miguel could enter the house. He went past them and on into the family room, seeming so familiar that she couldn't help raising her eyebrows at Alex. Shrugging helplessly, he followed his cousin.

"What's up, Miguel?"

The older man dug a piece of paper and a wad of bills out of the baggy khakis he wore, then handed the piece of paper to Caitlin. She blinked down at it in confusion when she realized it was her birth certificate.

"Where the heck did you get this?"

"Luz figured you'd like to have your I.D. back, so she contacted your parents and had them fax over a copy. Now you can take that to the motor vehicle office and get a replacement license."

Caitlin turned the paper over in her hands. This didn't look like a fax. It looked like her actual birth certificate, right down to the fancy blue border and the watermark shaped like the state of Arizona.

Once again, he seemed to detect her astonishment. "All right, so Luz might have cast a minor illusion spell on it so it would look right. But it'll pass muster with the MVD. Just take care of it today, since the illusion won't last forever."

Since she wasn't sure what else to do, she nodded. At the same time, he gave her the folded-up wad of money, neatly rubber-banded together so it would be easy to carry.

"And that's five hundred dollars. Your parents wired that down as well."

She'd been worrying about having Alex pay for everything, but Caitlin hated the thought of her parents having to send her money. They helped out a little with her school costs, but she'd been paying for her own room and board, had supplemented her McAllister clan stipend by tutoring in English part-time and picking up some hours at one of the coffeehouses in downtown Flagstaff. All right, she'd been using money from all those sources and her other side project, the one nobody, not even Roslyn and Danica, knew about.

"Thanks," she said, realizing that she really should have called her parents yesterday sometime. Yes, her phone was gone, but she could've borrowed Alex's. Well, the money would help to replace her phone and a few other necessary items, and she'd try to be as sparing as possible with the rest.

Alex spoke up for the first time. "This is all great, Miguel, but why couldn't my mother have just brought these things over herself? Why did she have you come all the way from Mesa to do it?"

Miguel's expression sobered abruptly. "Well, actually, she's up in Scottsdale right now. Maya had a stroke last night."

"What?" Alex demanded, and Caitlin went very still, a shiver of cold running across her skin, even though it was warm enough in the house. "Why didn't she tell me?"

"Because she had about a hundred other things to take care of?" Miguel answered, his voice seemingly unruffled, although the way his brows pulled together told Caitlin he wasn't too thrilled with Alex's tone. "And I'm telling you now."

"How is she?"

"As well as can be expected. Valentina went up to assist Manuela, and the two of them got her stabilized, were able to stop the bleeding in her brain. She's very weak, though, and doesn't seem able to speak."

Alex let out a small, tortured sound, not even a groan, and Caitlin wished she could go to him, put her arms around him and give him a comforting hug. But since she wasn't sure how well that would go over with Miguel, instead she stayed where she was, that same icy fear seeming to move inward, snaking its way through every vein. Foreboding…but what was its source? Was it only her worry about what would happen if Maya took a turn for the worse?

Looking uncomfortable, Miguel went on, "They're watching her carefully. If they can't keep her stabilized, they're prepared to move her to a hospital. But we're all hoping that won't be necessary. Besides, since I was coming down here anyway to check out the neighborhood where the kidnapping took place, ask around a bit, I volunteered to bring these things over to Caitlin."

"Thank you," she said again. "I appreciate it. And I'm very sorry about Maya."

"She's tough. She's survived worse than this," Miguel remarked, somewhat cryptically.

No way was Caitlin going to ask about that comment. Not with Alex looking stricken, and somehow pale and pinched beneath the usual warm brown of his skin. He did seem to gather himself enough to say, "I'm glad you're following up on that, Miguel. So you'll call me if you find out anything?"

"Oh, I'll find out *something*," Miguel said. "Just a question of when. I'll be in touch." He looked over at Caitlin and added, "Very nice to meet you, Caitlin."

Then he went out. His footsteps seemed to echo on the travertine floors, and then a moment later, she heard the front door shut. She looked over at Alex, who hadn't moved.

"Are you okay?" she asked at last. "I'm really sorry—"

"It's all right," he cut in. His tone was more brusque than she'd ever heard it before, but she thought she understood why. "Miguel was right— Maya is tough. And in the meantime, we've got stuff we need to do."

All right, so he didn't want to talk about it. She knew it was probably best not to push things, so she nodded. "Okay. Let's go to the MVD and get me street-legal."

She wished he would smile.

But he didn't.

CHAPTER TWELVE

THINGS WENT FAIRLY QUICKLY AT THE MOTOR VEHICLE department, all things considered. The whole time they were waiting, Alex tried as hard as he could not to think about his grandmother, about what she must be going through right now. She'd always been so strong, so vital. These last months had been brutal enough, but with this stroke? What if it turned out she couldn't ever speak again? What if she were paralyzed? What would the clan do then? When a *prima* passed away, it was one thing. Time-honored mechanisms were in place to ensure a more or less uneventful transfer of power. But when the head of a clan was incapacitated…that made things far more complicated.

Funny how the more you told yourself not to think about something, the more your brain just kept grinding away at it.

Caitlin seemed to sense his inner turmoil, but, unlike a lot of girls he knew, she didn't try to make him talk. That was one thing about Lana that had finally driven him nuts; she'd never been able to leave things alone, always wanted to keep picking at him to find out what he was thinking. His own fault for dating a psych major, he supposed, but it was still annoying as hell. Caitlin, however, couldn't have been more different. She sat next to him as she waited for her number to be called, but she was quiet, watching the people around them, letting out a soft sigh every once in a while when the toddler with the woman in the next row of chairs let out a particularly ear-piercing scream.

No, even the most efficient motor-vehicle office wasn't exactly a day at the playground.

Eventually, Caitlin's number was called, and she went off with her magically altered birth certificate and story about how her purse was stolen at a club, and that was why she needed a replacement license. At least she'd be issued a new one right away without having to wait weeks.

Alex watched her, saw the way she smiled and chatted with the tired-looking woman at the processing window, and despite everything, he found himself falling for her even harder. Caitlin was going through her own hell, and yet there she was, somehow managing to act as if nothing more horrible than a stolen purse had happened to her over the past few days.

And then she was coming toward him, flashing her new driver's license and smiling. It was a subdued smile, as if out of respect for the blow he'd just suffered, but he could practically feel the relief pulsing from her.

"Great photo," he said, and found a smile of his own tugging at his lips. Might as well find the enjoyment he could in the little things. And she did look great in her photo.

"You think?" she asked, and angled the license toward herself so she could scrutinize it more closely. "I guess it's not too bad. I was squinting like hell in my old one, so maybe Matías did me a favor by making me leave my purse behind in that house."

That might be going a little too far, but Alex didn't bother to contradict her. He could tell she was, like him, trying to make the best of the situation. Getting up from the uncomfortable plastic chair where he'd been sitting, he asked, "Well, now that you're legal again and have some cash, is there anything else you need? We might as well take care of it while we're out."

She seemed to consider for a few seconds, head tilted to one side. "Probably a new purse and wallet, at least. I tend to overpack, so I brought enough clothes for five days. I suppose I could get a few things, just in case."

"You can always do laundry at my house," he offered, and she sent him a grateful smile.

"I might have to take you up on that. But in the meantime, if you know someplace to take me shopping that won't break the bank, that would be great."

Actually, he'd already been thinking of taking her to Nordstrom Rack, partly because it was on the way home, and partly because she could get decent stuff there while making her money stretch a little further. He suggested the store, and she nodded.

"Sounds great." To his surprise, she got up on her tiptoes and gave him a quick kiss on the cheek. By then they were out in the parking lot, standing next to the Pathfinder while he dug his keys out of his pocket. A wave of warmth went over him, and in that moment, the world looked just a little bit better than it had a few moments earlier.

He'd wait to see how long that lasted.

Caitlin hurried as best she could at Nordstrom Rack, which was difficult because she'd never gone on one of her clan's shopping trips to Phoenix and therefore didn't have more than a fuzzy idea of what she was getting into. The local Walmart it most definitely was not.

But Alex had already spent almost an hour with her at the MVD, and so dawdling here while looking at the dizzying array of tops and jeans and sweaters and accessories was not really being fair to him, especially when he'd just gotten such awful news about his grandmother. True, people bounced back from strokes every day, and Maya had not one, but two healers looking after her. Even so, Caitlin had no intention of making things worse by going on a crazy shopping spree. Well, semi-crazy. Five hundred bucks sounded like a lot of money to her, but she knew it could go very quickly if she wasn't careful.

So, a cute pale blue wallet marked down to ten bucks, and a very cool bone-colored suede purse with silver studs for the unbelievable close-out price of only thirty dollars, and then a couple of extra pairs of underwear and a new bra, just in case. All right, so she chose pretty, flirty pieces in nude satin trimmed with pale pink ribbons, but they were also way marked down, so no one could accuse her of not being practical. And if she was thinking about Alex possibly seeing her in them, well, who could blame her? She hadn't forgotten about Roslyn and Danica, nor about Maya…but she also hadn't forgotten that kiss she'd shared with Alex the night before. Might as well be prepared.

Luckily, he'd gone off to the men's shoe department, mumbling something about taking a look around. Caitlin sort of doubted he really needed anything. More likely he was making sure he stayed far out of the way, just in case she did end up buying some "unmentionables." Which she had, so thank the Goddess for his discretion.

Eventually, he caught up with her just as the clerk was handing over her bag of goodies.

"Find everything you needed?" he asked, stepping ahead slightly so he could open the door for her.

"I did—thanks." When they got to the car, she'd get out the wallet and tuck her new license and what remained of the five hundred dollars into it. For now, they were both just shoved into the pocket of her jeans.

They stopped at the rear of the SUV so Alex could open it up and stow her bag inside. Just as she was handing it to him, a strange droning sound seemed to pound through her head. At the same time, the busy parking lot around them tilted, flickered, and then *shifted*, changing into another scene entirely. Caitlin retained just enough of herself to put out a hand and lay it on the Pathfinder's side, the metal the only thing anchoring her to the here and now.

Because she could feel the vehicle, but she couldn't see it. Instead, she was in another small, dim room. Daylight tried to peek around the cheap roller blind that blocked the window but wasn't doing a very good job of it. Caitlin could see her arms, but they weren't *her* arms—these arms had a faint tan, whereas she had the true redhead skin, the kind that burned and then peeled, and stayed ferociously pale. More than that, the arms she saw now wore bandages in various places, and in between those bandages were the long, angry red lines of scabbed-over cuts.

That wasn't the worst, though. She looked down and saw the dark blonde hair that fell over her chest, nearly obscuring her breasts—but not nearly enough. A pair of brown hands cupped those same breasts, and she could feel a man's body against her, holding her, his breath hot on her neck.

But even that wasn't the worst. That was raising her head and looking into the face of another man, not the one holding her, and realizing he was above her, and in her, thrusting inward as she wrapped her legs around him, moaning in ecstasy while the first man continued to fondle her breasts.

"Oh, Goddess, Roslyn, wake up!" The words came out of Caitlin's mouth before she realized she was even saying them, and the shopping bag fell from her fingers.

"Caitlin!" Alex's voice, very close, urgent. "What are you seeing?"

"No," she whispered, closing her eyes. "No, please, no."

Hands settled on her shoulders, shaking her, but gently. "Caitlin. You have to tell me what you're seeing."

Her breaths leaving her in short, panicked gusts, she somehow managed to open her eyes and stare up into Alex's worried face. "It's Roslyn."

"You saw her? Where is she?"

"I don't know." A blink, and the last vestiges of the vision had disappeared. A woman walking past gave the two of them a curious look, but then shook her head and kept on going.

Alex gathered up Caitlin's discarded shopping bag and stuffed it into the cargo compartment of the Pathfinder. "Let's get you in the car, okay?"

She nodded and allowed him to guide her over to the passenger-side door, which he opened so she could climb in. That was something she just barely managed to do, her limbs were trembling so violently. But at least she was in the seat and he was buckling the seatbelt for her, since she clearly couldn't manage to do it herself.

Without saying anything else, Alex got in on the driver's side and started up the SUV. He backed out, then said, "Can you talk about it?"

Could she? Caitlin didn't know for sure. All she knew was that, while the vision with Matías had been bad enough, this was far, far worse. She hadn't been able to see the face of the man holding Roslyn, but it had to be Jorge, since the one—her brain stumbled on the concept, then kept going—the one *fucking* her had clearly been Tomas. Roslyn, with two guys? She was admittedly a flirt, and sort of flitted from boyfriend to boyfriend without much sign of slowing down, but a threesome? That was not her style. Especially with two men like Jorge and Tomas.

"It was bad." Alex's words were a statement, not a question.

"Yes." She let the syllable hang there in the air for a minute, not sure how she should follow it up. Was she even capable of describing that scene to Alex? She'd have to at some point, but not here. She couldn't imagine having that conversation while riding around in a Nissan Pathfinder. "Can we—can we talk about it after we get to your place?"

"Sure," he replied, and went silent after that, guiding them back to his house. If it seemed like he was going a little too fast, cutting it a little too close on a couple of yellow lights, well, she couldn't really blame him for that.

About ten minutes later, they were pulling into the garage. By then, Caitlin's shakes had subsided enough that she was able to get out of the car herself. Still quiet, Alex went around to the back and retrieved her shopping bag, then went to unlock the door and let them into the house.

"Why don't you go sit down, and I'll get you some water?" he asked.

She sort of doubted water would fix any of this, but she realized they had to start somewhere. Besides, maybe it would help to settle her stomach, which was churning so badly she was afraid she might throw up. "O-okay."

So she went into the family room and took a seat on the couch, trying not to think about how Alex had kissed her right here in almost this very spot. Actually, she was trying very hard not to think about much of anything at all. She'd have to tell Alex what she'd just seen, but in the meantime, she was going to do what she could to keep her mind blank.

A minute later, he came into the room, a glass of water in either hand. He set one down in front of her on the coffee table, then settled himself next to her. Because he'd brought her the water, she knew she should drink some of it. The glass felt far heaver than it should as she lifted it to her lips, but at least her hand wasn't shaking anymore.

Alex sat waiting, dark eyes full of questions. He didn't speak, though, seemed willing to remain quiet until she could find the words to express what she'd seen. The problem was, she didn't know if there *were* words. That is, if three people wanted to get together, fine. She had the vague impression that one of the artists in Jerome had that sort of arrangement with his girlfriend and his best friend, although no one really talked about it. But all three of them had gone into that pact willingly and with their eyes open. You couldn't say the same thing about Roslyn.

"Is she—" Alex finally ventured.

"No." Caitlin set down her water and shifted on the couch so she was facing him. As hard as this was, it would've been even more difficult if she'd been with someone less sympathetic, instead of someone she knew would give her a comforting hug as soon as she showed that she needed it. "She's—she's alive. But…they've been hurting her."

He didn't say anything, only waited, full lips slightly compressed as he processed what she was telling him.

"Cutting her, I mean. Whatever magic they're using, whatever spells they're casting, it's obvious they're still doing it. She had bandages all over her arms, and in between, scabs where the cuts have started to heal—" Caitlin broke off as the horror of it came back to her all over again. "How could someone do that to another person?"

"She's not a person to them. She's a means to an end," Alex said. Then he drew in a breath. "Shit, that sounded terrible. But you know what I mean. If they're firmly set on this path, then a few cuts and some spilled blood aren't much to them. And also… although I don't know much about the mechanics of the whole thing, from what I've heard, it sounded like you don't need huge amounts of blood for those rituals. They might be able to keep at it for some time." Pausing, he seemed to study Caitlin's face. "There's more, though, isn't there?"

"Yes." Oh, Goddess, would she really have to tell him everything she'd seen? Even as she asked herself that question, she knew the answer. He had to have all the facts so he could pass them on to people who were more knowledgeable about these sorts of things. Trying to cover it up wouldn't do anyone any good, least of all Roslyn and Danica. Once again, Caitlin prayed that her friends would have no memory of what had happened to them, that once they were rescued, their time with Matías and Jorge and Tomas would only be a bad dream.

But that was the future. She had to focus on now.

"She was...with Jorge and Tomas. The way Danica was with Matías," she added, just in case Alex didn't make the connection. "One was holding her, and the other was—"

Looking shaken, he held up a hand. "I get it. Jesus." For a few seconds, he was silent as he attempted to absorb what she'd just told him. "I've never—I've never heard of anything like this. I mean, the blood rituals are one thing, but...."

The words trailed off, and the horror in his expression told her everything she needed to know about his opinion on the subject. There were a few guys she'd known who probably would have tried to laugh off the matter with a flippant remark about consenting adults, but there was certainly no consent in either Danica's or Roslyn's situation.

"We have to get them out of there," Caitlin said, anger at her herself, at her limited abilities, rising up again. What was the point in seeing these terrible things if they couldn't give her any concrete details, any information she could actually use?

"I know that, but since we don't know where they are—"

"Then we have to go to someone who might." An idea began to form in her mind, one so audacious, so completely out of left field, that she knew Alex would be sure to protest. "These guys are obviously good at covering their tracks, but if they really did come from Simón Santiago's territory, then the logical thing is to go directly to him and make him tell us where his warlocks are holed up."

"You're not serious." But the way Alex was looking at her told Caitlin that he did realize she was serious, even if he didn't want to admit it to himself.

"I'm totally serious."

"But—even if we did do such a crazy thing, how do you know he'd have any information? I sort of doubt Matías and his buddies filed a flight plan with their *prima*'s consort."

Well, that was possible, but even if he didn't have the exact information, Simón might be able to give them a better idea of where to look. People they knew in the Tucson area...something. Anything. Surely their clan leader would have access to knowledge she and Alex wouldn't even know to look for. It had to be better than stumbling around in the dark while her friends were tortured.

"Isn't it worth a try?" she asked at last. "Do you have any better ideas?"

His troubled silence told her that he didn't. Since he didn't seem to be offering any protests, she went on,

"Do you know where he lives?'

"In Pasadena, I think. I'd have to get the address from my mother." Then he gave Caitlin a penetrating look, those dark eyes suddenly far too piercing. "And what am I supposed to say to her? She's got her hands full with Maya, and now I have to tell her that we're going to be running off to California to interrogate Simón Santiago, and could I please have his address?"

Put that way, her suggestion did sound pretty terrible. But there was that feeling in her gut again, the one telling her this was the right thing to be doing. On the surface, it seemed like a crazy plan. That didn't mean it wouldn't work.

"And that's exactly *why* we should be doing this. I suppose technically she should be the one to contact Simón, since your grandmother isn't well and she's the *prima*-in-waiting. But she doesn't have the time or the energy…and I think it would be best if Simón didn't know we were coming. Just a feeling. He'd wonder why Maya wasn't contacting him, and start asking questions…."

Alex still looked pretty grim, but at last he nodded. "All right. Obviously, these 'feelings' of yours are a little more than just that. I'll let my mother know."

"Thanks, Alex."

To Caitlin's surprise, he leaned forward and kissed her on the cheek. Gently, but even so, that delicious warmth curled low in her belly again.

She'd definitely been right when she said he was distracting. Too, too distracting.

Just as Alex had expected, his mother's reaction was not exactly encouraging

"You want to do what?"

"Go and talk to Simón Santiago. If these are his warlocks—and I think they must be, because they're sure not any of ours—then he should know something that would help us find them. We need to, *mamita*," he added, trying not to sound too desperate. "What they're doing to those girls…it's bad.

Very bad." *And please, God, let her not ask me for any details....*

Whether she'd picked up on his urgent desire to avoid discussing exactly what Matías & Co. were doing to Danica and Roslyn, or whether she was preoccupied enough with her own troubles that she didn't have the energy to go into any more details, Alex didn't know for certain. But his mother sighed, then said, sounding very tired, "All right. I'll get his address from your grandmother's book and email it to you."

"Thanks so much, Mom."

Her tone sharpened as she replied, "You be respectful, Alex. Simón has perhaps let things get out of hand the past few years, but he is still the consort of the Santiagos' *prima*. What has happened to Caitlin's friends is terrible, yes. However, their current situation is none of his doing. Keep that in mind."

Alex wasn't sure he entirely agreed with that. All right, it wasn't as if Simón had told the rogue warlocks to come to de la Paz territory and wreak as much havoc as possible. Even so, if Simón had been more vigilant, he might have seen the cancer growing within his own clan and taken steps to counteract it. If he even could, that is. He'd been more or less running things for years, ever since his wife became an invalid, but Alex was a bit fuzzy on how that

exactly worked. Simón wasn't a *primus*, but a consort, and so didn't have access to his wife's powers.
Not precisely, anyway.

"I will," he said. "You don't have to worry about
us. We'll be extremely diplomatic."

"Oh, I worry," his mother told him. "I worry a
lot. But I can't leave Maya's side, and if there's even
the slightest chance that Simón might have information that could be helpful, then it's best you should
go. I have to hope that he'll see you, the grandson
of our *prima*, going to him in person as a sign of
respect. This is not the sort of thing that can be handled by a phone call."

That angle hadn't occurred to him. But his
mother knew far more about inter-clan politics than
he did. She had to, as the *prima*-in-waiting.

He just worried that she might not be waiting for
much longer.

But he didn't give voice to his worries. Instead,
he thanked her again, said that he and Caitlin
planned to head out very soon, and hung up before
his mother could throw any roadblocks their way.
Maybe it was crazy to be leaving for such a drive
with the day half over, but Caitlin kept insisting there
wasn't a moment to lose. They'd get into Pasadena
at almost ten o'clock, far too late to go see Simón.
No, that visit would have to take place in the morning. If it was fruitful, though, they could get back on

the road immediately afterward and be in Tucson by dinnertime.

That was assuming everything went according to plan. A pretty big assumption, he knew, but they had to start somewhere.

His phone chirped, indicating he had a new email. He opened up the message and saw that it was from his mother. Simón's address. Perfect.

Caitlin had been waiting in the family room, pretending to watch TV. As soon as he entered, however, she turned off the television and looked up at him expectantly.

"I've got it," he said. "I'll program the route into Siri, but it would probably be easier if I went hotel-hunting on my laptop. Come on."

She followed him into his office, where his MacBook sat on the desk. He opened it up, went to a booking website, then found a few prospects not too far from where Simón's house was located. Since Alex had never been to California, all the streets and districts were unfamiliar to him. As far as he could tell, though, it was only a mile or so from Pasadena's downtown section to the Santiago house.

The hotel room—he flicked a glance over his shoulder at Caitlin, who stood a few feet away. "Two rooms?" he asked. Just because they'd kissed once, it didn't seem as if he should presume as to their sleeping arrangements.

She shook her head. "No, that's just wasting money. Um…a room with two beds?"

Well, it would have been nice to hope for more, but he'd take that. Anyway, this was a quick fact-finding trip, not a romantic getaway. "Sounds good." He selected the room, entered his information, and pushed the button to finalize the transaction. "We're probably lucky we were able to find someplace at such late notice." A glance at his watch told him it was almost three o'clock. Since the room was guaranteed on his credit card, a late check-in wouldn't be a problem, but they still needed to get going. "How soon can you be packed?"

"I'm already packed," she replied, and seemed amused by his surprise at her answer. "I mean, I've been living out of suitcases anyway. I just went and got a few things together, and then closed everything up while you were on the phone with your mother. Took me just a couple of minutes."

Maybe he should have said something about presuming too much, but really, her efficiency was only a benefit here. "Well, I don't know if I'll be that fast, but I'll do what I can. Why don't you go back out to the family room while I get my own stuff packed?"

"Sure." Her entire aspect seemed brighter now, less weighed down by those troubling visions. Alex guessed it was simply knowing that they were taking the next step in finding her friends, rather than sitting around and waiting for another vision to come to her.

It did feel good to be doing something. Whether it would end up being constructive, well…they'd just have to see what happened. A lot of things could be waiting for them in California, and he had to hope they could handle whatever they might encounter out there.

CHAPTER THIRTEEN

THEY DROVE WEST INTO THE BRIGHT AFTERNOON SUN. Caitlin squinted and wished she'd thought to pick up a pair of sunglasses at Nordstrom Rack. She had her new purse with her new wallet and I.D. tucked into it, and she supposed if it got really bad, they could pull off at a gas station where she could buy some cheap glasses.

In the meantime, though, it just felt good to be on the road, to watch the desert landscape flash past as they left Tucson and headed toward Phoenix. She'd known in her heart that this was the right thing to be doing, and yet she'd still had the thought in the back of her mind that Luz would try to dissuade them, tell them that going to California was a terrible idea. According to Alex, though, she had caved pretty quickly.

They hit the Phoenix sprawl just as rush hour was starting, but for the first part of it, the traffic wasn't too bad. It wasn't until they got to the other side of downtown and were caught with everyone else trying to get to the western suburbs, to Goodyear and Glendale and Avondale, that Alex had to slow to a crawl.

It was excruciating, to say the least, but Caitlin knew there was no point in complaining about the time they were wasting. They couldn't change the traffic patterns—although she thought that would be a handy talent for an urban witch to have—and eventually they did come out on the other side, leaving the suburbs and their planned communities behind them as they headed into the open desert.

The sun blared right into her face and she raised a hand to block it, as it was now low enough that the visor wasn't doing much good to protect her. Alex glanced over and asked, "You managing okay?"

"It's a little bright. But I'll live."

"There's a spare pair of sunglasses in the glove compartment. One of the arms is a little loose, but it's better than going blind."

She opened the glovebox, and, sure enough, there was a pair of somewhat wobbly Ray-Bans in there. "Thanks," she said gratefully as she settled them on her nose. They were heavier than the cheap drugstore sunglasses she usually wore, but they'd do.

Alex nodded. "I probably should've thought of them sooner. Sorry about that."

"It's okay." He had enough on his mind; he shouldn't have to worry about babysitting her. And really, she had been all right until the sun dropped just low enough to be a problem.

Seemingly abandoning that topic, he said, "We should be getting into Blythe right around dinner-time. You want to stop there and get something to eat?"

Part of her didn't, just because she wanted to get to Pasadena as soon as they could. But that was silly, because they wouldn't be able to see Simón Santiago until the following morning anyway. They'd grabbed some tacos at a hole-in-the-wall place not too far from the motor vehicle office, but that had been hours ago. By the time seven o'clock rolled around, she knew she'd be starving. "Sounds good. Any ideas?"

"Not really. I've never been this far past Phoenix before. Uncharted territory." He glanced over at her, the warm western sun flashing off his teeth as he grinned.

Even though impatience was still dancing through her, to the point that she'd had her feet press-ing against the footwell, as if that would make the SUV move faster, she couldn't help smiling in return. "Well, I guess we'll have to take our chances."

Another grin. "Or hope that I get a good enough signal in Blythe that I can find something promising on Yelp."

"That works, too. My powers of divination aren't really designed for picking out restaurants."

He nodded, still smiling. That smile slowly disappeared, though, as he stared out at the road ahead. "Do you feel like we're missing something here?"

Caitlin didn't bother to ask what he meant by that. "I feel like we're missing out on a whole lot of somethings. Do you want to be more specific?"

"Matías. What's his endgame? What's he using all this dark magic for?"

"Besides getting laid?" A grimace pulled at her mouth. The words had slipped out before she could stop them.

His tone grew gentle, as if he knew just how much that part of her friends' current situation upset her. "Yes, besides that."

"I don't know." She stared out the side window so she wouldn't have to look directly into the sun. The golden-brown landscape rippled past, broken by manzanita bushes and cactus and the odd ocotillo, its strange undersea-looking branches tipped by bright orange flowers. "That is, I don't know if these are the same guys who had a run-in with Connor and Angela a few years ago, because obviously they didn't exchange names. If they are, it might just be a grudge thing—I mean, they kidnapped witches from both clans, so that has to send some kind of message. But….." The words trailed off, because she knew deep down that this wasn't anything as simple as a grudge, that Matías' actions spoke of a far deeper motivation than merely trying to get back at the *prima* and *primus* of the McAllister and Wilcox clans.

The thought tickled at the back of her mind. Was Matías somehow behind Maya's mysterious wasting illness? But she'd been sick for months, according to Alex. Then again, they really didn't know how long the warlock had been lurking in de la Paz territory. Caitlin waited to see if she'd experience that strange inner nudge, the one that told her that her suspicions might be right, but she felt nothing. Probably better to tuck the idea away for now. They were already doing everything they could to find Matías, and adding to Alex's worry wouldn't help anything. Besides, those inner twinges weren't infallible; so far she hadn't experienced anything she could call a false positive, but they also didn't chime in on every single notion or idea she might have.

He spoke then. "But you don't really think it's just a grudge."

"No." She turned back toward Alex. By then the sun had begun to slip down behind a range of jagged mountains to the west, so the light wasn't quite so painful. "I can't say why for sure."

"Another feeling." It wasn't a question.

"Yes. So far those feelings have been mostly right, so I'm willing to go with following this one for now. I just wish that one of these stupid visions would show the front of the house or apartment or wherever it is they're holed up. Something where I could see a street number or an address. That would be a hell of a lot more useful than seeing them—" She broke off then. No point in going over it again. Alex knew what she was talking about.

He gave her a grim nod. "That's the tough thing, I guess. Some powers are easier to control than others. Mine's pretty concrete—I mean, all I have to do is imagine that shield coming up around me, and it just appears. But when you're a seer...when you're tapping into time and space and all that...it's a lot less cut and dried. So I don't think you can give yourself too much grief over not being able to pinpoint it the way you'd like. At least we know more than we would have if you didn't have that power at all."

True, Caitlin thought. *And maybe I could have lived a long time without knowing some of it.* She didn't say that to Alex, though. Instead, she pulled in a breath and looked ahead, at the unending ribbon of black pavement that lay ahead of them, and hoped they wouldn't reach their destination and discover this had all been a colossal waste of time.

The signal on his phone kicked back in as they entered the town limits of Blythe, so Alex handed it over to Caitlin. "Can you find us someplace to eat?"

"You like barbecue?" she asked.

"Sure."

"Then how about this place?" She angled the screen toward him so he could see some images from the restaurant she'd selected. The pictures various Yelpers had added to the site showed barbecued ribs and brisket sandwiches and an assortment of other dishes, all of which looked pretty damn good to him, considering he'd only had a couple of meager street tacos to keep him going for a good chunk of the day.

"Sounds good. Can you get the navigation started?"

She pushed the screen to start them on their route. Her fingers just barely brushed against his as she gave him back the phone. Even that light touch made his heart start to pound, but he did his best to ignore the way she'd gotten his body to react. No, that wasn't even fair. He was getting himself all hot and bothered. Caitlin probably had no idea that even her lightest touch was enough to make his blood seem to boil.

The restaurant was just off the freeway, and he pulled into the last remaining parking space before shoving the phone into his jeans pocket. Thank God the bulge had subsided. "Did you bring a jacket?" he asked, looking at the thin knit top Caitlin was wearing. It might have been fine for a bright, sunny day in Tucson, but now that the sun was down, it would be much cooler here.

"Yes," she said, then pulled on the handle to open the door. "It's in my suitcase, though, so you'll need to pop the back so I can get to it."

"No problem."

They both headed to where their luggage was stowed, and he watched as she opened up the larger of her two suitcases and got out the jacket. After shrugging into it, she said, "What about you?"

The air was cool, but he thought he could manage. "I'm fine. Let's go eat."

She raised her shoulders, as if to say, *your funeral,* and then followed him into the restaurant. Well, diner. It was the sort of place where you ordered at the counter and then had someone bring you your food. Not fancy, but it definitely smelled good in there.

From the way Caitlin took an appreciative sniff, it seemed she felt the same way. And although she had to be even more apprehensive about what they were going to find in California than he was, it didn't seem to have affected her appetite. She ordered a pulled pork sandwich with a side of mac and cheese, while he opted for sliced tri-tip with steak fries.

"Obviously you're not one of those girls who only eats salads in front of guys," he joked as they sat down.

She rolled her eyes. "Nope. I like to eat."

Alex couldn't help wondering where she put it, since she was fairly slender, except for her chest. *Built like a swimsuit model,* he thought, wondering what she'd look like in a bikini. He had a feeling he wouldn't find out anytime soon, even if they were headed to California. No beach trips in their future, that was for sure. But if this had a happy ending, maybe he could convince her to stay a few days more at his place, swim in his pool, before she went home. Or would that even work? She was on break from school right now, but he didn't know for sure when she had to go back.

His phone rang then. Frowning, he pulled it out of his pocket, then looked at the number on the display. He didn't recognize it, although the number did have a Phoenix area code. "I'd better get this," he said apologetically, and Caitlin nodded.

"It's fine."

He accepted the call before putting the phone to his ear. "Hello?"

"Alex, it's Miguel."

"Oh, hey, Miguel," Alex replied. Across the table from him, Caitlin lifted an inquiring eyebrow, and he shrugged. "What's up?"

"I have a little more information. I don't know how much of it's going to help, but I figured I'd pass it along."

"Anything would be great. We haven't been able to get much more on these guys."

Caitlin seemed to tense, and she leaned forward slightly, as if she expected by doing so that she'd be able to overhear what Miguel was saying. Alex wasn't sure it really worked that way, but maybe she'd be able to pick up a little bit.

His cousin said, "Well, I went back to the neighborhood where the McAllister girl says her friends were taken. I did some asking around, and it turns out that someone down the next street did actually see them as they were leaving. Thought the girls must be high or something because of the way they were wobbling around."

Not high…just under some really nasty mind control. But it was better that the neighbors thought Danica and Roslyn were on drugs. A couple of loaded college girls was a lot easier to explain away than dark spells and darker talents.

"Did the person who saw them notice where they went?"

"They got in a black late-model car. Sporty. One of those updated muscle cars. Wasn't sure if it was a Mustang or a Camaro or what. But flashy enough that they noticed. The neighbor, a Mrs. Herrera, said she thought they were drug dealers because of the car and the tattoos and the way the girls were acting. Anyway, because she lives around the corner from the house the guys were using, she really didn't see where they were headed. Back out to the main road, obviously, but after that, who knows?"

Who knows? That was for sure. Alex wondered if the car was really theirs or if they'd stolen it. They wouldn't even have to do something violent like a carjacking. No, Matías' talent would lend itself pretty well to walking up to someone in a parking lot and asking for their keys. Maybe eventually the vehicle would be reported as stolen, but by then they could have ditched it or switched out the license plates or something.

"Any way to figure out if the car was stolen?"

A chuckle, and Miguel said, "Already ahead of you. I did search the stolen vehicles database. Cars like that are a tempting target, so they do tend to get ripped off. But Mrs. Herrera also said it had paper temporary plates, although the car was parked far enough away from her house that she couldn't see the actual numbers. That narrows it down, because it means the car was stolen somewhere in Arizona. They don't use paper licenses like that in California. Turns out the car is a Dodge Challenger and was taken from an auto detailer three days ago. Tucson P.D. is on it, but I have a feeling that the paper plates on this car were taken from someone else's, and they probably haven't even noticed. I mean, most people don't memorize those temp things the way they do a real license plate."

No, they probably hadn't. Alex knew that when he'd bought the Pathfinder, he couldn't have read back the code on those temporary plates if his life had depended on it.

"So anyway, unless those boys get pulled over for some kind of traffic violation, I doubt the police are going to catch up with them. I let our guys know to pay extra attention when they see a vehicle like that, and word's gone out to the rest of the clan to keep an eye out. If they're holed up someplace and not venturing out much, they might still be hard to track down. But if they go out for beer—well, someone might notice."

"Thanks, Miguel," Alex said, and he meant it. That wasn't just "some" information; it was extremely valuable information. And it might just lead to someone finding those bastards.

"No problem. If I find anything else, I'll let you know, but that's all I've got for now."

"It's plenty. Thanks again."

Miguel hung up then, and Alex set down the phone. Caitlin gave him another one of those expectant looks. He loved how one of her brows was just slightly more arched than the other, giving her a sort of charmingly quizzical expression.

"So someone saw them in a car?"

"Yeah, a stolen Challenger." Speaking quickly, he filled her in on Miguel's side of the conversation.

"And when he says 'your guys' are going to be paying extra attention, he means the de la Pazes in Tucson?"

"Well, them and the people we actually have on the police force." Both her eyebrows went up at that reply, and he continued, "We have a couple of clan members with the Tucson P.D., and then more in the Phoenix area. It's kind of cheap insurance to make sure any witchy things we don't want noticed get swept under the rug. Don't you do that in Jerome?"

"Not really," she said. "I mean, Roslyn's older sister Jenny worked in dispatch for the Cottonwood police department for a while, but she decided she really didn't like it that much, so she quit. I think the Wilcoxes might have some of their family in law enforcement, though. I can't remember for sure."

Alex figured if the de la Paz family was canny enough to make sure a few of its members were carefully placed in the local police and sheriff's departments, then you could bet the Wilcoxes would have done the same thing. Simple insurance. He wasn't sure why the McAllisters hadn't done something similar, but maybe they figured they were isolated enough in their little hillside town that such measures weren't necessary.

Lifting his shoulders, he said, "Well, it just means we have some eyeballs in places that count. I don't know if that's going to be enough, though. It depends on how often they might crawl out from wherever it is they're staying."

Caitlin didn't appear to like that notion very much. She seemed to slump in her chair, and some of the hopeful light went out of her eyes. Alex was about to reach out to her, maybe to lay a comforting hand on her arm, but the waitress showed up right then with their food, so that was the end of that idea.

They ate quietly after that, Caitlin apparently preoccupied with her own thoughts, while Alex worked at the problem in his own mind, attempting to see if there was some angle he hadn't thought of, something else the clan members back in Tucson could do to track down where that stolen Challenger had been taken. Other than blanketing every street lamp and stop sign with "stolen car" signs, or maybe taking out a bunch of Craigslist ads, he couldn't think of anything. And even that wouldn't really work. All it would probably do was alert Matías and his boys that the de la Pazes were closing in on them.

As he and Caitlin were winding down to eating the last of their sandwiches, she finished chewing and asked, "How far is it from here to Pasadena?"

He paused to think about the route, then replied, "Couple hundred miles, I think. So...around three hours left to go."

A nod, and she ate the rest of her pulled pork before lifting her napkin to her mouth and dabbing at it, then wiping off her hands. Actually, for as messy as that sandwich looked, she'd done a pretty good job of not getting it all over herself.

He finished his sandwich as well. Since they'd paid for the food when they ordered, all he had to do was dig in his wallet and get out a five for the tip. After he laid it on the table, he asked, "Ready?"

For a second, Caitlin hesitated. Then she said, "Yes, I'm ready."

Unfortunately, she didn't sound very sure of herself.

CHAPTER FOURTEEN

Spending this much time with Alex—being in the car with him for hour after hour—was turning out to be more difficult than Caitlin had expected. She seemed to be acutely conscious of everything he did, even if it was something as mundane as asking her if she wanted him to turn on the heater as the night deepened and the drive across the desert became increasingly chilly. The sound of his voice, the way his strong fingers wrapped around the steering wheel...everything. She even fancied she could detect the faintest hint of whatever aftershave he used, something very light, sort of citrusy. Clean-smelling.

Are you trying to drive yourself crazy? she thought with some irritation, shifting in her seat for what felt like the hundredth time. It wasn't the Pathfinder's fault; the car seats were extremely comfortable. No, it was only her, reacting to Alex in a way she knew was just wrong. *Wrong*. Bad enough that they'd kissed, when they should have been focusing all their energies on locating Danica and Roslyn and bringing them home. But that kiss seemed to have kindled a fire in Caitlin, and she had no idea how to put it out.

He'd been quiet, although whether that was because he was trying to focus on the unfamiliar roads, or because he'd sensed that she really didn't want to talk, she didn't know for sure. And was it actually that she didn't want to talk, or was just worried she'd say exactly the wrong thing?

At least it wasn't dead quiet in the SUV; as they were leaving Blythe, he asked if she minded if he turned on the radio. She'd said that was fine, and since he chose a station that played the rock and alternative music she liked, it helped to fill the silence without being too intrusive. The problem was that even the music couldn't distract her from the man sitting just a foot or so away from her.

And what was she supposed to do when they got to Pasadena? She'd already agreed to share a hotel room, so there was no backing out of that arrangement.

You shouldn't have asked for separate beds, she told herself, and that thought had to be the craziest thing that had crossed her mind yet. She'd barely known the guy for two days. And now she was okay with sleeping with him? That was just...no. Never mind that she'd never slept with anyone. Her big dark secret. She'd come close a few times, but always something in her held back, told her it wasn't the right time. Her boyfriends hadn't been too thrilled with her, that was for sure. In fact, the guy she'd been dating at Northern Pines—a civilian—called her a "cock tease" right before he dumped her. But she hadn't been teasing him. She'd *thought* she wanted to, had told herself that the whole situation was ridiculous and that it was time to lose that unwanted virginity. She wasn't some *prima* holding out for her consort, after all. At twenty-one, she thought she was way overdue.

And yet...she still couldn't make herself take that final step. Until now. Well, she hadn't taken any steps, beyond that one kiss she and Alex had shared, and yet she wanted to. The intensity of that desire shook her. She'd never experienced anything like it before. For some people, it might have been enough to throw aside any remaining reticence they might have possessed. But could she do it? Could she take that final step?

She was afraid of the answer, but in her heart, she knew exactly what it was. Never mind that it was truly insane to be considering such a thing when her friends were being held captive by an insane warlock, when she'd only met Alex the day before yesterday.

What did she know about him, really? A few things about his family, about where he worked and how a few of his dreams had been thwarted. She knew he was attracted to her. But how deep did that attraction go? As deeply as hers did?

They'd passed through the outskirts of Palm Springs, and Caitlin had barely noticed, she was so preoccupied. It wasn't until they crested a hill some miles past the desert town, and the bright, glittering lights of the inland suburbs were laid out before them, that she realized how much ground they'd covered. Surely it couldn't be that much farther to Pasadena.

But it was, as mile after mile passed by in the dark, the freeways around them widening and yet at the same time growing more and more congested, even though it was far past what she would have thought of as rush hour.

She must have let out a sigh, because Alex said, "Not too much more. Maybe another half hour."

Half an hour until she was alone with him in a hotel room. So many thoughts and questions had been chasing themselves around in her head, she couldn't keep them straight anymore. She nodded, then blurted out the first thing that rose to the surface of her mind. "So what's with your house, anyway? Does being a store manager really pay that much?"

Even though he'd been keeping his eyes on the road pretty much the whole time, he swiveled his head toward her and gave her a startled glance. "Um...what?"

"I'm sorry," she said at once, mentally kicking herself. Yes, she'd been wondering about the house ever since the first time she set foot in it, but did she really need to have asked that question? "It just—I'm a dork. Never mind."

He actually grinned. "I don't think you're a dork." Something in the way he said the words sounded almost like a caress, and Caitlin found herself daring to hope that maybe she hadn't completely screwed up. "Actually, I suppose it's sort of an obvious question. My grandfather—my dad's dad—passed away a few years ago. He left each of us grandkids a chunk of money. So I bought the house...and this car." Even in the darkness, she could see the teasing glint in his eyes. "Are you after me for my money, Caitlin?"

"Very funny," she retorted, and he chuckled, albeit somewhat grimly.

"Wouldn't be the first time."

She wondered who those other girls had been, the ones who'd seen a guy in his mid-twenties with a solid job and a house that was already paid for, and thought he was a great prospect. Obviously, none of them had gotten their claws into him, but still. Alex was an amazing person. The house and everything else didn't even factor into it. Caitlin knew she'd feel the same way about him even if he was living in a crappy studio apartment and driving a ten-year-old pickup truck.

"Don't worry," she told him. "We McAllisters may not be as rich as the Wilcoxes, but we do okay. I get my own stipend every month—and I work two part-time jobs. I'm completely self-sustaining."

"Two?" he said. "And go to school full-time?"

"Well, I tutor, so that's not like going to a regular job, and the other one is only ten to fifteen hours a week. It's not like I'm doing a full-time gig or anything." She knew she should leave it at that, and forced herself to keep from mentioning her other source of income.

"Still." He seemed to think for a moment. "I put in a few hours a week at the store while I was in college, but that was it. My parents didn't want anything interfering with my education."

"You were doing a double major. It makes sense that you wouldn't have much time left over for a job."

"I suppose." Another one of those quick glances in her direction before he returned his focus to the busy freeway around them. "What are you majoring in, anyway?"

"English." Utterly boring, she knew.

"Really? What do you want to do—teach?"

"If I have to. But really" —she took in a breath, deciding she would tell him and see if he laughed— "really, I want to be a writer."

"Seriously?" Someone cut right in front of him, so he didn't have the luxury of looking over at her. In fact, she thought she heard him mutter a curse in Spanish under his breath before he went on, "What kind of writer?"

"Oh, you know." She sort of flapped at the air dismissively, then told herself if she'd been foolish enough to confess her dream to him, she might as well go all the way. "Novels. Fantasy novels."

He didn't laugh. "That's cool. Are you going to write about witches?"

"No," she replied, trying to sound severe but not being terribly successful about it. "I know they say write what you know, but...."

"But familiarity breeds contempt?"

She did chuckle a bit at that question. "'Contempt' is a strong word. And it's kind of hard to write fantasy without writing about magic, too. It's just a really different kind of magic."

"So have you written anything yet?"

And now she was about to divulge her biggest secret...well, except that whole thing about still being a virgin. "Yes. Three novels so far. I finished the third one in December while I was on winter break."

"That's impressive." He did sound impressed, and Caitlin relaxed slightly.

"I'm still editing it, but it should be ready to go next month sometime. And then I'll have that trilogy done and published, and I can move on to the next one."

"Wait," he said. "You mean you already have a publisher?"

Oh, boy. "Not exactly. These days, you can upload your work directly, you know? I'm in an online critique group to get feedback, and I trade tutoring with someone who's studying graphic design at my school, so she does my covers. I'm not selling a lot yet, but I make a couple hundred bucks every month."

"Wow." His admiration didn't seem at all feigned. "I had no idea."

Neither do my parents, she thought. The books were published under the pen name of C.J. Marsters, and her royalty payments directly deposited into her checking account, so no one knew—except Tracie, the graphic design student who was brilliant at typography and Photoshop manipulation, and not so great at writing term papers.

"I don't talk about it, really," she confessed. "Even Danica doesn't know, and we're roommates. She just thinks I have to write a lot for my classes, and since I'm an English major, it makes some sense."

He changed lanes, edging over the right, and she realized he was getting ready to exit the freeway. So they were almost at their destination.

It wasn't until they'd pulled off onto a feeder road that ran parallel to the highway and were waiting at a red light that he asked, "Are you ever going to tell them?"

"Eventually." She hesitated for a moment, watching houses that wouldn't have looked out of place in Jerome pass by outside the window. This part of Pasadena appeared to be fairly old. "It's just—if I say anything now, they'll think I'm taking time away from my coursework. And I'm not. I'm really careful about that. And also…I guess I'm hoping I'll start making some real money from it, once I have my trilogy done, and then they'll have to take me seriously."

"You really think they wouldn't?"

"Did your parents, when you said you wanted to go into local television instead of working at the store?"

"Ouch." He shook his head. "No, not really."

They turned left then, passing back over the freeway and into a much more commercial area. An impressive-looking building fronted the street they were currently driving on, and Alex turned again, this time onto a much smaller street so he could head into the hotel's underground parking garage.

When he took the ticket, he looked at the prices and winced. "Twenty bucks a night just to park? We really are in the big city."

"If it's a problem—" Caitlin began, and scrabbled in her purse for her wallet.

"It's not a problem. It's just highway robbery." He took the ticket from the machine, and the automated gate arm in front of them lifted.

At least there was a parking space not too far from the elevators, so Alex pulled in there and turned off the engine. It only took a minute or so to unload their luggage, and then it was time to check in.

By then it was past ten o'clock at night, and the lobby was almost deserted, except for the woman behind the front desk and a bored-looking bellhop standing duty by the sliding doors that opened on the street. He gave the two of them the side-eye as they passed, and Caitlin wondered if he was annoyed that they'd parked themselves in the garage instead of using the valet service out front.

No time to worry about that, though, because Alex had moved purposefully to the front desk and was giving his information to the woman there, along with his credit card. Caitlin waited off to one side, trying to look as if she checked into hotels with guys all the time. All right, not *all* the time, but at least she didn't want to give the impression that she was doing something illicit.

The transaction settled, Alex turned back toward her. "Looks like the elevators are down that hall. We're on the tenth floor."

She nodded, mostly because she didn't know what to say. All of the easy dialogue they'd shared during those last few minutes of the drive melted away as if it had never existed. For each floor the elevator ascended, she could feel her throat constricting and her stomach tightening just that much more. It didn't help that they were standing fairly close to one another in case someone else got on the elevator, close enough that she thought she could hear the beating of Alex's heart. Or was that hers, hammering away in her chest?

The room was large and clean, with a fairly spectacular view of the downtown Pasadena area. Caitlin went to look out the window and stared down at all the lights sparkling beneath them. How big was Pasadena, anyway? Bigger than Tucson? Smaller? She had no real sense of scale, because everything felt big to her, compared to where she'd come from.

"What do you think?" Alex said, coming up to stand next to her and look out at the night cityscape.

"It looks pretty from up here," she replied cautiously.

"True, but unless you want the whole world looking in, you might want to close the drapes." He reached up and grabbed a sort of plastic wand hanging from the heavy outer curtains and pulled them shut.

Right. She should have thought of that. But she'd never stayed in a hotel in her life—up until this past summer, when she transferred to Northern Pines and moved into the apartment with Danica, she'd never even ventured farther afield than Prescott. Her whole life had been spent in tiny Jerome and the small towns of the Verde Valley.

"So…when do you think we should visit Simón tomorrow?"

If Alex was surprised by her abrupt change of subject, he didn't show it. "Not until after ten. Maybe closer to eleven, just in case he isn't a morning person. That gives us plenty of time to sleep in."

Did he mean anything by that? Caitlin wasn't sure, and she definitely wasn't about to ask. "Okay," she replied. "I'll go ahead and start getting ready. You don't mind if I take over the bathroom for a bit?"

"No," he said, and then paused, gazing down at her. She tried not to flinch and look away, but it was hard. Those dark eyes seemed to be piercing right through her, seeing the crazy thoughts that had passed through her mind during the drive here. He continued, in a much different tone, "Thank you for telling me all that. About your writing, I mean. I think it's an amazing thing you're doing."

Her mouth went dry. How was she supposed to reply to that? Tell him she thought he was pretty amazing, too? Finally, she managed, "Thanks."

The word should have fallen flat, but he seemed to ignore how woefully inadequate it really was, and instead moved closer to her. Without truly under-standing how it had happened, she felt his hands holding hers, pulling her closer to him. And then he was bending down, those strong, full lips of his touching her mouth, kissing her, making her open to him so she could taste him once again.

Something in her seemed to break, and melt, and she was pressed against him, feeling his body on hers, one of his hands reaching up to run through her loose hair. The kiss deepened, and then he was picking her up and carrying her to the nearest bed, only a few feet away from where they'd be standing by the window. His weight was on her, and his hands moving up under her top, warm against her flesh.

A moan escaped her lips, and that seemed to be all the encouragement he needed. He pushed her shirt up even further, fumbled with the front hook of her bra. Then it was loose, and it wasn't just his hands on her, but his mouth as well, trailing feathery kisses up her stomach until at last he closed on her breast, suckling, and then she cried out even more, her fingers caught in his thick dark hair as she held him against her.

It wasn't the first time she'd gone this far, but it had never felt like this before. Warm, heavy pulses of desire flooded through her, heat growing between her legs.

"Oh, Goddess," she murmured.

He undid the button of her jeans, then pulled down the zipper. And then he was reaching down to stroke her, while she had to practically bite her lip from crying out at the sheer ecstasy of his touch, that strong finger caressing her right where she wanted it the most. The waves of heat grew stronger, and she felt it building in her, knew he was going to make her come right then and there.

Which she did, clinging to him as the orgasm flooded through her, blood surging through every limb and to her fingers and toes. Her head fell back against the pillow, and she gasped for air like someone who had nearly drowned. Maybe she was drowning. She knew she couldn't fight this anymore, couldn't tell herself it was crazy and that she had far more important things to worry about. Right then, Alex was the most important thing in her world. If that was wrong, well, she'd face the consequences later. But she also knew she had to tell him the truth.

"Alex," she said, once she felt as if she might be able to string two coherent words together.

He'd been lying next to her, holding her as the last of shudders had finished wracking their way through her body. Now he propped himself up on one elbow, dark eyes sharp and worried, as if he was expecting her to tell him that was all they could do, that they needed to stop this madness here and now. "What, Caitlin?"

"I—" Her tongue seemed to be stuck to the back of her throat. No wonder, really, with the way she'd been panting. She sucked in a breath and started over. "I just—I need to tell you something."

His mouth tightened. "What is it?"

Just get it over with! "I'm a virgin," she said simply.

He didn't quite pull away, but she could feel him go very still. "You're—seriously?"

"Is it that unbelievable?"

"For a girl as gorgeous as you? It's kind of unbelievable."

He called me gorgeous! a part of her mind burbled happily, but she forced herself to say, "It's not as if I really meant to wait this long. It just never felt right before."

He watched her, eyes half hidden by the sweep of his lashes, thick and dark as his hair. Then, finally, "Are you saying this feels right?"

"Yes. Doesn't—doesn't it feel right to you?"

His expression softened, and then he was pulling her close, kissing her cheek, her neck. Once again he caressed her, his mouth warm against the sensitive skin of her breast. She shivered, let him touch her, explore her, his fingers moving deeper. But then he paused, murmuring, "We don't have to go any further than this if you don't want to."

She shut her eyes, made herself pull in a deep breath. Then she blinked and gazed back up at him, at the sensual curve of his mouth, the dusting of late-day stubble against the warm tones of his skin. Every part of him seemed so perfect, so uniquely Alex, that she knew she could never have said this to anyone else.

"I want to. I do. Make love to me, Alex."

He let out a soft, soft moan, a deep, guttural sound that seemed to have come from deep within him. Without replying, he kissed his way down her stomach, moving lower and lower. When his tongue touched her, she had to grab hold of one of the pillows and grip it tightly to keep herself from screaming in pleasure. She'd heard how good that could feel, but she'd never let a guy do that to her before, make love to the most intimate part of her body, the touch of his mouth and tongue setting another series of those warm waves loose in her, streaming over her, until at last she let go of the pillow and knotted her fingers in his hair, convulsing against him as the orgasm struck her with the force of a tidal wave.

Then he raised himself on his hands, positioned his body between her legs. She could feel him pressing against her there, the heaviness of his arousal pushing her open just a fraction. Even that touch was so amazingly intimate that she let out a gasp.

Immediately, he stopped. "Am I hurting you?"

"No." She knew it probably would hurt some, but right then she didn't care. All she cared about was having him inside her, joining to him in a way she never had with anyone else. Still, she wasn't so lost that she didn't forget to send the mental prayer to Brigid out into the universe, the one that would protect her from any long-term consequences of this time with Alex.

Blessed Goddess, now is not the time. Bestow your blessings elsewhere.

When her mother had first told her of the charm, Caitlin couldn't help wondering if a witch saying it meant some poor civilian somewhere would still get knocked up instead. Now she knew the magic didn't quite work that way. But it would protect her, and that was the most important thing.

"It's—it's good," she went on. "Don't stop. Please."

That seemed to be all the encouragement he needed, because he pushed against her more. She could feel him sliding in, and there was a twinge, almost like a sharp tug, and then he was in her, all the way in, moving gently, as if he was still worried that he might be hurting her. To show him that he wasn't—not really, anyway—she wrapped her legs around him and pulled him closer to her, then began moving with him, her hips rocking against his as they found their rhythm, moving together, their breathing speeding up.

Time didn't seem to exist anymore. Nothing did, except Alex, his face above hers, eyes locked on hers in a kind of wonder, his expression seeming to say that he'd never thought they would come to this place, to this suspended moment where the world was gone and it was only the two of them, the push and pull of their bodies, the beating of their hearts, joining in a moment of perfect synchronicity, perfect harmony.

And then he groaned, his eyes closing, and she felt him pound into her as the orgasm hit him and he released, more warmth filling her as he came. She knew she wouldn't, not this time; despite her reassurances that he wasn't hurting her, she was a little sore. Just enough. But that didn't matter, since he'd already made her come twice before now, and she was sure he would again.

He went still then, and ever so gently pulled out of her so he could ease himself onto his side. Dark eyes scanned her face, hesitant, somewhat worried. "Was that—was that okay?"

Caitlin leaned over and kissed him, tasted herself on his lips, and a new spasm of desire went through her, even though she knew she needed to give herself some time to recover before they tried this again. "Way more than okay," she said. "It was perfect."

Some of the tension seemed to leave his body then, and he smiled at her. "I'm glad. And—I'm glad I could be your first."

Truthfully, she couldn't imagine having done this with anyone else. In fact, the very thought made a shiver go through her. "I'm glad, too." She paused, then said, "Although I think I'd better go get myself cleaned up."

He nodded, and she gave him another quick kiss before getting out of bed and going to the bathroom, where she washed up as best she could. That did feel a little better. Odd that when she gazed at herself in the mirror, she didn't think she looked all that different. Her hair was mussed and her eyes shining, but otherwise, she seemed to be the same old Caitlin.

Only she knew she wasn't.

She went back out to the main part of the hotel room and slipped under the covers next to Alex. It felt bold to be sleeping next to him like this, wearing only her panties. But she was tired now and didn't feel like rooting through her suitcase to find the tank top she slept in. Besides, this was better, in case they woke up in the night and wanted to make love once more.

Without hesitating, he reached over and pulled her against him, kissing her, but gently, as if he knew she needed to rest. Really, they both did—who knew what they'd be facing the next day when they went to meet with Simón Santiago?

"Comfortable?" Alex asked, and she nodded.

"Very." She was, too; the bed seemed to cup every part of her that wasn't nestled against Alex, and she thought she'd never felt so safe, so protected, so warm.

But as she drifted off to sleep, she couldn't help wondering if she was a terrible person for feeling so happy when her friends were anything but safe or protected.

CHAPTER FIFTEEN

WAKING UP NEXT TO CAITLIN LIKE THAT—WELL, IT WAS nothing short of miraculous. All right, so she'd slept in his bed that one night after the first horrible vision she'd suffered, but this morning was about as different from that one as he could have imagined. For one thing, when he shifted and opened his eyes, squinting at the clock, she had snuggled closer to him, her bare breasts pressing into his chest. That had been enough to distract him from realizing it was already past eight o'clock and that they really should get moving.

They got moving, all right…into one another, her hands on him, urgent, wrapping around his shaft and stroking him, his fingers slipping into her, feeling how ready she was for him. He'd pulled off her panties so quickly, he was surprised he hadn't torn them right off her body. Then they were locked together once again, a quick, urgent joining that was very unlike the gentle but intense lovemaking they'd shared the night before. Afterward, it seemed the most sensible thing to do was take a shower together to save time, although that might have been a slight miscalculation, considering the way they ended up clinging to one another yet again, her riding him while he sat on the floor of the bathtub and the hot water sluiced down over the two of them.

Eventually, though, they got out of the shower and finished the rest of their morning prep. As Caitlin was giving her hair one last flick with the brush, she asked, "Are we checking out before we leave?" Now that they were fully dressed and looking more or less like civilized human beings, Alex could tell she was a little diffident, not quite sure of how they should be interacting.

Well, that first "morning after" was always a little awkward, but he'd decided earlier that the best thing to do was act casual and hope she wouldn't misinterpret his off-hand manner to mean that last night hadn't been a big deal. It had been a huge deal... for him, anyway, and while he didn't claim to be an expert on women, he thought it had been incredibly important to Caitlin, too.

As far as the room went, he'd also been wondering what to do about that. "I'm not sure," he replied. "If we get the information we need out of Simón, then yeah, there isn't much point coming back here, since we'll need to get on the road back to Tucson as soon as possible. But if he's not there, or he won't talk to us, or whatever, it seems as if it would be kind of stupid to give up on the room and have to go someplace else if we end up being stuck in Pasadena for another day."

She frowned, then shoved her hairbrush into her weekender bag and zipped it closed. "I suppose that is kind of a tough one. And I guess we have to decide soon, since it's already ten and we have to check out at eleven."

"And we haven't eaten yet," he pointed out. As good as all that sex was, it had taken something out of him. He needed some fortification before they went to see the head of the Santiago clan. No way was he making that call on an empty stomach.

In the end, they decided to take their luggage to the car, just in case, then eat and see how things felt. The hotel had its own restaurant, so it was easiest to eat there and keep an eye on the clock.

"We won't need it," Caitlin said abruptly when they were some fifteen minutes into their meal, mug of tea halfway to her mouth.

"Huh?"

She shot him an apologetic smile. "Sorry. A twinge. My gut telling me that we aren't going to need the room. So I guess we'd better finish up here so we can check out."

Was this what it would always be like—getting little promptings from Caitlin's sixth sense or whatever it was? In a way, he supposed that was a good thing. Less chance of making a really heinous mistake. On the other hand, it would feel strange to have your life guided by some force you had no control over. No, that wasn't right. Not really. It wasn't as if her every waking moment was dictated by what her seer abilities might be sensing. They only seemed to show up for the important stuff.

And he probably shouldn't delve too deeply into why he'd just assumed that her life and his would be entwined from here on out. They'd slept together, and it was amazing…way more amazing than the time his high school girlfriend had lost her virginity to him, since Amanda had seemed to view the whole procedure as an ordeal to get over with, her hands squeezed into fists and her face tight with pain as he cautiously entered her. With Caitlin it had been so different, he almost found it hard to believe that she really had been a virgin. Well, except how tight she'd been. That had made her virginity fairly obvious.

Anyway, it was sort of a big step to go from spending one night together to thinking it was only the first of many more nights. He hoped it would be, though. Of course he wanted this whole terrible mess with Danica and Roslyn wrapped up, but at the same time, he prayed there would be some way for this to end in a way where he could still be with Caitlin. The few days they'd been together told him he enjoyed being around her as a person, and last night had only shown him that they were just as compatible physically. He'd never had these thoughts about another girl. But Caitlin was different. Caitlin was special.

"Okay, if you say so," he told her, since she was watching him, again with that one arched eyebrow, the one he thought was so adorable. "I'll check out as soon as we're done here. And then...."

"And then the Santiagos," she finished for him. She didn't look terribly overjoyed at the prospect, and he couldn't blame her.

It might not be exactly the same as walking into the lion's den, but it was definitely beginning to feel that way.

Caitlin wasn't sure what she'd expected of California, but Pasadena, or at least this part of it, didn't seem to quite fit. Yes, there were palm trees, but the beach was miles and miles away. And it wasn't sunny at all, but gray and damp-feeling, as if the clouds above wanted to start misting but didn't quite have the energy. Luckily, she'd packed a few tops with longer sleeves, just because she'd read that temperatures in Tucson could go up and down at this time of year, and she didn't really want to get caught off-guard and end up freezing her ass off. Even so, she felt chilled through, in a way that couldn't entirely be blamed on the weather.

The houses were beautiful, though, older, in a bewildering variety of styles—Spanish hacienda, Tudor cottage, colonial, all on large properties with lots of trees. This was obviously a neighborhood of people with money. Lots of money. It made sense, she supposed. The head of a clan always lived in a luxurious house, from the big Victorian up on Paradise Lane that had once been Great-Aunt Ruby's to the sprawling adobe building where Maya de la Paz lived. Something about this area felt more intimidating, though. Maybe it was all the Mercedes and BMWs she saw on the streets…and was that a Ferrari cruising past, sleek and low and somehow menacing?

Caitlin didn't know for sure. All she did know was that she felt woefully out of place.

Beside her, Alex looked relaxed and confident enough. Thank the Goddess for that. And thank Blessed Brigid as well that he'd been calm, easygoing this morning, not trying to put too much weight on what had passed between them the night before. Well, and this morning. Twice.

She winced and hoped that the evidence of their tryst wasn't written all over her face. It had been amazing, and she knew she wanted more, but there was a time and a place for everything. She wasn't sure last night had really been the best time for them to sleep together, but her body had overruled her brain on that particular issue. Now she and Alex shared some kind of bond, although she'd have a difficult time explaining what that bond exactly was. It couldn't be love. Not so soon. Didn't it take months and months to fall in love?

For some people, maybe. Actually, she'd always thought she was one of those people, someone who needed to spend a lot of time with a guy before deciding if it was worth going any further. For her, it had never seemed to be. But now she'd jumped into bed with Alex without even stopping to think it over. It was as if her body and soul already knew something that her mind kept refusing to acknowledge.

"Here we are," he said, pulling over to the curb in front of an imposing Spanish-style mansion with an actual turret to one side, a turret with large windows that overlooked the street. You couldn't see inside, though; the curtains were shut.

Caitlin's hands suddenly felt very cold. She wished she could blame her chilled fingers on the gloomy gray day, but she knew they were only evidence of a spectacular case of the nerves.

Alex turned toward her. "You ready?"

"Probably not," she admitted. "But let's do this anyway."

A flashing grin, one that sent an unexpected rush of warmth right to her core, despite their current circumstances. Then he undid his seatbelt and got out, while she followed suit.

A flagstone pathway wound up toward the arched front door. To either side of that door were terra-cotta urns with graceful drooping palms of a variety Caitlin didn't recognize. They matched the house very well, but something about them felt cold and artificial, as if they'd been placed there precisely because they did go with the place and not because the people who lived there particularly cared for them.

Alex reached over and rang the doorbell. The sound of the Westminster chimes sequence echoed dimly within the house, and Caitlin held her breath, waiting. And waiting. She cast a worried glance up at Alex, and he gave the barest lift of his shoulders.

"It's a big place. It could just take them a long time to get to the door."

True. Or maybe they simply didn't answer that door if they weren't expecting anyone, in which case getting in might be even more difficult than she and Alex had expected.

After what felt like an eternity, though, the door opened slowly, and a pretty young woman around Alex's age stood there looking at them with a half-startled, half-suspicious expression on her face.

Caitlin could sense right away that the other young woman was a witch, and so that meant she could also tell that Caitlin and Alex were no civilian canvassers, out to tell everyone in the neighborhood about *The Watchtower* or the Book of Mormon.

"What is it?" the young woman asked.

Alex smiled—the sort of smile Caitlin thought should melt just about any heterosexual woman's knees. The strange young witch seemed fairly impervious, however, and continued to stare at them, her expression not altering one whit.

The smile faded, and Alex said, "We're really sorry to just show up like this, but there's an urgent matter we need to discuss with Simón Santiago."

She blinked. "And who are you, to show up on our doorstep and ask for such a thing?"

Our doorstep. Caitlin wondered exactly who the young woman was. Simón's daughter? Most likely. She didn't know all that much about the Santiago clan, but she figured the *prima* must have had at least one child before she suffered the fall that put her in a wheelchair.

Alex's smile returned, albeit somewhat more subdued this time. "My name is Alex Trujillo, and my grandmother is Maya de la Paz. This is Caitlin McAllister. Her mother is one of the elders of the McAllister clan."

Once she'd been given these credentials, the young woman appeared to soften slightly. "Well...."

"Please. This shouldn't take very long."

A lift of her shoulders, and she said, "All right. You can wait in the living room. My father's out in the greenhouse. I'll go get him."

She opened the door the rest of the way and ushered them in, then shut it behind them. They stood in a large foyer with a wrought-iron candelabra hanging from the twenty-foot ceiling. All around were expensive-looking antiques and Persian rugs, and on many of the tables were orchids in a dizzying variety of shapes and sizes. That must have been what the young woman meant when she'd spoken of her father being in the greenhouse. The orchids were probably his hobby.

Caitlin and Alex followed her into the living room, which was a cavernous space with a wood-beamed ceiling and an enormous fireplace surrounded in Spanish tile.

"My name's Lucinda, by the way," the young woman said. "Can I get you some water or something?"

"We're fine," Caitlin replied hastily. They were already intruding enough. She certainly wasn't going to make Lucinda fetch them refreshments.

Alex nodded, and the Santiago witch seemed satisfied with that, telling them she'd be back in a few minutes, and to please have a seat while they waited.

"Wow," Caitlin commented after what seemed like a safe interval had passed. "This place—it looks like something out of one of those old black and white movies my Great-Aunt Ruby liked to watch. You know, where all the women have that perfectly waved hair and slinky satin dresses."

"Definitely old Hollywood. Or old Pasadena, I guess. But yeah, this place makes my *abuelita*'s house look like a mud hut."

"I wouldn't go so far as to say that," Caitlin replied.

A shrug. "I don't know. If my art history class hasn't failed me, I'd say that's a real Picasso hanging over the fireplace."

She wouldn't know a Picasso if it came up and punched her in the nose, so she'd have to take Alex's word for that. What she did know was that this place intimidated her. It spoke of money that had been around a long, long time. Yes, the de la Paz clan had been in southern Arizona since before the territory became a state, but the Santiagos had come to Southern California with some of the earliest Spanish settlers. Their roots went as far back as the founding of Los Angeles itself.

Movement at the entrance of the living room made both Caitlin and Alex go still, and she looked up to see a tall, stately-looking man in his early sixties standing there, surveying them, his daughter standing directly behind him. Crap. Caitlin had to hope he hadn't overheard any of their conversation, the casual way they'd been discussing the house.

Lucinda cleared her throat. "Father, this is Caitlin McAllister and Alex Trujillo."

At once the two of them scrambled to their feet. Another man might have told them not to get up, but Caitlin could tell at once that the Santiago patriarch was not that easygoing. His dark eyes surveyed them coldly, and she thought she detected a downward twitch to his mouth when his gaze rested on her for a few seconds.

Somehow she resisted the urge to put her hand to her neck. She thought she'd done a good job of covering up the marks Alex had left there, but what if she'd missed something? Simón probably thought she was a complete tramp.

"Mr. Santiago," Alex said politely. "I'm—"

"I know who you are," Simón broke in. Once again his gaze flickered to Caitlin, then returned to Alex. "What are you doing here in my territory without permission?"

So it was going to be like that. Caitlin could feel Alex wince slightly, but then he replied, his voice firm enough, "My apologies for that, sir. We've come here on an urgent matter and didn't have time to wait for the back and forth of getting permission. My grandmother is not well, and my mother, the *prima*-in-waiting, is occupied enough with caring for her."

Simón waved a hand. "I do not care for your excuses. You are here now, so tell me what it is you want."

Alex hesitated, and Caitlin said, "Mr. Santiago, we're trying to determine the whereabouts of three warlocks we believe are members of your clan. They—"

"And how do you know they're members of my clan?"

The older man's expression looked so forbidding as he asked the question that Caitlin faltered, not sure of the best way to reply. Was there a best way to describe the situation? She was beginning to think not.

Thank the Goddess, Alex stepped in. "Sir, we don't know for sure. We'd hoped you'd be able to clear that up. They certainly aren't members of the de la Paz clan, and although it's remotely possible that they've crossed the border from Mexico, I don't think that's the case. Their names are Matías and Jorge and Tomas, and they—"

At the mention of the three warlocks' names, Lucinda gave an audible gasp. Simón rounded on her, saying, "Lucinda, go check on your mother. You're not needed here now."

Without bothering to protest, she ducked her head and disappeared down the hallway. What the hell was all that about? It seemed obvious enough to Caitlin that Simón's daughter did in fact know something about the young men in question…and just as obvious that Simón didn't want her talking about it.

From the way Alex's mouth tightened, it appeared he'd come to the same conclusion. Maybe that was why his tone was far more clipped than usual as he said, "Mr. Santiago, these warlocks have kidnapped two of Caitlin's friends, a McAllister and a Wilcox. I don't think I need to stress how serious the situation is."

Simón looked very grim, although it could be that was his usual expression. "That is unfortunate. But I don't know what you expect me to do about it."

Right then Caitlin desperately wished they had brought someone older and more experienced with them. It seemed clear to her that the Santiago clan leader intended to stonewall two people he thought were beneath his consideration, and not worthy of being treated as equals.

She cleared her throat, and reminded herself that you caught more flies with honey than with vinegar. "Sir, if they did come from this territory, then any information you have could be helpful. You see, they're using some dark magic we don't completely understand, and—and they're *hurting* my friends, using their blood somehow—" On those last words, her voice caught, and she had to stop herself so she wouldn't start blubbering like an idiot in front of this forbidding-looking man.

His expression softened, but only a fraction. "That is a matter of grave concern, and I can see why it would upset you. But I'm afraid I don't know anything of these young men or where you might find them."

Alex rocked back on his heels, his hands straining against the pockets of his jeans. Caitlin got the impression he was doing so to prevent himself from grabbing hold of Simón's arms and shaking him hard to get him to tell the truth. The impulse was completely understandable, but she knew that would be the absolute worst thing he could do.

Then again, what Alex said next wasn't much better. "Oh, really? Because I could have sworn from the way your daughter reacted that she did know something."

At once Simón Santiago's brows swept downward, and his jaw set. "She is high-strung and easily upset. You misinterpreted her reaction. And since I have nothing of use to tell you, I think it's best that you go."

"Just like that?" Alex said, his tone disbelieving.

"I'm sorry you came all this way for nothing, but if you'd called—"

From the way his eyes began to blaze, Caitlin could tell Alex was really about to let loose on the older man. "It's fine," she said, laying a hand on Alex's arm and beginning to pull him toward the hallway, and from there to the front door. "We're sorry to have taken up any of your time."

At least, after resisting her for a second or two, Alex slipped his arm from her grasp and seemed to recover some of his composure. However, he wasn't mollified enough to offer any sort of parting remarks to Simón, and instead stalked to the front door, opened it so Caitlin could slip out, and then slammed it shut behind the two of them.

"What an asshole," he growled.

The sky had decided to start misting after all, letting fall fine needle-like drops that felt like pins hitting her skin. "I know. But we can't force him to tell us anything."

"No, that's Matías' thing." Alex still sounded extremely irritated, and Caitlin couldn't blame him. To have driven all this way, only to be treated with slightly more courtesy than someone trying to sell magazine subscriptions door to door?

She wouldn't call it a waste—not after what the two of them had shared—but she couldn't help wondering if they might not have been able to come to that point in their relationship in Alex's home rather than in a hotel room. Then again, maybe those neutral surroundings had helped to relax a few inhibitions. At this point, did it really matter?

All she could do was offer a shrug, and he added,

"Well, I guess your premonition that we wouldn't need the hotel room was right. I just wish I'd known it was because we were going to get sent packing like a couple of panhandlers or something."

"I'm sorry," she said, then went to him and took his hand. At least he reciprocated, wrapping his fingers around hers and giving them a squeeze, so she knew he was angry at Simón Santiago for being a dick and not at her for failing to accurately predict what would happen with this interview.

"Hey!" came a soft voice as they were climbing into the Pathfinder.

Caitlin paused in the front seat with her hand still on the door handle and looked over to see Lucinda Santiago hurrying toward them, coming down a narrow path that ran along the tall hedge that separated their property from the neighbors'. That path must have led to the backyard; as Caitlin gazed in astonishment at the young woman while she practically ran the last few steps to the SUV, she noticed a gate in a tall wrought-iron fence standing open.

Without asking for permission, Lucinda grabbed the handle of the rear passenger door and then opened it. She settled herself behind Caitlin before leaning forward and telling Alex, "Drive. Go around the block or something. We need to talk."

His eyes widened in astonishment for a second, and then he nodded and turned the key in the ignition. He pulled away from the curb, but sedately, as if he knew that peeling away in a screech of rubber would only attract attention. Once they were far enough away that the Santiago house was out of eyeshot, he said, "What's this about?"

"You know what it's about." Lucinda cast a nervous glance over one shoulder, as if to reassure herself that they were a safe distance from her property. "Matías Escobar."

So that was his last name. Whether knowing it would help them, Caitlin had no idea, but at least it was something. "So he is a member of the clan."

"Well...."

"Either he is or he isn't," Alex put in, turning left down another street, one lined with equally impressive houses.

"His mother was a refugee from El Salvador. She came here when Matías was really young, way before his powers began to manifest. Since she was a powerful healer, a *curandera,* my father let them stay in our territory, gave them the protection of the clan. I remember him saying once he wished she'd come a few months sooner, because that way she might have been able to help my mother after she had her fall."

Not sure how she should respond, Caitlin nodded. That would have been difficult, knowing his wife could have been healed, if only Matías' mother had come into their territory in time. As for Simón offering the woman shelter, Caitlin had heard rumors of such things happening occasionally, especially in the larger clans, but it wasn't common. "And then when your father discovered what Matías' talent really was...."

"It wasn't good." Lucinda's shoulders slumped, and she leaned forward in her seat. For the first time, Caitlin realized the other young woman wasn't wearing a seatbelt, and wondered if she should say something. But she decided not to, just because Alex was barely going twenty-five, and she didn't want to interrupt any of these revelations. "Matías' mother could control him...sort of...but he still got away with murder." Her mouth curled faintly, and she added, "Well, not actual murder. But a lot of bad stuff. He started hanging out with Jorge and Tomas, who'd always been trouble as well. Neither of them are particularly strong warlocks, but they started dabbling in things they shouldn't, digging up rituals that had been buried for years."

All this sounded pretty much in line with what Caitlin and Alex had encountered so far. "And no one tried to stop them?"

For a second, Lucinda didn't reply. Her fingers tightened on the seat back, the leather creaking slightly. "They were good at hiding what they were up to. Maybe they would never have been discovered if Matías hadn't gotten a little too sure of himself and started aiming too high."

"Too high?" Alex echoed, sounding puzzled.

A flush tinged Lucinda's warm olive complexion. "He thought—he thought because he had this power that no one else had, and could make people do pretty much what he wanted, that…he could be with me."

Oh, Goddess. No wonder Simón Santiago wanted to act as if he'd never heard of Matías Escobar or his friends.

Not looking at either Caitlin or Alex, Lucinda went on, "My father found out. He was furious. He'd expected more of me, wanted me to honor the clan by marrying one of my more powerful cousins, and Matías had—in his words—'ruined' me."

"Seriously?" Alex asked. "Isn't that sort of… medieval? I mean, you weren't the *prima*-in-waiting, were you?"

An immediate shake of the head. "No. So there was really no reason for me to be saving myself, except that that was what my father expected of his daughter. When he found out—that was about six months ago—he ordered Matías out of Santiago territory."

"Could he do that?" Caitlin asked, then shook her head at herself for the clumsiness of the question. Obviously, Santiago had managed to avoid Matías' own particular blend of mind control...the real question was how. "I mean, if Matías can make people do pretty much what he wants, how was your father able to keep enough control of himself to exile him?"

"You've met my father." Lucinda's mouth turned down in a wry smile. "He doesn't take orders very well. A lifetime of having it his own way, I suppose. So Matías' powers didn't have as much effect on him as they might on someone else. I, unfortunately, was pretty susceptible, since I've spent my whole life doing what my father says."

Caitlin murmured, "I'm sorry."

A shrug. "It's partly my own fault. But anyway, I don't know where Matías went. I do know that Tomas and Jorge hung around for a while after their ringleader was gone, but they disappeared about a month ago, too. If they're working together now, then I have a feeling Matías put out the call to have them come meet him wherever he was hiding."

While that was an interesting tidbit, it didn't exactly help solve the issue at hand, namely, Matías' whereabouts. Caitlin repressed a sigh and wondered if they'd ever be able to get a piece of information that would actually help them.

Alex must have been thinking roughly the same thing, because he said, "Does anyone know where he might have gone? Does he have any relatives except his mother?"

"He has a sister, Olivia. She lives in Temecula."

Caitlin's pulse speeded up a fraction. "Do you have her address?"

"Thought you might ask." Lucinda paused and pulled a small folded-up piece of paper from the pocket of the button-down blouse she wore. "She's a *nunca*, but she might help you."

"*Nunca?*" Caitlin repeated, wishing she'd taken Spanish in high school instead of French, which at the time she'd thought was far more romantic.

"It means 'never,'" Alex said, looking uncomfortable. "It's slang for someone who's born to a witch family but never develops their one singular talent, and instead can only manage the usual fire-starting and door-unlocking stuff."

"Oh." It did sound kind of rude when you thought about it. After all, it was just an accident of nature that some people's talents never manifested at all. It wasn't their fault.

"Anyway," Lucinda went on, "I'm not saying she'd sell out her own brother, but they never did get along very well. Probably because his talents were so strong and hers...weren't. She moved out to Temecula to get away from him, I think. Her husband's a contractor or something. A civilian."

She said the word so dismissively that she might as well have said he was an ex-convict or something. But that didn't matter. What mattered was that they now had the one piece of evidence that might lead them to Matías' lair, wherever that might be.

"Thank you," Caitlin said, and hoped some of the gratitude she felt was reflected in her voice, if not in those simple words.

"It's fine. Matías is...." Lucinda let the words trail off, her dark eyes haunted. "He has no limits. He wants what he wants, and that's it. So I hope you can catch up with him." Her tone changed abruptly as she addressed Alex. "If you turn right here, and then right again, we'll be back on my street. You can drop me off at the corner. I'm sure eventually my father will figure out what I've done, but no point in rushing the moment of truth."

"Uh...sure." Following her instructions, Alex maneuvered through the residential area and then came to a stop a few feet from the corner she'd indicated. As she was lifting the handle to let herself out, he added, "We really do appreciate your help."

"No problem." She got out of the Pathfinder, and for a second, her pretty face twisted into a mask of hate. "I hope you catch that motherfucker."

And she slammed the door shut and strode off in the direction of her parents' house.

For a second, Alex and Caitlin just stared at one another. Then she said, "You heard Lucinda. Let's catch that motherfucker."

CHAPTER SIXTEEN

ALEX SET UP THE ROUTE ON HIS IPHONE, AND HE AND Caitlin headed out immediately. The drive to Temecula would take around an hour and a half, depending on traffic, but since it was the middle of the day, he had to hope that wouldn't be too much of a factor. In the seat next to him, Caitlin was keyed up, tense. He couldn't blame her—this information about Matías' sister could be the break they'd so desperately needed.

Or she could shut them down just as heinously as Simón Santiago had. Alex supposed it depended on how close she was to her brother, how much familial loyalty she possessed. Once upon a time, he might have said that no one would cover up for a family member who'd done such terrible things, but after he'd heard about some of the things Damon Wilcox had pulled,

Alex wasn't so sure about that particular point of faith in human nature anymore.

"You okay over there?" he asked Caitlin, and she startled before sending him a tentative smile.

"I think so." Her head tilted to one side, and she continued, "That is, there are some things I'm *very* okay about. But I'm worried Matías' sister is going to tell us to drop dead when we ask for her help."

That reply made him smile a little. This thing wasn't resolved by a long shot, but at least Caitlin was telling him that relations between the two of them were just fine, even if nothing else was. "She might," he admitted. "That worries me, too, but we'll just have to see what happens."

Caitlin nodded and settled herself back in her seat, then glanced out the window. At what, he wasn't sure; the area the 10 Freeway cut through at this point in their travels was mostly industrial, and, coupled with the lowering gray sky, anything but inviting.

They drove on, eventually angling south on I-15. He'd propped up his iPhone on the dash so he could watch the miles counting down. About a half hour to go. They'd be pulling into Temecula at the tail end of lunch, but since he and Caitlin had eaten breakfast late, he wasn't going to suggest that they stop for some food. Better to head straight to Olivia's house and hope for the best. With any luck, Matías would have completely alienated her, too, and she'd be more than willing to give him and Caitlin any information she had.

Wishful thinking, probably. But he was sort of tired of contemplating worst-case scenarios.

Eventually, they pulled off the freeway in Temecula and wound through neighborhood after neighborhood of tract houses. Since he lived in roughly the same sort of area in Tucson, albeit one where the lot sizes were a bit bigger, he didn't think twice about his surroundings. Caitlin, though, was staring at the streets with wide blue-green eyes, as if her brain couldn't quite absorb the notion of mile after mile of nearly identical houses.

The tract where Olivia's house was located looked a little older, the houses a little smaller. A lot of the cars were parked on the street or in driveways, rather than being tucked into a garage. Alex saw toys lying out on lawns or sitting on sidewalks, but no kids. They were probably inside eating lunch or, if they were older, still at school.

By contrast, Olivia's home looked very neat and clean from the outside. No scattered Big Wheels or buckets of sidewalk chalk. The grass on the postage-stamp lawn was green and bright, and cheerful pansies grew in the flower border next to the front walk.

Seeing all this, Caitlin brightened a bit. "It looks nice."

"It does," Alex agreed, then pulled into the first opening on the street, two houses down from Olivia's place. "Let's hope she's just as nice."

Caitlin's face fell a little at that remark, but she only nodded and slung her purse strap over her shoulder before letting herself out of the SUV. He followed suit and met her on the sidewalk, and together they went up the walkway.

The front door had a bright flowery wreath hanging on it that partially obscured the peephole. Not that it really mattered; even a *nunca* such as Olivia would be able to tell from the other side of the door that the two people standing on the floral "Welcome" mat were witch-kind.

Since he was closest, he reached over and pushed the doorbell. A simple *ding-dong* sounded, none of that pretentious Westminster chimes crap. They didn't have to wait nearly as long this time for a response, either; a bare minute later, a young woman a couple of years older than Caitlin stood there, staring at them in some perplexity. She had a baby, maybe six months, balanced on one hip, and she was pretty in a rounded sort of way, probably still working to get rid of the weight gain from pregnancy.

"Yes?" she asked. Not "what is it?" Clearly she knew it had to be some kind of witch business for the two of them to be there.

"Hi," Alex said. "I'm Alex Trujillo, and this is Caitlin McAllister. We need to talk to you about your brother." On the way up the front walk, he'd resolved to get to the heart of the matter immediately. If she was going to shut them down, she might as well do it right away rather than waste any of their time...or hers.

But she didn't shut them down. She swallowed, sent a nervous glance up the street, and then said, "Come in."

He allowed himself the barest sigh of relief as Caitlin entered the house, and he followed closely behind her. The first hurdle cleared, anyway.

The rooms in the house were small, but, like the front yard, everything was neat and clean—not an easy trick with a six-month-old baby. He knew some of his own cousins had let their own places go to wrack and ruin the second a child came along. Olivia led them to the family room, then set the baby down in the playpen there. When she straightened up, there was a look of mingled fear and worry on her face.

"What has Matías done?" she asked.

Alex and Caitlin exchanged a glance. It seemed obvious the young woman was ready enough to believe her brother's guilt, so clearly she knew he was no angel. Since this was Caitlin's story to tell, not his, he gave her an encouraging nod.

She still hesitated for a second, then said, "I know this is going to sound terrible. But it's what really happened to me…and is still happening to my two friends." From there she launched into a terse retelling of how Matías and his two friends had lured her and Roslyn and Danica from the restaurant bar, and what had happened afterward.

During this entire narrative, Olivia's face had grown paler and paler. Alex had never seen Matías in person, so he didn't know if they shared any of the same features—whether the wide, slightly almond-shaped eyes were similar, or the straight, chiseled nose. But he knew their expressions could never have been similar, because there was nothing hard or cruel about the way she looked. By the time Caitlin was done, the other young woman had what appeared to be tears shining in her dark eyes.

"I am so sorry," she said at last. "He wasn't a bad brother to me when we were really small, but as he got older and his talents started to appear…." A shake of her head. "It was bad. And even worse when it became obvious I wasn't intended to have any true magic at all, except for the smallest, most useless things. He'd bully me, make fun of me…and then after that, he ignored me as if I didn't exist. I embarrassed him. He was meant for more, he told me. He was going to do great things." Her mouth twisted. "Yeah, like get the clan leader's daughter in the sack. Matías didn't skate out of that one quite like he'd intended. He'd thought Simón would make Lucinda marry him. But instead Simón told Matías to get out of our territory, and even Matías wasn't strong enough to take on the clan leader and the witches and warlocks in his inner circle, the ones who guard our *prima* against harm."

"So where did he go?" Alex asked.

The baby started making the little meeping and mewling noises that were generally a precursor to a crying fit, and Olivia went over and picked him up, jouncing him on her hip so he'd quiet down. "He went to Phoenix first, but he didn't like being that close to the de la Paz *prima*...he said he thought she could smell him or something. So he headed down to Tucson. He's been there for a few months."

"Do you have an address?" Caitlin's voice was tense, worried. They'd been denied that urgent piece of information so many times.

"No," Olivia replied, denying them once again.

Shit.

"But," she went on, "he gave me an address for one of those mail drop places, just in case I needed to send him anything. I don't know if it will help, but I can get that for you at least."

It was better than nothing. Besides, all those mail-box businesses required you to give a proper address when you rented a box. Maybe Alex could get his cousin Miguel on it, see if he could pry the actual address out of someone at the mail drop place.

"That would be great," he said. "It could help a lot."

Olivia smiled, appearing relieved that she'd been able to help them a little, if not as much as they might have hoped for. Baby still on her hip, she went over to a side table that had a small drawer and pulled out an address book. She flipped through it with her left hand and got to the correct page, then came over to Alex.

"At the top of the page," she instructed, holding the book open for him.

Sure enough, there was "Matías Escobar," writ-ten in a neat, rounded hand, followed by a box num-ber and a Tucson zip code. Alex pulled his phone out of his pocket and entered the information in his notepad app. "Thanks," he said when he was done.

Caitlin was still standing a few paces off, a trou-bled expression on her face. "Yes, thank you for help-ing us, but...."

"But you're wondering why I would help you at all?" Olivia went to the side table and replaced the address book in the drawer before turning back to face them. The baby began to fuss, so she lifted him from her hip and leaned him up against her shoulder. A soothing hand running up and down the child's back, she said, "Matías is my brother, but I know he's not a good person. And when he fell in with Jorge and Tomas, he just got that much worse. I'm not sure what their talents are, but I know they're not as strong as my brother. But they do seem to…I don't know…encourage him."

"So they are brothers?" Caitlin asked, the strain clear in her voice. Alex guessed she was remembering that terrible vision of the two warlocks having sex with Roslyn.

"No. Cousins—first cousins. Not cousins in the way the witch clans tend to use the word, where we all say we're cousins even though the connection may be four or five generations back."

Both Alex and Caitlin had to smile at that remark. It was so true—"cousin" tended to be shorthand for most clan relationships. It was just easier that way.

"Anyway," Olivia went on, "Matías is one of those people who's never satisfied with what he has. He always needs something more. He hates that our mother was a refugee witch, that we were only here in Santiago territory on Simón's sufferance. I wish I could tell you what he's up to, but we haven't spoken for a few months now. He doesn't approve of me, and I don't approve of him."

She sounded sad rather than bitter when she said this, and Alex could tell that beneath it all, she still loved her brother, even if she couldn't possibly defend his actions. Who knows…maybe she was hoping he would manage to redeem himself somehow.

The baby began to fuss again, and Alex had been around too many cousins with infants not to know what that meant. The kid was either hungry or needed to be changed. Whichever it was, he knew that was his and Caitlin's cue to get out of there. Anyway, they'd gotten the one piece of information they could use. It was time to be on the road.

"I'm so sorry," Caitlin said. Her eyes met Alex's across the room, and he gave her a very faint nod, just so she'd know they needed to wrap this up. "And we won't take up any more of your time."

Olivia didn't bother to protest. She was still caressing the baby, trying to keep him calm, but he was getting increasingly restless. Alex knew the screaming would commence at any second, and she had to want them out of there just as badly as they wanted to leave.

She only nodded and led them to the front door. Just as he was crossing the threshold, Caitlin already a pace or two ahead of him, Olivia said, "Alex, if you do find Matías—"

He paused and glanced back. Her mouth was tight with worry, her eyes strained. He could tell what she was thinking. "I won't do anything more than I have to," he told her. "We just want Danica and Roslyn back. What their clans decide to do after that...." All he could do was lift his shoulders. Truthfully, he'd been so focused on tracking down Matías that Alex hadn't much thought about what they'd do with the rogue warlock once they caught him. Well, that was an unwelcome chore he'd be more than happy to hand off to the elders of the McAllister and Wilcox clans.

"I understand," Olivia said sadly, then shut the door.

It was clear she never expected to see her brother alive again.

Caitlin remained silent as Alex maneuvered them out of the housing tract where Olivia lived and back onto the freeway, heading south so they could pick up Interstate 8 and take the southern route back to Arizona. The last thing she'd ever expected to feel was pity for a member of Matías' family, not after everything he'd done, but she couldn't help being sorry for Olivia. How awful to know that your brother was capable of such terrible acts, and also know there was nothing you could do to stop the justice that was surely coming his way. It wasn't as if Caitlin had ever been terribly close to her own brother, as they were two very different people with not much except their parents in common, but she did love him, was proud of his accomplishments. She couldn't imagine not being able to feel that way about a sibling.

While she was looking out the window, at the freeways that never seemed to clear completely, and the mass of cars around them, Alex said, "I'm going to call Miguel and get the information on the mail drop to him. If we're really lucky, maybe he'll have a lead for us by the time we get back to Tucson."

"Sounds good," she replied, although she had to wonder whether the de la Paz contingent in Tucson would wait for her and Alex to return, if Miguel actually managed to dig up something that would help in locating Matías. She had a feeling they wouldn't exactly stand on ceremony when it came to that sort of thing. After all, she and Alex had at least a six-hour drive ahead of them. She wasn't quite sure exactly how long it would take, since they'd traveled a different route when heading to Pasadena, but she knew it was going to require a chunk of time to get back to home base.

He pressed a button on his contacts list, then lifted the phone to his ear. Caitlin hoped no one was paying too much attention; didn't California have a hands-free law for mobile devices? But as she glanced out the car window, she saw one driver with her own phone glued to her ear, and another apparently putting on mascara, so she thought Alex was safe from scrutiny as long as a highway patrol officer didn't come cruising by at exactly the wrong moment.

From the long pause that ensued, Caitlin guessed Miguel wasn't picking up, for whatever reason. And that speculation proved to be correct, because Alex said, "Hey, Miguel, I'm checking in. Caitlin and I got something you might be able to use. I need you to check on this box and see if there's a real address attached to it." For just a second, he pulled the phone away from his ear and went to his notepad, then read off the information for the rented mailbox. After that, he transferred the phone to his other ear and added, "Can you call me and let me know you got this? We're on our way back to Tucson, but it's probably going to be close to seven by the time we get there. Thanks." He ended the call and set the phone down on the dashboard, presumably so he could reach it easily if and when Miguel got back to him.

"No answer, huh?"

A shake of the head. "No. He might be with a client and has the sound turned off on his phone. But I know he'll get back to me when he can. I just have to hope that it'll be before we get out into the open desert. God knows if I'll get any cell reception out there."

That didn't sound very good. She was about to ask if he'd ever driven this way before, then remembered this was his first trip to California, just as it had been hers. Not that they'd gotten to see very much of it. But although Simón Santiago had done his best to thwart their efforts, they'd still come away with one valuable piece of information. That was something.

She yawned, feeling something of the anticlimax hitting her after meeting Olivia, and Alex sent a quick glance in her direction. "Tired?"

"A little. I didn't get as much sleep last night as I probably should have."

"Sorry about that."

"I'm not."

The smile he flashed her then was so brilliant that she could practically feel herself reviving in its warmth, like a sunflower lifting its head to the life-sustaining rays of the sun. But as good as it felt, it wasn't quite enough to keep her from yawning again.

"Maybe we should stop in El Centro or Yuma or someplace, get you something to eat."

"I'm fine," Caitlin protested. "I'd rather just keep going."

"Is that a feeling, or just personal preference?"

She paused to think about it for a few seconds. "A little of both, maybe." On the way to Temecula, Alex had had to stop to fill up the Pathfinder, and he'd bought them some bottled water at the attached convenience store. The water would be enough to keep her going. She really didn't feel hungry, even though breakfast was hours and hours ago now. Something was telling her that they needed to get back to Arizona as quickly as they could, and stopping for even fast food didn't fit into that plan.

"Okay," he said. "And then when we get back to Tucson, I'll take you to the restaurant that invented the chimichanga. I have a feeling by then you'll be hungry."

"It's a deal," she replied. "I've never had a chimichanga."

"Then that's definitely where we're going." He was still smiling, but his expression turned serious as he added, "I think this time we're really going to catch him."

"I hope so." For whatever reason, the same sixth sense that was telling her they needed to get to Tucson ASAP was remaining quiet on the subject of Matías' eventual capture. It could be that conclusion was a given, now that they had a solid lead, but Caitlin wasn't so sure. The warlock was a ghost, elusive as quicksilver.

Alex nodded, then took his phone out of his pocket and set it in a little depression in the dash, one that seemed to have been designed to hold a cell phone. Maybe he hoped it would get better reception there, rather than buried in his pocket.

But there was no return call from Miguel, and as the miles slipped past, Caitlin could feel weariness taking hold. She reclined her seat to get more comfortable, and Alex turned down the volume on the radio slightly, as if he could tell she wanted to rest. That would probably be best. Just an hour or so of sleep while they cruised through the most barren parts of the desert. Then she'd be rested up when they got to Tucson, and they could figure out where to go from there. With any luck, Miguel would have gotten back to Alex by then, and they'd have a plan of action. Some way of catching up with Matías, who might as well be in the witness protection program for all the luck they'd had tracking him down so far.

Her eyelids slipped closed, and for a while it was just blissful darkness, the quiet of sleep. But then she heard voices, and although everything was still dark, she thought she knew who was speaking.

"...Man, you really need to switch them out. This one's just about tapped," came a male voice. Not Matías, but either Jorge or Tomas. Tomas, probably; he was a tenor rather than a baritone, his words sounding slightly nasal.

"It's not time yet." That was Matías, his tone clearly irritated.

The darkness behind her eyelids retreated, and Caitlin saw that the three warlocks were standing in a living room that had all its shabby furniture pushed up against the walls so there was room for the circle they'd drawn on the scarred wooden floor. Jorge and Tomas stood across from Matías, Roslyn between them. Seeing her, Caitlin wished she could scream, could cry out somehow, because that wreck of a person could not be her beautiful, vivacious friend.

Roslyn's long dark blonde hair hung lank, looking stringy and somehow thinner, where it had always been lush and full before, the kind of hair you might see in a shampoo commercial. Her arms were so criss-crossed with cuts, some still oozing blood, that Caitlin could barely make out the color of her skin. Shadows hollowed her eyes, and her cheekbones looked too sharp, too pronounced.

Goddess, what have they been doing to you? Caitlin cried inwardly, but the despair coursing through her wasn't enough to shut out the vision, and neither could she close down that inner eye so she wouldn't have to see any more of the wreck of her friend.

Jorge said, "I thought we were going to alternate. She's going to be useless real soon."

"She'll still be useful enough." Matías shifted, bending down to draw a symbol Caitlin didn't recognize along the edge of the circle. As he did so, she caught sight of Danica, who had been standing next to him. In contrast to Roslyn, who looked as if she'd spent the past two days being death-marched through the desert or worse, Danica appeared more or less unharmed, although her eyes were still glassy and unfocused, a clear sign of still being under Matías' spell. Her hair was brushed, and it even looked like she might be wearing some mascara and lip gloss.

Clearly, the dark warlock was saving her for something…but what?

Tomas and Jorge exchanged a black look, but neither of them said anything. So they were still following Matías' orders, at least for now.

He straightened, then went back to Danica and slipped an arm around her waist. She smiled and bent in toward him, nuzzling against his neck. "Say it, *mamita*," he told her.

"I love you, Matías," she murmured, the words partly muffled because she was trailing kisses up and down the skin of his throat.

In that moment, Caitlin was glad she hadn't eaten anything for hours, because otherwise she would certainly have vomited. Although she knew it wasn't really Danica saying those things, but rather the spell Matías had cast on her, she couldn't help feeling sick.

"Good girl," Matías said. He ran his hand down her hair, then pulled away from her slightly. He addressed his next words to his cohorts. "We're keeping this one because she's stronger. If we weaken her, too, we won't be able to use her when we need more power. Got it?"

"Yeah," Jorge said, although he still sounded annoyed. "But that's only because you let the strongest one get away."

Matías' black eyes glinted with malice. "I didn't 'let' her do anything. Yeah, she was stronger than I thought. But you know we couldn't go after her—not when she ran straight into that nest of de la Paz witches." For some reason, his mouth curved into a cruel smile. "Last laugh's on them, though."

Tomas and Jorge both chuckled, and Tomas said, "Let's do this thing."

He went over to a side table and picked up the knife that had been lying there, a long, wicked-looking thing with a slightly curved blade and a handle of some kind of black metal. Just seeing that knife in her mind's eye was enough to make Caitlin's blood run cold. There was something ceremonial about it, as if it had been designed for one very dark purpose. It was not the same as the knife she'd seen Jorge use before to cut Roslyn's arms. That one had been a regular switchblade, as far as she could tell. She hadn't known for sure, as she'd never seen one in real life, only on TV or in a movie.

"Put her in the circle," Matías commanded, and Tomas led Roslyn into the very center of the outline they'd drawn on the floor. She stared off blankly into space, as if she had no clear idea of where she was or why she was there. Maybe that was a blessing.

Then Matías began to speak in a language Caitlin had never heard before. It wasn't Spanish, and she didn't think it was Latin, either. Something old and cruel, something that seemed to turn her blood to ice.

Stop it! she cried out, but since the words were only uttered within her mind, they had no force, no way of preventing the dark warlock from performing whatever rite whose words he was uttering now.

Tomas handed the knife to Matías, who lifted it to his lips and kissed it reverently. Then he hefted it in his hand and, with one blinding motion, slashed it across Roslyn's throat. She collapsed to the floor, blood spraying the two warlocks, and across the circle itself. Once again the foul mist she'd first seen in that borrowed house a few blocks from the Trujillo store rose into the air, only this time it was dark, so dark, a black that was blacker than black, and seemed to billow and sway before it took on the vague outline of a man and went flying through a wall and disappeared.

All that remained was Roslyn's limp form, the life drained from her throat, and Danica standing by with a vague smile on her face. And the three wizards, wearing their own smiles, but of gloating malevolence.

Caitlin screamed.

CHAPTER SEVENTEEN

It was good that Caitlin could get some sleep. All this chasing around, on top of the worry about her friends that he knew continually weighed her down, couldn't be good for her. And he liked looking over at her, seeing the dark crescents of her lashes against her cheeks, the way her head was tipped to one side and her wavy copper-colored hair flowed over her shoulders.

Then her eyes snapped open, and she let out such a piercing scream that Alex's hands jerked involuntarily on the steering wheel, sending them over the lane divider for a second before he could get hold of himself and yank the SUV back where it was supposed to be. The eighteen-wheeler behind him honked once, probably to wake him up in case that knee-jerk reaction had been caused by falling asleep for a split-second. It hadn't, but between Caitlin's scream and that honk, Alex figured he'd be awake for at least the next twelve hours.

She was staring forward, eyes like saucers. The fingers of her right hand were clutching the handle of the passenger-side door as if it was the only thing connecting her to reality. Then tears began to trail their way down her cheeks. But she said nothing.

"Caitlin? What is it?"

No reply. Only that staring, white-rimmed look, like a spooked horse.

"*Caitlin!*"

At last she turned toward him. "She's dead," she whispered.

"What? Who's dead?"

"R-Roslyn. I saw it. I *saw* it!" Then she began to weep in earnest, burying her face in her hands, her slender shoulders wracked with sobs.

Oh, shit. This was bad. This was very, very bad. Her visions had never been wrong before, but Alex found himself compelled to ask, just in case there was even the slightest chance of a misunderstanding, "Are you sure?"

"Of course I'm sure!" she flung at him. "I might as well have been standing there with the rest of them, I could see it so clearly."

"'Them'?" Alex echoed, although he thought he already knew the answer.

"Matías and Jorge and Tomas. They'd drawn another circle, and they slit her fucking throat! I saw it!"

"Jesus." His hands were shaking, and he tightened his grip on the steering wheel. What the hell were they supposed to do now?

Keep going, he told himself firmly. *Even if Roslyn's gone, we still have to save Danica. And you can't lose it now—you have to be here for Caitlin.*

"I'm so sorry," he said at last. "We'll find him. Don't worry. We'll find him, and we'll make him pay."

"What good will that do?" she snapped, shifting in her seat so she was more or less facing him. "Will it bring Roslyn back?"

"No," he replied. Somehow he managed to keep his tone calm and even. What he really wanted to do was pull over so he could take her in his arms and hold her, give her the comfort she so desperately needed, but he knew that wasn't a good idea. For one thing, it wouldn't even be safe—there wasn't a rest stop in miles—and anyway, now more than ever they needed to get to Tucson as quickly as possible. "But at least she would have some kind of justice."

Strangely, those words seemed to calm Caitlin down. She swallowed, then said, "You're right. She's gone, but Matías is still here, and he needs to face the consequences of what he's done."

There was something very cold and hard in her voice, qualities he'd never heard in her speech before, but then again, even with everything she'd had to handle so far, this was the very worst of all, the one thing they'd feared but hoped would never come to pass. Alex risked a glance at her and saw that already the tears were beginning to disappear, and her pretty features were still, almost icy in their set fury.

"How much longer to Tucson?" she asked.

He blinked at the *non sequitur*, then said, after glancing at the clock, "Another two hours, probably. I'm speeding as it is, but I don't want to go too fast. The last thing we need is to get delayed because I got pulled over for a speeding ticket."

She nodded at that reply. Her hands were clenched in her lap, he noticed, the fingers knotted into one another so tightly that he could see her knuckles standing out white against her already fair skin. A tear dripped from her eye, but she didn't reach up to wipe it away, instead ignored it as it trickled down her cheek and then dropped onto her shirt, making a dark blotch on the pale green material.

Seeing that, he could feel the rage building in him as well. He'd never met Roslyn McAllister, but she was a friend of Caitlin's, a young woman who should have had her entire life ahead of her. She didn't deserve the fate she'd apparently just suffered. If Matías had suddenly appeared in the middle of the highway ahead of them, Alex would have floored it and let the Pathfinder turn the warlock into a dark spot on I-8. But it wouldn't be that easy.

It was never that easy.

They were just entering the outskirts of Casa Grande when Alex's phone went off—probably because they'd at last come in range of a decent cell tower. Sunken in misery, Caitlin startled, then watched as he reached over and lifted his phone from where it had been resting on the dashboard.

It felt as though someone else was watching him do that, though, because the only thing that kept echoing through her head was, *Roslyn is dead, Roslyn is dead, Roslyn is dead,* and she couldn't seem to focus on anything else. How could Roslyn be dead—carefree Roslyn, whose voice and gift for music could have given her far more material success if she'd chosen it? But she didn't care about money or fame, had loved singing in the local bars and restaurants and clubs, was friends with everyone she met, it seemed. If she'd ever had a secret, something dark and deep, Caitlin never knew about it. And somehow she didn't think Roslyn ever had. Hers was too sunny and open a nature for that sort of thing.

Alex's voice finally penetrated the fog in her mind. In sharp tones, he broke in, "Wait, Miguel—*what?*"

A long pause as he appeared to listen to Miguel's reply, which seemed to be fairly involved. Then,

"When?"

Another pause.

"You're sure of that?" Alex's jaw tightened, and Caitlin watched as he drew in a deep breath that sort of hitched its way down, as if he was fighting a constriction in his throat. "Okay. Well, we're in Casa Grande right now, so I was planning to be home in about an hour. But we can backtrack to Phoenix if—"

He stopped then, as if Miguel had cut him off.

"My mother said that?"

Another pause.

"All right. I guess she knows where to find me. And I hate to bug you about that address, but it's really urgent. Caitlin just had another vision, and... it's bad. Roslyn—one of the girls—has been murdered. We've got to find Danica before it's too late."

Hearing the matter stated so baldly made tears begin to sting at Caitlin's eyes again. She forced down a breath and told herself that weeping for Roslyn wouldn't change anything. The best thing they could do now was hunt down Matías and stop him. What would happen after that, she honestly didn't know. It was up to Angela to decide his fate, as Roslyn was a member of her clan. Somehow Angela didn't really seem like the Old Testament, avenging-angel type, but she'd never been tested like this before.

In a way, it would be easier if they could simply find enough evidence to send Matías to prison, but the witch clans had always policed their own. Sending someone with their kind of powers to live in close quarters with civilian criminals was a recipe for disaster in and of itself, and for a warlock like Matías, it would be a thousand times worse. If he ever managed to get as far as an actual prison, he'd have the whole place from the warden down eating out of the palm of his hand within a few hours. No, Matías would have to face clan justice, whatever form it might take.

Alex ended the call, this time slipping the phone back into his pocket. His profile might have been carved out of stone as he stared forward, and Caitlin wondered what on earth Miguel had just told him.

Finally she got the courage to ask, "Alex? What is it?"

His fingers tightened on the steering wheel. Without looking over at her, he said, "Maya is dead."

"*What?*" It was just too much. The passing of the de la Paz *prima* would have been blow enough, but like this, right after Caitlin had just seen her own friend murdered? And then her brain caught up what had really happened, and she realized Alex hadn't just lost his clan's *prima*, but his grandmother. "Oh, Alex, I'm so sorry."

"It's okay." He still stared forward, as if he risked losing his obviously shaky grasp on his composure if he glanced over and saw any expression of pity or sorrow on her face. "She didn't suffer. At least, that's what Miguel said."

"How…what happened?"

Alex pulled his bottle of water from the cupholder next to him, took a long drink, then replaced the cap and set the bottle back in place. Maybe he really was thirsty, or possibly he wanted to think over his reply before he spoke. "I guess she had another seizure last night. It was bad, but not so bad that Valentina or Manuela thought she needed to be moved to the hospital. And my mother apparently agreed, because she could have overruled them if she had to. At first they thought they'd made the right call, since she woke up this morning and seemed to be a little better. But then this afternoon…."

He was silent for a few seconds, and Caitlin could see his jaw working. She wished she could tell him that it was all right to cry, that he'd just lost someone very important to him, but she didn't know if he'd really appreciate hearing that from a girl he'd only met a few days earlier, no matter what physical intimacies they might have shared. Instead, she folded her hands in her lap and waited.

After a long moment, he continued, "This afternoon she seized again…and again. My mother called the paramedics, but…my *abuelita* was gone by the time they got there. There wasn't anything they could do, so they left. I guess my parents are making the arrangements now."

And what a lot of arrangements those would be. When a *prima* passed, it wasn't just a matter of calling the funeral home and setting that particular chain of events in motion. That was part of it, of course, but the entire clan network would have to be notified, and the *prima*-in-waiting would have to assume the title of head of the family and anoint her own *prima*-in-waiting. The young woman in question was always identified long before that, of course, as soon as the strength of her own powers made it obvious that she should be next in line, but it wasn't made formal until the new *prima* assumed her role as head of the clan. Caitlin wasn't sure how such things were handled in the de la Paz family, but with the McAllisters, becoming *prima* also meant taking ownership of the big Victorian house on Paradise Lane and living there. Angela had bent the rules on that quite a bit, as she spent at least half her time in a house she and Connor had bought up in Flagstaff. Was that what Alex's mother would do now? Be in her own home in Tucson part of the time and in Maya's the remainder of the year?

The silence in the car was so thick, Caitlin was surprised she couldn't see it surrounding them like a dense, choking fog, one that seemed to prevent her from speaking. She picked up her own water bottle and drank some, hoping that would help to clear the thickness in her throat. "Alex, I—"

"It's okay," he said. He sounded normal enough. Then again, she'd only known him for a couple of days. She had no idea what he was like when he was grieving. He didn't seem like the sort of person to bottle things up, but maybe he was right now, just because he had something else even more pressing that he needed to focus on. "At least she can't suffer anymore. We witches and warlocks all know that there is a next life to move on to, so it's not as if she's gone forever. I'll see her again someday."

Maybe that was something you could be fatalistic about when discussing the death of an older person, someone who'd lived most of her life… although realistically, Maya should have been around for at least another ten years or so, depending on how long-lived the de la Paz witches tended to be. However, Caitlin couldn't quite adopt that same attitude about Roslyn's death. True, her friend had passed the veil and moved on to another world, a place where she would no longer be in pain. But that didn't make it any less difficult for the people left behind, the friends and family who should have been able to see her grow into the woman she would have become…the man she might have fallen in love with someday and with whom she could have started a family of her own.

Those thoughts only made Caitlin want to cry again. But if Alex was holding it together after learning that he'd lost his grandmother, then Caitlin would do the same, even if the hurt inside her was like an empty, gnawing ache that wouldn't go away, no matter how hard she tried to ignore it.

"So…your mother is the *prima* now?"

He nodded, mouth tightening, and Caitlin realized that had probably been the wrong thing to say. Luz Trujillo would always be his mother, of course, but now, as *prima,* she also belonged to the clan as a whole. Their relationship would never be quite the same again. But since she couldn't take the words back, Caitlin only sat and waited, hoping Alex would answer and wondering what she would say next if he didn't.

At last he said, "She was with my *abuelita* when she passed, and the powers came to her without any problem. That's one thing that's gone right, at least. Or as well as it could, considering." For the first time he glanced over at Caitlin, and she saw that the hard set to his jaw had softened slightly. "It's rough. All of this is just…I don't get it. None of it makes sense."

That was the problem. Roslyn was dead, and Maya gone, too, and the "why" of either of those deaths completely eluded Caitlin. All right, she knew that Matías and the other two warlocks had been using Roslyn's blood as a power source for their dark spells, but what were those dark spells doing? What were they getting out of all this?

She settled back in her seat, thoughts churning. As much as she hated to admit it, Roslyn's death had served some sort of purpose…for the warlocks, if no one else. But this illness that had struck out of nowhere and then taken Maya long before her time… once again, Caitlin heard that whisper at the corner of her mind, the one saying Matías must have had something to do with it. Yes, she knew that millions of people died every day, often in ways that made no sense. In general, though, a *prima* didn't die of an undiagnosed illness. Primas tended to live longer than most people, whether civilian or witch.

For some reason, she heard Olivia's words echoing in her mind: *Matías is one of those people who's never satisfied with what he has.* He always needs something more. And then, in Lucinda's crisp, no-nonsense tones: *He has no limits. He wants what he wants, and that's it.*

The thought growing in Caitlin's mind was so terrible that she didn't want to voice it aloud, didn't want to acknowledge it. That would give it shape, and reality. And then….

Before she could lose her nerve, she asked, "Alex, who will be your mother's *prima*-in-waiting?"

Sounding puzzled, he replied, "My cousin Zoe. She lives up in Fountain Hills. Why?"

"And—and has she turned twenty-one yet?"

"Yeah. A few weeks ago. The consort hunt is already under way." He paused and gave Caitlin a very sharp look before returning his attention to the road. "What are you trying to say?"

"I'm saying…." She hesitated, but the truth of what she had been thinking was so strong now that she knew in her bones it was her seer's ability telling her to speak, to not doubt herself. "I'm saying it was Matías and the other warlocks who killed Maya. They've been casting these spells for months, weakening her, disrupting things in your clan just enough that no one would notice they were operating in your territory, right under your noses. For the big push, though, the spell that would kill her, they needed witch blood. So they kidnapped the three of us, and that's why they murdered Roslyn. I still don't quite understand why they haven't hurt Danica yet, but I guess I'll just have to be grateful for that and worry about it later."

"Jesus Christ." Alex looked like she'd just punched him in the gut, and Caitlin hated having to say these things to him, even though she knew it was vitally important for them to use every bit of information they had. "And so they wanted Maya out of the way, because then my mother would be the *prima*—"

"And the *prima*-in-waiting would be formally designated, and the clock ticking down to the time when she would bond with her consort," Caitlin finished for him.

Beneath the anger and sorrow, a flicker of confusion came and went in Alex's dark eyes. "Matías can't possibly think that he's her *consort*, can he?"

"I doubt even he's that full of himself." She shook her head, adding, "He doesn't have to be. He just has to be…with her."

"You're saying a *prima* doesn't have to have a consort? That's nuts!"

"I would have thought so, too…a few years ago." What she was about to say next was not common knowledge, but she thought Alex needed to hear it. The Wilcox *primus*'s kidnapping of the McAllister *prima* had brought to light a few truths that Angela had thought it better for the girls of her clan to know, even though the vast majority of them were not and never would be *prima* material. "It's best for a *prima* to bond with her consort, of course, just because then she'll have the full strength of her powers. But it's not as if she won't be *prima* if she's with someone else. She'll still inherit the title eventually. She just won't be as effective. That's why the *prima*-in-waiting is guarded so carefully."

"And so Matías plotted to get rid of Maya so my mother would become *prima*, and Zoe would officially be made *prima*-in-waiting, and then he could swoop in and take her, make sure she wasn't a virgin and couldn't bond with her true consort." Alex's hands knotted around the steering wheel so tightly that Caitlin was worried he might actually break the plastic. "That fucking bastard."

"I think so. At least, that's what my gut is telling me." In that moment, she hated those instincts of hers, hated the evil they'd made her face. "Matías wants to be Zoe's consort—he'll have the power and station he's always wanted, and he'll be able to control her any way he likes."

"And I have a feeling he'd make sure my mother had some kind of 'accident' in the near future so he'd be in charge of the entire de la Paz clan." Alex reached for his phone and stabbed a button.

"Are you calling Zoe?" Caitlin asked, hoping they'd figured out Matías' plan in time. Maybe, if he was still in Tucson when he cast the spell that killed Maya de la Paz. He'd have to go from there to Fountain Hills to get Zoe. Where the hell *was* Fountain Hills, anyway? She had a vague idea it was a suburb of Phoenix, but after that she was at a loss. But she knew it wasn't down in the Tucson area.

Phone against his ear, Alex shook his head. "I don't have her number. Normally, I'd call my parents, but I have a feeling they're both sort of busy right now."

Of course, Caitlin thought. *Luz just lost her mother, and now she's in charge of an entire clan...a clan under attack, even if she doesn't it realize it yet. And of course her husband will be with her to support her.*

"So I'm calling Miguel. He's got everyone's contact information."

That made sense. She waited as Alex sat there, expression growing increasingly dire. When he spoke, she could tell he was leaving a voicemail. "Miguel, we're pretty sure those warlocks are going after Zoe. Can you get in touch with her, with Uncle Luis or Aunt Andrea, and let them know they need to get her to a safe place? Maybe Jack Sandoval—he's pretty good with defensive spells. Or even up to my grandmother's house if there's no one else. My mother should be able to keep her safe."

He ended the call but didn't put away the phone. Driving with one hand, he went back to his contacts list and pushed another button.

"Who're you calling now?"

"Jack, the guy I just mentioned. I don't want to wait for Miguel to get that message I left."

She nodded. It was horrible being this far away, now knowing what Matías was up to, and also knowing there wasn't anything they could do to stop him, except put the de la Paz clan on alert and hope that someone would be able to intercept the warlock in time.

But apparently this Jack person wasn't answering the phone, either, and Alex blew out a breath in disgust. "Jesus Christ, it's Friday afternoon. Where the hell is everyone—at a titty bar or something?" he paused, then added, "Well, actually, knowing my cousin Jack, he *could* be at a titty bar."

Normally, Caitlin would have laughed at such a remark, but she couldn't laugh now. Not with what was at stake. She said, "Maybe you should try your parents after all. They'd want to know, wouldn't they?"

Alex looked less than thrilled at that suggestion, but then he inclined his head toward her. "Okay." This time he dialed the number directly, which made sense; that should be a phone number he knew by heart.

A second or two went by, and Caitlin's pulse accelerated slightly. Maybe they wouldn't pick up, were so immersed in dealing with the aftermath of Maya's death that they'd just let the call go to voicemail.

But then Alex said, "Dad?" and Caitlin felt herself—well, not relax exactly, but at least go a little less tense. "Hi—yes, Miguel told me. I was going to come up there, but he said it would be better if I went home for now. That's not why I'm calling, though. We just found out what Matías is doing. I can't explain it all now, but he's going after Zoe. He wants to be her consort." A short silence, and then

Alex replied, obviously in answer to his father's question, "I know, it won't be a true consort bond, but it'll be enough for his purposes. And there won't be anything we can do about it if he succeeds. So someone needs to get her away, and now. I don't have her number, but I know one of you must—okay, good, thanks."

He ended the call and set the phone back on the dashboard. "Screw this," he muttered, then got out of the fast lane and cut in front of someone in a pickup truck loaded with hay bales so he could get off at the next exit.

Over the sound of the other driver's indignant honking, Caitlin asked, "Alex, what are you doing?" The street they'd pulled off on had the incongruous name of Sunshine Boulevard, and seemed to be set in the middle of equally incongruous cotton fields. And here she'd thought this part of Arizona was just scrub desert.

"I'm not going to sit down in Tucson doing nothing while everyone else goes up against that bastard." They turned under the freeway and then sped up the on-ramp, heading north toward Phoenix. "There's got to be something I can do with this talent of mine."

She couldn't argue with that. It was true—Alex was quite possibly the only person who could face Matías' magical coercion and not be affected by it.

And she understood his need to be doing something. The dark warlock had murdered his grandmother. That demanded action…and retribution.

"Okay," she said, very glad that her voice sounded firm and determined, and not frightened at all. For some reason, she couldn't be all that frightened if she had Alex with her.

"Is it?" he asked. "You're not scared?"

"No," she replied. "I trust you."

Without speaking, he reached out and took her hand, holding it tightly as he raised it to his lips and kissed it. "You're kind of an amazing girl, Caitlin McAllister."

"Am I?" She didn't feel amazing. She felt worried and shaky. Not scared. Not for herself, anyway.

"Yes." Another squeeze of her fingers, and then he let go so he could put both hands on the steering wheel.

They were going way too fast, that much she knew. The speed limit out here in the boondocks was seventy-five, and they were probably going at least ten, if not fifteen, miles per hour over that. All she could do was hope the cops were otherwise occupied, because neither she nor Alex had Matías' neat little Jedi mind trick to talk themselves out of a ticket.

Alex's phone rang, and he grabbed it off the dashboard. "Dad?" He listened, then said, "We're heading back to Phoenix now. She's where?" Caitlin heard him mutter something that sounded like a curse, although not loudly enough that the phone would pick it up. "Well, in a way that's good. Maybe he won't want to try something in a public place. Did you get hold of Uncle Luis or Aunt Andrea?"

Obviously the answer was no, because Alex looked like he wanted to swear again, although he managed to refrain.

"Okay, well, we'll go straight there, and you can keep trying her cell. Can you give me the number, just in case?" He pointed at the glove compartment, and Caitlin opened it. Inside was a notepad and one of those little golf pencils. "All right—602-555-7823. Thanks." He lifted an eyebrow at her, and she showed him the number she'd just written down on the pad. "And papa, give *mamita* a hug for me, all right? I'm sorry I had to worry you two with this right now. I'll let you know if we can find Zoe."

This time the phone went into his pocket. Alex glanced over at Caitlin and said, "According to my cousin Zander—that's Zoe's little brother—Zoe went shopping with some friends. Civilians, which means they'll be no help. They're at a mall off Cactus Road. She was talking about going to the movies. That might be why she's not answering her phone."

"This just keeps getting better and better, doesn't it?"

"I don't know—if she's in a movie theater with a bunch of civilians, in a way she's kind of protected. I doubt Matías is going to make a move in a place like that."

Alex did have a point. Even a warlock as cocky as Matías couldn't very well attempt to abduct a girl in front of hundreds of civilians. His whole *modus operandi* was to coax, to persuade. Much more likely that he would wait until she was someplace else— walking back to her car, maybe, or separated from her friends when she went to the restroom.

"How far is it?"

"Maybe an hour. I guess we'll just have to hope whatever movie she's going to see is a long one."

An hour, Caitlin reflected.

A whole hell of a lot could happen in an hour.

CHAPTER EIGHTEEN

Alex did slow down to a more respectable seventy miles an hour once they reached the outskirts of Tempe. It was painful—after going almost ninety for the past forty-five minutes, he felt like he was standing still—but there was just way too much traffic and too many cops from various municipalities and counties around for him to be comfortable going faster. Even now he was speeding, but since everyone around him was also going around seventy, he didn't feel too conspicuous.

Caitlin was tense and quiet, her gaze flickering toward the clock on the dashboard what seemed like every other minute. Not that he could really blame her. He could almost feel the minutes flying by, each one an opportunity for Matías to catch up with Zoe and…what? Use his powers to lure her away from her friends, take her to a nearby motel, and force her into bed. Then she'd be his, and the unspoken rules of the witching world would make them bound together, even if he wasn't her true consort. That was how these things worked for a *prima*, and although he didn't understand precisely why such traditions had arisen in the first place, there was no changing them now.

His phone had remained conspicuously silent ever since his last conversation with his father, and Alex didn't know if that was a good sign or not. It did seem to indicate that no one had yet been able to get in touch with Zoe's parents, and Miguel and Jack were also maintaining their radio silence.

Alex saw the off-ramp for Cactus Road coming up, and let out a sigh of relief. "Almost there," he told Caitlin."

She nodded. "What's the plan?"

He didn't have a frigging clue. Get close enough to Zoe so he could cast his protective field and therefore render her immune to Matías' magic? Beyond that, he didn't know for sure, although he was hoping he wouldn't have to perform such a show of magic in front of a bunch of civilians. But if it came down to a choice between protecting Zoe or revealing his magical gifts in public, well, he'd make sure the *prima*-in-waiting was safe, and worry about the consequences later.

"What plan?" he quipped, but the joke fell flat as Caitlin continued to gaze at him, that one eyebrow of hers cocked at an ironic angle. Backpedaling, he said, "We have to find her first, and see if the three warlocks are together. I'm hoping they'll have split up, because the three of them together are more conspicuous. It would have been different when they were going after you and your friends, since it was three and three, but I have no idea how many friends Zoe has with her. Zander didn't know for sure."

"All right," Caitlin said. "I suppose we'll start at the movie theater and go from there. How big is the mall?"

"I don't know. I've never been to this one."

"Well, since it's Phoenix, I'm going to guess that it's bigger than the mall in Flagstaff, which is the only one I know." She paused, appearing to think over the problem. "How well do you know Zoe?"

"Uh…." It was time to turn off onto Cactus Road, so he did that as he considered Caitlin's question. "Not that well. I mean, she's my cousin—*really* my cousin, that is. Her mother is my Aunt Andrea. But they've always lived up here in Fountain Hills, while we were down in Tucson, and so we saw each other at all the family get-togethers and clan gatherings or whatever, but I wouldn't say we were all that close. I always got the impression that she wasn't overly thrilled to be chosen as the next *prima*, but she went with it because, well, that's what you have to do."

"And what's her power?"

"Nothing she can use to protect herself from Matías," Alex said bitterly. "She's a healer, *a curandera*, but beyond that, she has the greatest facility with potions that my grandmother said she'd ever seen."

"And no one brought her in to help Maya? I would have thought—"

"They tried, back when my *abuela* first got sick. The problem was, no one knew exactly what was wrong with our *prima*. Zoe can supposedly whip up a potion to get rid of a cold or the flu in nothing flat, and according to Jack, she makes great hangover cures, but...."

"But it's not the sort of thing that can counteract black magic. Got it." She didn't exactly sigh, but Alex could tell from the way the corners of Caitlin's mouth had turned down that she wasn't thrilled with his answer. "What does she look like?"

The question caught him off-guard at first, because it seemed to have come out of nowhere, but then he realized Caitlin was just moving on to the next order of business. "She's—I guess she's pretty. Not very tall...maybe around five three or somewhere? Her hair and eyes are dark brown, and she wears her hair really long, almost down to her waist." He smiled then, recalling a particular aspect of that hairstyle. "She got a little rebellious the last year, put a streak of hot pink in her hair. And a tattoo of the Pluto symbol on her shoulder."

"Why Pluto?"

"I'm not sure. Tell you what—when we find her, you can ask her."

"It's a deal."

After that, he had to focus on maneuvering through the crowded streets around the mall, then pulling into the shopping center's parking lot. Following the signs, he began to head toward where the movie theater was located. Right then his phone rang, and although he didn't want to get distracted, he knew he couldn't ignore whoever might be calling.

That person turned out to be Miguel. He didn't even give Alex time to say hello, but immediately said, "I talked to your father, and he told me what's going on. I'm almost at the mall now, and so is Jack."

Thank God. That was probably the first piece of good news Alex had heard all day. "We're here now. I'm about to park over by the theater."

"Okay. Do some recon, but if you do see those warlocks, don't engage until Jack and I catch up with you. *Comprendé?*"

Alex reflected that his cousin Miguel had watched way too many war movies, or played way too much *Call of Duty*. Still, his advice made sense. "No worries there. We don't even know for sure if she's still at the movies or not, but that's the only information we have to go on right now. If I see anything, I'll call you."

"Got it. I'm less than five minutes away now."

"Then we'll see you in a few," Alex said, just as Miguel ended the call. After sliding the phone into his jeans pocket, he told Caitlin, "The cavalry is coming."

"Thank the Goddess," she breathed.

"What, were you worried I couldn't handle it on my own?"

She didn't respond to the half-smile he'd worn while asking that question. Those big sea-colored eyes were fixed on his face and filled with worry. "They're *killers*, Alex. I've seen what they're capable of. It's not that I don't believe in your power, but I know they'll fight dirty if they get the chance." Her gaze faltered, and beneath the worry, he saw the anger seething in her. "What I don't understand is how they could even find Zoe. I mean, I doubt your family goes around broadcasting information about its *prima*-in-waiting's whereabouts."

"I've been thinking about that," Alex replied as he pulled into an empty parking space. Since it was late on a Friday afternoon—almost evening, actually—the lot was filling up, and they'd had to park farther away from the theater than he would have liked. "I have a feeling that either Jorge's or Tomas's talent is finding people, witches specifically. My grandmother's ability was similar, although in her case it was more knowing who was in her territory who shouldn't be there, knowing what all her people were up to. But the talent for finding things is a pretty common one, so it's not a big leap to go from that to being able to find particular people."

"That makes sense." Caitlin picked up her purse from where it had been resting in the footwell and shrugged the strap over one shoulder. "It would also explain why Matías was hanging out with them. He'd only keep people around who had talents he thought were useful."

"Yeah, which begs the question, what talent does the other one of the gruesome twosome have? Nothing friendly, I'm sure."

"Probably not."

They both paused then, neither of them apparently eager to open their door, even though Alex knew they needed to get going, that time was slipping away. He really didn't want to admit it to Caitlin, but he was scared. Never in his life had he gone up against anyone like Matías. There had been some scuffles with his older brother Diego...more roughhousing, really...and a few more with a couple of guys at school, but magic hadn't been involved in any of those fights, low-key as they were. Matías wouldn't hesitate to do whatever it took to make sure he achieved his objective of making Zoe his.

But they couldn't wait. Maybe stall a little, until Miguel and Jack got here, but if Miguel was only five minutes behind them, he'd be here soon, too. He was the sort of person Matías wouldn't spare a second glance for—slightly overweight, edging toward middle age. And Alex knew Miguel would make damn sure he didn't get close enough for Matías to sense that he was a warlock. Maybe Jorge or Tomas would be able to figure it out, if locating witch-kind really was one of their talents, but Alex had to hope they'd be distracted by the crowds at the mall and wouldn't be able to quite pin down who was pinging their radar.

"All right," he said, then opened his car door. "Let's do this."

Caitlin followed Alex as he walked toward the mall, and tried to ignore the frightened thumping of her heart in her chest. Without being too obvious, she kept glancing around, wondering if she would catch sight of the three warlocks, or of a girl with a pink streak in her long dark hair, but she didn't see any of them. Just masses of people intent on their own business, some leaving the mall, some entering. There did seem to be a flush of people exiting the theater just as they came upon it, but whether that was because the particular show Zoe had gone to see had just gotten out, Caitlin couldn't begin to guess. Her sight seemed to have deserted her for the moment, although, underlying her current agitated state, she could sense that this was where she was supposed to be.

"No sign of her," came a voice from behind them, and Caitlin jumped.

But when she turned, she saw it was Miguel, Alex's cousin, and with him a taller man, probably in his late thirties as well, although a good deal better-looking. In contrast to Miguel's untucked bowling shirt and baggy khakis, the stranger wore a dark button-down and newish-looking jeans.

"Hey, Miguel, Jack," Alex said, a visible expression of relief on his face. Not bothering to introduce her to the newcomer, he went on, "Yeah, we haven't seen anything, either. But we just got here."

Miguel nodded. "I have a feeling she was probably in the movie that just got out. It seems like the sort of thing she'd go for—teenage girl against the world, two guys fighting over her, all that."

He sounded almost amused, even though Caitlin didn't find anything terribly amusing about their current situation.

"But if that's true, the question is, where would she go next?"

Not being a mall-goer—before moving to Flagstaff, she'd never even set foot in a mall—Caitlin couldn't begin to hazard a guess. Alex surprised her by saying,

"Well, since it's Zoe, I'd say either the food court or Hot Topic."

Jack grinned, and one or two of the women passing by sort of paused to get a better look at him. From the way his grin broadened, Caitlin got the distinct impression that he'd noticed the attention he was attracting and was pleased by it.

"That's probably a good guess. Has quite an appetite, our Zoe. I'm not sure where she puts it, but…." He shrugged. "And if she's not eating, she's buying another T-shirt that's guaranteed to piss off my sister." Apparently noticing the expression of puzzlement that passed over Caitlin's face, he added, "Zoe's my niece. Luis is my brother. His daughter is a good kid, but sort of contrary."

Maybe that was a good thing. If Zoe was stubborn and used to getting her own way, then possibly she had a chance of fighting back against Matías' magic.

"Okay," Caitlin said. "So should we split up, or first try the food court, then Hot Topic?"

Miguel shook his head. "First rule—don't split up if you can avoid it. You two head over to the food court and we'll follow, just not so close that it looks as if we're together. Okay?"

There didn't seem to be much point in arguing with that. She had to admit that the four of them did make a sort of motley group, and would probably be less conspicuous if they walked far enough apart that it didn't seem as if they were connected in any way. The other two warlocks would be in eyeshot, and Alex right next to her, and she thought that should be safe enough.

Actually, even though it was sort of nerve-wracking to be surrounded by so many people—she'd never been that good in crowds—in a way it was comforting as well. She had a hard time believing anything truly bad could happen in a place with so much surging, cheerful energy. How could Matías possibly hope to pull off another kidnapping under all these civilian noses?

They came into the food court area, and a thousand sounds and smells seemed to assault her at once. She found herself pressing closer to Alex, and he slipped a comforting arm around her waist, pulling her against him. The warmth of his body gave her some courage, and she drew in a breath so she could look around and see if she could catch a glimpse of the warlocks. She knew this part was up to her; she was the only one who knew what Matías and Jorge and Tomas looked like.

The first person she recognized, however, was none of them, but Danica, standing in front of a fast food place called Charlie's Grilled Subs. She held a go-cup in one hand and was staring dreamily out at the crowd. Blood going cold, Caitlin realized that her friend wore the same glassy-eyed stare as she had in the hideous visions that had invaded Caitlin's sleep… only this was no vision. She forced herself to focus and saw that Danica was flanked on either side by Tomas and Jorge, but there was no sign of Matías.

What the hell? Where was he? And if he wasn't even near Danica, then why did she still look so strung out? It was possible the spells he cast took awhile to wear off, or maybe she'd been under his influence long enough that he could still put her in that semi-trance even when he wasn't in the immediate vicinity.

Caitlin leaned against Alex, making sure her hair fell partly across her face, just in case either of the two warlocks might look in this direction at exactly the wrong moment. Under her breath, she said, "Jorge and Tomas are here—standing over in front of the sub shop, with the dark-haired girl in between them. That's Danica."

His body went tense, but he kept his arm around her, maintaining the façade that they were just a couple out shopping at the mall, getting a little snuggly. "I see them."

Miguel and Jack stopped a few feet away and pretended to be scanning the food offerings.

"Charlie's subs," Alex told them in an undertone. "The two guys with tats with the girl standing
between them."

"Got it," Miguel replied.

In that moment, Caitlin's view of the food court
was blanked out, replaced by the parking lot, cars
shimmering under the rays of the setting sun. A man
and a young woman emerged from the glass-doored
entrance to the mall, the woman lifting her arm and
pointing, as if at one of the cars. The man nodded
and bent toward her, smiling, and then Caitlin saw
the flash of his teeth in the sunlight, the glimmer of
hot pink in the girl's long black hair, and she knew
the couple was Matías and Zoe, slipping out, so close
to getting away.

Where are they? she demanded of herself. *Just an
entrance isn't good enough. I need to know which one!*

She hadn't really expected the scene to change.
After all, her visions up until now had been terrible
about providing any sort of actionable information,
no matter how hard she'd tried to bend them to her
will. But then it was as if she'd been watching the
scene through the lens of a movie camera, one that
seemed to swing on one of those boom devices, and
the view panned to the right slightly, just enough to
show her that the store behind them was Dillard's.

How that had happened, she wasn't sure. Maybe she was just desperate enough to finally make her strange sight obey her, or maybe she'd now been using her power enough that it was becoming more malleable, more useful.

"They're leaving," she told Alex. "I just saw them. The mall entrance by Dillard's."

"Shit."

Miguel must have overheard, because he pointed directly ahead of them. "That way. You're in luck—it's the closest exit. You go after them, and we'll take care of these other two."

How precisely they were going to manage that, Caitlin wasn't sure, but Miguel didn't look overly worried. Hadn't Alex said earlier that Jack Sandoval was an expert at defensive magic? She'd have to let them handle the situation, as she and Alex had to catch Matías before the two runaways got in Zoe's car and disappeared. What had happened to the *prima*-in-waiting's civilian friends, Caitlin didn't know, but she figured Matías had somehow maneuvered Zoe away from them so he could get her alone.

Walking quickly, Alex led Caitlin through the crowded food court and out into the parking lot. They paused on the sidewalk to get their bearings, Alex scanning the lot to see if he could locate them, Caitlin doing the same.

It was not her eyes that saved them then, however. A vision came to her again, this time an image of Matías and Zoe approaching a pale blue Fiat.

"Three rows over. Blue Fiat," she told Alex, and they took off at a run, ignoring the startled looks from the civilians in the area. Right now, attracting attention was something they didn't have time to worry about.

Even at almost seven o'clock in the evening, the heat rising from the asphalt felt merciless. How hot had it been here today? Caitlin supposed that it didn't really matter, that her mind was distracting itself so it wouldn't have to focus on the confrontation ahead. Because there they were, Zoe tossing back her head and laughing, Matías again leaning toward her with a smile on his face, all easy humor now that he thought he'd won.

Because of the way he was bending toward Zoe, he didn't see Alex and Caitlin approaching. It was Zoe who spotted them first, her laughter dying as she apparently recognized her cousin.

"Alex? What the hell are you doing here?"

"Get away from him, Zoe."

Her face was a study in puzzlement. "What's your deal? Matías and I—"

The dark warlock straightened and turned in their direction, his expression growing black when he saw Caitlin. Just looking at him like that, seeing him walking in the sunlight when Roslyn was dead by his hand, made her almost physically ill. But she couldn't give in to any weakness now.

Before she had time to even worry about being afraid, a protective sphere shimmered into existence around them. Voice calm and cool, Alex said, "Zoe, you need to come in here with us. You have to get away from him."

The *prima*-in-waiting was a pretty girl, but in that moment her mouth pursed into a distinctly mulish pout. "You're not my big brother, Alex. You can't tell me what to do."

"That's right," Matías said, his tone coaxing, seductive. A tremor went through Zoe, and she turned back toward the warlock. "You don't have to do anything they say. All you have to do is get in the car with me so we can leave."

She blinked, but Caitlin could already see the familiar hated glassiness in her big dark eyes. "Okay." Reaching into the slouchy studded black leather bag she carried, she fished around for a few seconds, then pulled out a set of car keys. "My cousin always was a goody-goody."

"Zoe, please—"

The desperation in Alex's voice was clear enough, but Caitlin didn't know what he could say, not with Zoe outside the protective sphere and already under the influence of Matías' dark talents.

"He's a murderer," Caitlin said loudly, and Zoe blinked, then looked around uncertainly. Matías began to take a menacing step toward Caitlin, and then realized the dome Alex had cast would prevent him from silencing her. Scowling, he held back, hands clenched in fists at his sides, seeming to understand that he had to be careful here, or risk doing or saying something that would break his hold on the *prima*-in-waiting.

"Yes, Zoe. He killed your *prima*. And my friend."

A shake of the head, the pink streak in her hair turning almost salmon-colored in the ruddy light from the setting sun. "No, that's not possible. Maya is sick, but she's not dead. You don't know what you're talking about."

"It happened this afternoon," Caitlin said. She hated to be so blunt, but she also knew she had to keep talking quickly while Matías' hold on the other girl was wavering. "You were out with your friends. Your family's been trying to reach you."

"I-I was at the movies. I had my phone turned off." Tears formed in her eyes, and she said, "Maya is really dead? Then I'm—"

"Yes," Alex said gently. "You're the *prima*-in-waiting. That's why he wants you. To take control of you."

That seemed to be the remark which sent Matías over the edge. "They don't know what they're talking about," he growled. "They're full of shit, *chica*. I don't want to hurt you. I want to make you feel good."

"Like you made my friend Danica feel good?" Caitlin snapped, feeling bolder now that it was obvious Matías couldn't do anything to penetrate the shield Alex had conjured. "Did you get tired of her that quickly, dump her so you could go after Zoe? I saw how you left her with Jorge and Tomas in the food court."

The oddest expression flickered in Matías' black eyes. Anger, yes, but also a sort of confusion, as if he wasn't quite sure what precisely he felt about Danica. It didn't matter, though, because Zoe rounded on him, hands on her hips.

"Is that true? You had another girl, right here in the mall, and you left her to come with me?"

"I—" Matías straightened, and his jaw set. "Zoe, *chica*, I told you they're full of shit. Don't listen to them."

For a second, she wavered, and Caitlin bit her lip, wondering what the hell they were going to do if they couldn't extricate the girl from the warlock's spell. But then Zoe shook her head, as if trying to rid herself of a persistent ringing in her ears. Comprehension seemed to dawn as she took in the implications of what Alex had told her, and she whirled away from Matías, began to run toward

Caitlin and Alex, and the protective dome that enclosed them.

As quickly as she'd moved, it wasn't quickly enough. Matías' arm snaked out, grabbing her by the wrist and yanking her back toward him. At the same time, he reached into his pocket with his other hand, pulled out a switchblade, and pressed it against Zoe's side. Caitlin wondered if it was the same one he'd used to stab her.

"I don't think so," he said. His black gaze settled on her and Alex, partly obscured by the shield that surrounded them, even as Zoe held herself still, clearly afraid that if she made a single move, Matías would strike. "You try anything, and your *prima*-in-waiting dies."

Caitlin held up her hands, showing that she wouldn't make any attempt at rescuing Zoe. Not that she would know the first thing about how to even do that. She wondered how Miguel and Jack were faring with Jorge and Tomas, and whether they'd subdue them in time to get out here and be of any help. Goddess knows, she felt useless enough at the moment.

To her surprise, Alex just laughed and shook his head. "Not thinking very clearly, are you, Matías? Your whole plan revolves around getting your hands on Zoe. Without her, what're you going to do? You kind of shut the doors behind you in California when you nailed the *prima*'s daughter."

Hate glittered in Matías' eyes. "Fuck you, *pendejo*."

"That the best you can do? It's over, Matías. At this point, about all you can hope for is mercy from all the clans you've insulted—although I'd say the odds of that are pretty low, considering you've managed to get the McAllisters, the Wilcoxes, and the de la Pazes against you all at the same time." Still smiling slightly, he added, "Actually, that's quite an accomplishment. All three of the Arizona clans in one fell swoop? I've never heard of anyone else who managed that kind of feat."

Caitlin listened, aghast. Just what the hell was Alex doing? He had no idea how volatile Matías was, how he couldn't be trusted to react like a normal person. All he had to do was stick that knife into Zoe's side, and then where would they be? Caitlin was no healer, and she'd never heard of healers being able to treat themselves. Also, she'd seen the dark magic the warlock was able to summon. Maybe it wouldn't work without the ritual circle, but still —

Scowl deepening, Matías said, "You might want to shut your mouth, *cabron*. Unless you want me to make a hole in this little *puta*'s gut."

"*Puta!*" Zoe flashed, her temper obviously getting the better of her common sense. "I'll *puta* you, you asshole!"

One Doc Marten–clad foot came down squarely on his toes, and Matías swore. But Zoe had gotten him off-balance enough that she wrested her arm from his grasp and came running toward Caitlin and Alex. Now just a yard away—a couple of feet.

Then Zoe let out a howl of pain, and Caitlin saw that Matías had reached out and grabbed a hank of the girl's long hair as it streamed behind her. A grin of triumph pulled at his mouth as he began to drag her back toward him.

"Alex, do something," Caitlin pleaded. It was fine to stand here and know that Matías could do them no harm, but Zoe would be lost to them after all if they didn't take swift action. And as much as Caitlin wanted to burst out of there and go running to the other girl's aid, she knew even the two of them together probably wouldn't be enough to overcome the dark warlock.

Beside her, Alex shifted, gritted his teeth, and then raised his hands. She didn't know what he was doing…she didn't even know if *he* knew what he was doing. Not exactly. He made a pushing motion, as if he was shoving against an invisible force. Around them, the dome shivered, pulsed, and then exploded forward in a flash of light, seeming to pass harmlessly over Zoe but knocking Matías back against the Fiat, where his head slammed into one of the rear windows with a *crack!* Caitlin both saw and felt.

He slid to the ground, unconscious…at least, she thought he must be, as he was limp and not moving. Zoe stopped in mid-flight, pink-glossed lips open in a round "O," as if she still hadn't quite processed what was happening.

And then Alex was moving, going over to where Matías lay. Caitlin jogged along behind him, not because she thought she could do anything to help, but more because she wanted to confirm for herself that the warlock really wasn't about to get up again any time soon.

"Is he…?" she began, as Alex stopped and laid a couple of fingers against Matías' throat.

At once Alex shook his head. "He's alive. I'm not sure whether that's a good thing or not." He glanced past her to his cousin. "Zoe, are you okay?"

She put her hand up to the back of her head. "Well, I'm lucky that *pendejo* didn't snatch me bald-headed, but other than that, I'm all right."

Caitlin glanced past the car, saw that there were a few people at the end of the row shooting curious glances in their direction. All she could do was hope they hadn't seen Alex's last display, had only caught a glimpse of what looked like an altercation over a girl between a couple of guys in a parking lot. Otherwise, they'd have a lot of explaining to do.

"Hey!" she heard Miguel shout, and she looked over her shoulder to see him and Jack Sandoval approaching, Tomas and Jorge in tow, a bewildered Danica trailing along behind them. What they'd done to subdue the two other warlocks, Caitlin had no idea, but they both looked cowed, marching along meekly in front of their captors and keeping their eyes firmly locked on the ground so they wouldn't have to look at anyone…especially not their fallen ringleader. And Danica only stood there, hand to her mouth as she stared down at Matías' limp form.

"So you got him," Jack said, gazing at them in approval. Alex straightened and nodded.

"Yeah, I don't think he's going anywhere anytime soon."

Then Miguel glanced up the aisle, eyes narrowing. An electric cart with the words "Mall Security" on the side was moving toward them. "Alex, take Caitlin and Zoe and Danica, and get out of here. Jack and I will handle the mall cop."

"What're you going to tell them?" Caitlin asked, even as Alex moved toward her and took her hand in his. She clutched his fingers gratefully, still shocked by what he had done. Well, it seemed her powers weren't the only ones that could get amped up when under pressure.

Smiling, Jack pulled out his wallet and flashed a Scottsdale P.D. badge at them. "No worries. I'll handle it."

He turned toward the approaching mall security officer, and Alex began moving then, collecting Zoe by looping his arm through hers and dragging her back toward the entrance to the shopping center, while Caitlin reached out with her free hand and took hold of Danica. Her friend still seemed a bit bewildered, but came along without protest.

Blinking at the sudden turn of events, and trying not to worry too much about how out of it Danica still was, Caitlin looked up at Alex and demanded, "Why the hell didn't you tell me your cousin Jack was a cop?"

Alex sent her a blazing smile in reply. "Well, you never asked."

CHAPTER NINETEEN

THERE WASN'T ANYTHING LIKE A "WITCH JAIL," AND SO Miguel and Jack volunteered to keep an eye on the three miscreants until all the parties involved could be contacted and some sort of determination made about what should be done with the warlocks. After they'd fled the mall, Alex drove Zoe to his aunt and uncle's house in Fountain Hills, where they took in their wayward daughter while wearing expressions that seemed to indicate she was about to get read the riot act about talking with strange young men in malls. Even though he was feeling wrung out and not as relieved as he'd thought he'd be, considering that Matías and Co. had been caught, Alex had to force back a smile at the resigned look on his cousin's face. Clearly, she was used to having her parents give her grief over something or other.

Then it was time to backtrack to Scottsdale so he could finally meet up with his own parents at Maya's home. It was a house in mourning, the curtains closed, the mirrors covered, even the fountain in the courtyard shut down. A cowardly part of him wished he could have gone back to Tucson and taken Caitlin with him so they could spend some healing time together, but that was not an option. For one thing, they needed to stay with Danica until her parents could get down to Scottsdale and reclaim her. Throughout the whole car ride over here, she hadn't spoken, but only stared out the car window, and Alex couldn't help wondering if being continually under Matías' control for the past few days had done something to permanently mess with her mind. God, he hoped not. That would be the final blow. Alex told himself she just needed time.

As for Caitlin, she was looking pale but calm enough, although he knew she must be dreading what had to come next. Events had spilled over them so quickly that she hadn't had a chance to call home and let her mother know what had happened to Roslyn, but it was a call that would have to be made soon.

Luz came and greeted them in the foyer, then folded Alex into a fierce, brief hug. Now she seemed composed, but he'd seen the shadows under her eyes, the smudging of the eyeliner she wore, and knew she must have been weeping not too much earlier.

"Are you okay, Mama?" he asked her.

"As much as I can be, *mijo*," she replied. Then her gaze moved to Caitlin, and she went to her, taking Caitlin's hands in hers. "My dear, I am so sorry about your friend." A little pause, as Caitlin nodded, and then Luz turned toward her companion. "Danica, would you like to come sit down in the living room? I can bring you something to drink—some iced tea, or lemonade?"

Danica's hazel eyes still looked a little blurry, but then it seemed as if she made an effort to focus. "Um…yes. Yes, please." She glanced around her, obviously confused. "Where am I?"

"You're at Maya de la Paz's house," Caitlin said. "This is Luz, Alex's mother. You remember Alex from the car, right?"

"Yes." Her brows pulled together, and she frowned. "Wasn't there another girl?"

"Yes, my cousin Zoe," Alex said. "We dropped her off at her house a while ago. Remember?"

"Oh, right." Danica put her hand to her head. "I feel hung over. Did we go out drinking last night, Caitlin?"

"Uh…not exactly," Caitlin managed, and sent a beseeching look in Luz's direction. It was clear she didn't know the best way to handle talking about what had really happened to her friend.

"If your head is hurting, then let's try some iced tea," Luz said in soothing tones. "Just come on into the living room...."

They both went out, and Alex led Caitlin into the kitchen. "Do you want some tea, too? Or lemonade?"

She lifted her shoulders, looking so exhausted that he went to her at once and folded her into his arms, holding her close. At first he was worried that she was about to start crying, but she was very still as he held her, and only laid her head against his chest and breathed in deeply. A minute passed, and then she said,

"I wish I could have something stronger, but that's just me being a coward." She stepped away from him, gazing up into his face. Her eyes glittered, but he somehow knew the tears that swam there would never fall. "I need to call my mother. Maybe I should be calling my Aunt Lysette directly to tell her what happened, but I know I don't have the guts for that. Besides, my mother's her sister-in-law, and an elder. Maybe Lysette will take it better hearing it from her anyway."

"You're probably right," he said, trying to sound as comforting as he could. "It's the sort of thing your mother should handle."

She nodded. "I think I'll take that lemonade now."

Alex went to get it, and right afterward, his mother came into the kitchen. Her troubled gaze immediately settled on Caitlin.

"Danica's sitting down and seems calm enough. I can't tell for sure, but it seems as if she remembers very little of what happened to her over the past few days."

"Good," Caitlin said immediately. "I hope she forgets all of it. That would be the best for everyone."

Still looking worried, Luz went to the cupboard and got out a glass, then filled it with ice and poured tea from the pitcher in the refrigerator into it. "I'll get this to her, but we need to call her parents as well. Do you have their number?"

"I did, but the phone that had their number stored in it is gone. I'll have to let my mother know Danica's here and safe, and to pass the word on. I'm sure Connor must have her parents' contact information."

"That will do just fine," Alex's mother said. "But I'll need to get this out to her, and then I think it best you make your call as quickly as you can, so that you can come and sit with your friend. I'm a stranger to her, and she's in a strange place. She will feel better if you are near."

Caitlin nodded. "I'll call right now and be out as quickly as I can."

Luz offered her a reassuring smile, then took the glass of iced tea and headed back to the living room. After she was gone, Caitlin turned to Alex, her expression troubled but resolute.

"I guess I'd better make that call now."

He wished more than anything that he could do it for her—hadn't she been through enough?—but he knew this was her responsibility. "I'll get the phone for you." The cordless sat on a table in the hallway, so he went to fetch it, then handed it to Caitlin. She took it as reluctantly as if it were crawling with the Ebola virus or something. Seeing the way she hesitated, he asked, "Do you want me to be here with you while you call your mom, or would you rather be alone?"

The look in her eyes told him she'd rather have his support, but she surprised him by replying, "I'd better do it alone. I'll be fine."

There didn't seem to be much point in arguing, so he nodded and slipped back into the hallway while she stayed in the kitchen to make the call. Even so, he wasn't so far away that he couldn't hear bits and pieces, heard her reassuring her mother that she was fine, and Danica was safe, too. A long pause, and then finally she passed on the news about Roslyn, following it up as quickly as she could with the information that at least the warlocks had all been caught, and so now it was a matter of clan justice.

When Caitlin emerged from the kitchen and gave the phone back to Alex, he could tell she'd been crying. Not a lot—her makeup looked more or less intact—but her eyes were red, and she kept sniffling.

"My mother is going to let everyone know what happened, and she'll call Danica's parents, too. It sounds as if Angela and Connor will be contacting your mother soon as well. They'll—I guess they'll have a lot to do."

That was an understatement. He held his breath, waiting to hear if there was more. After all, so far Caitlin hadn't said one thing about what she planned to do next. It was Friday, the last day of her spring break. He was pretty sure she was supposed to go back to school on Monday. Only…would she, after everything that had happened this week?

Then she said, "And they'll be coming down to take me home."

His heart sank. Then again, what the hell had he expected? They were only about five years apart in terms of age, but the gap between twenty-one and twenty-six was a pretty big one in terms of living one's life. She had school to consider, if her parents would even let her go back. He could understand the impulse to want to keep her close, keep her safe.

He was feeling exactly the same way right about now.

They all ended up crashing at Maya's house that night. Sure enough, Angela phoned only about fifteen minutes after Caitlin had called home, and spoke to Luz Trujillo for nearly an hour while Caitlin and Danica and Alex sat in the family room and pretended to watch television. At least Danica hadn't yet asked where Roslyn was. Caitlin wasn't sure if she could handle that right now. Eventually, her friend would have to learn something of the truth, but Danica was too fragile right now, still nowhere close to herself.

Apparently, the McAllisters and the Wilcoxes had agreed that there probably wasn't anyplace safer for their two girls than with the de la Paz *prima*, and that was why Caitlin and Danica were told to stay put, and that a contingent from Jerome would be coming down in the morning to collect them and handle the whole Matías situation.

"Since it was already so late, and they wouldn't be here much before ten anyway," Luz said as she showed Caitlin and Danica to a pretty little guest room with two twin beds and plaster walls washed a warm rosy hue. "And I believe you already have all your things with you, Caitlin, and can share with Danica as necessary."

That was true enough; her luggage from the trip to California had still been in the back of Alex's Pathfinder. He'd brought it in, looking quiet and closed-off, and not very like himself. Caitlin wished more than anything that she could find a solitary moment to speak with him, to tell him that just because she was being ferried off to Jerome the next day, it didn't mean she wanted things between them to end. But maybe that was being too forward. Maybe he'd thought all along that this would be a short-lived relationship, something that grew up out of the intensity of the experiences they'd shared, but not anything that could possibly survive the long haul.

No, she didn't want to believe that. But unless she had a chance to talk to him, *really* talk, she didn't know how they'd begin to straighten all this out. And quite possibly it was ridiculous for her to be worrying about such things when Roslyn's parents had lost their daughter, and Danica kept looking around with that puzzled pull to her brows, as if she kept adding up two and two and getting five. Not to mention poor Luz, who had lost her mother that same day and had had no time to mourn.

Caitlin realized, as she climbed into the narrow, unfamiliar bed and Danica did the same in the one across from her, that Maya had died in this very house. In a different room, of course; Caitlin knew that the people from the funeral home had to have come hours ago and taken her body away, but it was still a creepy feeling. What if some residue of the dark spell the warlocks had cast to kill her still lingered, waiting to find its next victim?

No, that was ridiculous. Luz would have sniffed out anything like that. They were all safe here, and although it was terrible that Maya had so recently lost her life within the walls of this house, she'd still been able to pass on her powers peacefully enough. The hideous spell Matías had cast had done its evil work and dissipated. There was nothing left of it now. They could all sleep here peacefully enough, Luz and her husband David right across the hall, and Alex two doors down, on the other side of the bathroom.

Maybe thinking about where Alex was sleeping wasn't such a good idea. They'd only been able to share one night together, but it still had been the most important night of Caitlin's life. She wanted to be with him, to have him hold her close so she could feel the beating of his heart and the rise and fall of his chest, to know he was there to keep her safe. As much as she wanted those things, she knew she wasn't crazy enough to slip out of her bed and pad down the hallway to be with him. She wouldn't leave Danica—what if her friend woke up in the middle of the night and didn't know where she was, or had nightmares or something? Besides, Alex's parents were right across the hall. Caitlin knew she had to stay put, as much as she resented being here in this narrow bed when she could be lying next to him instead.

She stared up into the darkness and felt tears slip down her cheeks.

What if that single night she and Alex had shared turned out to be the only one they would ever have?

"I hate this," Angela said. They were all gathered in the living room of Maya's home, waiting for Miguel and Jack to show up with the three warlocks in tow. The McAllister *prima* had declined a seat and was pacing nervously in front of the fireplace. "I didn't sign up to be judge and jury and executioner all at the same time."

Connor had been standing nearby, and he came over and took her hands in his, thus making her stop her nervous pacing. Seeing them together, Alex couldn't help experiencing a twinge of jealousy. Not because he wanted to be with Angela; he knew Caitlin was the girl of his heart, even if circumstances did seem to be conspiring to keep them apart. It was just that Connor and Angela seemed so right together, so comfortable with one another. She held her husband's hands and looked up into his eyes, and her entire frame seemed to relax slightly.

The last time Alex had seen her, Angela had been just a girl, slightly too thin and nearly pretty, without a lot of confidence in herself. Now she was still slender but had filled out, and some sort of alchemy had turned the half-pretty girl he'd met into a very lovely woman. Was that a consequence of being with Connor, or would Angela have turned out that way no matter what?

Alex supposed it didn't matter at this point. She wasn't destined to be his, and the woman he did want, who sat on the sofa on the other side of the room, sandwiched between her parents, might as well have been on the moon for all he could reach her. Tricia McAllister had her daughter's same rich copper hair, although with a few streaks of gray around her face, and normally she probably would have been a very pretty woman. Now, though, she was frowning, her mouth set. On the other side of their daughter, Richard McAllister, tall and brown-haired, looked equally as grim. It didn't seem as if either of them was too concerned about Angela's scruples regarding Matías' punishment.

Apparently there had been some talk about the other McAllister elders coming down with them, but then the Wilcoxes would have had to send envoys as well. It also sounded as if Marie had wanted to put in her two cents regarding the situation, although since she hadn't really been that much help in locating Roslyn and Danica, Alex didn't much see the point of Marie being present. In the end, though, it had been decided that the three clan leaders—Angela and Connor and Luz—would handle the situation. Just as well, Alex reflected, since the living room was already crowded enough, what with Caitlin's parents and his own father being there, too.

Danica's parents had come down with the rest of the contingent, but had collected their daughter and continued on to Tucson so they could retrieve whatever of her things were still left at the condo, along with the Land Rover that had been parked there since the girls first arrived in Tucson. They'd looked shaken when they saw their daughter's condition firsthand, but they hadn't wanted to stay to see punishment meted out.

"It's better if I don't see those bastards in person," Joseph Wilcox had growled. "Because otherwise I'd be tempted to wring their necks."

Now, Connor shook his head. "I don't think any of us signed up for this," he told Angela. "Problem is, we have to deal with it, one way or another."

"I know." She looked past him to Luz. "I don't suppose you have any advice?"

"None beyond what I've already given you." Dressed in a black sheath dress, her hair in a low bun on the back of her neck, Alex's mother looked more composed than she had the day before, but still tired. He hoped that after Matías and his cronies were taken care of, she might finally have the time to grieve for her mother.

"That's what I was afraid of," Angela said. She fidgeted with the pendant she wore, a pretty thing of turquoise and what looked like smoky quartz. Unlike Luz, she was wearing jeans, but with a simple wrap top and boots. Too heavy for Phoenix weather, really, but they'd come straight down from Flagstaff.

A knock came at the door. "I'll get it," Alex said. It made sense. He was closest. And anyway, he was curious to see how the three warlocks had fared while being watched over by Miguel and Jack.

When he opened the door, he noticed at once that, besides the two men he'd been expecting, his cousin Oscar stood outside as well. Oscar de la Paz was a detective with the Tucson P.D., and Alex didn't have to think too hard about why his other cousins would have enlisted Oscar's help.

As for the three captured warlocks, well, they weren't looking all that good. Tomas and Jorge seemed to have shrunk in height, and still seemed to be unable to meet anyone's eyes directly. Matías did stare angrily at Alex, but the effect was marred by the two black eyes he was currently sporting. Whether they were a result of smacking into Zoe's car, or whether one or more of his captors had decided he needed a little roughing-up, Alex didn't know for sure. Either way, Matías wasn't in any condition to be attracting any more unsuspecting females.

"They're waiting for you," Alex told his cousins, and they marched the three young men into the living room, then stopped with them in the middle of the space.

He wasn't psychic or empathic, but Alex could still feel the wave of fury that radiated from the watching witches and warlocks as they looked upon the trio who had caused so much havoc. Angela had still been holding hands with Connor, but in that moment she let go and turned toward the three captives. Her green eyes blazed pure emerald, and her pretty mouth pulled into a flat line.

"Tomas Aguirre, Jorge Aguirre…Matías Escobar…your crimes have put you beyond the pale. No witch or wizard has dared to lift a hand against their own for generations."

Well, except maybe Connor's dear departed brother, Alex thought with some irony. *Although in that case, he never intended to hurt Angela, only make her his own. Even he wouldn't have stooped to the sort of foul magic Matías was using.*

She hesitated, and looked up at Connor. Looking very grim himself, he said, "And because you have committed crimes that haven't been seen for generations, we thought it only fitting that you should suffer a punishment that hasn't been handed down for generations."

Jorge and Tomas maintained their hangdog looks, but Matías glared at the *prima* and *primus* out of his bruised eyes, his mouth curling in a sneer.

"You can't do anything to us."

Luz spoke up then. "Actually, they can. I'm surprised word didn't get around about what can happen when you go up against a *prima* and *primus* working together."

For the first time, Matías appeared frightened, a muscle twitching in his cheek as he fought to maintain his current defiant stance. His two companions only exchanged puzzled glances. Obviously, they didn't have a clue as to what Alex's mother was talking about.

Angela said, her voice soft but her tone cutting, "You see, we all agreed that you should be punished for what you've done, but a civilian prison isn't much good when it comes to keeping someone with witch blood locked up. However, if your powers were taken from you...."

Matías shook his head. "You can't do that." The words were defiant, but Alex couldn't help detecting a note of worry in them.

"Oh, I think we can." She looked past Matías to Jack Sandoval. "Detective, why don't you let them know what they're facing?"

"Up to ten years each for kidnapping, but that's moot, since they're all on the hook for first-degree murder. Life, or the death penalty. I think I know what the judge is going to go for, once the particulars of Roslyn McAllister's murder come out." Jack didn't seem to take any pleasure in saying this. Maybe it was because of Tricia McAllister's white, stricken face. Roslyn hadn't been just a distant cousin, but her niece.

"I didn't kill no one—" Tomas began, and Jack overrode him, saying,

"Doesn't matter. You were an accessory to first-degree murder—a murder that followed a kidnapping, which means special circumstances. You're equally on the hook."

Looking pale, the warlock subsided, but Matías wasn't so ready to back down.

"You got nothing on us, *pendejo*."

"Well, about that—" He glanced over at Oscar, who'd remained silent during the whole exchange. "Want to tell him what you 'got' on him?"

"With pleasure." Oscar stepped forward. He was ten or so years older than Jack, with tired dark eyes that had seen too much. "We followed up the lead Miguel gave us and got a warrant for the address associated with the mail drop rented in Tucson. When we searched that residence, we found Roslyn McAllister's body."

Tricia let out a small moan, and Caitlin reached over and took her mother's hand in hers, while on the other side, Caitlin's father dropped an arm around his wife's shoulders. For herself, Caitlin looked pale but composed. Then again, she'd had a little more time to come to grips with her cousin's death.

Luz and Angela and Connor remained silent, waiting, while Matías clenched his hands at his sides and seemed as if he wanted nothing more than to lash out at all of them. But because he was surrounded and outnumbered, he stayed where he was, seething, while the two other warlocks appeared as if they were ready to have the earth swallow them up. Better that than face the combined wrath of the McAllister *prima* and the Wilcox *primus*...not to mention the stern justice of the civilian legal system.

After pausing a few seconds, probably to let everyone regain what they could of their composure, Oscar went on, "We also found a quantity of spilled blood and what appeared to be some kind of ritual knife with Roslyn's blood on it, along with fingerprints that we're certain will match those of our perpetrators here. We'll find out for sure when we take them in, but at the moment there's sufficient evidence for an arrest."

"Thank you, Detective," Angela said. Her gaze shifted back to the three captive warlocks. "You abused your powers to kidnap three innocent girls. Caitlin was lucky enough to get away, but even her escape wasn't enough to shock any sense into you."

Matías shot Caitlin a baleful glance, but she stared back at him, unmoving, and after a second or two he looked away. The interaction surprised Alex a little, but he realized Caitlin had grown into her strength the past few days. She wasn't as easily cowed as Matías probably thought she would be.

"And because you abused your powers," Connor went on, "you have no right to them any longer. You can see what it feels like, being the prey from now on." His eyes met Angela's, and she nodded.

They joined hands then, and the air in the room suddenly felt dense, charged with electricity, like the atmosphere before a thunderstorm. Alex could actually see the hairs on his arms standing up. It was difficult to breathe. The blood seemed to pound in his temples.

Still with the fingers of their near hands entwined, Connor and Angela raised their free hands, palms facing outward. And then it was as if some sort of pale light or energy began to drift out of the three warlocks, knotting itself into a heavy thread that connected with the *prima's* and *primus'* fingers. They both made a sudden tugging motion.

The *crack!* that followed was sharp as lightning, and Alex couldn't help wincing. In that same moment, all three of the captive warlocks let out a trio of unholy shrieks, further assaulting his eardrums. They sank to their knees, moaning, while Angela calmly caught that thread of light and squeezed it in her palm, where it seemed to disappear.

"It is done," Luz said.

None of the warlocks seemed able to move from where they were crouched on the faded Persian rug that covered the floor. Alex looked on in disbelief. Was it really possible? Had Angela and Connor combined their powers somehow to permanently remove Jorge's and Tomas' and Matías' magic?

Then Angela put a hand to her forehead and winced slightly, as if the effort had taken something out of her as well. "I didn't think that was actually going to work."

"But it did," Luz said. "They are harmless now—well, at least as harmless as men with souls black as theirs can be." She looked to Oscar and Jack. "They're all yours now."

"And we know what to do with them," Jack said. "I'm just sorry we can't prosecute them for what they did to Maya, but there's no evidence we can present in a civilian court."

Alex watched as his mother's eyes grew cloudy with unshed tears. "I understand. It's enough that they'll face justice for Roslyn's murder and the kidnappings. They'll never walk as free men after this."

It said something for how much the de-magicking—for lack of a better word—had traumatized the three warlocks that none of them said anything or even reacted as Miguel, Oscar, and Jack took them by their arms and hauled them to their feet, then pushed them out of the living room. Alex supposed they were about to get a quick one-way trip to the Tucson police department's central station.

Even so, he hardly felt happy about it. Yes, they'd been caught and would be going away forever, it looked like, but that wouldn't bring Roslyn or his grandmother back, wouldn't fix the glassy, confused expression in Danica's eyes. So much mayhem, and for what?

He couldn't help looking across the room at Caitlin. She still sat quietly next to her mother, but her gaze caught his, and she gave him the slightest of nods, as if to say, *This isn't over.*

The faintest flicker of hope stirred in his chest. Maybe he would be able to steal a chance to speak with her before her parents spirited her away.

It took some waiting, but while Tricia McAllister was speaking quietly with Alex's mother and father, and Connor and Angela with Caitlin's father, Caitlin slipped over to Alex and whispered, "Kitchen."

So he followed her there, wondering what she was going to say. As it turned out, she didn't say anything at all at first, but instead took his hands and pulled him toward her so she could kiss him soundly, a kiss that seemed to turn him all to heat and flame, despite the shocking show of power he'd just witnessed.

"I have to go with them," she said at last, after she pulled away. "And there's school and everything, but—"

"But you still want to see me?" he asked, wondering if that was being too blunt.

"Of course I still want to see you." The way she uttered the words made it sound as if their being together was so natural, she didn't even know why he was questioning it. "That is, if you want to see me. Maybe I was assuming—"

The only possible response was to reach over and bring her against him, to cover her mouth with his and show her that she wasn't assuming at all. Or maybe she was, but that was all right, because he'd been assuming the exact same thing.

As for the rest, well…he figured they'd work it out as they went along.

CHAPTER TWENTY

THE SUNLIGHT FELT FAR TOO BRIGHT, FAR TOO merciless, for such a solemn occasion. Caitlin couldn't help wondering how much hotter that same sun was down in Tucson, where Alex had gone home. But no, she shouldn't be thinking about Alex right now. This was the time for the McAllisters to say goodbye to Roslyn. Never mind that Caitlin wanted Alex with her so badly, wanted to hang on to him and feel his reassuring arm around her waist as she made her last farewell to the lighthearted girl who had been both her cousin and her friend. He'd had to make his own goodbyes to his grandmother just the day before, and his family needed him with them to share their grief. Both he and Caitlin had realized their families wouldn't understand the bond that had grown between them so quickly, would have thought them selfish to insist on being together when their clans needed them more. And so they'd reluctantly agreed to stay apart until things settled down, although every day away from him was its own kind of agony, its own measure of grief.

The McAllisters had gathered in the quiet corner of the Cottonwood cemetery where all the members of their clan were laid to rest, and stood quietly as the white coffin with its coverlet of pale pink roses and soft white lilies was lowered to the ground. Well, most of them were quiet. Cousin Lysette, Roslyn's mother, was sobbing, handkerchief pressed to her mouth, and Roslyn's sister Jenny was sniffling, her big blue-gray eyes—the eyes she'd shared with Roslyn—filled with tears. Standing next to her was her brother Adam, his arm around Mason's waist as she looked on, her expression stricken. Caitlin somehow knew that Mason was thinking about how that could have been her own sister Danica being lowered to the hard reddish earth, and how she was selfishly glad that Danica had somehow been spared.

Caitlin didn't really think that Mason was being selfish. At least one person had survived Matías' hellish plans, so why shouldn't be Mason be glad about that while at the same time grieving the young sister-in-law she'd lost?

Adam's face was tight, his eyes shimmering with unshed tears. Caitlin could see his jaw working, but he obviously didn't intend to let go of the tight rein he had on his emotions. He and Roslyn had always been close, closer than they were with their older sister Jenny, who was three years older, while Roslyn and Adam were barely a year apart.

Angela stepped forward and spoke quietly, talking about Roslyn's joy for life, her wonderful voice, her amazing talent with music. And then Caitlin heard the sound of a guitar being plucked, accompanied by her cousin's pure, clear soprano singing "In the Arms of the Angels," and she realized someone must have found a recording Roslyn had made and was playing it now from some source she couldn't quite see.

It was understanding that she'd never hear that voice again in real life, that she'd never see Roslyn's big blue eyes dancing with laughter, or the way she'd toss her long honey-colored hair in that artfully artless manner of hers, that finally brought the tears to Caitlin's own eyes. They streamed down her cheeks, and then it seemed everyone was weeping, mourning the loss of a girl who should never have been taken from them so young.

And if fury toward Matías Escobar burned in the hearts of some of the people around her, how could she blame them? The same fire burned in hers.

Since Alex wasn't privy to the goings-on behind the scenes at the Tucson P.D. or the local district attorney's office, he didn't know exactly what went down to send Matías and his cronies to the front of the line when it came to them going to trial. Somehow, though, they were arraigned within a few days, with the courthouse date scheduled for only a week or so after that.

When he'd called Caitlin to give her the news, she seemed relieved but not particularly happy. He hesitated, unsure as to whether he should press her on the subject, but then he decided to go ahead and ask anyway. "What's the matter? I thought you'd be glad to hear he's on the fast track to life in prison."

A long pause on her end. He wished he could see her face, but she didn't have Skype installed on her computer, which she claimed was really underpowered, and so they were talking on their cell phones. She'd finally gotten hers replaced after she went home; there had never seemed to be any time to do it during those feverish few days they'd spent together.

Then she said, "I don't think 'glad' is the right word. Of course it's good that he was caught and that he's going to get a dose of civilian justice on top of what Angela and Connor already did to him, but...that won't bring back Roslyn or Maya. It won't fix what's wrong with Danica."

Oh, hell. He'd been hoping in the back of his mind, between trying to adjust to a new clan dynamic with his mother at its head, and attempting to focus on work and not the ever-increasing need to see Caitlin while the world conspired to keep them apart, that her friend might be improving. "She's still having trouble?"

"Yeah." A little gust of a breath, as if Caitlin had let out a sigh she couldn't quite keep in. "I mean, it's not like she's in a trance anymore, but she still seems pretty out of it, and I guess she's been having a lot of nightmares, too. She had to withdraw from school, and her parents just came by yesterday to get the rest of her stuff. They're thinking about sending her to a therapist, although they're not sure because no one in either of our clans is a psychologist or anything, and it could get weird if she has to go see a civilian."

"Weird" was putting it mildly, Alex knew. There were certain things that had happened to Danica that weren't exactly proper for a civilian to know, and it was even more awful that apparently her ordeal hadn't ended when she'd been rescued.

But because he knew talking about it was painful, he didn't press for any details, instead asking, "So you're living in the apartment alone now?" Alex didn't think he liked the sound of that, although he knew Caitlin should be perfectly safe in Flagstaff. Her cousin Adam was living there with his wife Mason, after all, and it wasn't as if the Wilcoxes and the McAllisters were feuding anymore.

"For now." Another one of those little pauses. "That is, my lease is up at the end of June, so I'll have to decide by then what I want to do. But luckily, the money from my book sales is picking up, since I just published the final book in my trilogy, and that should bridge the gap. It'll be okay."

This girl never ceased to amaze him. She'd lost her friend, been through an ordeal of her own, and yet seemed to have dusted herself off and gotten back to her writing despite everything. "That's great news," he said. "Kind of surprising, but—"

"Not really," she cut in. "I was really close to being done anyway. It seemed like the best thing I could do was focus on the writing...and my classes, obviously. It wouldn't have been honoring Roslyn to quit any of it. Besides, no way was I going to give Matías that sort of power over me."

When she put it that way, Alex could understand how she felt. Letting that warlock interfere with her life any more than he already had would only be allowing him to continue to disrupt her plans and goals and dreams, and clearly Caitlin was a lot tougher than that. He also realized then that, however much he missed her, he couldn't interfere. She needed to finish out the semester, if nothing else.

Afterward...well, he had a few ideas about that.

She tried to tell herself that it was all okay, that this separation from Alex didn't get more and more painful as spring wore on toward summer. True, he had come up to visit as often as he could, and in the beginning, Caitlin had had the selfish thought that she was almost glad she was living by herself now, since at least it meant she wouldn't have to hide their nighttime activities from anyone else. Yes, it was awkward squeezing in with him in her full-size bed, but still so much better than sleeping alone. But then he'd have to go away again, to attend to his own responsibilities, and she was left telling herself it was okay, that she'd see him again in a couple of weeks. It was never enough, but it was better than nothing.

Even more promising, Alex told her in mid-May that he'd submitted his resume to a local station in Tucson, and they were very interested in talking to him about an assistant marketing position. Caitlin had been thrilled for him, although he'd only shrugged and said, "Well, it's not a job offer. And even if I do get an offer, I still have to deal with my parents and the store."

Oh, right, that. "I find it hard to believe that there's no one else who can manage it," she protested.

A shrug. "Manuela could probably do a great job. The real question is whether my parents will let her. She's not a Trujillo son."

Since Caitlin had grown up in a tight-knit clan herself and knew all too well the weight of tradition and expectations, she didn't force the argument any further than that. She could only hope that Alex's father would come to realize that his younger son's happiness was a lot more important than whether a Trujillo was in charge of things at the family *mercado*.

It was even more difficult to determine whether anyone in their respective clans was particularly happy about hers and Alex's burgeoning relationship. Her visions hadn't gone away—she'd woken up one night after having a nightmare about the hillside beneath Rory Lightman's house giving way, and phoned her mother immediately. Tricia McAllister had passed on the warning, and Rory got his family out before half the house slid down the hill. At least the incident had proved that Caitlin was willing to do her part as the clan seer, even when off at college in Flagstaff, but she had a feeling they really wouldn't be thrilled if she announced that her relationship with Alex Trujillo was getting serious and that she might not be staying in the northern half of the state for very much longer.

She wouldn't make that announcement, though, because she didn't know for sure if their relationship really *was* that serious. Sure, he'd come up and spend a weekend here and there when he could make the time in his schedule, but she really couldn't count that as an extreme escalation of their relationship. And she couldn't even reciprocate, because her ancient Toyota could barely make it back and forth between Flagstaff and Jerome. No way could she drive the poor thing all the way to Tucson and hope to have it survive.

On Memorial Day weekend, Alex made the slog through traffic to see her, since it was her birthday that Sunday. They had a large, noisy lunch at the Haunted Hamburger with as many family members as they could squeeze in amongst the tourists, but after that Alex took her back to Flagstaff. He seemed unusually quiet on the drive home, but Caitlin didn't want to make anything major out of that. A few hours spent around her relatives would be enough to wear anyone down, even someone who was used to being part of a large extended family himself.

After they got back to the apartment, though, and Caitlin got them some iced tea, Alex asked, "So what are you going to do about this place?"

"What place?"

"The apartment."

"Oh." She handed him his glass of tea and settled herself down on the threadbare sofa. It seemed Alex had finally decided they were going to have "the talk," and she wasn't sure what she thought about that. Or maybe it was more that she did know what she thought...what she hoped for...but didn't want to admit it to herself. "Well, I can afford to stay, if I decide that's what I want to do. My parents aren't thrilled about the whole thing, but no way am I going to bail out with only a year of college left."

He appeared to absorb that remark, dark eyes thoughtful. Instead of coming to sit next to her, though, he went over to the sliding glass door and looked outside. The view was about the only decent thing in the apartment; you could see pine trees and a glimpse of Humphreys Peak off to one side. But Caitlin had a feeling Alex wasn't really looking at the view, no matter how pretty it was.

Turning around so he could face her, he said abruptly, "I want you to come to Tucson and move in with me."

"What?" Even though she'd been halfway hoping he might make such a proposition, now that it had come, she felt blindsided.

"You heard me." He moved from the window and stood in front of her, a pleading expression on his face. "We've been trying to make this work, but God, Caitlin, you live four hours away from me, and that's on a day with good traffic. Besides, this place is a dump. Wouldn't you rather live in my house?"

Tone wry, she asked, "Oh, so now you're trying to save me from living in a shithole apartment, Mr. Protector?"

"Of course not." His mouth twisted, and before she could even register what he was doing, he'd gone down on one knee in front of her and was pulling a box out of his jeans pocket.

No—he couldn't. This was ridiculous. They hadn't even known each other for three whole months.

But Goddess...she wanted this. She wanted *him*. She wanted to be with him.

Obviously, Alex didn't think it was ridiculous, even if he did look adorably silly, perched there on one knee in front of her. Voice earnest, he said, "I want us to be together, Caitlin. I want you to come home with me. I want it to be *our* home. I know you only stayed there for a few days, but the house still feels empty without you." He opened the box. The ring inside was white gold, with a glittering round-cut diamond in the center surrounded by smaller diamonds.

It was beautiful. It was perfect. But still she could only sit there, staring at him, all the words she loved so much suddenly deserting her.

He paused and stared up into her face. "Is it—is it too soon? I've been trying to make myself wait, at least until you were done with school, but Caitlin, I don't want to wait anymore."

At last she found her voice. "I don't want to wait, either. So—yes. *Yes.* It's crazy, but yes."

That flashing smile she loved so much lit up his face, and he slid the ring onto her finger. It fit exactly right. And that was how she felt about Alex...he fit exactly right.

He pulled her toward him, and she was kissing him, and then they were on the rug and their clothes were being flung this way and that, and his mouth was on her, his fingers stroking her, and at last he was inside her, and she knew this was the most perfect thing in the world, being with Alex, knowing he loved her and would always, always make sure she was safe.

Afterward, once they'd gotten themselves more or less pulled together, they settled back down on the couch, Caitlin with her head on Alex's shoulder. She knew she should call her parents to tell them the news, but she wanted to work out a few more things first.

"What about school?"

"Transfer to U of A. It might be a little hard this late in the game, but my clan has a few people who work there. I'm sure some strings can get pulled so you can still start in the fall."

The McAllisters weren't all that good at string-pulling, so she'd have to take his word for it. But the University of Arizona was an excellent school, and most of her coursework should transfer straight over, since both universities were part of the same system. And if she ended up having to take an extra semester to get caught up, well, it wouldn't be the end of the world. After all, she'd be living with Alex. That would make everything a lot easier.

But still, her conscience pricked at her. She'd just come to terms with being the McAllister seer, and now she was going to pack up and go off to de la Paz territory?

"The clan elders won't be happy about their seer going to live outside McAllister lands," she said. "I mean, I've just started really functioning as a seer, and now I'm going to bail completely?"

Alex lifted an eyebrow at her. "You're going to Tucson, not Siberia. And this is the twenty-first century. Haven't your clan elders heard of Skype? Facetime? Email? I don't know, a telephone?"

She stuck her tongue out at him, and he laughed.

"Now you're just teasing me."

"Maybe I am, a little," he admitted. "But you brought it on yourself."

That could be true. But she had one last question to ask. "What about a job?" she asked.

"What about it?"

"I won't feel right, freeloading off you."

At that remark, he pulled away slightly and gave her a very direct look. "First of all, Caitlin, I wouldn't call going to college full-time exactly freeloading. Besides, I thought you said your book sales were picking up."

"They are," she admitted. It wasn't as if she was going to hit the *New York Times* bestseller list anytime soon, but her monthly earnings had inched past fifteen hundred dollars or so.

"Well, then," he said, as if that covered everything. "It's not like I need you to help me with a house payment or anything, and if you're earning your own money, then you'll be able to buy the little things you need for school and whatever. Isn't that enough?"

She watched him carefully for a few seconds. He was telling the truth. All he wanted was her with him. Nothing else. No strings.

"I love you, Alex Trujillo," she said.

Another of those blazing smiles. "That's the first time you've told me that."

No, that couldn't be right. But she reflected on the time they'd spent together and everything they'd talked about, and she realized she never *had* said those three important words aloud. She'd thought them plenty of times but never quite got the nerve to say "I love you" to Alex, always telling herself that it was too soon, that they needed more time together. A silly notion, really, to believe that you had to spend a set amount of time with someone before you could take that next step. She'd known almost from the beginning that there couldn't be anyone except Alex, that through all the fear and terror and worry, he'd been there for her, the one person, the one true match to her soul, that she'd thought she would never find.

Taking his hand, she pressed it against her cheek. "Well, I do love you."

"Oh, I know. And I love you, too. I think I was in love with you from the moment you collapsed in my arms in the store." She gave him a disbelieving look, and he went on, "It's true. I didn't know who you were or what kind of trouble you were in, but I was…drawn to you, I guess. And even though I knew I had other things I should be focusing on during that whole nightmare, I couldn't stop thinking about you. About being with you."

Caitlin could understand those feelings all too well, because she'd been thinking the same thing about him. What they shared wasn't exactly like a consort bond, because that sort of connection was only for a *prima* and her soul mate, but it seemed something almost as powerful had brought her and Alex together. Her mother had said it was like that for witches sometimes, that they were somehow able to recognize in another person the quality that would make them their perfect pairing, but Caitlin had dismissed the notion as overly romantic, and had thought it couldn't actually be like that in real life. Not when she'd had such bad luck before when it came to men. *Or guys,* she amended mentally. *Before Alex, they were all just guys.*

He was something different, though. Something special.

She tried to keep her tone casual as she said, "I couldn't stop thinking about you, either, but I just thought it was because of your outstanding gorgeousness."

"Oh, now you're going to give me a swelled head."

"That's not such a bad thing," she responded, moving her hand down to the crotch of his jeans.

He gusted out a breath. "That's dangerous, Caitlin."

"I know," she said. But he made no move to rub against her and escalate things. She withdrew her hand and asked, "What is it?"

"You're going to think it's crazy."

"I grew up in Jerome, Alex. It takes a lot to make me think something is crazy."

Smiling, he took her hand and kissed it. Shivers ran down her spine, and she could feel her pulse beginning to speed up. Funny how even the little things he did could cause such a strong physical reaction in her.

"The next time we're together, I want it to be in the house. Our house. I know it'll take a while to make the transition, but—"

She leaned forward and kissed him. "I don't think it's crazy. Besides, I know you hate how your feet hang off the edge of my crappy little bed."

"So you're willing to wait?" He sounded surprised, and she couldn't blame him. At least half the time, she was the one who initiated things between them. He'd once said he didn't know what blazed hotter, her blood or her red hair. Then she'd teased him for only being attracted to her hair, whereupon he'd taken it upon himself to prove that there were actually a great many things about her that attracted him.

"Oh, hell, no, I'm not waiting. Not that long, anyway," she replied at once, pushing herself up from the couch and thinking furiously. "I can pack a few things, and come back for the rest whenever. It's not like I have to be here for school—finals were last week. And if we leave in the next fifteen minutes, we can be down in Tucson in time for a late dinner. You still owe me that chimichanga, you know."

She headed off toward the bedroom, Alex only a few feet behind her so he could get the duffle bag he'd brought up for the weekend. Clearly, he didn't want to wait, either. And why should he? They'd both been waiting their entire lives for one another.

The time for waiting was over.